"A profound, and profoundly affecting novel. I don't think anybody could read it without being deeply touched. I was. I found it hard to resist—the ideas, the writing, the passion, the message. All resonated for me. A wonderful reading experience... I think anyone who picks up this book will be changed by it."
Jeffrey Moussaieff Masson, Ph.D., Author of *When Elephants Weep* and *Dogs Never Lie About Love*

"Sherrida Woodley bravely takes on the big issues between humans and the natural world: evolution, extinction, human hubris, technological arrogance and ecological survival. *Quick Fall of Light* shares Rachel Carson's fears for our planet and exhibits Woodley's own "sense of wonder," as well as her sure instincts for mystery and suspense. Nature lovers have a new advocate."
Linda Lear, Historian/Biographer and Author of *Rachel Carson: Witness for Nature*, 2009.

"*Quick Fall of Light* is a powerful archetypal tale that bores deeply into bone and blood. It is an important message for our age, because it connects us with the mysterious essence of the natural world, a connection we require now more than ever."
Larry Dossey, MD Author of *The Power of Premonitions*

"This is the riveting story of a possible plague and the haunting loss of the passenger pigeon. Woodley explores a future world of global extinctions and how we might survive a pandemic of bird flu. A prophetic mystery and an environmental thriller, *Quick Fall of Light* will keep you reading and wondering."
Brenda Peterson, Author *of Animal Heart*

"This book has everything! Great characters, vivid language, a shocking resurrection, and birds. I loved it!"
Sy Montgomery, Author of *Birdology.*

"A most original story line created by a fine writer."
Hope Ryden, Author of *God's Dog* and *Lily Pond*

"*Quick Fall of Light* is the perfect book: an exciting thriller with heart and a powerful environmental theme. I stayed up all night finishing this one."
Dale Peterson, Author of *Jane Goodall: The Woman Who Redefined Man.*

"Woodley delves into mystery as deep as the Northwestern Rain Forest to capture an intriguing story of pandemic and murder, apocalypse and redemption, a story that compels vital and necessary reflection."
Sheila Nickerson, Author of *Disappearance: A Map: A Meditation on Death and Loss in the High Latitudes*

"Especially relevant in today's world, *Quick Fall of Light* gives us a vivid picture of a stark and critical future. Set in an America devastated by a pandemic, the complex and unique characters race to find a cure. With a narrative of power, intense and moving, *Quick Fall of Light* grips the reader with beautiful and light-handed prose. This first book by Sherrida Woodley is an ambitious effort of mystery and history."
Sylvia Robison, Poet, *The Poetry Diner*

"It is a time of plague, and a bird brought back from extinction could be the savior of humanity. The bird escapes, and must be found, has a special bond to the widow of a murdered scientist who pursues it, putting her own life in danger. There is action and mystery here, and an emotional trip for the reader. I enjoyed it."
James C. Glass, Author of *SHANJI*

QUICK FALL OF LIGHT

SHERRIDA WOODLEY

Gray Dog Press
Spokane, Washington
www.GrayDogPress.com

Printed In The U.S.A.

ISBN: 978-1-936178-18-6

DEDICATION

To my husband, John, who opened the door,
to Jessica and Deanna, who gave me reason,
and to Dorothy, who for a long time fed the
pigeons.

ACKNOWLEDGMENTS

I would especially like to thank two authors who recognized the significance of the 1918 flu epidemic and wrote extensively of their caution to mankind—John M. Barry, who wrote *The Great Influenza* and Katherine Anne Porter in her novel, *Pale Horse, Pale Rider*. Even now, over forty years after her death, I want to thank Rachel Carson for her unflinching look at our changing environment, at extinction, and at the role of future corporate stewardship.

And always my gratitude goes to Sylvia Robison, who encouraged me to achieve, Lorna Lynch, who produced the tools, Virginia White, who showed the way, Kathleen Judge, who treasured our friendship, Kris McCauley, who repeatedly told me it could be done, Virginia Meyer, who had the book savvy, Petrushka Pavlovich, saying it was all in the focus, Sabrina Budik, who showed the kind of courage, and my mother, who never gave up. A special thanks also to Russ Davis, who saw potential in the middle of a storm.

My grandmother survived the 1918 flu. My grandfather came home from WWI to tend to her. They lost many of their peers and some of their family to that first great flu epidemic.

"What's in that place?"
"Birds," he said, as if transfixed by the very word.
"Birds that went extinct almost a hundred years ago."

CHAPTER 1

Nothing so simple, so unrestrained would ever happen again. Josephine Russo looked at her underwear folded as if they'd been pressed, then centered exactly on top of her jewelry case. For over four months she hadn't touched them. Two blue panties with white diagonal stripes and one solid pink. They'd worked their way so far into her everyday consciousness she hardly saw them anymore. Like wallpaper or the etchings on paper towels, she looked past them. It wasn't until this moment in the clarity of early morning sun she considered them for what they really were—the last undisturbed remnant of her husband's existence.

Robert Russo never folded his own shorts. She suspected he took care of his half of the laundry exactly the way he always had. When they married fifteen years ago he'd been doing his own clothes twenty years before that. His first wife told him his dirt was his dirt, to apply and remove. Josephine never expected the same, but it came with Robert, along with cleaning the birdcage and making lasagna twice a month. He folded her underwear even as he wadded his up in the top vanity drawer. He'd done it again the day he died.

Josie pulled the hasp to the door of the birdcage and stroked Fritz in a deliberate tug of his tail feathers. He seemed entranced by the mauling. This time though she touched him without watching his eyes close and his beak barely open. "For you," she said, "I hope there's never harm." Her other hand hovered over the underwear her husband had dutifully placed within reach. *I can't stay. Not anymore*, she thought.

Last night Josephine Russo had decided to leave. She dug her old backpack out of the hall closet, and in it she pushed jeans, a sweatshirt, three sets of Rob's socks, a first aid kit, bug spray, a nail file, a book of matches, five jerky sticks, a small bottle of lime Gatorade, and the *Book of Common Prayer.* This morning she added a couple more things, a red flannel head rag and the panties.

For a few minutes she left Fritz alone with Peone, the two doves used to her comings and goings. Their silhouettes, dark inside the sun's hovering glow, pecked effortlessly at seed they'd scattered. If they missed her husband they made the adjustment between themselves to accept Josie's gratuities. There was no premonition, no scuffling about in the cage over what was about to happen.

Like I told you, I'm going away for a bit. Josie crossed through the note she'd started. "Again," she said aloud, hearing in response only the click of seeds. *It's just a vacation, Mom. I need some time away. I'm not sure where yet, but you'll hear from me. The birds love you, almost as much as they loved him. Be careful. Whatever you do, keep away from public rest rooms, taxis or bus terminals. Don't even take flowers to Dad's grave. You know what they keep saying about not knowing exactly when it's going to get here.* "You're so paranoid," she said to herself. *I love you, Mom. We'll get through this.*

The sun shone between the wire strands of the birdcage cutting itself into precise beams that illuminated the black-bordered diamonds on Fritz' wings. He was bent over preening, like an actor who only wants the camera to see his good side. No bigger than a mouse, there was a certain ego about him. Not so for Peone, the adoring mirror of his splendor. She seemed only to want to duplicate him.

Right now, Josie continued, *I need to find what's left of my husband's spirit.* His spirit, more than anything, had transcended a disappearance more than a death. Rob had folded clothes before he left for the small airstrip outside town. Something so mundane as to seem comical. To him it was as simple as priorities. He'd taken off for a routine trip just inside the Olympic National Forest, the report said. They'd found him hanging upside down in what remained of the cockpit of a white Cessna, the tail separated in small fragments strewn a quarter mile between tree limbs. From the air, they said it looked like the severed tailbone of a fish. He would've survived a mistake, Josie told herself. This was something different. It was compression.

Two clumps of red geraniums, oddly brilliant in their stark white pots, made the living room seem too airy, too untouched by her sadness. They hadn't been blooming when Rob left. Above them on a white paneled wall was a charcoal depiction of a Blackfoot peace pipe. Fashioned after a rare original, it was covered with spiral hide wrapped around the stem and black horsehair in the center inset with six human teeth. On each end were feathers of a golden eagle. Such a pipe she knew was able to compel peace. With it, the Indians thought of the soul and of death. She studied it, as she used to when she first began teaching, and she thought of the teeth.

Over time so many things came together—like these bits of her childhood and the death of her husband. When she was little she asked her mother what happened to animals when they died. Laurinda told her about compression of the sea under its own weight and explained some people believed ships that sank and whales that died never reached the bottom. Maybe they drifted forever. But then a scientist named Rachel Carson wrote a book saying that didn't happen. In the very deepest basins of the ocean were the teeth of sharks and the hard ear bones of whales. There were pictures of tiny odd-shaped bones in the red clay of the ocean floor. Immense pressure, she said, is what caused them to keep going down as far as anything could go. Compression, it turned out, could swallow the bodies of living things.

For Josephine, her husband's death had become a symbol, a powerful icon of subdued, marginalized loss. The faculty he'd worked with remembered him with a small bouquet of chrysanthemums sent to the house the week after his death. The Chairman of the Ornithology Department at the University of Washington sent her a bound copy of a cross-section of Rob's field notes on wild finches. A couple of his old birding buddies made it to his memorial. But there was nothing to distinguish his death from his life. There wasn't even curiosity. She plunged the underwear deep down through the jeans and sweatshirt, past the prayer book, into the bottom of the backpack, then stared at the top of the jewelry box. Robert was gone. Even his intentions. She shuddered and her sigh became a sob. "I can find you less and less."

*   *   *

Laurinda would find her daughter's note that evening, long after Josie caught the ferry from Anacortes. She would hold the birds, one at a time, inside the torn paisley smock she wore when she cleaned their cage. Peone would flatten between her breasts encompassed in the undiluted smell of deodorant and the deep valley of her salt-rich skin. In this time, when nothing else was safe, she'd fuss over the doves in her everyday routine. They weren't to blame, she'd whisper, for avian flu or for Josephine's predictable departure. Robert Russo was to blame for it all.

CHAPTER 2

Anacortes, a pale dot in the intense map-green that represented the west side of the state of Washington, was a town beginning to suffer a slow and terrifying withdrawal. In the midst of an elaborately contrived image of old growth forests with tree stumps the size of grain silos and rain-soaked moss draping from overpasses, the community at the north end of Fidalgo Island had always thrived on tourism. It had only half as much rain as Seattle because it lay within the Olympic Mountains' rain shadow, and it boasted a fishing fleet the largest in the state. But Anacortes, like so many cities bracing themselves for a medical catastrophe, was starting to shut down.

Robert's death had coincided with the first few cases of avian flu infiltrating the east coast of the United States. On February 3, 2009, a small town in New Hampshire reported three of its residents had succumbed to a virus so strong it kept them from finishing a dog sled race they'd been training for at least two years. The only woman competitor told friends she'd awakened that morning feeling woozy, and two hours later she was found dead, almost nude, face down in a snow pack. Two men, also sledders, were hospitalized with body temperatures of 104 degrees. The realization became immediate news prophecy. That Americans were in a fight every bit as ominous as any world war. And every face, every heart, every person was on the front line. The next morning Robert read the headline that now all of America was headed into the darkened wood of disease. He reminded Josie to keep the first aid kit close at all times and called flight service for an update on weather. She watched him leave, a red flannel rag tied around his head as if he was a biker instead of a pilot. He threw her a kiss and loaded his wolfhound, Kerrie, into the car with him. Josephine watched them drive away, then round the corner onto DeSmet Boulevard, her husband ramrod straight in the eye of a storm.

There had been a full quarter of a year since then. The pandemic moved in ways similar to a forest fire, depending on forces inherent to its existence—atmosphere, opportunity, even the peculiarities of individuals. The predictions were usually dire, and for that reason certain odd formalities had overtaken communities. For instance, most of New Jersey had enforced limited access on their major beltways. This, alone, seemed to deter unnecessary traffic along the coastline. The effect was a slowing, an unsettling abandonment, as if one was watching the re-enactment of the fall of Rome. The flu hunkered down in the valleys of the Blue Ridge Mountains and exploded into world view, killing a long-time anchor of a major news network. It struck with such force in Sioux City, Iowa, the town tried to enact a self-imposed quarantine by burning pyres of bed sheets and hospital linens in every city park, fires that drove the Midwest to compare the event to a back fire set against a prairie inferno. The flu would engulf, pause, and move steadily westward. Anacortes, Washington, as yet, had not seen one flu-stricken citizen, but the island town grew consistently more isolated, as if it could protect itself by secession.

Josephine drove the Outback into the ferry's stall, relieved there had been enough room aboard the single operating craft to take her across Admiralty Inlet before the next four-hour wait. Normal schedules had been abandoned since the cutback in service, and the Townsend Ferry was now used as much for shuttling cargo between Whidbey Island and Port Townsend as it was for ferrying cars and people. The San Juan Islands were poised between the United States and Canada, as fragile appearing as if they were biscuits placed in a diplomatic stew. On any map a line ran longitudinally west of their combined mass delineating British Columbia from the State of Washington. That line had become accented with the international menace of bird flu. Ferries running between Seattle and Victoria were moored indefinitely. For the first time in over a century a bell in the tower of St. Thomas' church rang daily offering solace to an island awaiting plague while Canada had withdrawn into her own uncompromising retreat.

Few people left their cars. Large metal bins between stalls separated passengers with no more than two cars together either side-by-side or front-to-back. Touring decks were consumed with freight. The engines shuddered and plowed through the water's strong current. Some people left the San Juans for good in a silent migration that brought them together with their extended families for the first time in a generation, and so they continued to keep to themselves. The last hurdle was the opening to Puget Sound. Josie pulled on a heavy knit sweater and tied the flannel rag around her head, then got out of the car. In the wind that bore down she felt a mist, water infused with the smell of ocean held deep in the throat of an inland passage. She burrowed her face deep into the sweater, then peered into the car window. Robert's laptop was concealed under the backpack, a last-minute, impetuous move, she thought, yet impossible to leave behind. In it were years of his observations spirited away in files indecipherable without a computer. It was all she had left of him. She looked for one long moment at the edge of the plastic carrying case, pressed the car locks, and walked away.

Crates labeled *Boeing* blocked the passenger deck entrances leaving just enough room for people, single-file, to enter the ferry's topside. What had once been an open room, a wide vista-dome encountering the water and weather of the inlet, had become a storage facility. Hand trucks were belted to appliances, both used and new. Car parts divided by heavy plastic sheets bordered the deck like statuary. No one would want to sit here anymore among the hardware of freighters. So Josie made her way to a table made from a rusted trunk placed on its side, the only thing she could see worth saving. It bore the patina of steerage, the only survivor from years aboard vessels. She ran her hand across the hexagonal pins protruding rivet-like the length of the trunk and imagined their fastidious power to hold. They never gave up, even in the dark misfortune of neglect. It seemed to her now that things were so tenuous men finally brought out the survivors, the things that withstood, even though these same people continued, trip after trip, to haul the mediocrity of tonnage.

Josie instinctively turned her head to the side, following the path of the ferry through its high-striding pace. She felt it bully its way through the inlet's traffic, smaller craft piloted by a new breed of entrepreneurs. The mosquito fleet, they were called, doing what the ferry was doing. Moving families and cargo and animals across waterways abandoned to the ingenious. No more were the days of timed departures and arrivals. The Sound had become a flotilla of boat-people.

In the early morning sun the ferry's windows trapped heat. The room seemed like an airless jar without escape. Josie pushed her sleeves up and wound the flannel scarf around her wrist, then pushed her mind into acceptance. She was in a moving box plowing full speed over the top of annihilation. There was resistance and obstacles. Anybody could make a mistake. It was the pilot, the one she didn't see, the one no one ever saw, who would have to pull it off. He might never tell another living soul if he misjudged the submerged geography of glaciers or sideswiped a freighter. She wound the scarf tighter. Pain and heat boiled through her. *This is what her husband felt*, she thought. This and the last swift flash of regret.

When the National Transportation Safety Board interviewed her two days after the accident they asked her what she knew about his flying habits. Did he ever take her? Why did he have a dog in the cockpit with him? Did her husband have epilepsy? They would only remark that Fraser, Washington, was not the place for one who might be disoriented because of disease or stress. The strip aligned with a patchwork of trees logged out on either side. "He was attempting an approach close to sundown. We suspect conditions were confusing. Perhaps the sun, shadows, something in the downward descent contributed to his miscalculation."

"What do you mean, miscalculation? My husband made that trip probably a hundred times. More. His dog went with him. Robert was healthy. Nobody believed he was fifty-nine." Then Josephine added, "He studied wild finches. Long term for the University. They wouldn't have let him fly, believe me, if they hadn't trusted his ability. They couldn't afford to lose him."

She thought about it now, shaking inside, the cabin around her no longer able to stifle her doubt. The way Robert's colleagues, his friends, had shrunk from view, disappearing behind routine. No comments, a peculiar, noticeable absence for a man who'd prepared a small but tight community of ornithologists. She'd heard them call it a fascination and not just a fact. Time after time he'd felt the air rush with gray-crowned rosy finches in pursuits he called relentless and often lonely. Josie knew he somehow managed to land at sea level and find a small, rare bird in the higher ground of the Olympic Peninsula. Pictures. Documentation. There was proof. But there were no witnesses. Or in her mother's standard phrase, "There's never been anyone welcomed into Robert's elitist world unless he's found someone as enamored as you were."

The wind on the other side of the inlet seemed to tug, finally loosening its sideways slap against the ferry. Josie drove her car across the grated metal plank in the exodus of riders moving from an island to a peninsula. If they went far enough, they would enter a cloud-enshrouded forest where huge tracts had consumed themselves over hundreds of years, feeding on blue-green needles of Sitka Spruce and water-logged bark of Western Hemlock. Layer upon layer the forest had stolen from the mighty to grow the mightiest, the leaners and the runts pushing from the bottom, nursing the consumption. The forest primeval. Some called it the Big Acre. It was, perhaps, the only true intent left for Josephine Russo.

CHAPTER 3

Ediz Hook, its rocks smooth and round as ostrich eggs, clamped to the north side of Port Angeles. It had a simple grace, the way it jutted from the land side of the straight in a natural barricade. At the same time, it lured the curious and the intrepid who wanted to walk the last deteriorating tendril of land. It was here, on this hook, that Robert asked her to marry him.

"No place to sit, no comfort in standing." He'd pressed his lips into her hair, bracing his thick-soled shoes between rocks and balanced as if it was such a little thing. "If I was to tell you it's going to be like this," he said. "We're not well suited, not where we are, not with our ages. You know, Josie, it will always be a disparity."

She rubbed her head against his jacket.

"Do you want to be with me right now?"

"Nowhere else," she'd said.

The hook, bleached in sun, held, still with no attraction, no lights, not even a bench along the last thread of land between the town and the straight. Josephine unzipped the backpack beside her, centering her gaze on the highway marker. One hundred seventy-two miles to Fraser. "This is how long it's lasted, Robert," she said, feeling down along the bag's curve until she found the medic kit. The road narrowed and took its way steeply into the long slope southward to the topmost rim of the Olympic National Forest. She remembered that time with him when she kept expecting to see delineation in this deep, green Disney world of mammoth trees, their limbs covered in velvet moss sleeves stretching, entwining Medusa-like. She expected the gloom to deepen until the trees became the road, until their very mass overcame the tenacity of men. There was a chance they would take them to the edge of the world.

Two vials wrapped in tissue paper were pressed inside the box along with bandages, sting-kill, and an eyedropper of Mercurochrome. A placard had been taped to the inside of the lid. In Robert's handwriting, dates were aligned beginning *July 2008*. Then, *Vial #1, 22 percent*. Four more times he'd tracked his exchange. *September 2008, Vial #2, 39 percent. November 2008, Vial #3, 54 percent. January 2009, Vial #4, 82 percent*, and another in January, *Vial #5, 98 percent*." Josephine traced the outline of the containers. She looked ahead to the transparent figures of trees, one becoming thousands, hidden from view by the highway's configuration. She'd never questioned her husband's cache. Like so much of America she was relieved to have something, some antidote to rely on. Pharmacies insisted there was enough Pass-Flu for every person in the United States, but what they'd continued to underrate was denial. People were dying, even though they'd been warned. Cautions were everywhere, breaking news, billboards, and postings on doors of all medical and government facilities.

Entire families seemed determined to go it on their own, sometimes erupting in suicides, other times struck down in a random stream of death known as "God's March." To Josephine the term had become just another human judgment, this time in the face of a plague. As if only by way of the flu were human souls, no matter how possessed, able to join in some kind of universal sanctity. No one, not even the drug companies, could keep up with re-assortment. The virus had detonated, but that was not the worst. In a gallery of mutating possibilities, the hobgoblin took to a numbers game. Every time the anti-virus was perfected for a newer, more deadly strain of bird flu, a nucleotide would change and a protein would flip over. The antidote, expensive and limited, would be phased out, causing the next wave of production. Over all the months since the flu's appearance in humans, and especially since the outbreaks of swine flu, the virus had mutated three times, each time taking the unsuspecting, children and young adults, in particular. Then, it would begin the slow business of random firing around an updated serum. Through all this Robert had kept bringing in every new generation of Pass-Flu when most of his country was still waiting for the last expiring update.

So little was ever spoken. This time description was in the form of a placard in a first aid kit. Usually it was notes, spiral notebooks. Cryptic, precise handwriting. Formulas. The man was thousands of words into detail. Like interminable debt, they lingered until she took them in cardboard storage boxes to the University. It was their debt now, the volumes of writing, some of it his pure obsession with the spell of flight. *There's one*, he'd written. *Too young yet. Faint wing-bars and patches. Pushes off and plunges. Wings vibrate. Skims cliff, bladelike. Lands high cupping wings, stalls. Feathers, a starburst, drift away.*

He would never explain to anyone what happened that day on approach to Fraser. Someone else, also objective would do it for him. Sheriff Miller leaned toward her the day after the crash, his clipboard a collection of paper and sticky notes. She noticed he hardly breathed between sentences. "Your husband was a careful man, Ms. Russo. Flight service every time, log book up-to-date. Even had a Metzger map among his sectionals, all plotted out with his routes and such. No one seems to want to believe it was his fault, what happened. But, you know, they'll check everything. They really will," he said, barely touching her arm, his fingers settling like gum against her skin.

Josephine rolled down the Outback's windows, looking for the Safeway store she remembered was about mid-way through Depot Springs. She pulled into the lot, now isolated from the road by a chain-link fence. There was a parking area to one side of the store. The rest was overtaken by tents and awnings of different sorts, resembling a farmer's market. People filed through at a steady rate. Some wore masks. A system of allowing only a few people at a time in a store had been established several weeks ago almost everywhere in Washington, and she watched as one-by-one customers were channeled through the entry met by a health-care worker with a clean mask and a net grocery bag. The sight made her cringe. Nothing, not even this, could stop a cough or a bead of sweat from splashing through the hot air, a deadly froth across plastic and cardboard. Still, there were people who believed it wouldn't happen to them, not yet. They purchased their South

Beach Diet Jello and insisted on Camels instead of Marlboros. They shuffled from the store pulling their masks into loose toys around their necks and net bags expanded into morbid obesity.

When she'd been here with Robert a lifetime ago, they'd made love. Everyone from school thought he'd taken her out of town as part of a field assembly, a gathering of students and teachers, birders, and professionals who'd actually met over a hundred miles away in one of the gateways to the Hoh River Wilderness. They all believed she'd been invited into a world few really understood. At eighteen, Josephine's determination seemed already honed. Her dark eyes never completely stopped searching for birds, at least when she was around Robert Russo. The noncredit class he offered evenings and weekends revealed only the beginnings of obsession. Quiet, deeply affected by wildlife, particularly birds, his mystique lay in his lonely inquisitions within the rain forest. Stroking his mustache, he'd move from desk to desk asking each student to write what mattered about birds. What difference did it make to study them? If some shorebirds only stopped briefly on their way to or from northern breeding grounds, then why did we try to identify them?

Josie couldn't remember anymore what made her stop trying to impress him. After that weekend when he finally reached across the car seat to touch her, she moved differently. Her skin, pale, freckled with careless dots of pigmentation was enough to make him pause slightly over her, seemingly curious about her description of the silhouettes of hawks. She watched him move through the halls intent in conversation, then turn his body toward the room she always studied in. His passing was a signal. He moved, he spoke, he gestured, and she took it all in. He waited in places for her. Average places. Parking lots, mall entrances. No places with birds.

* * *

Heat, sullen and heavy with the smell of wet salt had slowed the store's traffic. At least that's what Josie assumed until she saw a car turn the corner from the parking lot and swerve toward the first row of tents. The driver's door was open, and at slow speed it appeared to slice through the tent's metal frame like a can opener. For a minute she could see the driver, a young man hunched over, his head bobbing up and down between the floorboard and pavement. A group of shoppers surrounded him, stopping the car. He disappeared in their mass. She knew, without getting any closer, that even while they managed someone's mistake they were struggling not to touch him, pulling their masks tight across their faces. Some of them would regret what they'd done. Others, she thought, might have only a few hours to remember.

Maybe it was because of what she'd just seen, a man sick or drunk or both, Josie felt a crippling flash of heat behind both eyes. It was enough to make her put her head down over the steering wheel and glimpse the shape of her feet on the dark carpet below. She moved them carefully back and forth, afraid of nausea, yet more afraid she wouldn't see movement. If she was sick, truly sick, symptoms would engulf her. There would be no recognition of someone else's dilemma, not even the will to run. Her feet wouldn't be important anymore.

The object was to fix her mind on finding the last path of her husband. She pulled a group of sectionals out from under the seat, the Metzger folded between them. When Miller had given her things that had made it through the crash, he must've thought no one else would care. He must've believed they weren't important. Investigators didn't need red flannel head rags and unused maps to solve a pilot's mistake. *They were wrong*, she thought.

Deep lines ran crisscross, perforating the terrain map in the familiar places Robert had folded it. Smudges, pencil checks, circled numbers, and small tight arrows marked the common trails of a man once he was on the ground. They told a story she could only guess. Trying something, back tracking, warning, moving a little west. She couldn't see where he'd been, not really. The map consisted of green lines, slow growing loops tightening into deep cuts and turrets thousands of feet high. There were few names where he went. Sometimes there were marks, more like squiggles, as if he was indicating a discovery of his own—a valley maybe, or a cliff, a swallow or an eagle. It was a glimpse of his secrets. She rubbed the broken edges of her husband's map while moving her right foot effortlessly between the brake and the accelerator, then began the last stretch of highway to Fraser.

CHAPTER 1

In the white-hot light of a weekday afternoon, Martin Pritchard took a long look across Camden Park. It had been one of the warmest days he could remember, but he had a bet with himself it would grow hotter. He knew it would happen within the next hour. The sizzle of pavement would grow mushy, and at least three thousand human feet would pound it down another hundred-sixty-fourth of an inch. Las Vegas, he knew, was sinking.

Pritchard kept squinting, trying to find a small clutch of people within a honeycomb of palms and blooming yucca. The park was blocks long, paralleling the north end of the strip, sometimes as thin as a bicycle path, then mushrooming into the wild borderland between Vegas and the desert. A group of landscape artists from Boulder, Colorado, saw the potential in developing a natural pathway within easy walking distance of the casinos and had set about inventing the city's real oasis over the last five years. There were those who claimed it increased tourism by forty percent. Pritchard didn't see it that way. What he saw attracted to Camden Park were losers.

"Look, there's only so much of me," he said, holding his cell phone several inches in front of his mouth. There was something phobic about his measured distance, as though the phone itself was a living microbe. He started to cough, then smiled, his lips and teeth drying out, causing him to cough again. If he did it long enough and perpetually enough, he knew she'd hang up. But lately, more often than not, Elsa simply asked him to cover his mouth when he addressed her, even over the phone. He'd better get used to it, she'd say.

"Dammit, I've checked out the works. Fraser and Hennings in two fuckin' days." Pritchard concentrated his entire body into a line of intent. Around him desert willows tittered softly, their leaves wafer-thin parchment in the growing heat. He kept waving the phone in front of his face as if clearing away the menacing caller, then finally put it to his ear when he saw the back of his daughter's wheelchair. At least a dozen people gathered at a picnic table alongside her. She sat at the right end, her head a mere blip above the seat. A woman seemed to be cutting something on her plate.

"It isn't that easy, Martin. There are some losses going on right now, things we weren't expecting. Our specimens are . . . uh, having problems. We might need you to go back and do a pick up. This week." Elsa, fastidiously prompt, enunciated the final two words.

"You're shittin me," he said, slapping the phone shut. Pritchard slowed his pace toward the party in front of him. He moved cautiously, as if the trees and the grass had become an African plain, and he was well advised to remain hidden, then stopped beside a gigantic agave, its spines segmented in perfect lethal unison.

As far as he was concerned, the woman and the girl could stay there for the rest of his life. He could watch them, neither aware of how close he was. Martin Pritchard was normally hard to miss. Over six feet with hair the color of ripening Hungarian peppers, he often wore shirts blazing in pinwheels. He favored all shades of blue and brown which suited his flamboyance but also kept him attired within bounds. He detested T-shirts and made the claim no one, especially women, should be lured by chest hair. He was a contradiction, a man dressed to go anywhere in the world, yet resistant to simple convenience. In the diminishing cover, he turned the cell off.

Shanna must've colored her hair again, he thought. Pulled straight back into a ponytail, it was the blondest he'd ever seen it. But there was no mistaking her adoration for the young woman seated in the wheelchair. She moved about, spooning food onto Rachel's plate. He knew there would only be about three things on there. Pudding would be one of them, even if Shanna had to bring it herself. Texture, how food felt, was everything to a girl like Rachel.

Over the last half year he'd kept track of them through Shanna's website, the only means he had of following them. He was continents away delivering anti-virus to medical centers throughout Europe, the Middle East, even parts of Asia. He'd planned on coming home at least three months ago, but Elsa sent him back, always with the promise the epidemic would turn around quickly with another update. First it was Beirut, then Gaza, and finally a Palestinian refugee camp in Jordan where the flu had overtaken the only treating doctor and his two helpers. The drainage systems, he'd been told, were to blame. But Pritchard was a representative of Colzer-Bremen, the largest pharmaceutical in the world. And he knew this particular flu didn't discriminate between refuse-strewn camps or the fastidious King Faisal Hospital.

Shanna looked up, her wariness apparent in the way she leaned across the table, then moved her body away from the food and even her daughter as if she'd caught scent of intrusion. She found Pritchard with her eyes. He could feel a pinch below his right elbow and knew within minutes his forearm would go numb. She could freeze him, virtually stop him in his tracks. This was the second time in twenty-four hours she'd caught him following her.

Pritchard turned away and began a long stride away from the agave, the picnic, and the lives he'd been studying. He reached in his pocket for the cell phone, then watched transfixed as it fell from the claw of his steadily contracting hand. In his haste, he stepped on it, snapping it into the air, a blunt, irritating projectile. He fumbled and lost it again in the flurry to use his useless hand. That's when he saw her close, the blur of her making everything stop.

"I think you better get to a doctor," Shanna said, her hand reaching across his trembling fist.

"Whatever for?" Pritchard took the phone with his other hand, rubbed it on his pants, then started to press buttons. "I can manage. Look I'm sorry. I shouldn't have done that back there." He couldn't look at her. Distance was permission for Pritchard, to take her in. This close he kept looking at her toe nails, a shiny opaque pink painted in a symmetrical arc.

"No, you shouldn't have. Sneaking around, checking up on us. How'd you know we'd be here?" Shanna took the phone from his hand holding it in silence. "Oh, not hard," she said, pausing. "It's just a matter of checking the car lot, right? Driving past, checking the website. Instead of just calling and asking to see us. It's just easier to stay in the groove, isn't it? Skulking around behind me."

"You won't see me. You won't let me see her. You wield the power, just like always." Pritchard held out his left hand putting it in front of her, expecting anything.

"Give me your right hand," she said.

"What for? You know what it looks like."

"No I don't. I haven't seen your right hand in years."

"Look," he said, finally able to find her face, peculiarly calm. "I haven't changed. It's still the same old shit." He pulled his hand out into the open air, the fist spasmed, clenched in a perfectly round, white orb. Blood oozed from his palm.

"Get to the doctor," she said, handing him the phone, turning away. "She can't see you like this."

CHAPTER 5

Two men circled a plane, bobbing up and down under a wing, then opened the canopy to crawl inside. They seemed totally preoccupied as Josie drove to the side door of a hangar, the only building mid-field. Robert had always called this place Fraser Strip. "What kin' I get ya?" one of the men yelled.

"Oh, I'm trying to find out something," Josie said, "Just some information."

The taller of the two loped across the pavement, his shadow swallowed by tall grass adjacent to the blacktop. He had sunglasses on, even though clouds had settled over the airport in a broad, gray spread. He didn't try to remove them, just stood in front of her, a man preferring his anonymity or simply more comfortable in these times of illness covering his eyes rather than his mouth. "Fred Deaver," he said, putting out his hand. "Club owner and general wing-walker. Would you like some coffee?"

"Um, sure," Josie said, pulling her car keys. "Can I leave it unlocked?"

"Yup," he replied, "Some folks leave their cars here for days. Only the shore weeds try to break in."

Josie noticed a square of short-cropped grass alongside the building big enough for a car, a rim of blackberry thicket overtaking the edges. A well-worn tire path led into the space and settled there.

"My name's Josephine Russo," she said, walking through the door as the man poured a trickle of mid-day coffee. "And I'm here looking for ghosts."

Fred turned slowly, taking his glasses off as he offered her a mug of something that resembled grease. "You're the wife?" he said.

She concentrated on the dark liquid that congealed on the sides of the mug, the stain undulating across other stains, maybe a layer left behind by her own husband, then watched helplessly as her own tears fell into the mixture. She knew Fred would see them, and he would be making an assessment. She was standing there with a man who knew what had happened. "Yes, I am . . . was."

She watched him shift his weight. He groaned and cleared his throat.

Josie wanted to sit down, wanted to let down. Anywhere. She backed herself against a countertop strewn with open maps and started pushing paper further behind her.

"Look, you need to sit down." Fred's hands were all she saw, pushing away more paper, end-for-end sectionals that had covered a plaid sofa next to her. She seated herself, stiff and upright, wondering what this man would do to keep her contained.

"I'm sorry, this may not be what I should've done," she said.

"It's not you," he said. "It's the whole thing. So sad, I mean."

Fred moved to the large front window of the hangar. He cleared his throat again, then coughed in the way of a long-time smoker. She wondered if he had any idea what a cough meant anymore. She covered her mouth with her fist and put the mug of coffee on the floor. "I still don't know much. There's been an investigation. You probably know about that. I guess it's closed now, and I've got what was left." She rubbed the sweat rag around her throat thinking how she wanted to wrap it tight around her nose and mouth.

Fred kept to the other side of the room, mostly with his back to her. "Did you mean what you just said? I mean you used the word 'ghosts,' didn't you? Like more than one."

"Maybe I did. Inadvertently." Josie studied his hips, now eye level to her. How lax they seemed, even disjointed. He seemed to be a figure receding, and her grip lessened on the scarf. "My husband had taken our wolfhound that morning. Kerrie was in there with him."

The door opened, and the second man plunged through waving a dipstick upward like a wand. "It's low again," he said, taking a long look at Josie.

Fred pulled a can off the shelf above him, then outstretched his arm to his friend. Without a glance he said, "Wilt, this is Ms. Russo."

Wilt backed up as though he wanted to exit as quickly as he'd come in. He was young, barely twenty, and already had the look of a man who'd found his calling. The coveralls he wore weren't orange or tan. They'd started out gray, probably sometime before he was born and were now a mechanic's camouflage. Gray-black, invisible. "I'm sorry, ma'am," he said, looking at Fred. The older man twitched his fingers for the boy to stay.

"We don't know much either, Ms. Russo. Just your husband was inbound that day, same as always. It was later than usual though, almost dark. Had his reasons, I guess, but it can be tricky. Pilots complain of haziness, vertigo sometimes because of it. You know the shore ain't over twenty miles from here."

"Where did he go down? Where exactly did he go down?" Josie felt a bead of sweat slide down the side of her ear, yet she couldn't move.

Fred told the boy to push the door closed. The room darkened and the men kept themselves on either side of the window, away from each other and away from her. Wilt stood with his hands straight at his sides, his head turned toward Fred and the out-of-reach oil can. "About seven miles due east. We heard about the site, but neither of us ever saw it. Wasn't our plane, you know. Guess it was the University's. That and the Land Rover. I mean . . . I don't know how much of this . . ."

"It's okay," Josie said, sensing how close she was to knowing what Robert had been doing here. Even this boy knew. "I've often wondered what my husband's work really was. I know what it meant to him. The field notes stacked up on our dining room table. For years. But so few people really knew him. Sometimes, like right now, I think that includes me. Doesn't it?" She looked at Fred hoping she could see something, some embarrassment that would tell her what she suspected.

"We don't know anything," the boy said, his hands now clenched in front of him. "We told the transportation people everything that could help."

Almost as if Fred was acting in reverse, he signaled Wilt to open the door again. Shorebirds swirled in the vast cut between them and a dark line of trees on the other side of the runway, their cries piercing, like old women laughing at gossip. Wilt turned and left heading straight into their frolic, the oil still sitting on the bench.

"He's right." Fred pushed the door back with his foot, then grabbed the handle. "I have to go help him, Ms. Russo. I don't know what you came here for, but there's nothing at this end. We beat this thing up, the investigators and us, trying to figure out what happened. It's been a quarter of a year. You'd think people would let this thing go."

The grass overtaking the parking spot seemed less noticeable as Josie pulled away from the hangar. Fred and the boy disappeared inside the plane plugging real or imaginary leaks. The horizon beyond them rounded in soft, almost translucent hills, a minor cleft in the upward climb to the rain forest on the other side of the field. It was here where the change took place, the drama of her husband's life. When he left Anacortes that last day, he never reached Fraser Strip. He died someplace smothered and unseen. But it was here where it was deciphered and became history. It was here between these two men.

* * *

The road out of Fraser had disintegrated into a long avenue of sorrow. Miles of stumps pushed out of the ground, insistent and barren, as if a force had stripped them of their belongings. Somehow they reminded her of natives who'd lived here for hundreds of years before smallpox took its deadly turn, leaving them corpses washed up on beaches, piled in villages. Indians and now trees. Josephine watched the road as one who wishes to ignore the burnout of a way of life. She thought of her mother and her never-ending warnings. "I can't believe in a man like Robert," Laurinda said the night before the wedding. "He left a family behind for this. It's wrong."

Josephine had studied her mother's fussing in the mirror. She fingered each of the eighty-five buttons running down her daughter's floor-length dress, indenting each silk-covered tab as if to more tightly compress Josie's figure into the boyish image of her father. One long drape of white accented her chestnut hair, softened by ocean humidity and sun streaked by long hikes in her lover's forest. She looked at herself against pale ivory. Studied her eyes, dark and slightly defiant in the reflection, and realized she was separated from her father only by a veil as transparent as her mother's disapproval.

"What do you think you're doing?" Laurinda said.

"I love Rob. If you insist, I'll be his mistress, his slut. But I won't stop sleeping with him."

Josie could feel her mother's hands poke each button as if one of them was capable of turning this whole thing off. She kicked the front of her gown. Laurinda looked up. "It's been my misfortune to have to shoulder everything since your father died. The business, debt, now this. Why are we making a mockery out of this event? This should be the happiest day of your life, maybe even mine. Instead, I'm mourning for what my daughter's getting into. You took this man away from his home. You could rue the day, Josephine."

She remembered staring at the top of her mother's head, wishing she'd just stop fuming. "You're prognosticating, mother. You don't know what it's like to be the second one."

It seemed like a cry for help now that she looked back on it. Her mother didn't know what it was like. There were things about Robert's first wife and her mother that were almost identical. Both were accomplished CPAs, both had one child, both married the first man they fell for. Then they both lost something. Laurinda watched her husband succumb to pancreatic cancer when she was less than thirty-five. Josie couldn't remember much of it anymore, just his thin fingers reaching out from under the covers, barely touching her hand. But Deb didn't seem to watch anything. When she found out about her husband and Josie, she took her son and drove to Michigan. Child support alone was enough to rent a two-bedroom apartment. The memory turned into the moment, disengaged from the litany of her mother's suspicions. Josie grabbed the Metzger, shaking it until she tore it in half.

* * *

Mile Marker 112 began as little more than a turn-out off the highway which now grazed the seaward side of the Olympic Peninsula. Where it met the national forest, the road had begun the dramatic change into wilderness. The suddenness of growth almost concealed the state's green marker sign. Josie pulled onto the logging road engulfed in the cloak of hard-edged spruce and hemlock, giants shrouded in mist. Within yards, her car disappeared, absorbed into the untouched margins of a scarred landscape. She stopped, straining to see something defined. There was nothing on her husband's map about this cut-off, at least not by this designation, but she had to start somewhere. And, slowly, she was realizing she hadn't been able to depend on him for a very long time.

Conditions, by now, determined which side of the road she kept to. Tree roots bulged on either side of deep ruts crossing in front of her, indomitable veins plucking water and light from beneath her. The Outback yawed like a boat. She looked in the mirror, watching the scene behind her liquefy everything, even the giants, into fog. Then the road evened out, and a clear-cut loomed like an old graveyard. She went through almost ten of these cycles, the forest bands getting thicker between cuts. The trees had become monoliths. Finally, the road seemed to dead-end. Two trails splintered off, each of them barely visible once they curved into the deepening gloom. A white truck was parked just short of the right trail, its tailgate down, side windows partly open. Josie got out and felt the hood. It was cold. She wondered what anyone would want to do out there for so long. In the forest's last assuring pocket of space, she put on the heavy sweater and shouldered the backpack, then grabbed the laptop. There was nowhere else to go, she decided, nowhere but out there.

CHAPTER 6

Somebody had left a note on Pritchard's front door to let him know the community well had gone out for the second time in less than six months. He peered through a kitchen window into his own house, then through the front door pane. Lake Mead shimmered beyond. Every time he walked in, he knew it might be for only a night. Until Elsa booked him for another stint somewhere in a flu-infested world. Lighting a cigarette, he methodically inhaled, and slid down the outside of the condo's persimmon-colored door. Then he started counting toes between the leather straps of his sandals. "One little piggy's for Elsa. Two little piggy's for Shanna. Three little piggy's for fuckin' flu which..." and he paused, holding that toe the longest, "I couldn't get even if I wanted to."

He pushed the house key into the lock above his head and opened the door still with his back to it. Pritchard believed that routine was the thing that killed most people, so he made a point of approaching the expected unexpectedly. He also was too drunk to care how he got in, especially if there wasn't any water in the house. "Perfect," he said scraping a brown paper bag across the counter. "Perfect welcome home for an asshole."

He grinned and pulled the bottle just far enough out of the bag to assure himself it was full, then dropped it back in with a thud. He threw his cell phone across the room, a projectile hurtling toward the lake beyond the window. It fell short, landing somewhere in the carpet-padded cat tree he bought Rachel last Christmas. Pritchard poked around in it for a few minutes, then gave up. The gun harness around his midsection pinched. As he unfastened it, he rubbed the shallow, sweaty dent in his skin and shook the gun loose for the first time in three days. Old habit and probably a bad one, he stuck his pinky down the barrel while he eased the trigger back and forth with the other hand. He could feel both hands now, the way they used to be. The arrangement was peculiar, a man so comfortable plugging the barrel of a gun that he could rely on his fingers to remain compliant, even though less than an hour ago in front of his wife they'd twisted into demonic pincers.

That's what Martin Pritchard still called Shanna. His wife. They were married, he believed, the only way men and women ever truly are—in the middle of adversity. They were married because there was a world blowing itself up in front of them, sparing them time after time. They were married because they were left to wonder why. He didn't know then, like he did now, they were married because they'd been awakened from civilization.

Pritchard could feel numbness begin its steady climb up from the third "little piggy." He stretched his leg across the couch, forcing it taut as if ironing out a charley horse. Sometimes, if he could stay uncurled long enough, the feeling would convert to a spasm, maybe two, then the leg would go to sleep. He moved fast during those first threads of numbness. It was that or go to the ground.

Sometimes, like now, he could smell it again. Shit and chemicals, the smell of the Persian Gulf. Everything had been collared or sprayed. Chemicals killed and then for a few weeks performed miracles. You shit them out, you hoped, before you went home. In the month-and-a-half he was there with her, he took the toxoid just like Shanna did. One tablet every eight hours. At just under ninety doses, he could detect the first signs of a hand tremor. He ignored it and watched for signs in her. But he never saw her get sick until the last few days she spent at the dispensary. She told him it wasn't the men. It was the babies, the Kuwaiti babies they were vaccinating against tetanus, diphtheria, yellow fever, typhoid, poliovirus, and sometimes more—babies, their arms turned toward the unflinching light, absorbing vaccines at the rate of a man. That following December Rachel was born with Addison's disease. Shanna said it wasn't anybody's fault.

For awhile Pritchard slept. The lake began to settle into an evening calm, and when he awoke its presence in the grand window behind him reflected in elongated, shivering bands across the walls and ceiling. The image reminded him of what he'd seen in the Olympic Mountains once. Aurora borealis crashing through the night sky in rolling silver sheets, condensed and magnified over the coastal mountains of Washington state. It could've been Fraser, he thought. It was clearcut even back then.

When he awoke again he could hear the sound of an engine far off on the lake. It was just breaking daylight. The steady whine relaxed Pritchard. He raised both hands flat open and tremorless in front of his face, then twitched each finger once back and forth. He interlocked them and pulled. It seemed better than a few hours ago, and probably, he thought, he could get by on the computer.

In the soft gray of early morning he stared intently at the last message he'd received from Hennings.

"It's not that I'm getting flaky, young man, at least not at this late date. I've been at this, you know, since I was old enough to tag along after my father. But there's something you need to know, even if you're making plans to stay with Colzer-B until retirement (or through the ravages of the flu). I've debated sending this on, but you're the messenger, so to speak. Perhaps you can decipher what needs to be done. Please read attachment." Again, Pritchard read the two lines, now over three months old. *Don't, under any circumstances, allow any more specimens to come here. They will surely die if you do—R. Russo.*

The sound of the motor stopped. The boat scraped the nearby dock, then bumped once and caught. They'd probably have the well fixed by now, Pritchard thought. Jobs around here were un-dignified, but so simple. So unlike what seemed to be taking over his life. He'd thought about those two sentences, how they'd drift-ed through his thoughts overriding the edge in Elsa's demand that he go to Fraser and then to Hennings himself. "Check with the locals at Fraser," she'd said. "See if you spot any disturbance. Any-body, and I mean anybody, inquiring about Russo or the project. And, when you're finished with that, I need you to run a check on things in Nebraska."

Now, she wanted him to go back to Hennings' place. Just like yesterday, Curtis would greet him at the barn, an old man with the bluest eyes he'd ever seen. He'd snap his suspenders, roll those blue eyes heavenward, and let out the most plaintive whistle

Pritchard ever heard. And then it would start. The commotion and the tittering inside the barn. "Gots to let 'em know there's company afoot," he'd say. "They live for company, you know."

The lake had become aquamarine. For a few minutes in the morning that could happen, when the sun split through the overheated atmosphere and turned the water into an inland lagoon. In the clarity, Pritchard could see the cell phone glistening in the lowest level of the cat tree, quiet but demanding. He wondered how many weeks Elsa would've kept Russo's message at the top of her in-box. Stewing about it and the effect it had on the old man in Nebraska. There was no doubt she'd monitored Russo's e-mails, maybe for months before he died. She knew about the warning. In fact, it probably was the reason for bringing Pritchard home.

"Folks got some concerns back at the lab," he'd said. "In fact, they're even a little worried about you, Curtis. So they asked me to bring you this." Pritchard pulled a vial from his pocket. Written neatly on the label was *January 2009, Vial #4, 82 percent.* "She knows about Russo's e-mail to you. I'm supposed to ask you where you stand, you know, as the supplier. That's what I'm supposed to ask," Pritchard said, watching Hennings' face for any sign of recognition that it was the one and only Elsa he was referring to. He held the vial within reach but made no offer to give it to the old man.

Hennings tipped his head once up and down, then said, "It makes no difference to me what you do with that, son. None of us is probably long for this world anyway."

The barn, by now, had come alive with a kind of collective tension. Pritchard distinctly heard the sound of wings flapping against the loft door directly above them. He looked up, and when he did, Hennings took the vial out of his hand. "I'll take it for my family," he said, patting Pritchard on the arm. "I been ordered to do a lot of things over the years. Even Robert gave me some instructions there toward the end. You know what he wrote about not sending any more birds. I'm wonderin' if that's why he died."

The old man peered up at Pritchard, then let out another whistle. The barn went silent. "It's been my experience it's best to leave other people's problems to them. That's how I've kept this place out here all these years without question. No one hardly knows I exist. So, except for them," Hennings said, tilting his head toward the loft, "Ain't nobody goin' to care whether I live or die. Including Elsa."

It was Hennings' way to wait for things. At just over age fifty, he had inherited his father's birds. For thirty more years he kept them sequestered in the same barn his father built during the Depression. He was just now getting around to taking a vial of Pass-Flu. But ultimately, the buck stopped with him. Curtis Hennings was stirring things, old things. E-mails from Russo. And now implying he'd pass up the vial, give it to someone else. Pritchard scanned the outline of the barn, listening for the occasional curious flurry.

"I don't think you have an option here, Curtis. Take the vial when the time comes, if it comes. Otherwise, you're going to become her problem. And we both know what that spells for them." Pritchard walked around one corner, then glanced above. "Ever get that roof fixed?"

Hennings barely nodded. "Just before the first snow last fall."

"No leaks, then?"

"Nope," the old man had said, smiling at the structure before them. "She's as sound as a battleship."

Still vaguely intrigued with the old man's reply, he squinted now to see his cell phone's menu and realized he had fifteen messages. He put his gun harness back on and scrolled through them. One-by-one the demands were compiled in an order sometimes no more than five minutes apart, all of them from Elsa. They stopped shortly after midnight. Wondering what made her stop then, he rubbed the barrel of his gun on his leg before he pushed it in the holster. The night's sousing seemed to quell the spasms, but he knew they'd return. The only decent thing war had ever done for Pritchard was chemical, sending his extremities into long or sometimes short sequences of palsy. But therein was the blessing. In the midst of an epidemic, often in the middle of a community's fomenting death, he'd experience the bloody aftermath of his own hand clenched inward. Yet he never got sick. Not with the flu. Pritchard believed it was still the seeping poison of the Gulf that protected him. It had permeated his nervous system years ago, and maybe even his cells no longer had room for a killing virus. So he took a very deep breath, then walked out his front door into the withering heat of another day.

CHAPTER 7

Anybody who came here would have to love the obsessive soak of months of rain. There was a musty collection here,
layer-upon-layer of something reminding Josie of an old library.
A permeating dampness that broke apart the spirit of newness,
and storm after storm turned it into a quagmire of fading, broken pieces. The trail, what there was of it, had been scraped into
long grooves that stopped just short of the white pick-up. A pile of
mid-sized logs lay there, reminding her of stranded whales in the
salty mist of death. The forest, without sun, seemed unaffected.
It was hardly noticeable what had been taken, and she knew the
trees that remained would deform themselves to reach the scarce
more light. Everything here choked for more room and always,
no matter what, became nourishment. Licorice ferns and lichen
drooped in opulent swags connecting trees—huge trees, web-like
in stifling interconnection. In this soundless world governed by
the weight of tons, soaked in generations of rain, Josephine could
simply blink and lose her way.

She followed the grooves, sometimes deep, puddle filled dents
at times fading to mere scratches in the interminable moss. She
looked behind her watching her footprints sog into collective holes,
one after another disappearing into the oblivion of this place. It
was never this easy before. The night her husband died she'd loosened the lug bolts on two of the Outback's tires. She drove for days
without anything happening, then tightened them when the investigators finally left her alone. She'd thought she wanted to die.
It could change so quickly, what a person wanted, really wanted.
They could wake up on this side and cancel everything.

This was the penalty, she thought, the past stirred up when
Robert died. Even her mother sensed it, and except for an occasional slip, stopped her tirades against him. It was worse than all

the forbidden. The way she'd made love to him in his car less than a mile from where his son was doing homework on the front steps. How she'd begged him to leave them, to run away with her before Deb put it together. "I'll never say no to you, I'll never wear out," she'd said, unbuckling his belt.

Overhead, densely pointed spikemoss funneled drops into rivulets, as if someone was squeezing water from a sponge. It parted Josie's hair into a limp, heavy tangle. Water soaked through the rag around her neck and down her back. The sweater, by now, was saturated in the same quiet cycle of absorption as the ground, and her backpack was the only protection she had. She shivered and moved it to the front of her. Then she put the laptop case against a stump.

It would be the best thing to leave it here in a wilderness that consumed everything, she thought. Every good intention, every miscalculation. The long wait would be over. Leaving her husband's secrets locked in a box in the same forest in which he died was one way she could let go of whatever he had been doing. Josie looked upward into the low gray sky above her and began to cry. She raised her fist for just one moment, cold rain sliding down her arm, then felt her feet plunge deep into water-logged moss. There was no one to tell, there never would be, what it was like to be the second one—a bookend wife for a man like Robert.

Rain fell soft and slow around her, returning seamlessly to the protective gloom of coastal fog. The trail inched ahead past waist-high sword ferns and the mulching decay of stumps. It scoured lower limbs off giant spruce and punched through rotten cedar, their remains hunched together as graceless as old men. An opening appeared within the dull, lifeless haze. More downed logs were visible, some of them butted end-to-end. It was here, when she was concentrating most, she could feel something move steadily toward her.

The quiet that had been so penetrating seemed to crack right in front of her. Completely still, Josie strained to see, to sense. Nothing was helping her, just the terrifying bumping of animal against trees, trees against each other, amplified by the bizarre shuddering of timber directly in her path. Josie saw a dense cloud of vapor, then heard a series of low, impatient snorts. The moving animal was dauntless. Then she realized there were two of them. For a moment steam enveloped her, then a looming, suctioning nose. "My God, it's eating me," she screamed.

Nostrils collided with her forehead scraping upward, warm, blowing impatiently, then pulling away from her. "Stand quiet," she heard a man say, his voice steady somewhere behind two immense horses. Heads bowed, they waited while Josie wiped her forehead, then rubbed the sweater's cold sleeve across her eyes. No longer facing them head-on, she could see lines and hitches cabling them together. But it was more than that. From a moment ago when she'd felt the startled nose, the animals had transformed themselves into patient dignity. The man came up beside them sliding his hand along one massive shoulder, then unsnapped the front of his jacket. "Christ, lady, what are you doing out here?" A prominent furrow between his eyes deepened as he pulled a handkerchief out from inside a layer of rain gear, then handed it to Josie.

"I'm not sure, anymore," she said, grateful for the warm cloth against her face. "This place is a labyrinth."

She watched him check the straps crossing the horses bodies, tinkering with a large ring dead center in the middle of each one of their foreheads, seemingly preoccupied more with their state of mind than hers. He continued, bending over to check their front hooves. "On this trail there's no way to get lost, Miss. Besides, if that's what it really is, a labyrinth as you call it, you couldn't get lost anyway."

After going completely around his horses, patting and checking each as he went, the man came up to Josie, hands covered in the sticky sweat of animals. "Name's Sterns, Gary Sterns. I'd shake your hand, Miss, but I've had it across them some," he said, gesturing toward the horses.

She looked at what he'd given her, a torn hand rag, probably part of a flannel shirt, then handed it back to him, watching him clean his palms and pull the cloth between his fingers. This time he offered his hand to her. "You're pretty soaked. Do you have a car nearby?"

"Look," Josie said, ignoring his outstretched fingers, "It's not that I'm usually this unfriendly, but I'm not out here to have somebody take care of me."

Sterns retracted, not just his hand, his whole body. Like a man deflecting a blow, he turned his back to her walking back into his animals, putting the rag in his pocket as he went. "Suit yourself," he said.

By now, water funneled in grooves between downed logs. It ran from high to low as if it was stream fed, as if its sole purpose was to wash away this man's trespass. Josie walked around Sterns and his animals, readjusting the backpack between her shoulders, and felt seepage run down her back and through the waistband of her jeans. She tried to quicken her pace as she got clear of the horses, even though her shoes disappeared in pools of dished-out moss. The whole tangle reminded her of rotting slippery kelp.

"You go through there," Sterns yelled, "You're going to need bolt cutters."

"What?" she said, hardly pausing.

"You're going to need something to get through chain link fence," he said even louder. "I've got some you can use."

Josie turned around and once again watched Sterns, now loosening some of the harness of his horses. He seemed inured to the way they shifted their weight, their hooves kneading the ground like dough, squirting water high up his legs. Finally, he looked at her looking at him. "You keep headed that way you're going to run into some kind of compound. There's no way through it," he said lowering his voice. "Though I've given it some thought."

"Bolt cutters?" Josie said, pulling a solid mass of hair out of her mouth. "I'm trying to find where my husband died. I just want to find the place his plane crashed." She began to sink, feeling herself lose control. There was no place to sit except a ragged stump. The upper part of the tree, still attached, snagged her backpack. Josie fell, her back striking the hard wood. For just a moment she looked up and thought she saw the edge of blue sky. The next thing she saw was Sterns' face, his hand cupped gently behind her head. "What's your name?" he asked.

"Josephine," she said at the edge of her breath.

Sterns smiled, then looked into the canopy above them. "It's getting late. I've got to get Jed and Liz to the road. Friend of mine's bringing in a horse trailer. You okay for the walk down?" Josie put her hand on the back of her head where his had been. She knew it was going to be difficult to convince this man of what she had to do. He'd let her know repeatedly how acquainted he was with things here. He just had no idea she didn't really care.

They began the walk back together, the horses ahead, massive creatures incongruous among lichen draped in folds of velour around them. They said nothing, the silence somehow offset by the plop of hooves and their own inner thoughts. Then Sterns spoke and made her re-think almost everything about coming here. "I've been logging some in here the last couple summers," he said, looking from side-to-side. "It's the best way to log, you know, with horses. They don't hurt. You've heard all the controversy about heavy equipment. It's true. Horses, mules, on the other hand, they're graceful movers."

She watched Sterns, how he connected with the animals he obviously loved. How he held the lines, loose swaying threads, as if to give them complete decision.

"I don't mean to disregard what you're doing, Josephine. If your husband died back there, then you've got a ways to go. This trail peters out in a couple hundred yards. Beyond that . . . Well, I wouldn't recommend you go it alone."

"He wasn't a logger was he?" Sterns continued, raising his voice in a question while at the same time she felt certain he knew who came and went even in the deepest reach of the forest.

"No," she said, shaking her head. "He was an ornithologist. He died in February in a small plane accident somewhere in the Hoh wilderness." They continued to walk down through the gloom, drizzle evaporating into steam off the huge butts in front of them. Not too far off Josie could hear the slamming of metal.

"I'm sorry," Sterns said, tightening his grip as the horses began to twitch their ears. He paused as if to give it all time to sink in. "Lady, I don't mean to be setting off any alarms, but that compound back there. Did your husband know about what's in it?"

The question pierced. For just an instant it titillated her, this stranger's assumption about Robert, that he would've known something about a place so remote. Josie stood there, holding herself rigid in the gray drench between them.

"Look," Sterns said, as if wishing he'd left it all alone, "I can't say for sure."

"What?" Josie said, bracing her hands in front of her. "Don't you dare stop now, Mr. Sterns. What's in that place?" She dropped her hands, stiff and cold, to her side, then rubbed them one over the other in steady repetition.

"Birds," he said, as if transfixed by the very word. "Birds that went extinct almost a hundred years ago."

Josie could feel herself tighten. Her legs, her neck, even her mouth drew into a thin, cold line. The forest's drench was pulling from her in the same way it tapped through hundreds of feet of firs and hemlocks, pulsing downward until it became no more than a fine, insistent spray. With each of his words it was dawning on her she had to retrieve the laptop before it, too, succumbed to this desolate sinkhole.

"There's more," he said, barely pausing as she pitched off onto the trail's stumpy outgrowth.

Frantic, Josie groped through the air, swinging her arms back and forth as if she could push the gloom to the side. "Hold them back," she screamed. "Don't let the horses come this way. The laptop. Shit. Oh my God, Robert. Where did I put the laptop?"

CHAPTER 8

As Sterns pushed the trailer door closed, Gilbert asked him if they were going back up to the same cut the next morning, even though for days they'd logged just off the Mile 112 trail in a consistency that needed no explanation, just persistence.

"I don't think so," he said. "If you don't hear from me by five, giv'em an extra wafer and go back to bed."

Gilbert Arneson had logged with Sterns for the past seventeen years. He seemed puzzled why his partner was considering taking a Thursday off, even though they were expected to get another five inches of rainfall overnight. He tilted his head toward the fogged up windows of the idling Outback. "She doesn't have anything to do with it, does she?"

Sterns didn't want to lie. Gilbert went all the way back to his childhood and probably knew him better than anyone ever had. They grew up in Missoula, Montana, in the shadow of a local mountain with the letter *M* embedded in white gravel near the top. "There's somebody buried up there," Sterns used to say, poking his buddy in the ribs. "Whoever did it marked the spot better than anything else around here."

"Why haven't the police gone up to take a look then?" Gilbert would ask.

"Because that's the way a murderer figures he can get by with it. Leave it right up there for everybody in town to live under."

They'd gone back and forth that way for months, Sterns finally irritating his friend to the point where Gilbert had gone to the police reporting his friend's suspicion. The joke didn't warrant investigation, but embarrassment lasted for almost a year. When Gil finally started talking to his friend again, Sterns swore he would never tell him another lie.

So, now he simply said, "It's a lot of extra work slogging around in this shit. There's that other parcel closer in to the hot springs. You know, it might make more sense to check that out." Sterns busied himself behind the seat of his truck wondering if he could keep the woman he'd just met willing to talk to him. She reminded him of a little girl somebody'd hosed down. Maybe God was doing his job, cooling her off. Making her think about what she was about to do. "Hey, Gil," he said, as his friend put his truck in gear, "Just stay in tomorrow. I'm goin' in further, and I want to check it out first. Call you tomorrow night."

He watched the tail lights of the trailer blink and fade, tiny red flames snuffed as if someone had blown them out, then pulled a canvas tool bag from storage, preoccupied with how young she looked. *A woman in this day and age named Josephine. After some other one, maybe her grandmother. Wonder if that's what attracted Russo?* he thought.

Sterns found a bright blue parka behind the far seat and checked it for tree pitch. He could see her through the car window, head down, completely withdrawn. He wondered if she was crying. *What was she doing bringing a laptop into the rain forest? Then dropping it off in a wallow along a logging road. Maybe she was sick*, he thought. Sterns took his own parka off and put on the blue one, while keeping the first one wrapped close around his middle. It was warm with long hours of work, and he hesitated, even knowing she could drive away without warning. The ornithologist he'd met that day in Fraser had on a waterproof padded jacket, wool trousers, and hiking boots. Strictly top of the line. If she was his wife, she might've never smelled a man's piled-up sweat, the slightest trace a signal that he didn't keep himself clean. The logger watched a bead of water run consistently off the center of his left eyebrow and knew it was too late to change first impressions.

He knocked on her car window. She looked up from the open laptop but for a moment didn't seem to see him. The way the rain cluttered the space between them, he couldn't tell if she was crying. Sterns fidgeted with his canvas bag. He wondered if she was reading something about her husband. Maybe some report about where he went down. He'd heard the guys from the airport talking about it. The poor bastard didn't stand a chance, they said.

Josie lowered the window, still looking at the computer. He could see the screen was blank. Her hands shook as she kept pushing keys, and although by now the car was warm he sensed it was her whole body that was shivering.

"I need to show you something, Ms. Russo," he said.

The woman's hands steadied, and she seemed to straighten in her seat. She looked at him, the precarious bulge around his waist, at the canvas bag he dropped alongside the door. "How do you know my last name?" she said, holding her breath against the invading dampness.

"I met your husband once," Sterns said. "He told me he was an ornithologist. The only one I've ever met. I admit it was a long shot, you being his wife, but when you told me he died out here, then I knew." Sterns looked up, mostly so he wouldn't have to see the expression on her face. The shadows of late day hastened darkness. Now, the only light, what little light he could depend on, came in thin downward shafts. He strained to see if the trees were swaying above them.

"You met Robert?" she said, finally closing the laptop. "It's been so long that anybody's mentioned him. Anybody who knew him out like this. What was he like?"

He could hear the desire in her voice. She wanted him to tell her something she already knew or maybe she wanted to know something only a stranger could tell her. Some small kindness, something characteristic about the man she'd lost.

"He loved birds. Finches, I think he called them. There was a place he'd been going to study them, I guess. When I saw him, it was a day a lot like today. Said he was on his way back home. That was probably almost a year ago."

"He told you then. About the birds. You knew about the birds."

"Well, yes," Sterns said, sensing her confusion. He kept weighing the difference between them—her in this alien world of old growth with a laptop and an unfinished love story and him with an obsession he'd never told anyone about. It was bizarre, whatever was happening. But it was urgent, and for the first time in a long time Sterns let himself go. "But it's not about those birds that's really important. I think your husband knew that. I need you to get a better look at that compound, Josephine."

He pulled the inner jacket out from under his own and offered it to her as a man would hold out a peace offering. She opened the door, but the computer remained on her lap. Again, she began to shiver, seemingly unable to set it aside. "I can't get into Robert's computer. Everything's probably in there. Maybe whatever you're talking about. I've never been able to get into it. I've never wanted to until now."

Sterns knew she was probably right. The laptop could tell them the whole of it, hidden in files as obscure as the chain-linked aviary he'd been looking in for months. He wanted to tell her what it was like to climb a tree, almost 200 feet in the air. To look across a barricaded jungle so many times he knew just where the afternoon's elusive light would fall, and exactly where one bird always found it. He wanted to tell her what he'd discovered there under the tight mesh of an almost imperceptible far-flung net. Instead, he wrapped the coat around her, retrieving her knotted, limp hair in his hand. "Your husband's work isn't lost," he said. "But I need to show you something soon before we lose the chance."

CHAPTER 9

Josie kept close behind Sterns. His body seemed to float through the carnage of downed trees, sometimes several gnarled feet of them that had to be scaled in increments like the pyramids. They'd run out of trail several minutes ago. The way ahead, wherever that was, was fiendishly off kilter amidst exaggerated spools, sawed off giants that merely used the vertical space to start again. There was a silence here, an oppression of green. To Josie, the forest was the equivalent of intractable ocean, a vacuum that occasionally buried its invaders.

The place he stopped was differentiated from the rest only by eight-foot high chain-link fence. In places, a person might've attempted to walk right through it. Concealed by lettuce lichen and moss crocheted within its wire strands, most of the fence had turned into another ungodly obstruction, no different than the log-jammed course they'd already traveled. The first thing she thought was how incongruous it was, far fetched as the Great Wall of China. "Why would somebody put a fence up here?" she asked, "No matter what you've said, this doesn't make sense."

Sterns turned to her, then looked straight up. "Before I met your husband, I thought the same thing. But that day when he was headed back to the airport he said something that made even less sense. He said the Olympics hold secrets. *Overlooked*, he said. That's why he was in here."

She could see him swallow, his Adam's apple dominant in the upward tilt of his neck. He seemed mesmerized. Then his mouth opened catching light rain like a little boy snatching snowflakes. "I've got a place I've been going to for the last few months. Nobody's known about it." He paused. "Until now."

Sterns pushed through undergrowth of huckleberries and sword ferns, his path slowly opening into a widening trail, someplace she could tell he'd trekked many times. The duff of spongy ground absorbed their footsteps, and over-and-over again he looked behind him to make sure she was there. He seemed more tense than a few minutes before. Finally, he put his canvas bag at the foot of a tree. "There's no other way to show you what I mean," he said, this time looking at her, his eyes half closed in the relentless sprinkle. "We have to go up."

By now she realized there was a long rope hanging from some-where above, attached to someplace high in the tree that Sterns was unwrapping from the base in front of them. She watched him pull things from the bag, a bewitched, ingenious Santa hooking and snapping things into place before his descent into darkness. But this was no trip downward he was planning. The rigging was meant to hoist. Finally, he put his hand within a simple fold of plastic attached to the rope's end. "A Bosun's chair," Sterns said. "It holds me, so I know it'll hold you."

"You have to be insane. You can't possibly think I'm going up there. My husband, if he was doing anything with this project from hell, died hanging upside down in trees just like these." Josie could feel her hands gripping the outside of the jacket he'd given her, holding on as if to skewer herself into the ground. At the same time, she wanted to run, so there she was lifting one foot, then the other, strangely preoccupied with the snapping of rings and a belt he kept adjusting around his waist. He measured rope, pulling it around the trunk, then tied it off in a separate loop around his body. His concentration kept shifting between riggings until he turned to face her.

"There's nothing even vaguely similar about it, Josephine. I don't know what happened to your husband. I'm truly sorry about how it ended. He seemed like a good guy. But isn't it possible he'd want you to do this? Isn't it possible there's nobody else who can figure out what he was really doing out here? Or maybe, they just don't give a damn." She could feel his disapproval, his eyes lowered again, searching the bag.

"If what's inside that fence is what I think it is, it's the greatest discovery among people of your husband's profession, people of conservation, maybe even people all over the world that's happened in at least a hundred years. But, personally, I think it's bigger than that. I think it started out as the secret of the Olympics. Now, it's the secret of mankind."

After he handed her work gloves, he placed a pair of binoculars around Josie's neck. There was such determination in his face, his lips as blue-gray as the weather that curtained them off from humanity. For a moment she remembered the long hours of distrust, how for months she'd ignored what her husband's life was all about. She'd been the one to withdraw from him, not the other way around. She'd let him come here time after time, never asking beyond his simple observances of mountain finches. She'd watched him drive away that last morning of their lives together convinced his considerate habits were the guilt-ridden burnout of a failing marriage. Now, she was finding out everything about her husband, especially his silence, was in keeping with some greater service. That, perhaps, he was as trapped as whatever was hidden behind the fence.

It's so wrong, she thought. *Every reason I'm here is because I'd given up.* She could feel her own helplessness right in front of her, provoking her to depend on a stranger.

The man pulled upright, having strapped metal spikes to his boots in a familiar, commonplace motion. He pulled the dangling rope over to her, holding it between them, waiting. "Rigging's the easy part," he said, "Get used to the feel of the rope, its thickness, how it feels in the rain. Because right now there's no doubt it's the biggest reason you're going to be safe up there."

"I can't go," Josie said again, clutching the thick line, then flapping her gloves in the deepening perfume of the ancient, towering tree.

"I'll be beside you all the way," Sterns said, pulling the chair open. "When you pull," he touched her hand and the rope, "you'll go up, and the rigging will lock you in place. You can't . . . I promise you, you won't fall. Not even a slip."

Somehow, she knew what this was all about. Trust. Allowing someone to help her through just a few moments. Not alone for just a few moments. She studied the bark, so close she could see the way it layered in clefts that pushed deep inside the trunk and forged upward hollowing out a dark, impenetrable world inside. A place of spirits and wood nymphs, a place Sterns never even considered. She touched the brown husk of three hundred years, tracing her fingers across unfinished creases and the abrupt, slow collision between time and tree. Josie climbed inside the chair the logger steadied for her and realized nowhere else in the world could anything like this bear the weight of her tired soul.

"Pull once, now again," she heard him say. "Just relax. Take your time." Sterns wrapped his rope around the tree, then leaned back. "When I started doing this last summer, I picked this tree because I thought it would give me the best vantage. After all, I was snooping. Trying to figure out what was going on in there. But after a while I realized it was a choice I'd made for other reasons. Sometimes you spare a tree when you're logging, and you can't explain why."

He adjusted himself to stay eye-to-eye with Josie. She pulled, he spiked. She stopped, he leaned back. There was a lightness about him, a quality that reminded her of a trapeze artist. She couldn't look down as she listened to words, disconnected, trailing wisps of the man who played in trees. "I bet you swing from branches too," she said, startled at her own impudence.

Sterns grinned and hiked up the tree ahead of her. "Keep it up and you'll be up here alone," he said. "Or maybe I'll just keep you in the tree forever."

Josie could feel blood rush to her head. She started to squirm, kicking her feet against bark, jerking the rope, unable to go any direction but up. She watched him slide back down, so agile he stopped as if he'd pushed the tree out of the way. "I'm sorry. Wrong time to be glib," he said. "Please stay up here with me. Just a little bit longer. There's a platform." He pointed directly above them. "It's really very comfortable. Maybe even somewhat dry."

She looked up, past lines of bark that resembled strands of horizontal writing stretched endlessly above her, a Rosetta stone reaching the sky. A divider seemed to cut the tree off. Light haloed around it, corona-like. Sterns reached across the trunk, working her onto the platform. He told her to focus the binoculars while he kept himself anchored with his own rope. By now, he'd returned to his quiet resolve. "Just point them over in that corner," he said, gesturing toward an opening peculiarly radiant in the forest's dimming light.

She realized looking through the lens that it was a corner of the compound, literally an edge. From where she was, it was obvious there was an inside and an outside, as though someone had trimmed inside the fence but left the fence line itself entangled in a filtered web of young incense cedar. Nothing seemed obvious in that moment besides the canopy enveloping the entire area below her, a second canopy below the trees' own, mesh secured tent-like every so many feet to the chain-link itself. It stretched away from them in an overhead dome spread between the tops of trees. Over time it had collected the remnants of the forest's eccentricities. Needles protruded from the netting like porcupine quills.

Josie had an eerie recollection of Indians who'd died in a forest like this, single or huddled in groups, bound together in the mass death of smallpox. "What is this place? There's nothing to fence in or out. It gives me the creeps."

"Be patient," Sterns said. "There's a lot to see once you really settle in. Now look way off to your left. Do you see it?"

A small building, barely visible in the paisley overlay of shifting shadow and light became more noticeable because of the parking area beside it. Josie trained the binoculars on a car adjacent to the building, a nondescript SUV with a University of Washington logo on the side. A Land Rover. Unable to steady herself, she pulled the glasses from her face. "That's Robert's car. I know it. What do you know about this place?" she demanded. "What secret lives here?"

CHAPTER 10

They sat there, two people balanced above a mystery. The magnitude of the forest, its pall over the dwelling below instilled a sense of complete alienation, as though they were invisible from any perspective. Sterns didn't whisper, and Josie didn't ask to go down. They discussed the scene below them as though it was without detection and so were they. "Your husband wasn't studying the passerines," Sterns said. "He was using them as an excuse. He was studying the order Columbiformes."

"You amaze me, but you don't flummox me, Mr. Sterns. You're talking about the most common bird on the planet—a pigeon. No doubt, they have their idiosyncrasies, but my husband's devotion, I hardly think so. We have a pair of doves. He could've learned anything he needed to know from them." She thought about what she'd just said, talking about the doves as if her husband still existed, as if that world still existed. Sterns seemed unfazed.

"I don't mean any common, feral pigeon, Josie. I mean something altogether, well, shall I say unknown to most of us. Look over in that opening below us now."

Josie trained the binoculars on the spot he'd first pointed out. There was motion, whirling as if insects or small birds were cavorting in the diminishing rain. Even here, there was a feeling that creatures celebrated in the final moments before a setting sun. She looked closely, turning up the scope's power. There was nothing besides the settling of waist-high sword ferns. Then, a tail protruded from between lower fronds, a slender blade that barely moved. She waited, steadying the glasses against her knees. The tail disappeared and a breast appeared, soft orange-russet and very showy. The bird seemed to parade into view, all of him. He had the bearing of a magpie, uniquely adept. Facile. Josie watched him preen, then peer over his shoulder. She saw his brilliant red eye.

"This can't be," she said between breaths. "What I'm seeing is impossible. Somebody's played a terrible trick on you." She looked at Sterns who kept his concentration on the bird below.

"I've seen him from the beginning. Always the same place, always apart from the others. But there are more," he said. "And there's no doubt in my mind what they are." He pointed across the compound. Three or four birds, smaller, fluttered together grouping on one moss-laden branch of a Sitka Spruce. They made infrequent clicking noises as though they were tapping the end of another's beak. Something startled them, and they rose in a tight lateral circle, obviously aware of the barrier above them. The male watched but made no move to join them.

Josie let the glasses fall. She stared at Sterns, who kept watching the ground. In her mind, she sorted through the years of her husband's cryptic notes, the boxes she'd barely opened, then carted off to the University when he died. She flinched thinking about the laptop she'd almost thrown away. In the deepening gloom, she pulled at the rope above her. "This has got to be somebody's Fantasy Island. Someplace for dreamers," she said. "Get me down out of this damned tree."

Sterns reached out in the quiet way of a man calculating a woman's intentions. He took her rope hand, holding it until it was still. By now, he'd pulled the hair back out of his face, and she could see the lines of time in his forehead. The realization struck her that he was no fool. "I've done some homework, Josie. The passenger pigeon died out in the early 1900s. Just about the time the 1918 flu epidemic was starting to build-up in the human population. Those birds are some connection, I think, from that first great deadly flu to this one. Everyone I've seen in that compound has on a lab coat, and those birds you see below us are what you think they are. Even without the flu theory, those pigeons are priceless."

"Because they're passengers," Josie said.

Sterns nodded, then let go of her hand.

* * *

In the encroaching darkness, Josie watched the mysterious rhythm of birds confined not only horizontally, but vertically. She thought of her mother and the two doves she adored. How she'd let them nibble her chin in the evenings when, for a few minutes she let them out. They never moved far from her, cautiously waiting for her to lift the gate into the domed cage, satisfied to feel freedom in inches. It was this way below her in the abrupt, nervous flight of birds, wings folded before they could fully extend. Only the solitary one made no attempt to fly. She watched him, his spare effort, and began to cry.

"It looks horrible, doesn't it?" Sterns had returned to a patient observer, in spite of the downpour and her anxiousness, somehow at home in the heights of the giant hemlock. "But I don't know if something this . . . well, controversial, could've made it anywhere else. No one comes here, except the workers. I've never even seen anybody in the aviary itself." He paused, seemingly absorbed in the sight below. "It's so absurd. We're up here looking down at him," Sterns said, as if hypnotized by the preening, flightless bird.

Josephine swallowed, unable to say anything between sobs. She wanted to recover, to push away from this place and this man who'd lured her into his private fantasy. But she was dependent on him, his equipment, even his overly stimulated imagination. He clung to the tree with only his boots and a rope, and she couldn't figure out how to get off the platform he'd steered her on to. He seemed content to let the rain wash through to his bones. "What makes you think it's a him?" From somewhere unexpected she coughed hard, then raised the glasses for the last time.

Sterns pointed straight down. He jabbed his finger a couple times into the air, determined that she pay attention. The bird's behavior was persistent. Josie could see the long tail, kite-like, spread across the moss-infested corner of the compound. There were moments when it stiffened and caught in the fibers of the spongy plant. Compulsively, Josie coughed again, and when she did the bird pivoted into view. Like a dancer he seemed to turn on an outward leg, assured, almost buoyant. In that moment she understood why he didn't fly like the rest, why he didn't veer from the net in repeated attempts. It would simply be a waste of energy.

"I see him now," she said, infinite sadness threading through her words. "What's more, he sees me."

It made her shiver. How his head turned side-to-side, feathers a steely, fading blue like layers of accumulated snow. Searching until he saw her. A look, maybe, of not forgetting, of observing with effrontery. A bird completely still within a forest prison. Any scientist would've said there was no way to know what he was thinking. But she knew, by now, Robert might've come the closest.

CHAPTER 11

The emergency room compounded Pritchard's phone problems. He usually avoided filling out paperwork by paying some other patient to do it for him. The last time had been an obese young woman who told him when she was feeling better she was in training to become a med tech. That, legally, it really wasn't such a good idea to have a stranger privy to your personal information. Upon which, he'd offered her his Colzer-Bremen business card and a hundred dollar bill for fifteen minutes of her time and clean writing.

But this time Elsa had already called him twice by six thirty in the morning, embarking on a rant about how he should never turn off his phone, how frustrating the night before had been. The emergency room lot was full. He walked to the entrance from a side street pacing his steps between her emphatic sobs, rubbing his blood-creased hand against his trousers.

"We're having a catastrophe here, Martin. Overnight, the entire flock has expired. Perished. Over sixty birds, Martin. I'm heartsick." Then her voice raised an octave. "But that's not the worst. While I couldn't reach you, two people were videoed in a tree just outside the compound. Overhead, brazenly sitting on a platform. By the time they were noticed in this mess, staff couldn't do anything about it. My God, cages of dead birds. It's like they all died on cue. Devastation." He could hear her breathe, gulping between sentences.

"Videoed? Have you I.D.'d?"

The E.R. was a mass, a swarm of bodies. Through the partly open door he could hear coughs, and the resonance of a tide of impromptu gurgles. The room seemed to rattle. He couldn't get past the smoke-tinted doors, turning back toward the street where a new stream of victims came up the narrow sidewalk forcing Pritchard to arc away from them on the manicured lawn. He looked like a man avoiding a jet stream.

"It's Russo's wife. That's the woman," Elsa said, holding the phone so close she blasted fury. "And, we're still trying to type the man." Then she added in a voice oddly composed, "They weren't just out for a joyride, Martin. Out of all the death, one bird is truly missing. Not dead. Missing. It's the one studied most extensively by Robert Russo. That bird, without all the others, has made us what we are today."

"You think they stole said bird," Pritchard said, finally stepping back to the walkway, wondering what difference one survivor could make. Already the E.R.'s were in trouble, some of them virtually locking their doors to keep never ending vileness out.

"I'm sure of it," she said.

For a moment he looked up at the sky frozen in the white-blue of desert morning air. After a bit it would turn colorless, a dome of suffocation. Nothing would move and even less now that air conditioners were being limited to four hours during the hottest stretch of the afternoon. He wanted to distance himself from its stifling contagion. Wrapping his hand in a handkerchief, he tied it off hard to stop the clawing. He took two painkillers, started his car, and pushed the air conditioning on high. "I'm on my way to Wilson's Bridge," he told his boss. "A couple hours, I'll be there."

Normally, he would've assured her that he'd fix the problem, that he'd get to the bottom of it all. But Pritchard lingered over Russo's intractable words, and he wasn't going to say anything until he saw the damage himself. Until then, he didn't want to hear her side of the story, not another word.

* * *

That same sky had turned gray, and the plane seemed to wedge itself clean between layers of cloud. Almost three hours they'd been in the air, partly due to a headwind lumbering out of the Gulf of Alaska. "No one's apt to figure out what's happened for days," the pilot, Danny Mellon, said. "You'd like that wouldn't you?"

Pritchard smiled, then gently tapped one of the altimeters. "No flight plan, no cell phone, no doctor's orders. Right now I'm a man without a country."

The plane made a steep, sweeping turn, then settled into a constant downward pull. Regulations had become so much chaff, soft as confetti. Men like Pritchard, men who continued to travel above the monster that devoured below them simply disregarded what had once been regimen. They weren't clandestine. They were somehow free to appear without notice into a world losing a grip on order.

He'd spent the trip thinking about how things were playing out. Russo's note to Hennings right before he died warning not to send any more birds to Wilson's Bridge, that they would surely die. How did he know? And, why was his widow now picking up the trail? Were they in cahoots all along? It was tempting to blame it all on Elsa, the whole goddamn mess.

"You know, people above me make these arbitrary decisions," Pritchard said to Mellon. "They move through some delicate issues as though they know what they're doing, and when it turns to shit they call in Martin Pritchard. Here I am trying to run down a pair of thieves in the middle of a goddamn plague. What the fuck difference does it make who stole the bird? Live bird, dead bird. Right now, looks to me like they'd be better off without the goddamn things." For a moment he thought of the Nebraska barn a couple days before, the chortling life within, and how quickly it could be silenced.

"Yeah," the pilot said, pushing levers, "Shoot the feathered bastards. I'll be here when you're ready to get back out."

The door to the aero club was locked. Normally Pritchard would've checked in with Fred before he took the car the seven miles to Wilson's Bridge. Today, especially he would've asked the pilot again if someone had shown up over the last couple days, a woman maybe. About middle-age. Probably still smarting over her husband's death. He peered into the lightless building, then walked to the SUV parked alongside.

Between storms, the road out of Fraser still retained a web of torn canopy. Cones, heavy as hand grenades, crunched under the tires, some of them bursting into saturated mist. Whenever he drove in here he had the feeling the jungle would never recover from the slow rot of death. Nothing survived here, didn't even leave a trace, once Pacific squalls drew enough energy to splinter thousand-year-old spruce and heave ocean-going salmon fifty miles inland. It was a hell of a place for what had become a high-tech research network. Wilson's Bridge didn't exist anywhere, on any map. Until now it had blended into the vast, untrammeled waste of the Olympic Peninsula as mysterious and detached as the land mass itself. If anyone had come upon it, Pritchard suspected they would have been immediately put off by its benign appearance and the fear of surveillance.

As he swiped in, the gate arm shuddered upward in a ludicrous thump. Somehow a rail fence with a hinged gate and padlock would've made more sense. A concrete lab recently painted a dark redwood stain was barely visible, nestled off to the right side of the road. The whole establishment continued to disappear more as time went on, as though it was being absorbed intentionally. Colzer-Bremen had promoted invisibility. The facility and the people in it did not exist.

Morris sat at the main desk, a tall man with a slightly exaggerated smile who never seemed to have to go to the bathroom or was tempted by the candy machine at the end of the hall leading to the aviary. He let loose with a short stuttering cough as Pritchard approached. "Good seein' you, Chief," he said, regaining composure. "Not the best of circumstances right about now."

"Yup," Pritchard said. In long-standing habit, he rubbed his leg with his briefcase.

Morris acknowledged by waving him through, then caught the slight sign of a limp in the visitor. "You doin' okay, Chief? Don't want you hurtin' yourself out there in the compound if I can help it. It's empty as a whore's funeral anyway."

"That's what I've heard. Nothing but disaster since last night, huh?" Pritchard leaned against the door frame. "Anything you can tell me about this Russo woman?"

"Do you one better than that."

Morris brought up the video on one of the screens above them, the faint outline of two people, silhouettes until he detailed their faces. Pritchard studied the woman, her body being manipulated onto an almost imperceptible shelf by a man steadying her. Though she was noticeably uncomfortable, she was beautiful in a singular way. He detected a simple agility despite her slenderness trapped inside a bulky jacket. Mostly, he noticed her penetrating eyes which, even at the camera's distance, were unusually wide as if she was enthralled with what she was discovering. They both seemed fascinated with one corner of the aviary, pointing with binoculars, disregarding the camera trained on them. It seemed so blatant, so practiced. "That's the southwest corner, isn't it?"

Morris nodded his head.

"Tell me, Morris, why would some woman crawl up a 300-foot tree at almost dark with a guy who's obviously made himself to home up there before? Even bigger question. Why hasn't anybody caught him before this?"

The security guard began another cough, then covered his mouth as he pointed to the eighth screen out of the panel. "Well, doubtful that you knew, but that camera was out for the past six weeks. We just got Beeker out here to fix it the day before this happened."

Morris turned to look at Pritchard, who began to kick the door jam with a tap that escalated to an irritated punch. "The goddamn camera was out. Jesus Christ, it's a wonder the widow didn't turn the whole works loose weeks ago. Who's the monkey with her?"

"We're still working on it, man." By now, Morris grabbed for the white towel he always kept beside his keyboard, burying his face. He peered above the edge in a kind of mock concern. "We've heard a rumor, Chief, that she stole a bird. Frankly, I'm not so sure. There's plenty of space out there. He could be dead like the others. But there's no blip for Number 522 and hasn't been since last night."

In the back of his mind, Pritchard began a run-down of reasons why this could all be happening. He kept going back to the warning from Russo that birds were going to die and that Hennings, himself, was calmly awaiting his own death. Pigeons seemed to be more important to these two men than their own lives, even the lives of their families. The woman in the tree, however, might have an agenda of her own.

He looked again at the close-up still of Josephine and said compulsively under his breath, "There's only one reason, Morris, for this particular woman to have been here. One woman, one bird. But there's more than one pharm lab in this country. And now that she's got herself a passenger, she's on her way."

CHAPTER 12

Wilson's Bridge began as the Hennings Project sometime around 1919. In the last-ditch attempt to save the passenger pigeon, several men had collected males and females containing them in makeshift colonies hoping nature would take its course. One man, Burt Hennings of Darby, Nebraska, actually saw the potential of early intervention. Rather than seeing the birds as one body requiring acres of natural forage, he confined them early on to a barn sequestered between two ruddy hills. Protected on all sides, he foresaw the structure as housing generations of pigeons. Unlike the other do-gooders, he pinned all his hopes on a prolific food source, earthworms, which he fed his colony from the beginning. And, from that first day, Hennings had success.

Through Hennings' ingenuity the birds multiplied, and within months he'd come to the attention of Theodore Roosevelt, then president of the United States, who was creating his own conservation dream. Few people had any idea what had been accomplished by an old man in an outpost in Nebraska, but the Roosevelt machine eventually wanted to be a silent partner in the preservation of birds that had once filled the North American sky in rolling, massive clouds. The Olympic Peninsula, recently annexed to the list of Teddy's national wildlife preserves, contained the ingredients for continued, undeterred success. The passenger pigeon, already declared extinct, was quietly relocated to the primal outback of the United States where it could be studied without fear of further destruction by a few individuals willing to donate their lives to its secret recovery. Burt Hennings saw this as a recovery for himself and his son as well. Over the remaining years of his life he continued to quietly raise pigeons, some of whom, from time-to-time, were shipped to Washington State. The son learned from his father the secrets of diligence and complete, unfortified withdrawal. The barn in Nebraska and the outpost in Washington endured around a generational secret.

In 1951, the unknown project in the Olympic rain forest was renamed Wilson's Bridge after an American ornithologist and the obvious "bridge" it had provided between a bird long regarded as extinct and the truth of the matter. Men came and went without saying what they knew, but one thing was certain. There would come a time when a government's secrecy, no matter how uncharted, would require a system of gatekeepers. The passenger pigeon, though inconsequential in the development of the atomic age, to a core few represented something beyond the power to destroy. It represented the holiness of life.

It was in the early 1970s that Colzer-Bremen began the slow take-over of Wilson's Bridge. By this time the facility, weakened by bureaucratic indecision, seemed most vulnerable to discovery. An attempt at a surveillance system was thwarted by an ornithologist who warned that any unusual activity within the bird sanctuary, now almost sixty years old, could result in major decline, maybe even die-out of the pigeons. The project left unattended seemed doomed to repeat the fate of the passenger. As Hennings himself had warned, "The knowledgeable few over time will diminish, and the bird once again could perish."

Colzer-Bremen, a pharmaceutical based in Hapsburg, Germany, was gaining momentum in a specialized expertise, something they termed "drug mining." Even at this point, their long-term interest was in epidemics and the indistinct biological connection between man and other life forms. Wilson's Bridge offered a database for stabilizing and reversing a species' extinction. The pharmaceutical struck a lucrative deal with the conservationists and promised to keep furthering their mission. In 1980, they hired Robert Russo as their administrative ornithologist. At thirty-two, he was the soft-spoken, intense champion of a bird that had overcome untold adversity, and by the age of forty he was lead professor of the Management of Ornithological Sciences at the University of Washington. Colzer-Bremen realized he was the perfect liaison between their Seattle base and the ecological concerns of the millennium. He might even be the one who would eventually tell the world about the greatest conservation achievement of all time.

But it was Coltzer's breakthrough in pandemic medicine that kept Robert Russo at Wilson's Bridge. It was this specialized process that was the real reason he managed a flock of birds in the secrecy of a forest in the Pacific Northwest. And, somehow, it was the source of his disappearance.

* * *

As Pritchard approached the sliding doors admitting him to the first tier of the research facility, he felt a gnawing apprehension, a feeling of slowly being lined up for a pinning. That's what he saw in his mind's eye. Someone virtually lining him up under lights, stretching his limbs until the contracture in his hands would make him scream. It was this place especially that could bring it out. The smell of disinfectant, the intense lights, the cloistered warmth. In blood red, the words *Potentially Hazardous Substances* gleamed above the door to Lab A. At least three hooded workers moved about in anxious concentration, shielded from the night's calamity in their plastic stretch suits. No one looked up.

In the past when Pritchard came through he would stop here watching the infinite beauty of injecting a bird. Somehow, it appeared exotic to him, the way the pigeon was barely hobbled while she rode an escalator of sorts, a tramway that took her through a dusting and release, then entry into a glass prism dimly lit in filtered blue light. There was a sense of hypnosis, as though the bird was without a will of her own, as though she never noticed the repeated inoculations and blood draws. She succumbed to the light, the warmth. Stupefied, she nestled into soft lint embedded in the slowly moving track. No human touched her. Instead, a robotic arm gently nudged the pigeon into a blanketed transport cage where her wing feathers would turn the color of snow under a winter moon.

But today there were no birds, no soft hum of filtered light and cozy bedding. Pritchard wondered what they'd done with all the bodies. He pressed the button opening the double doors to the aviary and entered the fenced rain forest. A gentle slope dominated by Sitka Spruce and sword fern descended into the aviary's natural, almost invisible canyon, a geologic anomaly that preserved the fate of Wilson's Bridge. After half a century, the canyon had been modified into a series of catwalks and trails allowing entry beneath trawler netting spread between natural supports. The man considered the possibilities, entering a honeycomb that would eventually take him almost two hundred yards in length and half that in width. It was usually filled with the cackles of birds doing bird-things. Nests built stair-stepped two hundred feet in a tree, much as they'd been during the heyday of the passenger, were hidden in tight-bundled needles of fir. Club moss and lichen pinched into and draped from some of them reminding Pritchard of the strangeness of this place, how it couldn't be separated from the green web around it.

Normally, somebody would've been in the aviary tracking a particular bird, taking a reading on nesting pairs. He wondered how often Russo had come through. *Years of documentation*, he thought. *The old fart was probably as tired of the grind as I am.* Pritchard climbed the first series of stairs to a catwalk paralleling the west side and entered a trail soaked hard in constant drizzle, yet persistent, a winding snake of footprints. Even in the middle of morning humped roots became tentacles and fungus burgeoned from trunks like sticky yellow eyes in the gloom. A woodpecker tapped insistently ahead of him. Camera number eight, eye level to Pritchard, stared into the southwest corner below, then began a slow rotation to the trees above.

He imagined the scene from the night before. Two average people, as much as a couple hundred feet in the air, looking down on a forest without end. *No way*, he thought. *To catch a bird in this shit you'd have to stick your finger right down his craw.* He looked upward sizing up the situation, the tree with the platform, the long haul for a woman and began to laugh, then in one weightless leap jumped to the forest floor. Still laughing, he poked at the chain link with his foot, tapping it as though checking for wall studs. Nothing moved, but a dark mound near the fence corner caught his attention. Maybe a blowdown he thought or part of an amputated root.

Pritchard stooped closer as he reached the disturbance, a section of duff pulled away from the fence. Links had been crimped toward the inside, and underneath their upturned prongs downy fuzz lined the solitary exit. "You conniving bitch," he whispered, rubbing a white tuft between his fingers. He looked up, imagining the man lithe, coordinated with ropes and pliers, the camera mute to his trespass. He wondered what Josephine Russo promised him, then remembered the video that identified her. *Everything*, he thought. The improbabilities began to chase through his brain as he walked back to the lab. The fence links had been rolled upward as if the couple had some greater plan in mind than immediate capture. Why create a neat opening at ground level when the pigeons were amenable to being handled, when they'd come to anyone holding an earthworm? With one slit of the fence they could've emptied the entire compound in ten minutes.

Russo's office was buried in the ground, one full tier below the lab. Though the ornithologist had been here over twenty-five years, Pritchard had never seen the man or his room. He'd only heard about the "birdman" through Morris, who said Robert Russo was quiet, proficient, "and his shit doesn't stink." The apple green of the prominent wall was offset by a brown plaid chair still sitting behind an immense square table centered mid-room. Apparently drawers on one side constituted filing cabinets. A computer keyboard was attached to the front. The placement of a large eyebolt in the center of the black surface was even more peculiar. A mahogany credenza occupied the entire length of an adjoining wall, and small basement windows let in a bare spicule of light. No wonder the man was always in the field.

Pritchard touched or opened everything, finding little to associate with the man or his studies. No doubt, Elsa came in here one night and cleaned out what remained of Robert Russo. He double-checked for a stray camera. Nothing he could find, but he knew she'd probably monitored this room obsessively as she grew more suspicious. He'd been told the University was responsible for Russo's participation in the project, that all data about the survival of the species was to be analyzed by them. Colzer-Bremen provided the lab and the research funding. They were fulfilling an old commitment to keep the passengers a secret, and for that alone they needed an expert in security, something Pritchard considered himself to be a natural at. But for the last eight years the lab had also been perfecting an anti-virus for avian flu from the birds themselves. This had increased his responsibilities, compounding them until he was distributing Pass-Flu in places like Spain and the Sudan more than he was on the west coast of the United States. A convenient absence, he was coming to believe—one that matched, incident for incident, with Elsa's torrent of ambition.

Finally, he sat down in the chair opening drawers still containing a few articles, mostly about the extinction of the Ivory Bill woodpecker. Incredible waste of time, he thought, running through swamps after extinction's proven she's won. "She does win, you know," he muttered, slamming the top drawer. He heard something rattle from underneath. A series of four cables fanned from a wiring harness in the middle of the table. Like spokes of a wheel they were evenly spaced, each ending in an electrical connection at the table's edge. Pritchard looked at the contraption appearing before him and knew there was more.

Once again, he went through it all, the desk, the empty credenza, then opened the door to a tiny closet converted from an old furnace cubicle. Four plasma monitors were stacked there neat as boxed oranges. It bothered him that Elsa must've known about this, because she did, and she was audacious enough to leave it. There was nothing he could do, no way to figure out this man's game. He could track down Josephine, and before an hour was over she'd tell. But the irritation was Elsa, her panic and her ever-present agenda.

Pritchard fixed his attention on the eyebolt. He thought of his mother's dog, Randi, they used to tether in the front yard with one of those metal skewers. The neighborhood kids would taunt her, then started re-locating her, anchoring the rat terrier to a neighbor's fire hydrant, then in their alley. The last time they stashed her inside the cab of a bulldozer where she died in hundred-degree heat. Someone gave the skewer back to his mom, who pounded it into the ground by the mailbox. It occurred to him now no one ever touched it again.

Skewers, eyebolts. They allowed limited movement, probably, in this case, only about the table in front of him. He hooked each monitor to a cable, then fantasized what this was all about. Monitors meant information and possibly pictures, and pictures of passenger pigeons were prohibited for obvious reasons. Russo could've used this room to perfect a procedure, to simulate a lab component. Considering the man was a scientist, and even more a bird lover, Pritchard instinctively looked to the ceiling directly above the eyebolt. He noticed a tile was off center, one corner slightly smudged, then stepped onto the table to remove it. Three plastic covers had been placed on top of the tile just to the right. Two CDs in the first cover were labeled *Training Modules I and II*; *III and IV* were in the second cover. One CD labeled *Final Module* was in its own plastic case. He inserted the first CD in the computer. Just one monitor came up, the one in front of him. Robert Russo began by explaining the exceptional abilities of pigeons in general. *"Like all birds, they have extrasensory abilities to navigate over long distances. But what makes pigeons unique,"* he said, *"is their cognitive strategy."*

Russo spoke in monotones, his head often tilted downward as though he was studying a script. Even when looking directly at the camera his lips barely moved, making the plausibility of listening for very long well beyond Pritchard's attention span. Russo continued with the theory of "Umwelt," the way birds interact with the world. He lost Pritchard in less than the allotted time of a television commercial.

Training Module II was far more implicating. This time Russo was holding a hooded bird on his sleeve much like a falconer. He mentioned the passenger pigeon's ability to memorize hundreds of pictures and remember them months later. *"They can rotate images in their mind's eye. In addition, they imitate successful behavior strictly by observing."*

With the bird still securely perched on his arm he continued to discuss migration—how birds are genetically programmed for time-distance and even time-direction—how they're aware of the passage of time. He talked of the racing pigeons of the great wars. Pritchard fast-forwarded, watching Russo's interaction with the bird. Finally, the ornithologist pointed to tag Number 522 located on the left foot. Pritchard returned the speed to normal and watched the hood being removed from the bird's head. "*Specimen 522 is otherwise known as Gem-X,*" Russo announced. "*He's the most exceptional passenger pigeon in this flock. Highly intelligent, he has been trained to leave this facility at the appointed time. He and I know when that will be.*"

Pritchard paused the CD studying the motionless image of Russo and Number 522. This was the missing bird, according to Morris. The most exceptional one of them all, according to Elsa. He put his hand in his pocket retrieving the down he'd held a few minutes before at the broken fence line and realized it had, at this very moment, become a talisman and a horrendous prank. He rubbed it between his fingers while at the same time switching to the fifth CD, the one, he assumed, that would pull it all together.

An intercom went off. Morris bellowed Pritchard's name throughout the compound saying he needed to report immediately to the security desk. Reluctantly, Martin Pritchard pushed away from the computer, throwing the CDs in his briefcase as he slammed the door to a man's entire life. For a moment he contemplated the power of Colzer-Bremen and the claim it held on Elsa and others like her. Even with what little he'd seen, he knew Russo was a doomed man.

CHAPTER 13

Morris was combing his hair when Pritchard walked around the corner into his cubicle. His desk was clean except for a picture of two children sitting in a swing and a nameplate he kept inching toward the desk's edge. "The dude with the brunette in the tree," he said. "His name's Sterns. Gary Sterns. Goddamn mule team logger out of Seattle. A nothing, a nobody."

"Well, he's somebody now," Pritchard said, kicking Morris' chair to get to the monitors. He flicked on the broad-faced view of the man dangling effortlessly alongside a tree.

"He's at the RV park just as you make the turn off the main road. Been there off and on all summer. Looks like he's done some cuttin' real close to us." Morris snickered and added, "Guess he shaved it a little too close."

Pritchard wasn't listening. By now his thoughts were way beyond an RV park, even beyond the pair of intruders. Like usual he had been picked for a job. What was unusual was that it was only the last half. He kept blinking at the wavy video, then stared at the workers now back in their regular clothes, a few leaving the lab.

"Do you think you should ask'em?" Morris asked. "Maybe they'd tell you."

"Tell me what?" Pritchard snapped.

"Maybe they'd tell you what they found."

He could tell Morris what they found. Without the fancy names, the genus, the phylum, all that shit. They found almost a hundred years worth of experiment gone haywire. They found birds strapped to conveyor belts, carcasses sprinkled across a canyon that doesn't exist, at least on any map. They found a mistake in somebody's concoction. What they didn't find was the only thing now that mattered. "You wanna know what they found, Morris? They found you a job."

Morris' face looked blank, even frozen. "That's good, sir, I mean, I guess that's good."

"Number 522," Pritchard said. "I want his TEL-ID frequency and a portable scanner."

"Yes, sir," Morris said, starting a run for equipment and maintenance.

"Then I want you to kill the platform. You know what I mean, Morris? Kill their fuckin' treehouse."

* * *

The high towers of Colzer-Bremen's Seattle office did little to improve the skyline. Castle-like in architecture, the pharmaceutical's U.S. stronghold had been designed by a German architect and held the distinction of being the first building on the West Coast designed to withstand the initial seaward invasion of global warming. Surrounded by a forty-inch thick buttress, the building's office suites began on the ninth floor. Everything below that was parking garage and docking facilities. A small craft could access the short inlet that coursed its way to the "moat," an ingenious watery access to the building's dock. Much like a canal, water was raised and lowered, depending on rainfall and coastal conditions. It was a fortress in a world lacking chivalry.

Pritchard hadn't phoned ahead. He told the pilot to point it toward Boeing Field, then rented a late model red Mustang at the airport. It was one o'clock in the afternoon on the worst day of Elsa Dupree's life. She would be paying off the debts of Russo's murder, and Pritchard wanted to present her with another insurmountable bill.

He found her waking up from a nap. She'd been in the suite all night, presumably making arrangements to tail the thieves and restore order at Wilson's Bridge. Two rosy indentations punctuated her left cheek. Although she was in deep conversation with someone, she looked like she was talking to herself. Back and forth, he thought, from phone to earphone. A marathon mouth.

"Did you check the RV site?" she finally said, looking directly at him. Her eyes sparkled from lack of sleep, and she kept rubbing her nose.

"What for? I'm going on twenty-four hours behind them."

"Well, good, good. They're way gone anyway, Martin, way gone. But I've got a bead on them." She smiled, pulling her hair back, her skin tight beside her eyes. She was good looking once, Pritchard thought. Maybe before she had hair.

"You know you remind me of the goddamn Pentagon," he said. "Sets the bullets right alongside the diplomatic silverware. Keeps it simple, within the budget, attractive no matter what the fucking occasion."

Putting her hands over her ears, Elsa said, "Get to the point, Martin."

"Camera number eight, that's the point. If I'd been here that bastard would've been working, and the visitors would've been apprehended, whenever," he said, dropping his briefcase to the floor. "In fact, Russo's widow wouldn't have shown up at all, now would she?"

He watched her align herself perpendicular to the long contour of her desk, suddenly revitalized by his accusation. "I don't deserve this right now. Not from my best representative. I haven't needed you like this for six months."

"Yeah, that brings up another point. You want to know what I think when I hear your exclusive birdman is dead, and Hennings wonders what his last message was all about? Something about not sending any more birds here. I think you got yourself a little revolution going on. Seems to me you wanted me out of the way for a while, so you could do your own intelligence. Right?"

Elsa glared at him, then ruffled some papers in front of her. "I've had to persist in keeping our program above board despite the fact you were needed in the Middle East. If some people disagree with my methods, they're not the ones lined up to take the hit."

"No, but when you found out what Russo was e-mailing to Hennings, he was the one lined up, wasn't he? I mean fatally?"

She winced, shaking her head as though Pritchard had cuffed her, then got up from her desk and walked to a series of small windows overlooking the Sound. Daylight poured against her skin in an emotionless profile. "Robert Russo was losing it. Over the last few weeks I've had it on authority the man was attributing characteristics to those birds unheard of, except maybe by visionaries or shamans. He was letting his opinions override the tremendous pressure of our business, endangering the business, the entire flock. In fact, as you seem to be aware, he had the audacity to e-mail Mr. Hennings that he shouldn't send any more birds to Wilson's Bridge. That they would all die."

Pritchard re-read the lines in his mind. He heard the warning from Elsa in a different way. The way she was talking about Russo's infatuation with the pigeons. He'd seen it himself in the training module, a man obsessed with the idea he could manipulate a wild bird. Or a man whose obsession had rubbed off on his wife, who was right now doing something about it.

"It's been so easy to cut me off, hasn't it? Keep me peddling the stuff in places that don't know whether it's flu or malaria they're boiling in. I come back to a mysterious message from a dead man and then talk to the supplier who tells me he doesn't care if he lives or dies. You know what happens if Hennings dies, right? Even if he just stops feeding them. I gave him a vial and I'm still not sure, now that Russo's gone, he'll keep on with us."

"You'll convince him," she said.

"Has it occurred to you it might be too late? When you decided to watchdog the biggest medical breakthrough since the polio vaccine, you left yourself wide open for the competition. My guess is the widow and the bird are headed to Haviland right now. Sucks, but Hennings might've cut a deal with 'em too." Pritchard shook his head back and forth, then stared at the Haviland calendar Elsa insisted on keeping above her first bank of files. Right about now he wondered how she could tolerate the intrusion, even though most of the time it seemed to fuel her edge.

"Lots of things have occurred to me over the last few hours. Hennings is nothing. You hear me? Nothing. But I'm going to give you an idea of what I had to put up with while you were gone."

She reached upward, drawing a long, curved curtain across the turret's windows, then spoke in the present tense as if she was seeing the thing reveal itself. "Russo tires, becoming agitated. More time is lost to his wild imaginings. Orders come in to provide 98 percent anti-virus because of a new outbreak in Melbourne, Australia. H5N6 has serious contra-indications when injected into birds with less than two weeks incubation since the last update, but we don't know this because Russo doesn't tell us. Doesn't tell us it will become deadly at the next update. In January, Russo insists the birds will be fine. And they are for five more months until there's another re-assortment, and we have to update again. Then we have what happened last night." She paused, rubbing her forehead, then indented her fingers against her temple.

"You've distributed 98 percent then?" Pritchard traced the number in his mind, followed its course back to the lab and the room he'd just seen. The eyebolt, he thought. However Russo got this far had to do with innovation, something Elsa had no truck with. He watched the expression on her face morph from distant to coldly defensive. "Actually, no. We never finished the run. Russo made off with the only four vials."

He wondered, now that he was hearing all this, what it was that led Elsa to finding a solution to the Russo problem. Impeccable in everything he'd ever done for Colzer, she'd once accompanied him to the White House, to a dinner with the President and a cross-section of medical entrepreneurs too young to know they'd be commandeered, one by one, into the economics of medicine rather than the ethics. Russo had been her golden boy. She'd saved all the accolades for him, finally purchasing a new four passenger Cessna for his unlimited use and flight instruction to keep him current. He'd never missed an appointment, it was said, to fly into Fraser to keep to the ruse of studying finches in the dark interior of the Olympics. Never, until that day in February when she paid somebody to fray a cable or plug a tube. The reasons, however many there were, were simply not adding up to match the ornithologist's former record. "So you were going for 100 percent. That's why the flock died last night, yes? Because you couldn't wait. And that's why Russo warned Hennings."

Elsa returned to her chair, sitting so far back in it she appeared to have deflated. He thought for a moment she might be finally overcome with the irritation in his voice. "I believe Robert Russo finally realized what he'd done, the mistake he made. He was the ultimate authority, you know. About passengers he knew everything. Not a soul doubted him, Martin."

"You did." Pritchard watched her, the way she reflected his stare.

"Yes, I was privy to doubt. But that's my job. I had no idea we would lose the entire flock in one foolish decision by the best man, perhaps the only man on the planet who understood the workings of this particular bird."

"I know of only one such particular bird anymore," Pritchard said, this time flipping the briefcase's handle. "I believe he's referred to as Gem-X."

"How'd you know that?" she said. "His name, I mean?"

"Intelligence," he said. "You used to trust me at it." Taking the down out of his pocket, he placed it in Elsa's hand. "That's what you've got left of him."

Elsa breathed on the frail softness. He relished the idea he'd found something that, for all her surveillance, she'd missed. That she couldn't verify all he'd discovered in Russo's room. Elsa could only fantasize and slowly lose her grip.

"So you want me to chase down one beady-eyed bird within the range of his worthless telemetry." Pritchard said. "You guys could barely find him in one aviary. I'm supposed to find him out there. Not to mention he's probably in a car, no wire, maybe even dead by now. Besides, what if she's got the vials, even one? Seems to me 98 percent could get her as much money as any passenger. Especially now that nobody's ever going to see your all-hallowed 100 percent."

Elsa raised her eyebrows. Once again, she'd become the inveterate professional. "I doubt she has the vials, Martin. I doubt anyone has. Russo was insistent that the batch was tainted. He quit the run at four, saying the birds had been too stressed. He couldn't be sure of the quality, and I knew when he said that it meant he would destroy the serum like he sometimes had in the past. We've never had a safety issue with our anti-virus, and if Russo was good for one thing, it was product safety. What he wasn't concerned with, however, was Colzer's reputation, our trustworthiness within the industry."

Pritchard could feel himself losing his scant little patience. "Trust? You really think this outfit's got anybody's trust? How long's it been since you checked in with the survivors when last count was one hundred twenty million dead? Have you even contacted the media to tell them what this thing means to you and your company? You act as if you've done everybody a big-ass favor by giving them vials of Pass-Flu, most of them out-dated. Safety issue? How'bout your moral issue?" Finally, he stepped back as if to observe her more scrupulously. "You knocked the old boy off too soon, didn't you? You didn't use the diplomat. Me, the one who does it right. Now, you're picking through the bones."

"There are no instructions that come with this job," she said, wiping her hand across the desk, papers settling around her like a dune of desert sand. "There's only the willingness to lead and keep the lead. When we couldn't make that Melbourne update, we lost credibility. We promised 98 percent, something we'd never come close to before. Then, Russo said it wasn't going to happen. All by himself he could shut down the world's supply from Colzer. But not from Haviland Pharmaceuticals. Don't you see, Martin? There's technology. And no one can keep it all to himself."

"What I fear most is that Haviland gets the bird Ms. Russo has stolen. Alive or half-dead, if they get that passenger we've lost the game. The rest of our flock has completely expired. Even if Hennings sends replacements overnight, it'll take weeks to bring them up to speed. Gem-X is not only the best, he's the answer. Every procedure was tested on him first. Every successful anti-virus update was because of his stability. Dr. Russo was doing something to that bird. I suspected it then. I know it now. He was given that same update, and he's still alive."

Reaching forward she pulled a check out from underneath a perfectly clear paperweight. She'd written it for five hundred thousand dollars. "You bring me the bird," she said, "Alive—I'll match it."

Pritchard shook his head feeling slightly maniacal. "It's a farce."

"I've called in the Feds," she said, undeterred. "They're turning a satellite for the next twelve hours, Pritchard. They'll track that bird for us. In fact," she said, facing her computer, "Ms. Russo and her friend are on the Washington/Idaho border right now."

"Then why don't you have them apprehended?"

Elsa closed the lid on her computer and finally pulled the earpiece from her ear. "Because no one knows how far this has gone, Martin. There's all kinds of suspicion, but in this destruction no one knows for sure what's happened to Gem-X. That's the way I want to keep it. You have to understand that."

Finally, he heard the resonance of truth. That she was systematically undermining standards that had been time honored before the flu's devastation through the pharmaceutical empire. Pritchard lifted the check from the table. Even on half-power, Colzer-Bremen would be demanding an accounting before very long, and he realized everything, even this, depended on his willingness to do exactly as she wanted.

"A pigeon that thinks he's a falcon, two jerks, and a dead man with a plan. Sure I'll take it on," Pritchard said, staring at his boss. "As you've relied on for years, I do it all, including groveling. But you do only one thing for me. The only thing that matters. You take care of my little girl, Elsa. You make sure she gets everything she needs."

CHAPTER 14

The road into the RV park had been graveled into an unending loop of small campsites, all of which were empty, except for Sterns' twenty-eight-foot trailer. Josephine drew the Outback alongside his pick-up but kept the engine running. She'd had time to think on the way out of the forest in its nightfall, trailing behind the logger's flickering brake lights. His jacket, now warm from the heat from her body, smelled of pitch and the acrid exhaust of a chain saw. She could see him switching on the truck's dome light searching for something on the seat beside him. Planning something, she thought.

"I don't know about this," she said, rolling down her window, speaking to Sterns as he walked to his trailer. "I keep wondering if I should just go back to Anacortes. My mother's there. Alone."

Sterns unlocked the door and flicked on the kitchen light. His comfort was evident in the way he bobbed up and down on the trailer's step, switching on an outdoor floodlight so bright she turned her face away. She fiddled with the car radio punching the button from station to station but could get nothing but scratching buzz. All she heard from Sterns was, " . . . little bit. Maybe I can help with something. Been getting wireless here for months." He disappeared inside. Lights came on, curtains were pulled open.

Josie turned the car off, then picked up the laptop. "I need to give you your coat back anyway," she said, as she peered in the open door.

He signaled with his hand, gesturing through the warming air. "Come on in. Keep the coat on for a while. Maybe I can fix something to warm you up faster."

"No, don't. I really have troubled you enough."

Sterns wiggled down on his haunches pulling a frying pan out of a lower cupboard. He stayed that way, crouched down, but stopped his search. "I don't mean to sound crass, but I think we've come too far to just pretend goodbye. It's not that I feel comfortable with you either. You've got some pretty peculiar actions, leaving a perfectly good laptop in the woodpile. Then taking a trip with me, quite frankly, somewhere I've never even talked to anyone else about. I think that makes us, what's the word? Simpatico."

Josie watched him begin to peel potatoes, slicing them in a perfect line. He didn't look at her but opened up his own laptop, tapping, then peeling, only stopping to catch a glimpse of the weather. "It's going to dry up tonight. So I guess you could get a head start home and be there in time for late dinner with your mom."

"I'm thinking about it," Josie said, feeling queasy, suddenly slightly off balance. "No offense, but until now I thought I was hungry."

"Come on." She noticed he paused to watch her. "Come on in. Give yourself a few minutes to decide."

She walked in leaving the door open and put the laptop alongside his. The tiny room, warm in the glow of hurricane lamps, enveloped her and rushed like light wine to her head. She eased her way onto the couch behind the table vaguely aware Sterns had closed the door, then removed his coat. For a moment all she heard was a spatula scraping against a frying pan. Then she closed her eyes.

"It's not the bleakest news," Michelle Matsen reported. "CNN has it on good authority, in fact the leading virologist at Atlanta's CDC, Dr. Peter Schemmel, stated this afternoon that fear-based medicines like amantadine might not be altogether lacking when some people can't be provided with the latest update of Pass-Flu. In fact, he says, there are people who will do just as well on the old stand-by anti-viral."

"Bullshit," Sterns said, "That's why an entire continent of people has already packed it in." He turned up the volume on the small TV mounted on the wall above the couch. Josie felt the head rag still damp around her neck and clutched at it, braiding it between her fingers. She watched Sterns serve them both equal portions, potatoes, toasted bread, and fried sausage. His hands moved in a blur of agitation until he closed his laptop, then carefully re-aligned hers in the table's mid-center.

"He's just trying to restore hope," Josie said, putting her el-bows on either side of her plate and shoving her fingers through her hair. She couldn't eat without first letting go of the tiny, pure doubt about what this man, for some reason, had shown her.

"He's covering for the pharmaceuticals, the whole medi-cal racket. There's nothing like saying something, even if it's a negative. Right now nobody's going to argue." Sterns stopped, his mouth half full. He watched her pull the red rag tight across her forehead. "Are you okay?"

"Could you please switch that thing off?" She looked at her plate, contemplating pushing it toward him. "I guess now I'm stay-ing for dinner."

"I'm sorry," Sterns said, turning off the broadcast. "I get go-ing. You know, my buddy Gil doesn't cook. I do it all. It's just habit more than anything."

She sunk down further into the couch, the warmth from his jacket the only thing at this moment she trusted. Josie pulled it back over her shoulders and snapped the tab near the neck, seal-ing herself off. "Up there this afternoon . . . You've put together something incredibly audacious," she said. "If only I could believe in it."

Slowly, she edged her laptop alongside her plate. "I've come here hoping to retrieve whatever I can from my husband's com-puter, Mr. Sterns. That's all. Thanks to you, I'm ready to tap into whatever he might have documented. But I don't know if I want to share all or any of it with a stranger. Should I be grateful? I mean for what you've shown me? Truth is, I'm not near as willing to show you the view from this computer as you were willing to show me the view from a tree."

Saying nothing, Sterns pushed himself away from the table and finished his dinner at the sink. He seemed embarrassed as if he was increasing the distance by simply turning his back to her. To Josie, he blended into the pale ivory of the trailer's birch panel-ing, mute and no longer controlling. She began the search through the first of Robert's notes, a file dated five years before.

It still seems impossible to me, Robert began. *These birds, one flock numbering in the billions, taking days to pass overhead, should've been so decimated. I've looked at their bodies over and over again trying to imagine what it must've been like to watch them. Speed, maneuverability, sixty miles an hour through a beechnut forest. Above it, but through it as well. Like something from Star Wars.*

Lots of theorizing has gone on about what happened. I'm sure some of it's right. The mass extermination by gunning, bludgeoning, burning, even netting. There's a longstanding opinion that between changes in agricultural practices eliminating part of the food supply and the mass murder of millions of passengers their will was broken, their mindset fragmented into barren, flightless colonies. But there's something else that happened sometime in the late eighteen hundreds. Avian flu was cooking in the background, unnoticed and deadly. It infested birds by the thousands, even horses, and pigs. There it gained momentum. In most animals, it simply and assuredly killed them. But in the passenger pigeon it took at least one more turn. The flu, more than anything else, drove them to extinction.

Josie looked up eying Sterns. She watched him pull a can of shaving creme from one of the upper cupboards along with a package of pink razors. He brought them down sequentially, silently, then opened the razor pack with his teeth. "Can I ask you something?" she said, holding her finger in the middle of Robert's notes.

"Sure." He continued to the bathroom with a razor in his mouth and the creme and a washcloth in his hands.

"When you were sitting up in that tree did you ever feel like you were spying?"

He stopped in a way that anchored his legs in that confined space like pedestals. For the first time she realized how lanky he was, how his body suited the demands of a high climber. "Yes." He paused. "But as you've seen, I couldn't stop."

"I see why. Already." Josie patted the seat next to her as if asking Sterns with the only voice she had left. He approached the couch side furthest from her, sliding in until he could see the screen. She noticed he was hardly breathing as they read on.

The 1918 flu took its toll. But at the time, even human death was underrated. The focus was on World War I, not flu victims or the

death of a bird species. What's interesting is we know of no other popu-
lation that so noticeably disappeared off the face of the earth as the
passenger pigeon, and it did so only about ten years before the devas-
tating outbreak in man—exactly in the time frame of the incubating
disease, as it re-invented itself, gained potency, and continued, along
with man, to waste an indigenous, highly successful bird. That's why
all the valiant tries to save the passenger were for naught, that is, ex-
cept for the efforts of Mr. Burt Hennings of Darby, Nebraska.

Josie sensed this was only a trickle of the information she'd
ignored since her husband's death. She was opening a wasteland
of his private thoughts, the only place he could ever go with what
he knew. He'd left it sitting there in their bedroom while he flew to
his death. Only now, after his colleagues had collected and stored
the incidental life of the man she lived with for almost twenty
years did she finally discover the coincidental. The only part of
Robert's life that really mattered had translated to indifference,
even indiscretion. Yet, now, so effortlessly it was coming to light,
sentence by sentence, that her husband was involved in a secret
so compelling he'd sidestepped his marriage, maybe even his full
potential, to barricade himself from detection. A deep ache began
behind her eyes as she strained to read on.

The man was a genius. He never said a word but kept a small
flock of passengers alive in his barn for at least nine years before their
final fate was decided. Quarantined, ultimately grounded, the birds
should've died. But Hennings was an expert on the family C. He'd
raised doves from the time he was a boy. He knew that in order to keep
them strong and willing to breed he would have to gain their trust. He
would have to provide an alternative to their nomadic lifestyle.

And so it began, Robert wrote. *Only now have I started to under-*
stand what he must've gone through. Curtis has written me accounts
of what his father tried on those birds, one at a time. He logged every-
thing meticulously. Earthworms days one through four, meal worms
days five through eight, ground acorn mixed with mineral salts, salt
peter added to spring seed mix. He built boxes in the barn, then open
wire cages in which he could keep individual pigeons, finally attach-
ing the cages to a series of overhead wagon wheels in which he would
rotate the birds in a kind of makeshift daily flight pattern.

"It must've been beautiful watching it work," Sterns said. "Complicated and thankless. Why did Hennings give almost ten years of his life for it?"

His question ran through her mind. She remembered the idea of cages. How Robert always moved the doves from one corner of their bedroom to another, two little unobtrusive figures following the sun. "It was his whole life," she said, "Not just ten years. And then it was his son's life."

Josie began reading aloud, clearing her throat several times. She sensed Sterns' engrossment. He leaned in toward her, his breathing still paced. "*But all this still doesn't really answer why this last remaining flock of passengers didn't die when the rest were eradicated by disease. How was it that the thirty-four paired birds Hennings collected didn't die of avian flu while the rest of North America's great flocks probably succumbed to some level of it? This is the way it's been explained to me by Paul Garner, professor emeritus from Berkley, now serving as lead consult pharmacological specialist of Colzer-Bremen labs in Schenectady, New York.*"

"*In studying pandemics, and the 1918 one in particular, epidemiologists began the process of trying to retrieve remnants from that great outbreak or any event that seemed to converge with its happenstance. The passenger pigeon's collateral extinction became an interesting sideline, and DNA testing opened a small back door to the bird's genetic make-up. By this time, Hennings' original flock had long been used as seed to provide a conservation-based additional flock on the Olympic Peninsula. But, in the effort to recreate conditions from the monster epidemic of 1918, Colzer-Bremen Pharmaceuticals obtained the right to pursue testing of the secret colony in Washington State. And from that, they derived a phenomenal discovery about Hennings' flock of passenger pigeons.*"

"*The viral blueprint of the 1918 flu from its inception to its final devastating re-assortment was encrypted in layers like geologic strata or rings of a tree on one section of a gene providing a genotype undisturbed through several generations of birds. Like a tablet hidden in a cave, the flu's origins had lain dormant for almost one hundred years in a living descendant of insatiable plague. The birds had not only survived, they were capable of decoding the next great pandemic of flu. And they were certainly capable of preventing it."*

"So Colzer-Bremen began the process of 'drug mining,' a difficult and rather unprecedented approach to extracting the genetic key from each viral mutation the 1918 flu underwent. Passengers were routinely tested from 1980 on in a program as secret as the original saving of the species. I came on board when they inquired with the University of Washington about my overseeing the health of the flock at Wilson's Bridge. They could only speculate as to what extent the passengers could provide current and reliable updates in the case of a new pandemic. But they knew they had the edge on every other pharmaceutical in the world. And so did I."

Robert's personal affirmation at the end of the first file took Josie by surprise. It was as if he was sitting here explaining to her what had been in his life for over twenty years. The sense of honor he would've felt. How unreachable she'd been. Now, she realized the internal struggle that paralyzed him at times, the unexplained absences, the lack of apology. He couldn't discuss this with anyone, so he'd left it in a computer his wife would ignore, then almost destroy. She'd come close to eliminating him from her life even with this second chance.

She began to cry, the tears slow, steady, alongside her nose, making her whole head feel as if it was a series of tributaries, all running down her throat. She coughed and tasted a tinge of blood. "Kleenex," she said, reaching across the table, straining forward. "I can't get up," she said. "I know I'll pass out."

Sterns pulled her back, and for a moment she felt him hesitate, his energy focused on keeping her there. She didn't look at him. Her eyes were still fixed on the monitor, but she couldn't separate words anymore. The screen began to split, first into two long lines that seemed to divide and subdivide like a computer version of pick-up-sticks. Headache encircled her eyes, making it hard to keep straining, and there was a feeling of shrinking visual space. She wondered if in a few more minutes she wouldn't be able to see, just like when she had chickenpox years before. She pulled the head rag down over her eyes and held it there.

"Do you want to lie down?" Sterns finally asked, patting her shoulders through the coat. "I can't do much, but I don't think you should be going anywhere. I shouldn't have taken you up that damned tree."

"Yeah, right, you spy. You've infected me. No, I don't mean that. Not flu," she said, feeling his touch slightly lessen. "Right now all I want you to do is keep reading. Please."

So Sterns began again, this time reading a second file as he unearthed a handkerchief deep inside his pockets. She felt him unfold it in her hands, saying without saying that it was clean. Head down, she held onto it and the head rag in a tight, sweaty grip. "*There is, to my way of thinking, a perpetual Oz of this operation. Curtis Hennings is now almost eighty-one years old. I've kept in communication with him about so many things over the years. The way the birds seem to meet on some unexplained cognitive level, how they advance through inoculation after inoculation, low coos, maybe raising a wing, but no miasma, no dread. There is one, though, Number 522, I keep thinking about. And I've told Curtis about. Gem-X, the meteor that bursts into the aviary whenever training is over, wings swept back, pushing for speed as if the boring route is only good for one thing. He's the one who tells me the most. Curtis says there's always one . . .*

Curtis once told me the secret of raising passenger pigeons. He said if it hadn't been for his father and his powers of observation, he doesn't think the birds would've survived. The fact is, there must be a leader. For years, everyone thought the passengers were team birds, eyes bulging from heads, beaks instead of brains, caught up in vast rolling flocks, as for the most part they were. But in the final breakdown some flocks seemed to determine a natural leader, and that too doomed the great numbers. Because if and when he was shot down, netted or bludgeoned, the rest were without a steadying force and often suffered the same fate. Hennings noticed this tendency early on and engineered a hierarchy that strengthened leadership and bonding. Gem-X is the purest form of Hennings' breeding strategy. He's the result of five to six generations of captive passengers."

By now, Josie laid her head on the table. She would moan and breathe through her mouth, then tap the table with one of her hands. She was doing this when Sterns stopped to ask her again what he could do. "Do you have anything with you, any medicine?"

"There's some aspirin in my backpack, but not yet . . . Keep reading, do not stop," she said, gritting her teeth.

Haltingly, Sterns read from the next document. *"Birds speak to us. More than any other non-human species. Even more than chimpanzees. After all, they have more to say. They are the voice of the stars and of the sun."*

Russo spoke of Gem-X and the nocturnal restlessness he would seem to experience at times. For this reason and perhaps others, he had often bathed the bird in soothing blue light. He mentioned over and over the bird's specialized neural wiring and his excellent visual memory. *"Curtis, I believe he communicates with me more through hunches than anything else. It's hard to explain (and sounds ludicrous), but there's a feeling I get sometimes of extreme fear, the fear that comes before extinction is the only way I can explain it. I wonder if it's a mass thing because I'm with these birds so much. But it's Gem-X who seems the most traumatized, the most stimulated. There's got to be a way to give him some assurance. Otherwise, I'm afraid for him—for his brilliance."*

One last file was the most updated, even though it was almost a year old. As Sterns opened it, he could see there was a different tone to Russo's notations. No longer invigorated, the ornithologist documented his thoughts in a kind of phraseology, even numbering his concerns as though he was struggling to keep things objective. Sterns skimmed quickly while Josie coughed in a tight, dry spasm. "I'm getting your backpack," he said. "You're not going to even understand this in a few minutes."

She waited for him to go out the door, then pulled up the head band. Her eyes focused on the screen's tiny print darkened in bold.

Over time the question of why Hennings' passengers didn't succumb to the 1918 flu has been obliterated by the question of how we can prevent a similar occurrence in man again. There is probably some law of immunology the birds out-maneuvered that first time. Perhaps it came through Hennings himself. But now, I'm afraid for this flock. There's been too much pressure on them.

    1) Inoculations, at least once every three months for almost two years.

    2) Twice weekly to daily blood draws.

    3) Titrations showing anti-virus depletion.

    4) Serum's impact inadequate for current outbreak.

    It's my job to protect this species. First and foremost. I'm not being listened to. If Colzer-Bremen decides to step-up production of Pass-Flu, they will look first to inoculations, bringing them closer together. Any less than three months apart, the birds will die on the next update. There is no sparing. The middle ground is gone. No one is listening.

    Underlined at the end of the alarm Robert Russo wrote, *Gem-X and I, however, have a plan.*

CHAPTER 15

The moon's faint light pierced the forest for the first time in a week of continuous overcast. Sterns watched the way it hovered, a celestial flashlight magnifying the upper branches of giant hemlock towering above him, then sinking, spreading itself in a glaze between campsites. It couldn't be a worse night, he thought, for its persistence.

He found Josie's backpack on the floorboard of the Outback buttoned and zipped every way possible. There was contrariness about her, he thought. To have ignored the laptop for months, then left it in the graveyard of timber slash without reading her husband's painstaking notes made him wonder about people, about females in particular. In a flash of remembrance he recalled a string of nights like this years ago when he'd gone out on Carolina's front steps, just to catch the long-forgotten scent of her climbing yellow rose. And study the shape of garden gloves that even yet, if he could hold them, would conform to the exact shape of her hands. She came back to him, he'd noticed, in shapes and scents, perhaps as part reflection of what suffering she'd been through. He considered the woman in his trailer, how little she reminded him of his old girlfriend, except for one commonality. Defiance, he'd have to call it. Refusal to submit to the relentless encroachment of disease.

Contents of the pack were layered neatly but certainly not things for the long haul. Matches, jerky sticks, but no aspirin. A sweatshirt and socks implied more of a sleep-over than an arduous walk to the place of her husband's death. It was as though she had known less than he did about the whereabouts of her husband's last minutes. The thought struck him that perhaps she never intended to find the point of impact. That she'd simply found it a place to head toward, but never find.

Sterns dug deep into one side pocket and drew out the first aid kit. The placard inside the lid, the updates listed there single-file, seemed to delineate a fixation with time and percentage. He still couldn't find any aspirin, but two tissue-wrapped shapes wedged in a corner were strangely conspicuous. *Pass-Flu, January 2009, 98 percent* was printed on the front of two vials. A small needle was attached to the head of each encased in a clear plastic bubble. Sterns pulled them from the kit, slipping them into his pocket, then re-folded the backpack as he'd found it. He worked the thought over in his mind that maybe she knew more than she was letting on, and that she might have something she wasn't supposed to have.

The day he'd met Robert Russo he'd been trying to find a metal clip, the kind usually connected to the end of a dog's leash, at Kiddner's Hardware. Eventually, everybody in these parts passed through Kiddner's, the only store in a logging town that still carried parts small enough to fit in your pocket. He'd been on his haunches digging through a box when a man in olive green snow boots stepped alongside him. The boots didn't move. Finally, Sterns got up, disbelieving someone would want that same exact spot in the store and for so long.

"Dr. Robert Russo," the onlooker began, still hardly moving. "Ornithologist, University of Washington." He put out his hand. "Your name?"

Sterns believed he must've looked perturbed, perplexed or both because the man named Russo took a step back and began to paw through fittings and more clips. "Gary Sterns. By any chance am I in your way?"

"Well, sort of," Russo continued. "Are you looking for parts for your pulley?"

"Pulley?" Sterns kept watching the man calmly stirring the box of parts.

"Southwest corner of a very secluded compound less than ten miles from this very spot," he said. "Very top notch operation you have. I'm impressed, but then I'm easily impressed."

Sterns could remember swallowing hard, so hard he'd coughed unexpectedly, fine spray settling across the stranger's hand and his sleeve. He'd felt a sweaty outbreak where only a moment before he'd been immersed in concentration. "Oh, Jesus," he whispered. "You know, Dr. Russo, we're both interested in birds. I mean I can't lie to you. What I've been doing . . . well I expected . . ."

"To get caught," Russo said, keeping his hand forward, the store's fluorescent light accenting the dimpled spray on his knuckles. "Look, Mr. Gary Sterns, I'm just a small part of a very big equation. One devoted to helping mankind in the most imminent way possible. No one knows really what goes on there, including myself, completely. But I'm afraid I've made a decision. A very arbitrary one at that. If you don't stop what you're doing in that tree someone much more hostile than I am might catch up with you. Probably not in the local hardware store either."

He could still feel the embarrassment, the teasing behind Russo's eyes. Even now, he recalled the man's amusement, yet his simple refusal to back off. A soft thread of light from above Josie's head traced across the campsite, and Sterns could hear her throaty hack while he sat inside her car. He realized he could never forget her husband's erstwhile warning. "There are hard times ahead, young man. Things that will call upon ingenuity not unlike yours. That place you've discovered is a secret, truly one of the great secrets of all time. Frankly, I think the day has come for revelation. So, I'm going to start right here . . . with you."

Russo had continued, hardly taking a breath. "Some days I study finches. The Olympic Rain Forest has them, you know. Wild mountain finches. But it also has other birds. Birds from another time, another place. A family of birds some would call the original superdove. E. migratorius."

He had stopped as if disassembling only select pieces of a myth. Sterns felt immediately he was about to meet this man's obsession head-on, but pared down in slivers, so an intruder could understand. "You've heard of bird flu, no doubt. Few people doubt its existence now that it's begun to swarm through birds and now people on this planet. It could be as devastating as it was in 1918. Because, Mr. Sterns, it's a lot the same. Frighteningly similar. The fact is what you've been taking in up there in that tree, those birds you've been so fascinated with, fascinate us too. In fact, they're keeping us all alive."

With that, Russo reached into his pocket and pulled out a sticker adhesed to an otherwise empty note. The logo, familiar to millions by now had stretched across TV screens and billboards for months. In fact, it was so commonplace the name itself seemed to conjure global relief. *Pass-Flu*, it said, *Will Ultimately Cure*. "It's time for me to go home," he said, abruptly ending the conversation while dropping the note that fluttered and disappeared under shelving.

A preoccupied stare seemed to cloud the face of the ornithologist as he turned toward the store's entrance. No longer the observer, he shuffled a bit as he walked away from Sterns, and it was only then he noticed that Russo collected an Irish wolfhound waiting patiently for him outside the front door. The memory drifted, detached from virtually everything else Sterns had ever heard about the flu and its voracious, unconquerable appetite. Again, he watched the outline of Russo's wife, the way she hunched and choked over the laptop, and realized the vials in his pocket were the remnants of something Russo had been talking about. *Keeping us alive* and his answer to keeping her alive.

"Will it?" he whispered into the Outback.

He found Josie, her head to one side, face-down on the table. Sweat beaded and drained from her face taking with it the deep fleshiness of her skin. As she looked up, her lips turned blue-gray, and her eyes stared motionless in a wash of tears. "That bird I saw. He was Gem-X wasn't he? My husband found something special about him." Her voice cracked, and he realized her mouth sounded dry, filling with fever.

"You need to rest," Sterns said, placing a wool throw across her lap. "You're getting sick."

"I know. I feel worse in a way I can't explain. The bird, though. He was doing something down there below us, wasn't he? Trying to get out maybe."

"Maybe. There was no aspirin. I might have some ibuprofen."

"Yeah," she said. "Robert was on to something they were go-ing to do to those birds. He couldn't stop them." She paused, hold-ing her breath, then swallowed hard. "Now it's my job."

"What do you mean, it's your job? You didn't know a thing about all this half a day ago, didn't even know what your husband was doing out here. You've caught something. Flu or something. Settle down, let the pills take hold." Sterns watched her barely part her lips to take two capsules with a small cup of water.

"Precisely," she moaned. "All the more reason to get out of here, out of your space. In the morning I'll be better, and you can go about your business."

"And where do you think you're going to make it to?

"Nebraska," she whispered. "Darby, Nebraska."

* * *

Sterns began the long night by moving Josie's laptop to a corner table in the living room, then gently re-positioning her the length of the couch. Every now and then he would hear her breathing, not the gentle in-out of sleep but a husky, penetrating wheeze that sometimes shook her huddled body. After what she said about Nebraska she hadn't raised her head again. He won-dered if it had somehow fulfilled a dream she couldn't awake from.

He wandered deeper into Russo's files, a man afflicted with more curiosity than sense. But that had been the way weeks be-fore the encounter at Kiddner's Hardware and something that had taken on a life of its own since the ornithologist's warning. Sterns had watched the emergence of Pass-Flu as a life-saving drug world-wide, it's praises sung from the CDC to every major network in a series of news releases for months before and after the flu entered the United States. He'd believed it all, but mostly, he believed he would never come face-to-face with it.

He put the two vials on the table and studied their composi-tion, a thin line of identical tubular volume and slightly amber color. He knew from numerous broadcasts that people weren't supposed to take a dose until they felt the first signs of illness. Otherwise, it would lose its potency and, in some cases, merely evaporate into nothing stronger than an antibiotic. It was a drug that required supervision. If you were alone, you could become sick so quickly you might not have the capacity to inject yourself. Obviously, Robert Russo had presumed he and his wife would be together in their decision to use it, or at least, if left to one of them, she was the one designated to take action.

He began reading, again studying the long-standing file notes Russo had documented as if he was journaling to a friend. In fact, it seemed often he was. He mentioned Hennings, starting thought-provoking statements with his first name.

Curtis, you and I know the passenger pigeon might've come through the greatest flu of all time if it hadn't been decimated by hunters. It held the genetic map of this epidemic because it had experienced that one. Unlikely thought I've had lately, but I wonder, is it possible its very demise sealed off the genetic mutations? Trapped them like bones in limestone. Maybe their death had to happen to give us what we know now.

It was as though Russo was documenting the substance of his e-mails to Hennings, keeping a log for his own tracings or for someone else to find. There was spirituality to his writing, not scientific, not factual, but as though he was confiding in someone with a greater understanding. He was outwardly quizzical. Peculiar for a doctor, Sterns thought.

Pneumonia. The captain of the means of death, Russo wrote. *Pneumonia impacting hundreds, thousands in Iraq with little relief from Pass-Flu. Should have greater efficacy, I'd think at 73 percent. Antigen drift is causing alarming rate of casualties. Has shut down borders but ironically hasn't decreased terrorism. Isn't this outbreak devastating enough?*

Sterns looked again at the vials, *98 percent, January 2009.* Colzer-Bremen's Pass-Flu had come a long way. He studied Josie's moving lips, the agitated pulse in her neck and remembered another truth about anti-virus. Medicine made no bones about it. They took care of their own first, admitting they couldn't save anyone else if doctors, nurses, physician's assistants, even dentists weren't provided the drug at every update. Russo had been part of that elite few, documenting his updates on a placard in a first aid box. Had he always left the box with his wife? And even if that was his neat way of storing anti-virus for her, why didn't he keep one with him at all times? After all, he was the birdkeeper of Wilson's Bridge, probably one of the most critically exposed of all its personnel. Sterns tilted a vial on its side, then shook it back and forth, undecided about what he should do.

He wanted to go to bed, to sleep through this strain, but instead opened a window and detected the faint taste of ocean salt permeating the coming night. He needed to think, to reason, and thought of calling Gil. But it was Carolina, her long-remembered, weakening whispers interspersed with doubt about what the vials were capable of that rattled Sterns, that sent him pacing the length of the trailer, opening windows, and feeling the presence of cloistered death. There had been no such vial of anti-cancer drug when she was dying. Nothing he could hold in his hand and deliberately consider giving her. Leukemia saturated her and finally washed over him in a paralyzing wave. He was meant to watch and only watch. Restricted to the sainthood of not interfering.

Sterns reconnected with the laptop, trying one more thing. Russo's e-mails, however many there were, were secure, locked behind a password the man probably changed every month. *E-migratorius* then *Superdove* seemed appropriate, words Russo had specifically spoken that day at Kiddner's, but led nowhere. Then Sterns typed in *Gem-X*. The screen indicated two e-mails were waiting for Russo, both from an address known as *Henpigeon*. Dates blinked alongside them of early February. *Close to the time Russo died*, he thought.

The messages were from Curtis Hennings, apparently sent at a time when Russo had already taken his fateful flight. There was no other explanation why these two had been left unread. Sterns hesitated, jiggling the mouse in agitation. He had unraveled things this far, but only because of Russo's willingness to confide. Opening personal messages might take him somewhere he'd regret. Or they might show him the intimate connection between these two men.

Don't, under any circumstances, allow any more specimens to come here. They will surely die if you do. The statement comprised the only notation Russo sent to Hennings on the second of February. It stood alone in stark formality that seemed uncomfortably precise, a command, not a suggestion.

Hennings replied in booming praise, deflecting the warning as if it was not even an issue. '*I understand the large hearts of heroes,*' he began. '*The courage of present times and all times.*' Whitman, my boy. He knew about courage like yours. Don't worry. We'll be fine.

The second e-mail was a stand-alone message from Hennings on the fourth of February. *Yesterday I wondered about you, the meeting and all. After what you said about the vials, I wouldn't let them out of your sight, Robert. May never happen again. Hold that bird steady, my boy. He means to fly.*

Sterns re-read the second message several times, each time sifting through the layers of meaning. Overwhelmingly, he was aware of Hennings' love for this man, then his brief, very electric insight. As easy-going as the old man seemed, he was ardent about the importance of the vials, probably the very ones Sterns now had. Hennings said a lot in those six sentences, no doubt, too late for Russo. But there was a feeling something was about to be unleashed whether he was dead or alive.

In the deepening hours, exhausted by recollection, Sterns first sat beside Josie on the narrow couch, then bent low over her, listening. Her body instinctively moved outward, and he watched her unfold an arm from somewhere inside the jacket. He could feel the fever escape into the air around him, and for a moment it soothed. Then she coughed. A gurgle pushed its way into her throat, and she stuck her tongue out. He couldn't believe what he was seeing. It looked as though fur covered it in a layer of dull white. She coughed again, then began to choke. "Robert," she screamed, "I can't breathe. No air. Is this where you are? Please, Robert, let me breathe."

Sterns propped her head on his chest and moved closer, pushing behind her. She squirmed trying to get away, then fell back, her hair sticking to his face in thin wet strands. He could smell her sickness, the way it soaked from the inside out. That was probably the reason she hadn't gone to the bathroom since she'd been with him. He shuddered under her cries but somehow forced his hand into his pocket.

Strange he would think of it now. He still couldn't remember the last time he'd seen the ring he'd given Carolina. She didn't have it on when she told him they'd have to call off the wedding. He never asked her what she did with it, just like she never asked him what he was going to do about the two funerals he was facing. All he knew was there wasn't enough time to be with her, to feel her heartbeat under his ear. Or gently place her arms over her head while he kissed her breasts. It wouldn't be right anymore, he thought. Because she was dying at exactly the same time they found his brother's body, what was left of it, embroidered within a parachute in the Rampart Wilderness. In that short summer so many years ago, their two lives had become one death for Sterns. He didn't see them separately anymore.

Sterns could feel Josie's pulse, her neck alongside his so close he wasn't sure if it was her blood or his he could hear. He forced a vial out of his pocket, then balanced it on his knee. He was aware for just a second that he was able to choose. To let it shatter on the trailer floor or even put it back in his pocket. It wasn't hopeless yet, he thought. Hopeless was waiting. Looking at her, a butterfly pinned to a white, motionless sheet.

"God almighty, forgive me," he said, prying his thumb under the vial's fragile cap. Hesitating, he shook it for the last time and in one decided motion plunged the needle into her forearm. "I'll stay with her," he said rocking her motionless body back and forth. "Robert, I'll stay with her."

CHAPTER 16

She woke him by slamming the trailer door. His coat was hanging on the hook above him, and the plate he'd given her last night sat on the counter alongside his toothbrush. Her laptop was gone. Sterns took it all in, even though darkness still pervaded the trailer. Only the small light over the sink gave him a clue she was leaving. That and the tinny slam of the door.

The Outback was running, the hum of its engine overtaking layer upon layer of insulated stillness. He watched her adjust the headlights bright to dim as though she was unsure of her preference, then wondered if she could even really see.

"Not even going to say goodbye?" he yelled. "You were pretty sick last night. Think you might be pushing it?"

Josie pulled at the door as though she wanted to close it before he could get to her. But it seemed too heavy or she missed the door handle and lost her balance, finally grabbing a small fir alongside the car door, sending it into tremors. Sterns pushed under her shoulder hoping she'd grab on. Instead she swatted him. "What do you care about this whole thing anyway?" she said, pulling away, her face obscured by a high-necked sweater and the red rag loose over her mouth. "You don't know anything about my husband that I wouldn't have figured out on my own. In fact, if you'd left me alone, I'd have made it to where I should be right now. I'd be there right now, where he died."

She turned her head, then her whole body away from Sterns. He felt the seat shudder, then noticed the backpack unopened on the floorboard beside her. She was so close to driving away, he thought. But it couldn't erase what he'd done only a few hours before. Bracing himself, he pushed away from the car, outstretched above her in the improbable hope she wouldn't touch the accelerator.

"You're a long way from home, Josie. And you're a long way from where he died. What you're close to is extinction. There's something happening here that, according to history, should've been finished a hundred years ago. Instead, it's still with us. Those birds, they're not just a figment."

"I know," she said through the chatter of teeth. "I know."

"Are you going to Nebraska?" he asked.

"When I can hold my head above the steering wheel, I'm going. I've stayed long enough, wasting time. There's an old man out there who knows everything."

Sterns looked up as far as he could, straining to find the outlines of needles against the gray Pacific sky. They could finally be distinguished, one from the others, as the sun burned through elevation and fog. This morning he could see them, imperfect clusters of disconnection. Then they blurred, receding into the damp ether above him. "It won't be easy," he said. "There's a lot of unrest. Nowhere to go if you get sicker."

For a moment he wanted to confess what would be happening inside her body. How something deadly enough to eliminate millions was hybridized into a 98 percent serum that could save her life. That he didn't know anything about it other than it was derived from an extinct bird he'd been told could save mankind. The night before he'd watched her slide into darkness where pure menace was waiting. The place where thousands before her had felt the epidemic rage, where blood became hemorrhage anyplace it could escape. Where eyes lost vision and putrid bloody foam would line her ears. Her uterus would bleed, and she'd lie in her own slow-filling death. He didn't know what he'd given her, but Sterns knew what the world had, and right now he didn't know which was worse.

Josie sat as upright as she could, holding her head to one side as if that was the only way to focus. Bags encircled her eyes in waxy gray mottling. Her breath reminded him of mildewed newspapers his grandmother used to keep packed in a chest-of-drawers alongside her house. If Josie left now the forest would swallow her. She would die in the direct path of her husband's stranded fear. "I can take you," he said. "At least part of the way. I grew up in Missoula, so I know I can get us that far."

Sterns watched her fiddle with the car's knobs and switches, trying them out as though she'd never driven it before. Wipers came on, then the hazard lights. Finally, she touched the key. Only the sounds of breathing filled the space around him, exaggerated and shallow. "I'm sorry if I've exposed you," she said, looking down, pulling the rag away from her mouth. "You must've thought about it already. What I've brought into your life, your trailer."

"Yeah, it's a little late for me. But why would you risk carrying it to an old man in Nebraska?"

"I wouldn't be carrying it to him," she said. "I'd take antivirus before I'd do that."

He could feel his lips now, how dry they'd become. It wasn't just the inside of his mouth. It was his lips, the hair in his nose, the lump in the back of his throat. There was nothing he could say. He had to wait, just wait through the long minute before she'd lean over and open the backpack. And then the first aid box. He waited, and she waited.

"It's not bird flu. It can't be. I'm better, I can feel it."

"What do you think is happening if it's not bird flu?" he said, pinching the vials in his pocket.

"My husband always warned me there would be this very thing when the pandemic struck. People who thought they were going to die from bird flu when what they really had was another strain. And then there'd be the people who were sure they'd never get sick. Period. You're one of them, aren't you?"

He thought of the horses, the way they'd spent their whole lives together. Never apart in the tangle of forest scree. Together in the darkness of a barn. Even their tails switched in unison. If one was to die first, and he knew that was the likelihood, the other would never hold a harness again. In the fine mist beginning to filter down through the black silhouettes above them, Sterns contemplated his losses. Disease and its nightmarish march through his life was no longer acceptable. He'd tried it with Carolina—stood by waiting while she let go. It might be his turn this time. But Josephine Russo, in spite of everything, might live, and Sterns, more than anything he'd longed for in years, wanted to be the reason why.

"I'm sure anything could happen," he said. "Bird flu. No bird flu."

"Die or no die," she said, tilting her face upward again, giving him a faint smile. "And it's a long way to go without knowing."

* * *

By the time they reached Snoqualmie Pass, four lanes of traffic had slowed to one. The Cascade Mountains had always gathered most of their might from seven thousand feet up, and since this is where Sterns and Josie were, the bottleneck was unavoidable. A five-mile-long ascent of cars and semis awaited some kind of mandatory check. Sterns' pick-up had pulled the wide lanes, trailer in tow, a diesel-growling steel insect for almost two hours before it came to a full stop behind an Oak Harbor tractor-trailer. The box in front of him hadn't moved since he edged up behind it.

"Where are we?" she murmured.

The diesel seemed to rumble with agitation, and after several minutes Sterns turned it off.

"Where are we?" she said again, this time pressing the electronic window opener which didn't respond.

"Snoqualmie. Maybe for the next week or so."

She didn't seem to fathom the situation. Sterns had watched her sleep since she got into his truck. Now, it was accompanied by a deep, grinding cough. Her skin had erupted into patches of roseola, vibrant streaks of flamingo pink that pushed through her hairline and down her neck. She kept putting her forefinger in her mouth, then rubbing it over her lips. "I'm so thirsty," she said.

"I know. We're out of 7-Up. I've got some diet coke."

She shook her head.

"Bottled water?"

No, again.

Sterns told her to honk if the traffic started to move and went back into the trailer. Everything from the night before, including the refrigerator, had been latched down with bungee cords. Nothing had shifted, yet he'd never taken this trailer on the open road before, and he wondered if it would pass whatever they were inspecting. He went through drawers and closets, looking, thinking, then thought of the vials and pulled the empty from his pocket, setting it on the counter in front of him. For some reason, in all the possibilities of a search, this is what worried him. It had from the moment he'd injected it into Josie.

A bar ditch strewn with collecting litter over the past few months was only feet away from the door. One toss and the canisters would disappear in a trough of plastic and Styrofoam. But there was something felonious in destroying the only evidence that might save her. He brought both vials together, one spent, one full, and knew one was just as irreplaceable, or deadly, as the other.

His first aid kit was mounted in an upper cupboard behind melamine plates and a stack of napkins. Sterns put both vials under some gauze bandages, then took two face masks from the box's contents. Following rules might work, he thought, as he dug ice cubes out of a freezer tray. By the time he brought her the zip-lock bag of ice chips, brake lights were blinking on and off the trailer in front of them. "Don't know what's ahead," he said, handing her a mask, "But you know what the story is on this."

She poured the cold slivers into her mouth and studied the mask. "Even Lewis and Clark did better than this. They at least had some thunderbolts," she said, pulling the elastic strap over her head. The cup adhered to the middle of her forehead, a third, pupiless eye.

"Thunderbolts. Is that medicine or a weather event?" he said, putting the diesel in gear.

"A purgative."

"What are you?" he said, searching the strained profile of her face. "I hate to ask, but are you a . . . Oh, Christ, are you a doctor?"

"I'm a teacher. American History," she whispered, ignoring his panic. "Or at least I was."

They moved a few feet. All the while Sterns kept thinking about what he'd done. He could see the corner of Josie's backpack behind her seat, the way she'd placed it within reach. Then he watched the trailer in front of him, its mud flaps gently moving like drapes. It was all so new yet, so confusing. This woman of another man, her life right now left up to him. He'd done everything, and he'd done nothing. He thought of the proof in his first aid kit, not hers.

"And you kill forests," he heard her say through the diesel's whine.

"What?" he pretended. "I do what?"

"You take'em down," she said through the mask, then rested her head on the seat.

"You really can't say anything new. I've heard it all. Most loggers have," Sterns said, hitting the brakes hard enough to screech. "But you don't know a damned thing about what I do." Quickly moving his foot to the accelerator, he realized she'd pried him open at the worst possible time. Traffic was starting to move downhill. Cars in front of him were gaining speed, and the ones behind were lining up in single-file aggression. It wouldn't last, he thought. He glanced at her every few minutes in a curious mix of frustration and guilt. Only her head moved back and forth, relaxed, as if she'd let go of the most putrid of her thoughts.

An orange sign warned to be prepared to stop in another mile. Rock debris was the explanation, and once again the space between cars tightened up. By now he could see the road had been split onto a paved outcropping in front of them, a place that normally would've been the only remaining shoulder through a vertical cliff bisected by freeway. Cement barriers had been removed. Only caution tape flickered along the edge of the drop-off. Cars, then trucks moved single file onto this spit of a trail, realizing for the first time in fifty years how close they were to falling off the middle of a mountain.

He felt his hands tighten on the steering wheel, and for the first time he wanted to pull over. To watch them all, the anxious ones, the confident ones, the tractor-trailers, the Greyhound buses, the SUVs, the ambulances, even the logging trucks pace themselves one behind the other. Anybody could make a mistake, and then no one would leave this line-up. Sterns kept re-adjusting his rear-view mirror, finally realizing it was only making things worse. He also saw himself for the first time since the day before.

Sunlight and stubble seemed to emphasize the thin line of his mouth in an unflinching division between his neck and his forehead. Under his whiskers were tiny indentations, the remnants of acne. He knew where they were. At one time he'd counted twenty-two on one side, thirteen on the other, and just as they had then, they stood out now as dark, flawed pinpoints. He rubbed his hand over the scars trying to feel if the hair was really thicker there, then pushed the skin up under one eye. Sterns licked his fingers, running them through his short brown hair. He thought about what she'd said and how he must look to her.

"You better close your eyes," he said, leaning toward Josie, but keeping his attention fixed on the situation around him. The car behind the trailer had disappeared into a blank spot, and the side mirror only reflected the endless line behind. She didn't move, but he heard her breathe in short, penetrating rasps, the mask now pushed to the side of her mouth. For several car lengths he divided his time, watching her sleep while they approached the reason for the delay. An accident had been barricaded off on what remained of the left side of the road. The detour to the right skirted thousands of feet of drop-off. The space in between was theirs.

Snoqualmie Pass had always been temperamental, a cut of highway high in the Cascade Mountains exposed to record-breaking downpours of rain and snow and to the fickleness of high-altitude boulders which could let loose on the terrain below. A series of nets protected some of the steeper rock faces. But they were only band-aids. Sometimes a rock would crash down on an empty freeway scattering like meteorites. This time it had missed the road entirely and instead destroyed a truck and fifth-wheel. The ensuing wreckage had included two other cars, all of them compacted in a single line as precise as the one Sterns was part of. No sign of life remained, no clothing, no man giving hand signals. Only yellow caution tape declaring the end of the road. He edged the diesel past, sensing the mountain's haphazard game. It was as if the vibration of hundreds of cars could set it off all over again.

And in the way of all things inconsequential, he continued, as they all did, without pausing.

At Sprague Lake Sterns pulled into a rest stop, the state of Washington having disappeared behind them in vast tracts of wheat and corn. Everywhere the wind blew across fields in a steady tow from the southwest, and the lake, a giant pothole in the prairie, churned blue on green. The water shimmered while scabland around it was beginning to starve. Irrigation, as promised, had become sporadic.

Josie had slept almost four hours, her head turning from side-to-side as though she was searching for air. Desperate for a break, Sterns touched her forehead, letting his hand rest on the side of her face for just a moment too long. Her eyes flew open. She ripped the mask away. It was then, full-faced, her lids heavy and swollen, he realized she didn't see him. He recoiled, then sat still, slowly waving a finger back and forth.

"What do you see?" he said.

Her face, blank, seemingly visionless, tempted him to stare. Not at the manifestation of her horrible disease, but at her. He'd spent a lot of time looking around her, putting her circumstances in his mind's eye. But there'd been no time to see the slightest cleft in her chin, the dark brood of her hazel eyes. She sat there now, unresponsive, her beauty translucent, short-circuited, reminding him of a cathedral of shattered glass. *You're a teacher*, he thought. *And I've gambled. With everything in your brain.*

Sterns stopped, longing for some way to relieve the pain of watching, of driving half a day to a deserted lake in a pasture with little hope of finding anything other than road blocks and death. If he could get her to Missoula then he'd call Gil with the news he was coming home. He'd take her to St. Patrick Hospital. They'd find room for her after he told them she'd survived 98 percent serum, after he gave them the empty vial. It would start there, her antibodies shipped to every major medical center in the United States, maybe all over the world. Then, too, she would grow better. But for now, swallowing seemed to take all of Josie's concentration, and she blinked several times but said nothing. It relieved him to see how she could fade into the netherworld of sleep after she'd been delirious, and he wondered if it was the anti-virus taking hold. Just the same, he watched for the simple things, her breathing or the turn of her head and promised himself he'd take her to Missoula, exactly as he'd told her early that morning.

The restrooms had been converted into one large building, probably intended to shelter a few families left stranded. Only one toilet remained, and it was dry. A torn sleeping bag was wadded up in a corner. The scene reminded Sterns of one of the first times he'd gone woodcutting with his father. They'd spent the day logging in the Rattlesnake at a time when it hadn't yet been parceled into acreage, serene and well kept. The road, parts of it, pushed up into high country, thick with Doug fir and Ponderosa, uncommonly lonely country, that eventually rounded into mountain tops devoid of much more than scrub alpine and a couple line shacks. Sterns could remember asking his dad to stop the truck just so he could see what was inside one. It was a dwelling no bigger than a cellar, and in fact, he could still remember how it looked as if someone had scooped out the hillside with a soup ladle or, at most, a garden hoe, then attached a small porch and a roof to give it the appearance of a house. There was really little there. Just a hole in a hillside and a façade to hide it with. He asked his dad what it meant, being built the way it was, and his father said it "wasn't nothing special. A place to hole up," he could remember him saying. "It picks the survivors."

As he opened the trailer door, heat pent up for hours engulfed Sterns, and the thought occurred to him that his home might've become an incubator of sorts, preserving a virus he knew he'd not only slept with, he'd embraced, breathing it deep within. Symptoms were different with everyone, and he knew from published warnings it could be days before he'd succumb. Or the next minute. A man in Toronto said he'd been working on his computer. He told his wife he watched the screen in front of him explode and kept asking her how he was going to get to an important meeting. She reportedly went to the bathroom to bring him damp towels, then collapsed in the shower and finally drowned in the tightening grip of terry cloth and her own congestion. The prime minister of Canada and his wife were dead so quickly, CNN reported, it was as though they were merely a political appetizer for a disease voracious enough to tumble world order. That had been a couple days ago. And, as his father would've probably said about this flu, it too was picking who was going to survive.

Sterns reached for his laptop, then switched, pulling Josie's up to the counter instead. He hesitated, knowing if he once started checking news it could lead to more checking, possibly of Russo's notes or conditions ahead, and he didn't want to leave Josie alone for long. He tried the TV and found the Pope and Billy Graham's Crusade, split-screen, blessing anyone who could hear. Katie Couric broke in with a news release.

"It's only been a week now, the CDC is telling us, since the second wave of flu has begun it's spread across the North American continent. We're learning what that means as we go along. Unfortunately, for most of us, that could eventuate in an extreme change in our lives. But, ultimately, we don't know what to expect. Dr. Grif Betcher from Haviland Pharmaceuticals is here to help us understand."

A red-haired man reminiscent of Charleton Heston overtook the screen, the furrow between his eyes T-boned by wire rimmed glasses. In the manner of a concerned bystander, he brought the public up to date on numbers, mentioning that the eastern seaboard had been the hardest hit with over two million seriously ill and another two million recently dead from the flu or secondary illnesses. No one knew exact numbers yet, he kept repeating, because this was a fast-moving disease. The Midwest was seeing outbreaks in Chicago and St. Louis, and the west coast in San Francisco and L.A., but vast populations in between were, as yet, still experiencing only sporadic disruption, as he called it.

"Haviland Labs wants to keep the public abreast of every new prospect in this tragic hour. Because this flu has an eerie resemblance to the 1918 variant, we've used that as the basis for our testing and formulation. Our competitor, Colzer-Bremen, has done similarly, we understand, with their production of Pass-Flu. But unlike their current serum, we have selected a measure that could exponentially double their output under the scrutiny of the most stringent FDA approval. This is no idle promise. But, Americans, there is no substitute for scientific analysis. Otherwise we create as much havoc as we are trying to relieve. At this time, Haviland Test Kits are being distributed in various cities. In the meantime, we're pushing production on aspirin, ibuprofen, and other over-the-counter medications. Shortages will be remedied."

Within seconds there was another update, this time from Colzer-Bremen. A woman named Elsa Dupree from the Seattle-based pharmaceutical began a slow, deliberate rebuttal. Increasingly, as she spoke she jettisoned diplomacy. Sterns concentrated on her lips, an immaculate red. "Our friends at Haviland have mentioned the 1918 epidemic. It's so true. This is a close cousin replicating itself in the cells of birds and humans, this time, that we can tell, without swine as the mixing vessel. But what they've failed to mention is the success rate of Pass-Flu, despite the current shortage. How it's already prevented the deaths of millions worldwide. How it's still protecting here at home."

"I've personally seen what this serum can do. How it can stop the disease in its tracks. Pass-Flu can microscopically flat line influenza that has undergone re-assortment at least twice since it broke loose in the United States about six months ago, an endemic process that renders a normal-functioning immune system unable to recognize the mutating virus. We have kept up with this drift, both here and overseas. And, we didn't do it with platitudes. Haviland Labs is behind the curve, the deadliest curve since 1918. Their confidence is taking time. And time right now is lives."

Elsa Dupree then said something Sterns hadn't been expecting. She stopped mincing words. "The 1918 flu took lives in the ugliest possible ways. People hemorrhaged, turned black from lack of oxygen, their bodies stacked like cordwood. But we learned the most from the ones who survived. They described never being the same. Though it spared their lives, flu scoured through their systems. Catarrh, some called it, black catarrh, caused people to vomit blood from their lungs. They wept blood. They felt a chill so cold they set themselves on fire. Some of them spent weeks without seeing. A few of them never walked again, and then, of course, there were those who never woke up."

"There it is," Elsa said, her words sure to be repeated at hourly broadcasts, "The worst that can happen might be that you continue to breathe. It might be that some treatment allows you to live, but it's too little too late. Haviland Pharmaceuticals could put us all at risk to carry the scars of bird flu the rest of our lives. They're powering up at the wrong time, folks. Unlike Colzer-Bremen's Pass-Flu, they haven't been treating the world's newest plague. We will continue to produce the needed serum at an astounding 82 percent efficacy. And we'll strive to increase that percentage."

The words, their brief, caustic truth tore through Sterns sending him into another fit of pacing and pushed him to the first-aid kit. Ninety-eight percent it said. Not eighty-two. *Of what?* he thought. Ninety-eight percent of an experiment, a mistake. Man had revived a bird, one that by all natural disasters was meant to die out, caged it, and had broken its blood into microscopic units of intentional poison. According to medicine and a desperate world, this had been safely admissible to the human body, up to and including 82 percent. How could anybody know what a higher dose, an off-the-record dose would do? All it was, Sterns believed, was a high stakes lottery against a virus that merely shifted a degree to rip through humanity all over again and might've never been in Josie in the first place. He threw the empty across the trailer expecting it to shatter into a crystalline mist. Instead, in the slight incline of the trailer it rolled back to him. Sterns pushed his thumb and forefinger deep into each of his eyelids trying to forestall the pain of a sob, then put the tube back in the box alongside the extra serum. It might douse the flu, he thought, but never, ever the memory of what he'd done the night before.

Sprague Lake glistened in the background, receding from Josie's side of the truck as abandoned as the rest stop. If she'd known it was just behind her he wondered if she would've wanted to stay there for the night. To run her feet in soft shoreline mud, to feel sunlight bake through the disease that had bullied her into muteness. He considered asking her, then watched her breathe in a kind of quiet vibration. Sterns put her laptop and a gallon of water between them and fixed his gaze on the road and his hands on the steering wheel. Everything so far in his life had pushed him into waiting. He'd receded from Missoula and death a long time ago, then cut through trees one at a time in a forest without end. It wasn't always easy delaying life, a real life, but it turned out to be productive and even safe. It wasn't until now in the confines of a cab with a woman he hardly knew that Sterns thought about the short measure of his own time and how little he'd risked. It occurred to him the rest of his life might be only hours instead of years. For a long time he considered the one remaining vial of serum, what it could give or take completely away. He imagined the sweat of his own fever and bloody foam claiming his breath. Waiting might be over, he thought. Just like it was for her.

CHAPTER 17

Las Vegas fanned out from under the jet's wings, a sweeping, controlled wildness that Pritchard chose over any other place to live. Sometimes there was a breeze here, a zephyr that began in the Sierra Nevadas, tumbling, scouring then finally descending into the basin that held Nevada's neon paradise. He watched the windsock crossways to the runway while the plane held straight, and lift slowly let go. All he said to the pilot as he punched out the door was, "Don't get liquored up yet."

Traffic beaded in tight, short strands all the way across town. Pritchard could only describe it as a sense of loosening when he got on the freeway after being in a plane. Tickets had piled up on his dresser a few months ago until he started using cruise control. And for awhile they moved the speed trap. So, for now, he reclaimed his view of the road at almost ninety miles an hour, opening all the windows, letting the trackless wind dismember anything it could.

Shanna's house, quartz white in the late afternoon sun and unusually long, looked as though it had been built for a large family or maybe an extended one. Her father had lived with her and Rachel until his death. In so doing he had left her with one more thing. A used car lot just off the strip in one of the oldest and worst neighborhoods of Vegas. She never considered letting it go. Instead, she worked at least six days a week, often sixteen-hour days and ran the business, some said, more like a ranch foreman than CEO. The rate of return was extraordinary, but so was the theft until she had a six-foot white block fence installed around the lot. Broken glass festooned the top accompanied by razor wire, and two Dobermans ran patrol every night below. Pritchard knew that's where she'd be until sometime after nine when she'd come home to curl up with Rachel and watch <u>CSI</u>. So he'd already picked

up the habit of coming by early most every night since he'd returned, and Rachel seemed to stick by the unspoken understanding that she wouldn't tell her mother.

"Hi Daddy," she said, her back to the front door, fuzzy slippers tipped out like ruby-colored floor dusters.

It bothered him she didn't even look, that she was teenager
enough, even in a wheelchair, to make bored assumptions. "You
know, Lady Slippers, it ain't cool to let in the riffraff. I mean just
do a wheely and take a look before you invite me in. Okay?"

Rachel nodded but didn't turn around. "Okay, Dad. Next
time."

The back of her chair, as hard as it was to look at, reminded
Pritchard of how fragile she had become. Shanna held off buying
it because Rachel wanted nothing to do with rolling around "in a
straight jacket." But when the flu first took hold in the U.S. Shanna bought her a power scooter, saying it was either that or wear a
bicycle helmet. So much fear surrounded chronic lightheadedness,
that most persistent of Addisonian symptoms, that Shanna had always restricted Rachel from standing in long lines or walking any
further than up and down a school hallway. Pritchard recognized
it was only by his daughter's determination that she walked at all.
But the fast approach of flu sharpened Shanna's governing to the
point of locking her daughter just once in her room. The action
had translated to inaction for Rachel. The only time she left the
chair now was to go to the bathroom and bed.

"What is it, babe?" Pritchard propped himself beside her on
the spiraled end-cushion of the couch. Rachel's skin, pale and
vaguely blue across her temple seemed thin as tissue paper. She
finally looked at him, her eyes clear, dispassionate. She held a box
of Kleenex in her lap, and there was a roll of toilet paper around
one arm of her chair. "You look like you might be getting ready to
blow this place," he said.

He grinned, holding his face in the toothy contortion she'd
always laughed at, then suddenly became serious. His voice, even
to him, broke as if it was strained through gravel. "You know you
could go anywhere," he said. "There's no restrictions on young
women of great beauty."

"I'm not going to leave this chair," she said, holding her spin-dled arms tight against her abdomen. "At least imminently."

"What's going on, my Lady?"

"What do you think, my Knight of Incredible Deceit?"

He wanted to laugh at the way she could work him even in the midst of so much introspection. How she could turn it off just like he could. But he waited, then said, "I think I've just come back from Seattle, Wah, a dirty little old man. I've been to see a woman there, my boss in fact, who tells me a bird just shit all over the entire organization. Can you believe it, Rach? I'm sure it's on me somewhere."

Pritchard got up checking his clothes for imaginary white blotches. He made quite a to-do out of it, asking her if she saw any such dung. "Now," he said, getting on his knees in front of his daughter, "What could be worse than that?"

"The bird flu," she said.

He scrutinized her, wishing he could pull from behind her expressionless face the real answer. Like always, she fumbled with her medic alert bracelet. "I'm craving salt, Daddy," she added. "I ate a whole can of olives today plus the juice."

"Maybe you need to double your meds," Pritchard said. "You know what the doc wants."

"Yeah, yeah, the glands and all that shit."

Pritchard couldn't believe what he was hearing. Rachel never swore. In fact, she never complained. Addison's had been some-thing life-long, more of an inconvenience than a disease. It ac-tually became more noticeable because of Shanna. Like juvenile diabetes or even hemophilia, people didn't understand that even though Rachel looked normal, she could be on the edge of destruc-tion. Sometimes in cold season she would be kept out of school for a month at a time just because of a strep throat outbreak in Henderson. It wasn't a raw throat and glassy eyes or even a cough reverberating through walls that worried Shanna. It was the fear her daughter would bend over some afternoon, sliding her books across the dining room table and fall to her knees in a coma. Or go to sleep at night with the window above her bed cracked just a little too far and wake up with her eyes crimped shut and her lymph glands as tender as if she'd swallowed a wasp.

Addison's didn't conform to a stereotype. It seemed to float through Rachel's body, an immunological time bomb set to destroy her adrenals. Over seventeen years she'd survived due to cortisone, curtailed stress, and lots of sleep. She'd managed to skip a full grade of school and achieve mediocre health. But Pritchard knew his daughter could no longer simply withdraw. Bird flu would find people with Addison's or diabetes or mononucleosis. Maybe not through their condition as much as through their medication. Everywhere pharmacies were running short of common antibiotics and name brand drugs. Hospitals were dropping one at a time off the supply lists. He'd never discussed it with Rachel. He knew she knew. In fact, she was probably far more ready than he was.

He concentrated on the fragility of her wrist, how she twisted the bracelet into a knot she was attempting to pull tight. "I'm the shit expert," he said. "Excrement is what you say. That's why you have a 4.0 and I have... Well, I have a maxed out credit card."

He pulled two one hundred dollar bills from a money clip in his pants pocket, recalling the panicked look on the bank manager's face earlier that afternoon. Now, almost half a million dollars was neatly divided between four deep pockets, some of the bills so large that just one would pay off his Mastercard. "Yes, they're real," he said. "And you better spend 'em before the banks go totally under. I say buy a whole goddamn olive ranch or orchard or whatever the hell it is." He could hear her sigh as if she was holding back some all-consuming annoyance. She let the bills sit in her lap. "Rach, it's not blood money. It's relatively clean."

For just a flash he saw a smile, then she scrunched the money into a small purse hanging around her neck. "This bird. Are you supposed to find it?"

"I'm thinking so. But not until I know you're ready to peel out."

"Daddy?" she said, elongating the word, cancelling everything else she'd just said. "I'm out of pills."

Pritchard pushed back on his haunches, falling to one side, hitting the floor hard with his left hand. So hard he could feel it fold in on itself and compress into nature's perfect involuntary spasm. He smashed it into his pocket, then stood up, his height like a column of dead-still air. "Does your mother know?"

"I haven't told her yet," she said, shrinking down even further in the scooter. "I didn't feel so good a few days ago and doubled up meds thinking I'd be able to get more. But Gretzel's Pharmacy is out, and they told me yesterday nobody in town has Florinef. They're rationing hydrocortisone. I'm down to one dose a day."

"I'm going to call your mother," he said, fidgeting one-handed with his cell phone, then shoving it in his daughter's hand. "Here, you call her. I want you to tell her what's happening. You're playing with fire, Rach."

She turned the cell face down, rubbing the back of it as though it was a worry stone. In one steady gesture she handed it back to him. "She'll try to put me in Santa Marista. They've got those portable things. What do you call them—DEPMEDS? They're bragging how they can house fifteen hundred more people every time they put up four or five more. It looks like Arlington Cemetery, except the crosses are white plastic tents."

"I know, I know." Pritchard shook his head back and forth, a swaggering head bob that often preceded a tantrum. Her description had brought back a memory so searing it made him, for just this one moment, her confidant. "Poor bastards die in a plastic womb probably thinkin' they're back inside their mama's . . . you know the place."

Rachel said nothing but looked at him in a steady, deliberate gaze. "You've seen a lot haven't you, Daddy?"

He turned away walking directly into an outpouring of sun across the dining room floor. The back yard radiated from the window in a geometric pattern of gravel, colored sand and river rock, a glorified effort at ancient art. At a row of desert willows a thin strip of grass bordered the back fence where a track sprinkler had crept to the end of its program. It sent a spray of water onto one round spot on the wooden fence. "Your mother's forgotten what water means. It's become just another commodity. Not like it was over in the Gulf."

As he walked out the side door to the yard, Pritchard could feel his hand loosen from a spasm to a steady cramp. He turned off the water, then unscrewed the sprinkler. He brought the whole device in the house, placing it directly in the center of the dining room table. A pond began to form on the oak veneer. "I know you'll be tempted to move it before she gets here, Rach. But don't."

His daughter leaned forward. The box of Kleenex slid to her feet. For a moment he thought she was going to get up, so he started towards her, both hands out, ready to catch her frailty. She caught his hands with hers, then bore down trying to stand up. He could feel the bones of her fingers and thought of cold, nervous talons. Pritchard knew he would never be able to hold her. "Let go," he said. "Please, Lady Slippers, let go."

She did it so effortlessly. Sat back in her chair as though she didn't need him in the first place. He looked at the long stems of her fingers, where they'd been on his skin and wondered if she knew as much about him as he did about her. "You think you'll be around for awhile?" she asked, leaning over for the box of Kleenex.

Pritchard shook his head up and down as he watched her fumble the box between her foot and her hand.

"Don't worry, Daddy," she said. "So will I."

*   *   *

Shadows darkened, turning the Mimbres Mountains into thick, undulating hide. At over three miles up, New Mexico became a writhing animal, exposed to wind and erratic bursts of flash floods. Its mountains looked like the spine of a dragon, its plateaus a segmented, fractured tail. Sometimes Pritchard caught sight of a basin floor the color of terra cotta, the soft disappearing belly of a desert beast. Terrain was becoming Mexican, both in words and in character. It was caliche and playas, juniper and prickly pear. Pritchard and the pilot, Danny Mellon, were on their way into the Columbus Stockyards Airstrip, a dirt road that paralleled the border fifty feet from Mexico. It was close to sundown when they made a low pass checking for cows on the runway.

"Mira Las Palomas." Pritchard screamed the song's refrain, a tight, throaty wail pitched awkwardly low against the whine of the landing jet. Hardpack runway rolled beneath them, a giant speckled monster about to dive into dust. Just once he looked at Mellon tightening his grip on the yoke. It was never like this, he thought, anywhere else but here. Where the heat, the wind, and the border slammed into each other, and the landing, when it was right, felt like a single moment of forgiveness.

Quien canta sus males espanta, Mellon sang, his face strained closer to the windshield, pulling throttles, then his voice trailing off into concentration.

Pritchard pointed to two small buildings. "Yeah, you prick. Sing away my troubles too while you're at it."

When Mellon finally stopped and released the door, grit showered into the cabin the consistency of pinched salt. It swirled and fell, then settled across the panel in a dense layer. Pritchard looked down and saw ground without life, a surface without height or color. A place that would just as soon spit water back into the sky. Knowing it could raise suspicion if they dallied, the two men began a quick pace to the border station.

"All I can say is you gotta want it bad to take on the Federales," Mellon said.

"Ain't nobody ever told you what cortisone does? It's better than a high, dude." Pritchard glanced once back over his shoulder, encapsulating the jet in one definitive memory. He knew if things didn't line up right, he might not ever see it again.

They crossed under the building's high dome, sunlight now abrasive in the absence of air conditioning. The doors to Customs were closed in front of them. Mellon reached across Pritchard's single-minded velocity, putting his hand out as though trying to restrain him. "Look, I don't know what we're doing down here. Yesterday you said we were flying back to Nebraska. Then you said something about Billings, Montana. I'm wearing out sectionals trying to keep up with you. But somewhere along the line we're going to get interrupted. My guess is it could be right now."

Doors clanged together, steely and final on the other side of Customs. A woman sat behind the counter, her computer monitor framed in lavender silk hibiscus. She looked up at the two men coming toward her, then concentrated on the screen while a stream of unintelligible Spanish seemed to emanate from all around her.

"All we gotta' do is get in. Ortez has cortisone. I know he does," Pritchard said, rubbing his forefinger over the top of his bottom teeth. "Just one night in this shit hole, Danny. Then we fly out to wherever-the-fuck, Montana."

* * *

It was easier than he'd thought. No one asked for placards, no one asked for an itinerary. No one was even in Customs the next morning. Pritchard left a note taped to the door. *Thanks to a world-wide epidemic, our stay was most gratifying. Gracias, especially to Senor Ortez.*

The take-off was smooth in the early light of Chihuahuan sun. Pritchard looked behind him at the disappearing town. He tapped the altimeter. "Higher," he said. "Ceiling it."

Mellon climbed and handed him the headphones where a broadcast first in English, then in Spanish, kept repeating in staccato monotone.

"A fire has broken out in Los Angeles, California, in an ever-widening threat to persons unable to be transported from the flu's epicenter. It appears to have been started by a civil disturbance when widespread panic overcame still healthy residents trying to escape the city's metro area. Already likened to the deadly toll of Katrina, the thriving west coast city has sent out a nationwide alarm. Hampered by black-outs and explosions, the City of Angels has also been likened to Kuwait during the Gulf War. Medical personnel trained in a variety of disciplines is trying to reach victims of both disease and devastation, but, at times, there simply is no access. Some city facilities are still functioning. No one has a confirmed report of casualties but estimated at least half a million. Interstates and airspace over Los Angeles, Ventura, and Orange Counties are cordoned until further notice."

Momentum transfixed Pritchard, his senses freewheeling. High above sickness that dispelled authority, and ignition, one of God's favorite weapons, he felt right at home. No longer in it, he could watch from above and hear the news from a place untouched. Elsa be damned, he thought. The world wasn't listening to her, to Colzer, to the White House. It was now up to the ones left unattended. The strays. Barely rattling a bottle of Florinef in his pants pocket, he set his eyes on the long low-line of a disintegrating cloud and realized he was at the apogee of what was about to happen. "Hell begins," was all he would say.

"Yeah," Mellon answered. "I wish we could keep us right here, my friend. In the sky, straight and level."

CHAPTER 18

Sometimes when Sterns was logging he'd think of chestnuts, their smooth shiny roundness a prototype for the perfect marble. How for centuries the method had worked. The nut surrounded by a burr-infested capsule fell to the ground, sprouted, and thrived. One tree could grow fat at seventeen feet in diameter. The tree of America, they'd called it. Suddenly in the summer of 1904 cankers appeared and spread their infection until every chestnut tree in the eastern mountains was diseased. Trunks atrophied but refused to fall. Somebody once said he thought *the whole world was going to die standing up.* That had been seventy years ago and a tree no one ever doubted would survive. It did, even now, at the roots in a curious refusal to give up but never stood its unlimited height again.

He studied the woman curled away from him, wisps of her hair the color of chestnuts clinging tenaciously to the seat between them, and prayed within his soul she'd survive. It all hinged on a strange pact with a creature programmed to contain, even revolutionize death. Eastern Washington faded behind him. Less than five hundred miles from home, there was nothing to remind Sterns of the wild trammel of the rain forest, its moss-infested cavities or roots the size of pier blocks. Here there was no comparison to Goliath evergreens. He was in the wide-open country between his homes.

The border patrol at the Idaho line forced him to stop at an inbound way station, the real meaning obscured behind the passing stare of a State Trooper, who contemplated Josie as though sleeping itself was an offense. Eight road workers foraged behind him, their heads and bodies swathed in plastic, bent over a long trench hammered ribbonlike across a two and-one-half acre parking lot. They unloaded some of the incoming semis, shoveling cargo out of covered truck beds and tractor-trailers. Cargo that slipped from their shovels in the heavy thud of carcasses that spewed a deepening layer of feathers over the workers as if they'd just succumbed to a glorious pillow fight. He knew the butchery would go unchecked and that at the end of a long day the men would be told to burn their boots and clothes until they melted over the bodies like pudding.

In the road climb away from the border, the sky above Idaho took on a look of purity. Its blueness thinned and mountains began to dominate, suddenly, as if Sterns was looking at the very spine of the state. The Bitterroots were the domain of a logger's dreams and his very conscience. He'd read a Nez Perce once said his people would survive in a place of forgetting. Until now they had, their lives surrounded with lodgepole and Douglas fir, cedar snags and sleepy willows.

Summer heat sifted through needles and earth. It permeated the space around Sterns and for a while he dreamed, the lucid state where the road becomes a trail, a winding fantasy between a man's pain and his pretend. He could remember the long desk in the hanger, his computer, a wall-length topography map of Montana in a memory as hidden from normal sight as a swath of clearcut on the backside of a mountain. It was unsettling to be this far out from a tragedy and yet suddenly remembering, feeling its tearing confusion. It was no accident he'd become the "killer of trees."

Josie coughed and pitched forward. Just as exaggeratedly she threw herself back against the seat, then relaxed as though the burst either relieved or exhausted her. It generated a disturbance wide enough to break Sterns' reverie, and he realized watching her she'd disturbed his whole world. The past and present swirled together and collided in this vehicle between him and a flu-stricken woman. He knew it could wear him out. So he took a long drink from the gallon of water, letting it slide out his mouth and down the sides of his neck. It soaked into the short hair around his nipples. Swiping the wet mouth of the jug, he reached across the seat to pat the soft curve of Josie's neck. She groaned. He did it again, and she spoke.

"The bird I saw inside the fence," she said, turning her head to look at him, then paused and wiped her eyes. "It's Gem-X. He's the only one left, but he's not alone."

Sterns slowed down, preparing to pull over. He hadn't seen her this alive since breaking camp that morning.

"Don't stop," she said, propping her feet hard against the glove box, then rolling down her side window. "Robert said to keep going. Trained him to keep going. Gem-X is out."

As he activated the hazard lights, Sterns continued to crawl toward the summit of Lookout Pass. He knew there would be a turn-out soon, someplace he could pull over if she got crazier. He wanted to put his hand across her forehead, lift the hair out of her eyes, to absorb what she meant even if it didn't make sense. But she was too far away. "Some water, Josie?" He shoved the gallon toward her.

She ignored him, concentrating instead on the rock face splicing into her side of the road and began repeating something that reminded him of a child's phonics lesson. "Al-de-bar-an," she said, enunciating each syllable as though it was the cornerstone of the word. "Aldebaran is the bull's eye. I mean it," she said, punching Sterns on the side of the arm. "We don't stop this truck until we get to Hennings."

Swerving toward the shoulder, he pushed the brakes, then turned, watching her irritation morph into undiluted concentration.

"All those months of vials. Remember?" she asked, peering at him. "Remember how you kept telling me you'd be replacing them? Twenty-two, thirty-nine, fifty-four. You made them disappear when a new one came in. And I let you. Wherever you took them off to, they disappeared."

She paused as if she was straining to see what happened, now, finally, when serum had her trapped in its devastating potential. "Every time it happened, every time you asked them for more, they gave. Then you'd throw it out, and they'd give again. Finally, you warned they would die." In a way now familiar to Sterns, she closed her revelation abruptly. "One bird. Hardly anyone knows what you've done, Robert. But he's alive."

Sterns didn't know what to say at first. The thoughts of deny-ing her hallucination kept him rational, but motionless. Finally, he pushed the gas, suddenly preoccupied with the crunch of stones under his tires, the lumbering, uphill climb. If he could just get her to Missoula, they'd know what to do. They'd know if she was losing her mind.

"Wait," she said.

Once again, he stopped unsure of how far to let it go until he called for help. Maybe at the summit there'd be an EMT. He could call ahead to St. Patrick's saying he was on his way with a woman delirious from the flu. But then he'd have to tell them everything, because Sterns knew what was happening was worse than that. He could see Josie fidgeting with the gallon of water, pulling it onto her lap, then flipped the door handle. "You know what I have to do," she said and added, "Give me two minutes."

He watched her kick the door shut, cradling the jug between her hands, then disappear behind the bulk of the trailer. Rearrang-ing side mirrors he thought he might see her, incoherent enough to let fly on the side of the road, but instead she left the gallon of water just outside a clump of serviceberries that absorbed her in one step.

Frenzy started in his chest, a wave of indecision that gathered Sterns in an all-out panic. Stabbing the keypad while concentrating on the thicket in the mirror, he punched *911* on his cell. The ring turned to a steady hum. *911 temporarily out of service* imprinted in a green glow, the number meaningless in a world of perpetual emergency. He opened the laptop. Immediately online, he brought up Russo's e-mail, then typed *Henpigeon* under New Message. The cursor blinked, unperturbed as the cold eye of a snake and settled in the upper left corner of the screen. Sterns waited, even opened his side door and got out as if considering a long uphill trek to the summit, then yanked the computer sideways on the seat while he stood facing it. *Mr. Curtis Hennings*, he began.

My name's Gary Sterns. I'm a logger out of Washington State. And I've got a lot of presumptions. Presume you know Robert Russo is dead. Presume you'll know what I mean when I tell you what's go-ing on. Long story short, I've been in the company of Josephine Russo,

Robert's widow, for about twenty-four hours. A horrible twenty-four hours.

Apprehensive, he re-read the confession and wondered what the old man would think. Would he just delete it as nonsense or regard it as a name-dropping set-up? He couldn't clear it out of his head how the world he'd known, the trusted routine of his animals, the daily respite of ancient forest was upended in a few short hours. Sterns focused on the words he was choosing, words of desperation. He choked and held his head down, feeling a stream of saliva pool at the corner of his mouth, then began again. *Mr. Hennings, I might've made a mistake. Please read on, as far-fetched as this sounds. Her life may depend on it.*

Josephine came into my logging camp saying her husband died in a plane crash some miles in. I told her it was impossible to get beyond a compound with birds. Another presumption of mine, but I'm sure you know the one. Neither of us knows much, but we do know what the birds meant to you and Robert.

Anyway, during the night she got sick. I mean what I thought was bird flu. She couldn't breathe. Delirious. When somebody doesn't know what's real. That's what she was. I've got no one to tell except you.

Sterns heard the distinct crack of summer-dried brush. In a keystroke he typed a thin line below his message, then added— *I gave her 98 percent Pass-Flu. She still doesn't know what I did. Sometimes out of her head, and it's been hours. Can't help her. At Lookout. All she wants is to get to you. Insists one of the pigeons has escaped. Am considering taking her to hospital in Missoula. Please, anything you can tell me?*

He watched her approach, the mirror reflecting her thinness, her steps deliberate, unbalanced. She took her time, then looked at him full-faced through the passenger window, a kind of detached stare so penetrating he hit "Send," then clamped the lid of the laptop in one succinct motion. Josie lifted the jug up through the window, and it occurred to him she might not get in. He reached across to help her when she dropped it, capless into the velour seat.

"What I mentioned back there," she said. "Aldebaran. It's a dawn-rising star. There was a time when it rose before the sun every June 21, just a flash, mind you. For hundreds of years it could be seen on this one day, a bright pinpoint, just before sunlight extinguished it."

Spellbound, he listened to her clarity after all the flu-infested babble. She was coming back to life, he hoped, her mind, or parts of it, keen with a teacher's ability to energize her student. Finally, she drew herself into the seat, concentrating on replacing the jug's blue cap while at the same time suggesting the impossible. "It didn't mean anything until now. It's no accident about us or the passenger pigeon. We're doing exactly what Robert planned," she said, wedging her sweater against the door. "He was working on it for years. He told me it's all about light."

Impatient, Sterns simply closed his eyes. If he could just shut her out of his sight, didn't have to look at what he'd created in that one horrific moment of decision. But he could feel her all over again. Her hair a wet knot under his chin, her body charged with convulsion. With a left-over virus, a god-awful 98 percent, he'd stopped the ugliness. But that was only half the work. Her brain was frying. He was listening to her pull it apart.

When he opened his eyes he looked at the trees in front of him, veterans of fire and disease. He noticed it here more than the peninsula where their mass shielded them, where they could regenerate under a shroud of mist, undisturbed some days, except for the slow wag of his team. It was here, near the Divide, that Sterns saw trees for what they really were. Individuals that could cut through a man, not a clean sideways or up and down but in effortless, increasing torture. Long after his brother was gone, he'd followed Mark's path in his mind, the descent a tight jump into a cavernous yawn of Ponderosa just to get close in. How a wind, barely shifting would've drawn ash into his face, forced him to cough, then maybe gag. Fire claims victims a million ways, Sterns thought, turning his head toward Josie. Just like the flu.

"Where are we?" she asked, now wadding the sweater behind her head, then looking at him as if she'd really understand the answer.

"The pass between Idaho and Montana. It's called Lookout."

He noticed she didn't blink, didn't hesitate. "It's a miracle then," she said.

"There have been a few today," he said, quite sure she wasn't hearing him anyway. "And there's been just plain shit."

"No, I mean it. It's a miracle."

A breeze came from behind her, toying with her hair, softening her gaunt, still whiteness. Her eyes searched for a sign of recognition. She must've seen something, felt something from a place far away from him. "The passenger. He's here. Right now. I just saw him."

In a moment of finality he watched her lean back and close her eyes, not needing his approval or his utter disbelief. It didn't matter one way or the other. He could hold his thoughts, whatever they were, until he burst open, ripe with the swarm of flu or drove his rig into hell. There was no one here who could tell him what to do. Sterns started again toward the top of Lookout. Every once in a while he took a downward look at the laptop, then a halting glimpse at the pale, sleeping woman on the other side.

CHAPTER 19

Her flu-dream always started the same way. *If I could just go back to the night I first suspected, I knew, something was wrong.* She wanted to go back, to repeal that segment of her life that no longer disappeared in normal sleep. It seemed more determined now to linger close to the surface of her memory, as if sickness itself had sharpened her doubt. So often night, without any other explanation, took her in a ceaseless loop of self-punishment. But now the unruly dimensions of fever seemed to lay her brain open, and helplessly Josie waited for the feeling that would follow, the invasion of dreams that would allow her, finally, to hear her husband's explanation.

In the half-light of a gray dawn she could see feathered bodies quietly folded like small umbrellas lined up on a counter. There was no deformity here. Nothing smashed, no feathers scattered in the aftermath of a tussle. Just rows of acquiescence. They lay still as soldiers in moonlight, the battle long over, a melding of blue and gray, north and south, win and loss. She saw the passengers as if she was a light above or maybe a constellation that barely disturbed their rest. She always, always asked what killed them and then immediately apologized. *I'm sorry for what's been done to you.*

Every time little changed in the room nearby. The slow drip of amber fluid into even darker bottles, the minimizing and sterilizing. Everything looked so clean even in the middle of decimation. A line of bottles, as neat as the line of birds began at one corner of the room and almost met itself three corners later. Close to 4000 bottles. Josie knew it was all that was left of the flock. Percentages were written, typed, even stamped on the labels. A trash can in the middle of the floor was labeled *Discards*. One by one a worker was picking up the bottles dropping each with a shatter inside the can. With each dream, the bottles were fewer but fatter and still lined the walls. The demand was endless even though the passengers were dead.

Above her she heard the first disturbance. Something flew back and forth, worried maybe. When she looked up she saw him. "A meteor" her husband had said, the end of a bloodline as old as North America. The bird possessed a frenzy that reminded her of a stalking mammal, that increased his diminutive size even while he bobbed back and forth on two red-orange legs. Wherever he stood he'd scratch hard, and she'd feel sand thrown in her face. He was getting even or maybe he was imprinting. She didn't know, but she watched him every time find a minute hole at one empty corner of the room and disappear. It was then she would sometimes see light, degrees at first, faint rays that elongated into an equator of sorts that divided the sky in half. Somewhere between atmosphere and earth's horizon an array of colors would coalesce into the sharp edge of direction, a single pure note of clarity. And she would know what he was following. But she didn't know why.

At Lookout Pass Josie's sleep was interrupted by knowing she'd seen Gem-X and not just in a dream. This time she'd seen a trailing antenna jutting from one of his legs, wire as fragile looking as cross-hatching in glass. It perplexed her, watching him strut between branches seemingly oblivious to the human device, as though it didn't matter what handicap they'd strapped on him. But she knew it transmitted information and probably the exact branch he was standing on. She reached up as if to coax him into letting her remove it.

What she touched at the end of her reach was Robert's face. They were in a garden back home four years ago. She remembered the time, not because of the day or even the place, but because of the unusual embrace he'd given her. And what he said. "Jo, what about a trip?" he said, reaching around from behind her. They were on their knees, her thinning the long stems of columbine, him enveloping her from behind. She savored its fleetingness, remembering how he used to pull himself the length of her body and take everywhere he'd kissed to her mouth. He hesitated, then put his cool hands up under her hair and on her neck. "I've been so busy for so long. I've got an assignment or I guess it's a mission in Nebraska. Some birding I need to do. I'd like you to come with me." She could remember how she sat back on her haunches, the dirt between her fingers thick and muddy, then reached behind her holding his waist. Robert didn't move but whispered, "Go ahead, wipe your hands all over me. Just say yes."

She should've known the love affair wasn't over for him. That should've kept her going—that and the two weeks they spent on the road. Pushing across mountains and Midwest plains once as far away as craters on the moon. Hundreds of stops, sometimes only minutes while Robert videoed the landscape and logged times, latitudes, elevation, even canyons and stream beds. The whole thing had been his voyage of discovery. And for her he'd bought pinwheels and corn dogs, drumsticks and chicken fried steak. He took her picture, he videoed her over and over saying she'd be the control through the whole thing. *Control of what*, she'd thought.

When they finally got to Two-Dot it was June 20. Summer was about to take over in the high Wyoming country spreading downward into the basins and rolling hills of the Great Plains. That night she'd bedded down with him on an outcrop, a grassy pedestal just outside of town at the remains of an old medicine wheel. Solitary rocks appeared to have been aligned by one over-seeing eye, then a series of smaller stones configured as spokes of a wheel. There was symmetry here, but primitive, as though the hands of these men had done the work of a master designer. Walking the knobbed stones for hours, finally covering his tele-scope, Robert couldn't sleep that night. He kept rolling back and forth in his sleeping bag murmuring numbers, checking his cam-era, whispering reminders to himself about what to do just before dawn. She remembered the slender strands of a pink sky giving way to light. "Watch it now," he said. "See this thing happen." Then the great red ball snapped the strands in perfect alignment with a lonely outer cairn.

She'd watched him roll up his equipment as neatly as he took voluminous notes. It was built in, his ability to concentrate for long periods while forming a theory, working up to a place in his mind where he could let it all go. Sometimes she knew he had to start all over again. Winning, losing, tabulating. She knew by his long disappearances into the Olympics. His disappearances some-where. But this time he'd relaxed while he took her further east than she'd ever been. And told her what he'd really wanted at the medicine wheel.

"A glimpse, a fleeting thing is sometimes the source of great journeys. Things hidden behind other things, earthly and human, that we don't understand. Not yet anyway. It's another star I was looking for, not our own—Aldebaran in the constellation Taurus. It's a lodestar to the ancient ones. I prefer to think of it as a beck-oning. Think it's in here," he said patting his camera. "A beam of extraordinary light from a star perhaps more glorious than our own. Over hundreds of years it confirmed the beginning of sum-mer, right down to the second. For the ancients, it set time. But now it will set time in motion."

She considered his eccentricity as they traveled beyond the brink of Wyoming into the lazy hills of Nebraska, the new summer blowing through the car between them. So much of his disposition naturally stopped short of explanation that she didn't question his absorption in an unnamed project. It was also a vacation, and some part of that seemed to register, even for Robert. For a while she dreamt she went on with him, following the middle line of the highway until it ended at a high barn, peeling red paint on the windward side, the last building for miles. The road ended there at the closed doors. She could see Robert's Land Rover parked right in front.

But when she opened her eyes she could see nothing of an old barn or his car. She thought hard, realizing the dream was merely what she wished she'd seen. In reality, four years ago in June Rob-ert had left her in Lanscom, Nebraska, telling her he had one last thing he needed to record. "Too mundane," he'd said, for anyone else to bother with and "perhaps the worst case of oversight in this country."

"I can't take you exactly there," he'd said, blotting the corners of his eyes with the open front of his shirt. "Otherwise, you'll want to move here and leave me back there." He'd laughed and cranked his thumb toward the west, then left her at the entrance to Plink's Mall. "It's business, Jo. Just comparisons between species, things like that. No one comes to Nebraska unless they want to get work done. Or unless they want to relocate here." He'd winked at her, then drove off, leaving her at a mall in the middle of a town of thirteen hundred people. "Back in two hours," he'd yelled over his shoulder. "Darby hardly exists."

She wondered what he'd meant, *Darby hardly exists*. He'd picked her up at the mall in precisely two hours with never a mention of where he'd been, and it seemed to her now that's when all her suspicion started. If he'd just said something. That it was a dusty junction in the road, that it had three local bars instead of the customary two. If he'd fiddled with paperwork or unrolled a map, she might've convinced herself there was validity to getting business done. All Robert Russo did when he picked her up was pull two tickets from his shirt pocket and told her they'd be leaving the rental car in Scottsbluff, because he had to be back home the following morning. And all she knew was the vacation was over, suddenly, as though Darby not only existed, it had made a decree.

Josie chewed the right corner of her lower lip, a boardwalk full of fever blisters her tongue peeled at until she bit them off one-by-one. Even in her sleep she could taste blood, wet and morbidly salty, and kept licking the corner of her mouth until she woke up, then touched one irritated canker. Some part of her wanted to look at the results of hours of chewing, another wanted to hide, especially from the man concentrating on the road in front of him. It was as though the country around them had turned up the heat, and Sterns was blasting his way through it.

A fly huddled in the crevice between the windshield and the dash. It kept spinning in circles, defeated against a crosswind from a side window. She watched its powerless rotation against a backdrop of straight-forward freeway and thought of her mother, always spinning, doing. Always with the answers. "He'll keep you chasing shadows," she'd said. All the while her husband moved straight ahead without her. From Darby into the Olympics. From birds to an outrageous medical breakthrough. Josie could feel the fragile dome of the blister break apart, a swill of infection run down her chin, then pulled the sweater from behind her. With it she caught Sterns' attention. She could feel it, even though she only leaned forward enough to see the fly lose his grip.

"Any better?" he asked.

"I don't know," she said, holding the sweater to the side of her face. "It's as though something's barreled through me, every part of me. My head, my backside, my frontside, back to my brain, and now out the side of my mouth." She patted the blister, then dropped the sweater to her lap. "Ugly huh?" she said.

He paused, but she knew he couldn't look for very long, not with his determination. And it would take away the embarrassment when she had to look him in the eye and ask him why he was doing all this. What made him take her this far? He didn't know what she'd seen. All he knew was there were some extinct birds in a forest he was working in. Not all that different from the Ivory Bill, she thought. Birds, even flashy woodpeckers, could eventually retreat in snippets of undisturbed wilderness. There would always be believers that one lone survivor, or maybe a mated pair could make it through extinction. That something with wits and a strong hiding ethic might make it through the disappearance of a species. As humans, we drifted into hope much too soon with far too little to show for it. But there was something to show for it this time. And it contained pictures of her.

"I've been this way before," she said. "I was on this road with my husband about four years ago. He was in search of something, something having to do with light and measurements. Precise measurements. He was planning something. I didn't know it then, just that he took along our camcorder, a camera, a telescope, and took notes continuously. And made me feel like I was part of it. Over and over again."

"Aldebaran?" Sterns said. "Were you part of that?" He asked the questions separately as though he was tucking them in as separate as mile markers.

"The star. Yes, I was part of it but didn't know much." She paused, then added, "And I know little more now."

"So why is this all about light?" Sterns asked, referring to words she'd said two hours ago and testing, she was sure, for a thread of coherence.

"No theories now. This is just what I know. Rob took pictures of every major landscape change between Washington and Nebraska. Freeway, mountains, canyons, passes, buttes, even radio towers and grain silos. I was in several of those pictures or videos, usually just a passing turn. He called me the control. You know what a control is?"

She considered looking at Sterns. To search his face for signs of recognition or disgust, to see what he'd do with scientific terminology. Instead, she readjusted the side mirror, pushing the knob to its extremes and waited for whatever he'd say. It was then she saw the oozing sore, a swollen ledge protruding from the side of her mouth. She kept touching it, fancying the mirror was accentuating its size. It reminded her of a plantar wart she'd had years ago. Not one lesion, but a colony clustered together ready to expand, to travel the curve of her mouth in a series of itching, infectious bubbles.

"A control is a thousand year old Doug fir with grooved bark deep enough for a kid to disappear in." Sterns said it with little hesitation, as if he carried the mental picture with him of the perfect past. She wondered if he'd ever been inside a tree. In a way, she thought, it did make him the control of his world. If he looked at things from within trees, the test was how to conduct his life in a business that hardly saw it that way. Confused and vaguely put out, she pushed the mirror away. She wondered if he'd complain, then leaned back pulling a strand of hair across her sore mouth. It put her in line with the mirror's momentary reflection, both real and strangely imaginary. Tail feathers protruded from a rolled-up awning over the trailer's front window. Feathers barely visible, yet slightly unkempt in the sixty-mile-an-hour wind, contained perfectly in the tube. The passenger wasn't moving on his own, she thought. Having done his own measurements, he fit into the awning as neatly as a well-folded burrito. Including the transmitter. Even in her bout of flu she knew that was no inconsequential feat.

"You've got the idea," she said, tacitly agreeing with Sterns, who, with one adjustment, could easily see the tail feathers for himself. "But when I look back at what he was doing, the kind of man he was, all of this points to a theory. A travesty he was trying to undo. In his mind, something about a star's rising corrected for man's mistakes—even his. I think he was just beginning to find that out about himself. That he'd made some terrible mistakes, and now he was trying to make it up to the flock, all sixty or seventy of them—by saving just one."

"And pictures he took of you made that possible?" Sterns said, breaking for a turn off the freeway.

His question stunned her. Dreams, brilliantly descriptive and repetitive had been her condition for the last few hours. Through them she'd witnessed a colony of dead passengers, each one a copy of the bird her husband called Gem-X. What had gone wrong? In some of the last notes before he died, Robert warned of a die-out. But the light she was talking about, she was seeing in dream after dream, was an experiment. An experiment begun four years ago on a trip oddly similar to this one. Even then her husband was building his test, shaping it through a bird called Gem-X. And he blatantly told her she was the control. *I was part of it*, she thought. *And I never asked what it meant, what I meant, to him.*

Josie curled outward toward the car door. She knew if she drifted dreams would overtake her, and she would believe. There were answers there, she thought. Answers to why ruffled tail feathers were poking out of the awning behind her. She relaxed. She wanted to tell Sterns to relax. Instead, she dreamed of holding a picture of herself standing in front of a small rock cairn. In the background was a subtle, rose-tinged dawn.

CHAPTER 20

Early morning seeped through the house. Pritchard studied the bedroom entrances from his vantage point, small clefts that disappeared off opposing sides of the hallway. Directly in front of him was the dining room table, the sprinkler on a lace place mat in the middle. He stood behind the glass slider, a man deprived by a simple pane of glass, then wedged it open with a pen knife. He placed the pill bottle on the other side of the sprinkler making sure to turn the label toward the inside of the room and continued watching the bedroom entrances as he backed away. Nothing moved until he saw the tip of Shanna's foot rounding the corner. She had a small black gun in her hands. "Want to sit down and talk about it?" she said, swiveling the gun in one steady motion toward the right side of the table. She pulled out a chair and looked at him with unruffled calm. "Talk," she said, motioning again. "You keep dropping off presents. What is it this time?"

She picked up the bottle of Florinef and set it down with a thump alongside the sprinkler. He pulled the slider closed behind him, never taking his eyes off the weapon she handled with such ease. She wouldn't shoot him, he thought. But she had all the earmarks of making one hell of a noise. "It's a re-fill," he said putting the penknife on the table in front of him. "I'll put mine down if you'll do the same."

He knew she could be stubborn about this. And he knew she had every right. Shanna seldom over-reacted. She just waited and dealt with the results. Put up a broken glass perimeter around her car lot when they'd stolen her blind. Fed her daughter daily steroids to protect her from her own body. Now, she was finally doing what the cops could've done months ago—arrested him.

He watched her hesitate, then place the forty-five tip-to-tip with the knife. They looked hopelessly mismatched. Dynamite meeting a sewing needle. "You've been visiting without a pass," she said. "And then you have the audacity to leave a puddle on my oak table. Damn you." She stared at him, her blue eyes defined by a series of small, coagulated dots of mascara. "I should call the cops."

Pritchard spread his legs apart, pushing them further under the table. He connected with her foot, then heard her pull it away in a peel across the carpet. "She told me she was outa' pills. What did she tell you? In fact, did she tell you?"

He could see her stiffen, pulling her overlarge T-shirt close around her abdomen. The cloth's indentation accented her breasts, and for just a moment that was all he could see. "I don't pry," she said reaching across to the pills again. "But I knew."

"Then why didn't you tell me?" he asked. "You know I can get what she needs."

"You're gone all the time, Martin. That doesn't mean you have a real job with a real pharmaceutical. That just means you travel. That you . . . dally with disease."

She spat out the last sentence with such force he could feel the words reverberate deep inside his skull. As though she'd said something he'd conjugated over and over. He began to lower his head. It was only a whisper once, he thought. But his doubts had magnified until he could no longer conceal them. One by one they preceded him, entering through the narrow doors of the dying. Everywhere he went they'd known, just like she did now. He might keep them alive. He might not. "What do you want me to say, Shanna? That I can save her life no matter what slime breaks loose. Right now I can find steroids in Mexico. It'll keep her going. I can keep her going."

"For how long?"

"For as long as she has," he said, slowly raising his head until he could watch her face, it's whiteness more like architecture than flesh.

*   *   *

He'd seen Dharavi long before he knew about insufflation. He'd been sent there less than a year ago at the request of Colzer's Advanced Serums Labs in an effort, they said, to stem bird flu in one of the world's worst slums. It was in India, they said, between a mangrove swamp and an upscale Mumbai neighborhood that a million people lived on a landfill arising from coconut leaves, rotten fish, and human waste. They were dying in such numbers that landlords were disposing of tenants' bodies in massive blazes stoked head-to-toe with corpses. Referred to as the *roll of human beads*, they eventually set fire to real estate which included a church and then spread to the Bandra-Kurla Complex, an affluent housing district just north of the slums. The flu had mutated through economic borders, and fire had melted everything together in an unrecognizable stink of communal life.

Right afterward, Pritchard entered a courtyard on the south end of Mumbai, hoping to disperse one hundred thousand vials of anti-virus to the slum below over the next week. The ever-increasing demand for Pass-Flu had depleted stockpiles, repeatedly sending Colzer into the dark chasm of choice. A month before they sent two shipments of a quarter million vials into Romania and Yugoslavia while parts of Egypt and Turkey were kept in a holding pattern. Now, India was getting the allotment for Alexandria. India, the place of abominable living conditions, had been desperate enough, crafty enough to practice insufflation. And because of that they'd managed to get this far without help.

The epidemic would eliminate slums first, the CDC had proclaimed. Even in the United States this would be the population hardest hit. But Dharavi was not without its saviors, Caleb Mitterand being the most outspoken. Originally a microbiologist, then trained in public health, he left New Orleans after Katrina's leveling to put himself smack on the edge of an outbreak. A slum would either vaporize or overcome any devastation. He predicted one slum in India, at least, would weather even a pandemic. So when Pritchard met him in the Bandra courtyard on a sweltering morning in September, Caleb had told him one hundred thousand vials of 54 percent Pass-Flu would never begin to stem the tide. "These people have done better on their own," he'd said.

He told Pritchard about the old women drying bird dung. Only from ducks, he said, where they believed the virus was *stored asleep*. Over days the waste was swept into piles where it was slapped with brooms until it became fine powder, spreading among residents who could never escape the fumes, even if they wanted to. There was no one who knew what had become of the practice. As suddenly as they began, the old women stopped, satisfied the virus had recoiled, and the next swarm would not stop at their simple measures. That's when the city of Mumbai had sealed off the infected slum, ringing it in barbed wire and threatening to burn it alive if anyone tried to escape. But they didn't have to threaten Dharavi, Caleb said. She would suffer her own pestilence, set her own fires. Fires they couldn't stop at the Bandra Link Road.

That's when the doubts began. Nowhere before had Pritchard been asked to straddle the line between medicine and its recipients. No matter what he said he couldn't get Elsa to compromise. "One hundred thousand units per week. No more, but it could be less. Convince them," she said. "Tell them it's the highest percentage we've produced thus far, and as far as anti-virus they're not going to slap their brooms and tell me things will get better their way. Stay there, Pritchard. As the virus mutates, and it will, this percentage won't work either. Convince Mitterand to make do. Percentages will be higher in less than a month. Another half million doses will be ready."

So he stayed and talked and watched while Shiva the Destroyer cast his hemorrhagic seed upon the slums. The nearby upper classes demanded the next higher percentage of Pass-Flu for themselves, and during the same outbreak were getting 82 percent. Pritchard delivered it himself. No one cared whether the lower castes were treated. Their bodies and their children's bodies were set on fire by the armed guards surrounding Dharavi, their screams carried high in the night. Higher than the constant traffic just beyond them. Quarantine had done little more than offend. Small bits of remaining bodies could sometimes be seen carried by vultures over the city of Mumbai, and the awful truth, Pritchard knew, was that no one could stop it.

So when the last shipment of 54 percent Pass-Flu arrived almost a month later Pritchard decided to go home. He kept hoping Caleb would stop his demands, give up on the World Health Organization and the CDC, and simply fly back to New Orleans to await the epidemic as it spread. "There's another shipment that's arrived, isn't there?" he'd asked Pritchard. "Is it 82 percent? Colzer doesn't have to know, man. You can divert it. For God's sake, we'll just take leftovers. Anything."

"It doesn't work that way," he'd said. "There's vouchers that prove where it goes. I can't mess with the stats. They'll cut you off, dude. You'll be back to suckin' in the duck shit."

"Don't let go of us, Pritchard. No one picks players in disease," Caleb said. "If Colzer turns its back here what do you think it's going to do in ghettos in New Jersey, barrios in El Paso? What do you think it's going to do with the whole goddamn city of New Orleans?"

That night Pritchard went through his provisions. Due to fly to Buenos Aires within days, he knew he'd probably never see Caleb again. But the voice he heard over and over was more than one man's or even one city's. It was the tap of a strange kind of conscience, an annoyance that Elsa would never be satisfied no matter how he distributed a quick, inadequate anti-plague. She would remain goddess behind the omniscient power of Colzer-Bremen. And she would never see a child burned to death before he could cough up most of his lungs.

So an hour before dawn on January 6, 2009, Martin Pritchard walked half way across a gated bridge between the city of Mumbai and the slums of Dharavi. He was alone, a backpack strapped tightly over his shoulders, a small Ruger tucked inside his beltline. A few of the guards had seen flu-infected birds fall out of the sky late in the afternoon the preceding day, and they blocked off the bridge with international pandemic tape and a chain. While that had been going on, Pritchard paid two men to re-label five hundred vials from the latest shipment, each one indicating 82 percent. The rest he left in a warehouse filled with bodies due to be burned within a few hours.

Midway across the bridge he could remember picking up the remains of a bird that looked a lot like a magpie, ivory bars on its wings in perfect chevrons. He pried the bird's mouth open with his forefinger. The chalky breakdown of a pellet had softened with saliva, swelled, and completely obstructed the bird's throat. Pritchard picked at it, then gave the bird a fling into the swamp below, impressed that Caleb's diversion had worked.

In the muggy gloom two cities were wrapped in the same fear, withdrawing from a bridge with only a piece of tape and a chain to protect them from one another. No longer would any Indian venture there, having expended all their remedies and all their faith in Pass-Flu. Pritchard knew this impasse could last for weeks, until the magpies decayed and the tape turned the pale lavender of a fading curse. Or until the WHO investigated the real reason the birds died.

He could see the outline of Caleb walking toward him, a manila envelope under his arm. Dawn was arriving, and the mangrove was coming to life under sewage and the corpses of a hundred stiffening birds. Caleb took Pritchard's backpack, then said, "So much death, my friend. Everything's blamed on bird flu. Even the birds below us. But you bring hope. And, I bring you the only thanks these people can give."

"They finally made good," Pritchard said, tapping the pack. "Not much, but you've got the best Colzer can give."

A look of relief passed over Caleb's face. He handed Pritchard the envelope, its contents a handful of coarse, gold-filled teeth. "Seems morbid man, I know. But as far as Dharavi is concerned, Colzer has now saved the only worthwhile souls of Mumbai. That, in spite of what you and I know to be one of the dreadful shames of India."

CHAPTER 21

The mid-afternoon sun seemed to light the country from below, as if Montana could be illuminated by its own geology. The climb into the Rattlesnake dizzied Josie, the elevation pushing colors to their extremes. The road twisted back on itself, each notch further up the grade past houses and barns, apple orchards, and a school. Once families kept the lawns trimmed and watered, and horses grazed the pastures to a constant green turf. But already summer was picking at the edges, turning grass to harsh bristle, and just like everywhere else in America incoming flu had decelerated constant upkeep. If it was possible, Josie thought, houses in the country had a particularly haunted look with swags of white sheets hanging at their windows and bales of hay barricading off driveways. Things were no different outside Missoula than New York City. The only thing trusted was community isolation.

Sterns finally made his way into the Rattlesnake Wilderness high above the homes and into a campground honeycombed with trails and the pungent smell of smoke. She watched him maneuver the diesel through connecting sites, past tents and chairs, fold-up tables, sawed off stumps, and fire pits smoldering between lines of soggy laundry. Nowhere was there privacy. People watched the outfit Sterns was trying to fit into an empty space between a bathhouse and the last loop of gravel road. They gawked at the Washington license plate, then continued to stare until he was backed in and turned off the engine.

"This reminds me of Steinbeck," Josie said, pushing the door open. "Are you sure this is where you meant for us to end up?"

"The last time I was here things were normal," was all he said.

She walked to the bathhouse. A trickle of water in a sink had several women scooping and filling former milk jugs. They moved away when they saw her mouth. She heard them shuffle out the open door as she locked herself inside the stall, then realized what Sterns must have had to look at for hours, confined in a place he couldn't leave with her oozing poison alongside him. And now she couldn't clean up, couldn't get rid of this thing that had invaded her mouth, her lungs, her breath, her hair.

When she got back to the trailer he was checking the whole outside, moving from tire to tire, the hood of the truck wide open. She wanted to disappear inside, to take up the entire twenty-eight feet alone with a bar of soap and a box of gauze. And then she decided that wasn't what she wanted at all. "It's not fair, Sterns," she said coming up behind him. "I don't even know why you're here. I'm sick. I know I've been sick for hours. And you act like this is a camping trip."

Checking his tire gauge, he pushed it in and tried again. "You wanted to go to Nebraska," he said. "I've got you this far. You're closer."

She puzzled at his sure-footedness. He wasn't saying anything about going further, yet he was checking all the extremities. She looked at the awning behind him. Nothing protruded. It was as though she was coming alive to reality, and it was no longer near as clear as hallucinating had been.

"I'm going to Nebraska," she said. "But you don't need to take me. I appreciate everything. But you don't need to."

Sterns kept working, moving around the truck in a methodical up and down pattern. "You need to settle down," he said. "You're right. You've been very sick."

"Is that all you have to say? That I've been very sick. Let me tell you, I'm getting well very fast. And I wonder why you're going through all this. Hours of driving, living in my breath. Why Sterns?"

He fumbled with hook-ups, then looked at the trees beside him. She wondered if he heard something flutter there. "I know what it's like to wake up crazy," he said. "I had to wait a long time to be okay again."

"So what does that have to do with what I've put you through?"

"Oh, I don't know," he said, leveling his gaze at her. "When you went up in that tree with me I guess I knew both of us were looking at the impossible. Finally, there was somebody who saw the impossible with me. At the same time. I knew I couldn't be crazy. Because you certainly weren't."

There was so little distance between her and Sterns she could see a reddish sheen come over the bridge of his nose, then he wiped his eyes with his shirt sleeve. He didn't look at her again.

"So I guess that means we're spending the night here," she said. "Together."

Sterns bent his knee to look under the trailer. "I'll be sleeping in the truck," he said. "Give me a few more minutes. Then I think we better check on things in Nebraska."

* * *

Blades of the window fan twirled in a slow whir behind her. Josie leaned against the sofa, the wind barely trembling across the top of her hair and realized she had to wash it soon, before it didn't move at all. She felt so dirty in this place, so cut off. But with a turn of her head she could see the bathhouse. When she knew it was empty she would go in and lock the door, and make the rest of them wait for her.

Sterns said nothing when he came in and placed a computer on the table. He went back and forth heating soup, finding crackers, and logging on. She wasn't hungry, and tomorrow was soon enough to find out about Nebraska. Every once in a while she would turn back toward the bathhouse watching for a rustle in the trees or the steady outline of a bird. Nothing happened except the breeze. Dreams had permeated her consciousness infused with something she could only describe as memory lag. She couldn't remember her mother's face but could see a metal strand on a bird's leg as thin as floral wire. His eyes, staring red orbs, had slowly bewitched her. And, without a doubt, she sensed he was nearby.

She noticed Sterns chewing the end of his thumb while he

concentrated on the laptop, then moved back and forth between it and stirring soup. *You think I'm going crazy,* she thought. *In that case, you should know people like me don't want to eat.* She pinched tighter into the rust-colored couch and remembered in particular the image of the barn in her dreams. Red eyes, red barn. For some reason, she felt a sudden, irked curiosity. "Do you think my husband was killed?" she asked.

She wanted him to hear her even though she could barely hear herself. She waited, remembering Robert's patience when she'd turn away from him in bed asking questions that didn't matter. Things like, "How close did you get to the finches?" instead of "How long before you tell me about her." Waiting, she could feel her belly tighten and a gruesome sweat break out across her back, pitching her back and forth between fever and shivering.

"I don't know much about flying," he said, "But I know it's extremely linear. Until it isn't."

"You didn't answer my question. Do you think Colzer eliminated him?"

There was a shoving sound, then a lid being snapped into place. She could feel his concentration now shifting to her. He barely paused. "I haven't thought about it very much, I guess. I've read things the last couple days that make me wonder what he was up against. I've wondered about what I would've done. But I've only imagined a man's secret drive—his mission. I haven't figured out his failure."

"Do you think he failed?" she asked.

"I don't know."

"Well, you brought it up," she said lifting herself out of the corner.

"I think the project itself was doomed. People meant well, but they've been dealing with a killer disease. Something misunderstood. Random. Like Powerball."

"What do you really think about Nebraska?" she said, putting her feet back on the floor, feeling the heat of her back escape through sweat and the incoming breeze. "About the old man with the pigeons. Tell me, Sterns. Don't you want to see what's left of extinction?"

She watched him roll his eyes to the ceiling and squint hard, examining an imaginary speck of truth. "It's a long way to go without an invite," he said.

She took his answer to mean he didn't want to go. Invitation wouldn't have made any difference. "The old man with the pigeons is alone now," she said. "For a while I thought he might just want to keep it that way. Alone with his birds. But you know what? He knows what happened to Robert and the flock in Washington. He knows whatever Robert was doing with Gem-X was clandestine. Mr. Hennings knows the way I walk, the expressions on my face, and the color of my favorite hiking boots. He's seen me a hundred times even though I've never met him."

She paused, watching Sterns for something other than calculation. "All the way through the experiment I was the control. I'm the entity no one accounted for and no one can get rid of. Robert somehow put me in his program, made me a part of the bird's escape. And Hennings knows it. In fact, he might have conjured up the idea himself."

It was farfetched, she knew, and pretentious. Something ordinarily she'd have detested in anybody, let alone herself. What did it matter what her husband did with the shots of her? Maybe he led her to believe, just for that short time, she was important. Maybe he figured he could buy time or that she'd forget. But Sterns was constantly questioning her, implying that although he was willing to take her to Missoula, maybe even Nebraska, underneath it all he questioned her reasoning mind. It was quite possible, by now, he truly doubted her sanity.

"Don't be so damned sure of yourself, Josie," he said, starting up from the table, reaching toward the overhead cupboard. "This thing doesn't move around one or even two people. It's high tech supremacy. Your husband and Hennings were bird men. They cared about something relatively insignificant, except in the game of medicine. The bird stopped flying a hundred years ago. No one cares about the passenger pigeon. Doesn't even know it exists. Its value is for one thing—venom. Its deadly immune component. Once this virus outmaneuvers 1918, the passenger might as well truly go extinct. It might be the one humane thing left to do."

Josie swallowed hard, the boiling fatigue of the night before layering her in another blanket of sweat. She stirred the soup with little intention except to watch it cool. Once more, he was thinking in his own track, oblivious to the impressions that had drifted through her hours of fitful sleep. "So now you think Gem-X, if he's not just my imagination, could be a disease carrier?"

"I doubt anybody knows the answer to that," he said. "But if you've indeed seen him, as you say, I'd give him a wide berth."

She laid her spoon alongside the bowl, then turned her body toward the bathhouse. Cinder blocks squared the building, bolstering it as though it would stand long beyond the grates and fire pits—that it would be studied someday for its inhabitants in the last days of western mankind. She considered taking her belongings and locking herself in it for the night.

"Hey, mister, see you're from Washington," a voice said just outside the trailer door. "Name's Ned Wanamaker. Wife Diane's here too. We've got a little sumpin' for you."

Sterns answered, opening the door just far enough Josie could see a small balding man extend a purple ribbon, the universal sign of flu, toward him. The wife was beyond sight, but several women were now heading toward the bathhouse, towels draped over their arms. Not one of them looked under fifty.

"We haven't seen a rig from Washington in here for weeks. Can we step in?" he said, putting one foot on the adjustable stairs. Sterns extended a hand toward the inside.

"Can't say it makes much sense to us," Ned said, waffling his thumb between him and Diane. "Folks come in here from the east, not the west." Diane nodded, her once jet black hair now intact for only the last squared-off inch, leaving the majority a cotton white. Besides the hair, there was a skunk-like quality to her, pointy chin with indented, almost invisible mouth and two very curious dark brown eyes. She remained at Ned's side in the manner of a small, disarmed animal on a leash. "Most folks is running from the worst of the flu. Heard Washington's still pretty healthy. So what's with your coming this way?" Ned persisted. "Nice rig though." His face lifted to the cupboards, and he leaned toward the closed-off bedroom.

"Family," Sterns said. "I've got family outside Missoula. We're just staying the night."

"Well, dear me," Ned said, "I should hope you'd turn around and go back home."

"Smells good in here," Diane added. "It's been awhile since we've had much other than pork chops. It's a staple around here with all the pigs."

There was a strange mix of curiosity and disenchantment, and Josie kept wondering when Sterns was going to let the neighbors back out as succinctly as he let them in. He caught her eye just once, moving his efforts back to Ned almost without pause. But that brief interruption was enough to rivet her attention.

"It's been awhile since we've been around real folks," Sterns said. "Something like this either draws them together or forces them apart. Looks like this place has pulled together."

Ned beamed and shuffled his feet one at a time, straightening himself to the top of his five feet six inches. His head wobbled back and forth with an air of self-imposed authority. "Well, I've been called the mayor of the Rattlesnake. Now that's a dubious honor, I can tell you. But truth is, this little community is strong, no matter what goes in and out of here. Those of us who stay are healthy."

"Most people have a house to stay or die in—whatever. But these people have been foreclosed on or just plain walked away, mostly since the economy was bad anyway. Some of them have been beat down so bad they got no family who wants them. One seventy-nine year old man was the only survivor in a Missoula nursing home. About three weeks ago they found all them folks stowed away in their rooms. Them's that could walk was hooked to their beds. All their shoes and purses, wallets and such was piled up in the administrator's office. He was nowhere in sight, and neither was the help. Most all the residents was dead. Except Axel. Even the administrator was dead in his home. There's the irony, you know. Nobody wins against the flu. Money don't mean nothin'."

"Yeah," Sterns said, lifting his fingers from the door jam where a wet film lingered. "I've been wondering how folks in

Missoula are doing through all this. I mean the regular ones. You know, the ones that don't make headlines."

"Oh, probably good as can be expected." Ned took off again. "You know none of these people use face masks. Never have, even when they was warned. We don't either," he said, gesturing toward the camp. "But most of us that's still here has had Pass-Flu or some derivative. You know what I mean by derivative?" Ned's face turned a shade redder, then he whispered, "Pee. We ain't got Pass-Flu, but we got each other's pee."

Wordless, Sterns studied Ned exactly as Ned surely wanted.

"You ain't never heard of it?" he asked.

Sterns shook his head back and forth.

"Well, we never did half-dose here. But we'd heard a long time ago that if you took the stuff, then saved your pee, you could give it to the next guy who needed it. Works fine," Ned said with a grin. "Haven't had to do it for a spell. It's like we're all immune."

"I'm happy for you," Sterns said, hardly moving his lips. "We didn't know what to expect out here."

Josie watched the two men, how intent they were, one simply overcoming the other with his word play. Ned hadn't looked at her once and bypassed his wife, leaving her to hunt the trailer with her darting glances. Finally, Diane settled on Josie in a probing stare. "You got a mighty mean lookin' blister there," she said. "How old are you?"

A bizarre state of amusement now accompanied Josie's irritation. She wanted to reach forward, extend her neck about two feet, and bite the woman. Instead, she subdued her urge and simply stared back. "I'm thirty-something," she said, holding onto a nearby pillow. "And I don't drink pee or take anybody else's shit."

Diane flicked her gaze to Sterns who began a slow motion toward the couple as if corralling them toward the door. "We gotta' get some rest," he said. "We're leaving early."

"Oh, and one more thing," Ned quickly added, patting Sterns on his outstretched hand. "We do have feral pigs out and round the campground. Turned loose off ranches down below. Remind me of javelinas. They can get mean."

As he walked out the trailer, the mayor looked both ways, held his hand up and out to Diane, who took it like the first lady she was, and said to Sterns, "We're having a vigil tonight, same as every week since we been here. You're invited, both of you. Bring a candle if you want." Then, without even a first or last glance toward Josie he added, "I'd head back where you come from, son. Looks to me like you got a sick one there. You got twenty-four to seventy-two hours to get a handle on it."

* * *

Cool dampness extended from the bathhouse, dampness that leaked into the ground, softening it into rich loam. From it, baby pines colonized along one whole wall, top heavy with the first impetuous growth of their lives. They could stay here forever, Josie thought. They could take their time.

She'd pulled clean underwear from a front pocket of her backpack, but it was the only thing she planned to change. Something drastic could happen if she made it all wash away. She might forget the tinge of disease and worse yet, so might he. The smell of her own body filled the stall, and she realized why she had to be alone to do this.

It took only moments for the soap to collect, to accumulate the hours of sweat and send it downward past her navel and the protrusions of her knees. For the first time in years she drew her fingers through bubbles, watching them escape, then replaced by a thin watery line. She worked them into her ears, down the slope of her neck. She moved the soap back and forth between her hands and into her groin. And she smelled aloe mixed with the pungent forest of the Rattlesnake.

It was all unanswered except for one thing, one overwhelming feeling that she was coming home. Robert had been here, somewhere along this road with her four years ago. There was never a time that had been better. But she'd been unable to discuss it with him. What he'd been doing out here was locked into a computer and a trusted partner. It was not extended to her. Yet, she was re-enacting parts of it.

Shower water pooled around her feet. Josie leaned over rubbing her legs, feeling the soft plunge of water above her and hesitated, letting it beat away her ache. It pelted her spine. A snap inside her head sounded like closing the bolt of a gun, and dizziness crept inward from the sides of the stall, maybe from the sturdy blocks of the house itself. There was only the water pipe to hang onto.

Hair hung below her, her own, beat under the relentless stream. She could see it waving back and forth. Maybe kelp or the cross-hatching of net. It fascinated her, kept her upright. If she could hang onto it she might be able to climb her way out. She could feel it lifting her, away from herself. She held on tight.

He came from behind her. She'd seen his hands first, palms pulling her hair back, steadying her head on his chest. He forced her to let go, to sink back and feel him. "Robert," she said, her arms flailing outward. "You're here, aren't you?" He didn't move except to hold her tighter. "Let me see you. After all this time, please let me see you," she said. She gurgled, that ugly sound of mucus when it's on the move.

"Get it out," he said. "Spit."

He loosened his grip and she pulled hard, in uncontrollable strength that comes from coughing. Off center, she grabbed his leg and looked up. There was no water now. Only his shape. Work gloves were tucked into the back of his jeans. They protruded like short, beige feathers.

"Oh, it is you," she said. "I knew you'd be here. I knew you wouldn't leave me alone in this." She crawled upward, her face against his leg. She could feel him caress the top of her head, then put his hand between her and his leg. "Don't," she said. "Let me touch you."

He stopped bracing her. She could feel him relax, even though he stood without helping. There was something inanimate, she thought. An angel that reaches down, then lets you come-to safely in bed. "You made me follow you here," she said, clutching his belt. "For this?" she asked, letting herself sink into the dark waiting pool of the shower. "Sometimes I wonder, am I supposed to die?"

CHAPTER 22

People like the Wanamakers would keep the Rattlesnake. They would hold the campground like a fort, Sterns thought. A stranger might enter this world and think it was Montana. But Sterns was no stranger. He'd never forgotten how this place lived apart from the rest, how it breathed separately. And taught its own.

Josie entered the bathhouse carrying a towel over her arm. It was concealing underwear, he knew, because he'd watched her pull it from her backpack, only briefly opening a side pocket. Sterns kept watching, bent low but well back from the trailer's side window and imagined how close she was to checking on her husband's final gift, the vials of Pass-Flu now in the cupboard above his head. He could hear the dense hum of insects chirring a single continuous note, and he knew, for him, the note was regret.

When he finally answered his cell, Gil sounded tired, even irritated. "Yup," he yelled toward the phone in a long-standing refusal to put the device to his ear. "You headed this way?"

Sterns could imagine him sitting at Ramsey's, his fork poised over a rib-eye and three baked potatoes. It was his one extravagance, always sometime the week following payday, and he'd want to hang up and eat.

"No, bud, I'm not. In fact, quite the opposite. I'm in Missoula."

"The hell you say. What's so damn important over there?"

Sterns could hear the clatter of chains, not utensils. "It's a long story, but I thought you better know where I am."

"Well, I get the idea." Gil paused, then said, "Trailer comin' in handy?"

It wasn't going to be easy to convince his partner of the reason this was happening. The years since Carolina's death had passed routinely between the two men. Gil spoke little of Abby, his wife, except to remind Sterns every Thanksgiving, every Christmas, Easter, and birthday she'd set a place for him at their table. It had gone on for so long, this parenting, there were times he simply accepted it must take the two of them to replace the woman he'd lost. But, eventually, he came to the conclusion it wasn't about Carolina. It was the other death, the loss of Mark, that kept things the way they were. The empty space grew narrower and had just about disappeared. Because over the years, from one job to another, Gil fit himself in.

Sterns took a long pause, studying Josie's influence, her rumpled sweater, her computer, even the extra soup bowl on the counter. This was nothing he could explain to his best friend. He hardly understood it himself. Her illness, it seemed, was part of what he'd searched for. Unlike leukemia, it was condensed and sure-footed. It didn't hide behind a screening or a smear and pretend not to exist. Her flu had defined itself within hours of his meeting her. It might still criss-cross through the rain forest in its own time. But it found Sterns through a woman. And, in this time of few options, overwhelmed with doubt, he'd done something about it. "I didn't hear that," he said calmly. "Look, she's not doing very good."

"When you think you'll be back?" Gil said. "I got things ready to go for tomorrow."

Sterns could sense it, the refusal to accept this sudden change, so he kept to a monotone response. "Not sure. Might turn around and come back in the morning. Or might continue on."

"Continue on where, Gary? What you doin', man?"

"I'm not sure," he said, holding steady. "All I know is you gotta' keep things going. For now, the business, it's up to you."

Gil waited, then cleared his throat. "You headed east?" he asked.

"I'm thinkin' we might."

"You better be sure, my friend. It's not just sicker back there. Now, there's a fire somewhere around the Black Hills. Heard it's got'em mighty buggered."

From under the weight of miles and his own beleaguered conscience, Sterns realized he had to say the thing to Gil he'd never admitted. Maybe it was because of Missoula, where disease and fire kept coming together. Or maybe it was the deaths themselves, Carolina's less than a week behind Mark's, that had sealed off the entrance to Sterns' ambition. The real terror wasn't in making the choice to go east. It was whether he could move at all. "When I left here, you remember years ago, I said I'd never come back. Now in less than a day, I'm here. From never to a day. When something sweeps over you that fast, it's driving the team, bud. I can't hold it back. Not anymore."

He could hear chains again, the sounds of horses working for a man they trusted. They knew he wouldn't be distracted long. "All's I can say is you're welcome to come back," Gil said. "Nobody has to keep gettin' in deeper. We'll be on the Nelson Fork when you get here."

The phone call left Sterns shiftless, as though admitting the truth to Gil had only set off more doubt. Doubt he'd started letting go in a message to Hennings over two hours before. As confined as the trailer was, it was distance from Josie, and he kept thinking she was needing it too, probably standing under a bend of simple galvanized pipe for the first time in her life. He imagined her, reaching up, letting water wind the length of her skin. It was easy to let himself wonder about her body. Such simple arithmetic compared to her mind.

A message from Hennings had come through by the time they got to the Rattlesnake, but he'd waited until he was alone to access it. In fact, he'd put it off until after Gil. It was getting harder to learn the unexpected, to shift into another decision. He knew he was in Missoula for the night. By morning, there was the freeway, and he'd be on it one direction or the other, alone or with her.

Straightforward, Hennings began his note simply. It picked up speed as he went. *Mr. Sterns: You've come to know a lot. My best guess is you've been able to retrieve a lot of Robert's data. That means his laptop survived despite his death. It also means the Pass-Flu he had also survived. I'm happy to say, you've done nothing wrong. In fact, you probably saved Josephine Russo's life.*

What's disconcerting is her disregard for her condition. She will survive the flu, but there could be other side effects. I think her preoc-

*cupation with Gem-X could be one of them. Hallucinations, I under-
stand, aren't uncommon with the avian flu. Contrivances about a mi-
grating passenger pigeon, despite what you've read, are moot. She will
need to rest as often as you can convince her. I doubt I'll answer all her
questions, even if she makes it to me. As for her imaginary bird, it can
hardly be expected to survive, even Ms. Russo's imagination. It would
have to fly over a thousand miles across the Rockies and down through
a shaft of unexpectedly good fortune considering there's a quarter million acre firestorm quickly consuming the Great Plains. In fact, I'm
not sure Darby will even be here in a couple more days.*

*Your thought about taking her to a hospital, well, I'll let you de-
cide that for yourself. From what I've heard, she has a better chance of
being treated by a small town veterinarian who might recognize the
anti-virus in her system without turning her into the Feds. That vial
you gave her is the strongest anti-virus ever produced. (Fact is engi-
neering it decimated the flock in Washington which is what my dear
friend, Robert, knew would happen.) That makes Ms. Russo a walking antidote to the bird flu, no matter how many times it mutates. It
appears the reason for this success is Gem-X.*

*Ultimately, I wish you both the best. Should you beat the odds,
I'll be here until it gets too hot to go into the kitchen—Curtis.*

Sterns read the message again, trying to separate the relief
from his fear. Hennings didn't sound like an eighty-year-old man.
He sounded like a scientist in his prime, a man counting his successes, not the malfunctioning of an experiment thousands of
miles away. He made no differentiation between the anti-virus and
Gem-X. They were one and the same. And yet, Sterns thought,
birds could never be absolved of this plague. Stumbling through
fragments of remembered conversation, he thought of what Josie
said miles back. Her comment that Gem-X was now the only one
left. Somehow, just like Hennings, she knew something had gone
wrong with the passengers at Wilson's Bridge this, despite her flu-
riddled brain, or maybe because of it.

A breeze rumbled across the roof, bowling a few pine cones
down its full length. Sterns fixated on the overhead staccato. He
even looked up, following the rolling, unpredictable thuds with his
eyes. A patchwork score of chatter reminded him of an elk bone

yard he'd found with Mark the last summer they were together, a place where they figured cows and calves were trapped in snow from the hard winter before. Wind funneled through the remains of eight or nine carcasses, an eerie clicking chime, just like now, that sent shivers through Sterns. And he realized, even from this angle, it was the invisible, solitary sound that made him ache to see his older brother.

He let himself follow a memory, an old one back in the house on Morgan Street. It was in the clothes chute, a dark hole of a place where he could hear Mark coaxing him from the widening cavern below. Telling him not to worry about the landing. "It's like that big orange pillow Mom's sitting on right now. It squishes out every time she sets on it. You think it's going flat, but the air inside it gots nowhere to go. It waits for Mom to get up. Then it poofs back up, just like the basement floor." That voice talked him through the falls, past the part where the chute narrowed and he'd feel it scrape his ribs, past the smell of paint and soap and damp earth. That voice got him into jump school. It took him right up to the Rampart Lake fire.

In a sudden, jarring invasion, something just beneath the trailer's back window let out with a yell. There was a second lurching screech and the crack of brush. Sterns looked out to see a pig make a stiff-legged circle around the bathhouse pursued by a man with a small rifle, the two of them accelerating in a slogging, comical dance. The pig jettisoned over a steep downward bank, bushes closing instantly behind him. The man, probably in his sixties, looked both ways as though crossing at an intersection, then stepped into the waist-high scrub. Nothing else moved.

It stayed that way as Sterns made his way to the bathhouse. For a minute he walked in the footprints of the pig, in some way sensing the energy of the hooves, desperate bites indenting the ground. He stood at the door listening to the faint hiss of a shower. Then, without much more than his own doubts, he knocked. Finally, he walked to the side where a small louvered window above Josie was the only decent eavesdrop. Water trickled in a constant stream. "Josie," he said, "Are you all right?"

He thought of her stamina. How it waned, then seemed to grab hold in bursts of undiluted clarity, each burst getting progressively longer. The serum wasn't one hundred percent, and hallucinations were to be blamed on the flu itself, according to Hennings. But the old man wasn't standing here listening to his own heartbeat pound in his ears. He would never have to watch her twitch sideways in her seat, rolling her eyes right past him claiming she'd seen a bird, extinct as a dodo, just beyond her reach. No other fool on this earth, Hennings included, would've punched that serum inside her. They'd have known she'd do better without it.

Even so, it wasn't without hesitance that Sterns opened the door to the bathhouse, seeing her feet, first one, then the other, dipping back and forth in water that swirled between stalls. Shafts of sunlight filtered through open rafters above her, giving him the feeling he was entering someplace forbidden to all but a team of elves or a young woman willingly caged by them. A scent of soap, apple maybe, made him think of her. He wondered if it was something she might've used when her husband was alive, and held back, seeing there was no door on either stall.

She moaned, lightening sharp. Her arms reached upward, stretching her body as if she was searching for a limb. Sterns watched and realized, even without the stream of water glossing her back, she was too young for the man he'd seen that day at Kiddner's. In fact, at that moment she looked more like a child, curveless, her sensuality something he'd only imagined.

Suddenly she bent forward and grappled for the pipe while studying the deepening water around her. She seemed to be considering what she was going to do to survive, then went down on her knees. Reaching above her, Sterns came from behind and turned off the water. Then, with little more than reflex he backed away, unsure what touching her would mean, aware she was barely conscious, but that his own feelings about her were fast erasing his inconspicuous life, sending him into the turmoil of his own heart. He watched her gulp as if the water was still running. "Robert," she said, her hand finding his boot. "You're here, aren't you?"

"Yes," he whispered, concentrating on the slip of gold on her left hand. She didn't move, holding the moment, he thought, too long. She started to look up, then began to cough. It shook through her, unleashed by the long warm shower, until her head fell back against his thighs.

Leaning forward, he cupped himself around her. Her coughs radiated into his chest, and she let them go as if the pummeling would somehow get easier with him behind her. Instantly, she tensed and began to pull away. "Let me see you," she warned.

If she could see at all in the dimness of the bathhouse Sterns knew she'd know, whether she said it or not, whether she could even sort it out in her fevered brain. She'd look at him with question, the cleft between her eyes the only thing that had grown as old as her husband, then accusation. It would never be the same if he kept pretending. So he said, "It's me, Josie. It's Sterns. I can't leave you here like this."

She turned toward him keeping her face down, some instinct pulling her arms inward, her bended legs closer to her body. She didn't look up but again sat very still. Finally, she put her head on Sterns shoulder, compacting her weariness deep into his embrace. "You made me follow you here," she said.

"I did, didn't I," he answered. "Would you like to leave now?"

He could feel her head barely nod. "Am I supposed to die?"

Sterns looked out beyond the two of them, holding the length of her, thin as summer sheets in his arms. He knew she'd grown into this disease while it continued to invade her. She'd slept the dreams of its making and wandered alone, unable to escape its cavernous waste save a few brief interludes of revelation. He'd waited, just like he'd waited once before, to watch her slip away into the pronouncement of death.

In the deadfall that skirted the far side of the bathhouse, just beyond the steep bank he'd watched the man and pig navigate earlier, Sterns saw a flash, then settling as if the creature there was hoping to blend. Feathers, uncharacteristically white, spread in two tiers below the cylindrical body giving his tail the delicate appeal of a petticoat. The bird was nothing indigenous. In fact, he was facing in such a way that wings V'd above his head gave him the look of a small cherub, roguish and curious. A small metal wire jutted from his leg glistening while he sidled back and forth, then became solid, as much a part of the Douglas fir as the brilliant afternoon sun.

Impatience filled Sterns, spurred on by his own imagination. He watched intently the woman he carried. She'd told him where the flu had taken her, how it moved through her mind and conjured the image of a bird. The dreams, until this moment, had formed his impressions of her. They overwhelmed his common sense and fed his guilt. And for a while, he believed they were his penance. But Sterns, in that fleeting instant, calculated the possibilities. If she survived, however she survived, it would be because of what she believed. By now it depended far less on the serum he'd given her, then what he'd just seen perched in a tree.

CHAPTER 23

It was at least a half hour before Pritchard spoke and then with an absent-minded quality, both edgy and superficial. "If you'd never been to Billings you could still find it, right? I mean I've seen a lot of airtime, and pilots always know where they are. Right?"

Mellon wagged his head in a persistent gesture, similar to a wooly plastic dog on a dashboard. "Yup, man. We always know where we are, and we always know we're lucky to get there."

An atmospheric pall, a subdued half-light that sometimes flickered in ribbons of falling diamonds, held Pritchard's mood. "There's something I've never seen before," he said, leaning closer to the windshield.

"Ash," Mellon said. "Beautiful until it clogs every moving part."

Fire stirred the air, adding its components in a series of heat-cracking explosions hundreds of miles away. The Black Hills, where it had begun, had taken on the char of a beginner's intensity. Its ownership hung in the smoldering wrack of boulders and trees. The Black Hills Fire had spread to nearly 250,000 acres in a matter of hours and moved south and eastward piercing the Great Plains, a giant scorching arrow that pushed itself outward while the jet moved windward. Unchecked, it was quickly becoming the biggest fire in the United States, sending its glittering embers thousands of feet high.

"Blasting whoreson," Pritchard said, his attention reverting back to his laptop. "As though fucking flu can't kill enough. But, then again maybe it'll make those thieving fools turn around and head right back into the hell they just drove out of."

He watched the slow steady blip just outside Missoula, the way it just sat there, a defiant eye staring back at him. He'd connected with the satellite tracking service on the way back from

Mexico and toyed with the idea of paying Mellon to take him any direction but this. Right now it might be easier to enter the toxic air space of Istanbul or Milan, to keep moving further and further into the viral net that blanketed the world than to act out Elsa's plot. She had satellites turned for a goddamnedable pigeon. She could titillate what remained of the healthy populations of the planet with 98 percent assurance she would cure them.

She practiced witchery, he thought. Witchery that over the months had first become tinged with a kind of orderly choosing. Not one billionaire had yet died from bird flu. Comment was that only a few members of Parliament could be counted among Britain's high losses, and out of almost two hundred Roman Catholic cardinals worldwide only three had died. Pritchard had heard about Colzer's stats. Built first by hemispheres, then by continental parameters, then by population densities, various ethnic groups, and finally occupations, the tables, by the time he was privy to their persistent rumors, were as outdated as the Pass-Flu he distributed. But the energy behind the numbers, the woman credited with "resourceful distribution," as Colzer saw it, was Elsa. Pass-flu updates had launched her. It locked her onto a fiendish path that more than once he'd swept clean for her. Millions died. Bodies were tagged and bulldozed, buried and burned, but Colzer-Bremen's worldwide achievement was extrapolated in neat, unflinching spreadsheets of success. Merely the incessant probability that they existed reminded him, in blood-chilling clarity, what he'd done in her name.

His mind drifted, somehow alight with the particles around him. This was the periphery that, by now, he recognized as a narrow, subconscious band of relative calm. In spite of Mellon's obvious concern, the ash captivated and pulled gently at Pritchard. Its weightless mass swirled about him, inflicting death way below, out of his sight.

For some reason he thought of Ortez again, the pharmacist, now almost seventy, who'd worked as a veterinarian most of his life, then switched over to filling prescriptions. There'd been a long-standing agreement between them. Pritchard could get any medicine the pharmacist might happen to have in Palomas, even though he'd never brought more than 39 percent Pass-Flu over that border and probably never would.

"We die in the lungs here," Ortez had said, "TB will be here when the flu is long finished with us."

And so Pritchard had brought him isoniazid. "Keep your tuberculosis over here, el medico. My boss says it's messy when it crosses the border."

"You think it's not messy here?" Ortez would say, counting his fingers. "Twenty-three dead last week, mostly ninos, the babies." That had been before bird flu's first wave hit Mexico almost eight months ago. Now, he thought, watching the ash accumulate in an immaculate line around the flight gauges, it wouldn't matter how much isoniazid he brought the pharmacist or how much burned-out anti-virus. The only thing that mattered was cortisone and his daughter's chance to survive.

A corner of one of Russo's training CDs protruded from the briefcase, an irritating reminder that reconnected Pritchard to the present. Yet, like one more artifact scattered across the floor of the birdman's life, it intrigued Pritchard, and he realized it, along with what he'd already seen, the eyebolt, the monitors and cables, the recorded preoccupation with training one passenger were direct links to what was happening below. He disconnected from the bird's motionless transmitter, then brought up the third CD. Instantly, the screen filled with a sliver of light, an eyedropper full compared to the intensity of sun that overcame it. Pitch bright luminosity re-entered the frame, a slow, earthly take-over of one steady view. What seemed to be a thin line of rocks or one spoke stretched beyond the camera's limits. An LED display in the bottom right corner contained a string of numbers. A date, *06/21/05*, and time, *05:24:06*. Pritchard paused the focus and thought back to the last thing he'd noted at Russo's desk ... *trained to leave facility at the appointed time.*

For a moment he wondered if this was more than just a man's off-ox scheme. True, Russo might've been pushing the limits of sanity, his doddering obsession with a passenger becoming more psychotic than scientific. But if the rationale had been to plan an escape for Gem-X, why allow the proof to fall into the hands of anybody, let alone Elsa? Pritchard imagined her indulging her senses in one sitting in Russo's office, re-attaching cables, propping her face against one fidgeting hand while she forwarded her way through hours of video. Training a passenger pigeon to do anything besides lying quietly in a blood-sucking incubator was sure to raise her question, and training him to escape was a death knell. Pritchard knew what he was watching had already been studied carefully by his boss, probably as carefully as she'd scrutinized Russo's flight plan across the Olympic Peninsula the morning he died. She'd used it as her logic to rid herself of a digressor.

He continued watching, couched in headphones, allowing the streaming video to play uninterrupted through a series of images, both eye level and aerial. Occasionally, the corner LED would identify the location. Inlets and lakes gave way to the helmeted lid of the Tacoma Dome. Puget Sound appeared, a continuous blue bead underneath an invisible wing, always on the left of the flyer. Lake Sammamish disappeared behind the rugged fence line of the Cascades, taking with it a glimpse of the freeway until it broke free again at Ellensburg. He knew it was Ellensburg because a woman he recognized as Josephine Russo stood at the city limits, one hand braced under the population sign while with the other she raised two fingers. She smiled in the way women do, he thought, when they're relaxed. When they don't put on make-up or comb their hair. He looked her over, all of her, and decided she didn't have a bra on either. He wondered what she knew, right then, that minute, and for the rest of the day until that night when she'd crawl in close to the old man she'd married and praise him for his ingenuity, then touch him with the soft underbelly of her hands.

A tinkling strain of *La Cucaracha* began, the cell phone at once demanding and irretrievable. Pritchard realized he'd locked it inside the gun sling on his lower right ankle the night before. That way he could say it was with him at all times but still choose to ignore repeated calls from Elsa. He watched the terrain below them, listening to the childhood song, swaying back and forth, until Mellon lowered his sunglasses and gave him an immobilizing stare. "She's on your ass, man," he said. "And if that's what cortisone does, I'm going to be too."

It seemed odd to imagine keeping time to catastrophe. But it had rhythm, always. In the sound of helicopter blades or the thud of a man's helmet against hot rock. Pritchard watched the road below them, straight as high-tension wire. A deer trail, he thought, in less than a year. If no one maintains it, it reverts. No different than the Gulf.

The ringing stopped. Elsa didn't know it yet, but she was drifting on the edge of a worn-out inner tube, he thought. Luxury was disappearing, even in Seattle. Everybody warned it would be water bubbling from underneath, from an ocean too full. Across walls, seeping around crossings, diverted by low income housing and manufacturing districts, draining through basements and into restaurants. But it was a simple virus that would reclaim Seattle first, sidestepping man's airtight, Hazmat, safety compliant, drug-tested technology until it putrefied every traffic artery and storm drain, silo and the underground city. The only thing it couldn't invade was plastic and rubber. Suited up for a plague was what Elsa was. Riding it out in a flood of human influenza, picking survivors. At least until yesterday.

"It's not cortisone," Pritchard finally said. "It's a long, I mean goddamned long shot. Russo's widow, I think maybe she's... what do they call it?... a mule." He laughed a short, hacking bark. "Which makes her a lot like me."

He fast forwarded through the CDs, watching for identifiers, towns mostly. Sometimes the view was from eight thousand feet, sometimes, as in Butte, he could see gouges where a mountain used to be. There was a refinery at Laurel, a locked iron gate at Custer Battlefield, a two-story hotel at Sheridan. Sky and road united in the center of a vast page of flight. He was observing indices, an exact reproduction, some of it with Russo, some of it with his wife, and some of it from satellite. But it was the end that would tell him everything.

It was unfortunate that the quality suddenly dropped off, as though Russo had messed with a filter or taken less care. Straining to see where the journey would end, Pritchard zoomed in the last minute of the fourth CD. There was a strange hue to the horizon darkening the border between earth and atmosphere until it seemed to boil dry except for a few glimpses of a large body of water, again off to the left. A lake's name was noted in the lower right corner, *McConaughty*, a place old man Hennings had mentioned as a west Nebraska landmark, an outgrowth of the North Platte not far from his ranch. It was here where the bird had been trained to fly, and it was the truth behind Russo's disappearance. The realization triggered Pritchard's earlier oversight. "How long before we land?" he asked Mellon as he pulled the cell phone from his ankle, then tapped the number to Wilson's Bridge.

"'Bout twenty minutes, more or less. Can't get tower. Out of service. I'm starting to hate those words as much as free flu shots."

Gray haze surrounded them. Far above, an omniscient eye might well be amused. Two men encased in an ash-filled bubble were running out of time. Mellon was nervous, and Pritchard knew that came with experience, and it was rubbing off. He wanted to get on the ground. "Yeah, Morris," he said, brief and loud. "Get into Russo's office. Now. There's a CD in his computer. Download to me. Pronto. No slugging through his stuff. In and out, man. Like with your date. Comprende?"

He waited, knowing it would be only minutes after he got it that Elsa would too. Her tireless hacking would take on new meaning. Whatever was in that final training module would tell her everything she couldn't imagine herself, and she might even hand over a slice of Pritchard's final half million dollars to Morris in perpetual thanks. But he didn't care. Because, right now, the competitor was a whole lot closer than she was. And, by the minute, he was getting closer to the bird.

The fifth CD began with Robert Russo shakily adjusting the camera until he was looking directly into it. "*Today is February 2, 2009. If you've found this, I'm dead and may have been for quite some time. Two nights ago my friend and colleague, Paul Garner, was found locked in his car at the bottom of Rexford Aqueduct just outside Schenectady, New York. There is a sequence here, part of a necklace I'd like to call it, that can't be ignored. With this CD you can break the chain of misconduct.*"

Russo then filmed a sheaf of papers on his desk. One-by-one he burned them over a wastebasket, then brought up on his laptop where he'd logged the results of all updates of Pass-Flu since the process began seriously in 1991. *"Most of this will be authenticated through Colzer's files. But beginning January 4, 2009, there was, I feel, a plan put into effect to update the passengers within a critical two-week period, a dangerous, I predict fatal, adjustment from the usual three-month span between updates. Following the planned inoculation on the 4th, a second took place on January 28, 2009, at precisely 1:59 p.m. It was ordered out of Colzer's Seattle office and was presented as a normal update for the newest outbreak of flu in Melbourne, Australia. But it was anything but normal. I watched all sixty birds inoculated with 0.5 cc. Pass-link, the name given the inciting virus. It was one of the hardest things I've had to witness in all my years as an ornithologist. Each passenger, including Gem-X, showed no alarm, no reaction. But the effects would be irrevocable."*

Russo went on to describe how he and Garner had discussed the precise nature of the mining of Pass-Flu. How it was to be governed by a methodical approach that required strict adherence to a timetable, no matter what the world's demands. Higher percentages were sought as the flu mutated and strengthened. But the source being what it was, a sensitive, highly adaptable bird, there was to be compliance with no less than a three-month re-inoculation schedule. In the meantime, countries were stacking up in holding patterns of indecision and political pressure. And where 54 percent had once been welcomed, now governments were insisting on 82 or better.

"I'm the guardian." Russo pressed his thumb and forefinger to the sides of his mustache and pulled directly down. *"I cannot authorize and did not authorize this latest passenger inoculation. And, that I know of, Paul didn't agree with it either. But here we are with 98 percent anti-virus on our hands."* He shifted his gaze to two amber-colored vials on the table before him. *"Or should I say, here I am with it. No doubt Paul's are in the bottom of the aqueduct right along with the rest of him."*

There was an interruption. The camera panned the cages of the passengers, soft bodies at rest under a subtle blue light. *"They'll all be dead by spring,"* Russo said. *"Perhaps, there'll be one survivor. I'll tell you about him in a minute. But, I predict Colzer will never get their 100 percent anti-virus. They can't," he added, "Because then the outcome moves to another level."*

"I've watched the flu spread around the globe," he continued. "Starting probably somewhere in the provinces around Bejing. Probably in some curious incident where a hen got caught under a farmer's plow or injured in a threshing, and he took her inside with him. Maybe she was his best layer. He gave her pablum from rice and pork fat, and she gave him death. Flu spread to the Middle East and the Ukraine, to Bosnia and Greece. In recent months it's passed through the ports of Dunkirk and Lisbon, to the slums of India and simply mowed down the Philippines. Yet, who receives the smattering of updates? The wealthier countries of Europe, Canada, Australia, and, of course the U.S. Is there a reason for that?" he said rolling the vials in his hands. *"Is there a reason why I'm one of the privileged?"*

"It's interesting that during my tenure with this process I've been left to manage the passengers. It's been my job. No, actually, my calling. Yet, just yesterday my office was investigated, and four training CD's of mine were stolen. That's why I'm replacing them, along with this additional one, in a less conspicuous place above my work area. Because I believe Elsa Dupree is now satisfied that I'm up to something, just as she's suspected for a very long time. So I say it, for once and for all. I've trained a bird how to thrive here—by showing him how to escape. And, I suspect that gives me about as much chance as Paul Garner to survive Colzer-Bremen."

Pritchard removed his headphones after pausing the CD, studying Russo's hands as they drew out small round spheres on a chalkboard above his desk. Perfect zeros depicted some kind of vaguely understood visual imagery, according to the ornithologist, where the lines met in flawless uni-connection just as they would in a pigeon's brain. What made some men so perfectionistic about the smallest details? Why not scribble, break all the colors in the box, scratch the board with that hideous sound of nails, throw the whole fucking explanation in the moat outside Elsa's window? "Bastard was going to die," he said aloud, unresponsive to Mellon's ongoing landing dilemma. "Here's the kicker. He knew it way before I did."

He thought of where he'd been in early February and the small round towers near Isfahan, their mud-brick silos abandoned for three centuries under the burning Iranian sun, pigeon towers that had been used to raise as many as ten thousand pigeons for their dung. Isfahan, her empty towers and her twentieth century fertilizer, was now dying with flu. Pritchard had been ordered to take them amantadine, a useless, distracting effort that Elsa had coordinated to get him clear of the pigeons of Wilson's Bridge and the men who knew everything about them. Russo's counterpart, this Paul Garner he talked about, gave Pritchard another jolt of recognition. It was no mere trade-off she'd planned—Russo for a scientific miscalculation or his entanglement with one bird. This was execution, Elsa-style, somewhere just short of detection and still alive with cavorting truth. Pritchard placed one finger momentarily to the screen directly over Russo's mouth, then re-activated the CD.

"*Years ago I read something Aldo Leopold said in his famous* Sand County Almanac. *It's the single most inspiring thing I've ever read about the passenger.*" Russo, obviously familiar with the verse, looked directly through the lens at Pritchard as if he had chosen another man's words specifically to convince him. '*The pigeon loved his land: he lived by the intensity of his desire for clustered grape and bursting beechnut, and by his contempt of miles and seasons.*'

There was a pause, more than likely for effect, Pritchard thought, but it intrigued him, and he replayed Russo's further comment twice. "*It was the contempt part, it is that part, I keep returning to,*" Russo said. "*I knew when I began training Gem-X it was his inborn disobedience that would save him.*" An instant smile crossed his face. "*He was a tom with an attitude.*"

Finally, as if humor had cleared the way, Russo drew S-shaped wave lines through one circle, a clock-work of short dits around another, then undulant waves emanating from the side of a third. "*Think of these circles as the passenger's head, the leading part of his body. Eyes, bill, a bilobed crop, a tongue, and a brain. And remember these and all other birds do not live in our sensory world. Theirs has been liberated through alchemy. I prefer to think of it as their one distinct advantage over us.*"

"*Not very simply,*" he said pointing to each sphere, "*they migrate much like the swing of three clock pendulums. One begins the process, very likely the visual pendulum with a thin beam of orienting light either at sunrise or sunset. The eyes lock onto a sequence of cues, anything from insects traveling the opposite direction to a row of aspens signaling a slope upwards into a canyon. Pigeons remember topography. That's how they overpopulate the more unorthodox portions of our world. Graineries, bus stops, Italian coin fountains. A system of remembering and rewards.*"

"*But, of course, things begin to get muddled with the swing of the second and third pendulums.*" Here, Russo bent over, possibly obsessing over a spot on his shoe. Or clearing his head one more time. "*Guesswork plagues us here. Magnetic fields, Coriolis effect, far-off odors, even low frequency sound from within the earth's influence. There's even talk of the third eye, the bird's pineal gland coordinating the whole show. But, after what I've seen, I believe it's more like proprioception. A sense of knowing where you are in time and space. Something acquired through past experience, aligned with environmental cues, finally topped off with a certain, sometimes fleeting success. To us, it doesn't take much stimulus to send a flock of birds into flying two thousand miles in four or five days. But we can't imagine what the POW goes through to write a book in his mind, page by page, every day for the three years of his captivity. Oddly enough, the process is similar. Where you are doesn't determine where you can go. It simply is a starting point.*" The ornithologist stopped, then, again, stared directly into the eye of the camera. "*Action converted to memory which is stored, then retrieved. Three pendulums in perfect synchrony.*" There was another ample pause while he looked away toward the whiteout window of his office.

"*I know little more than what I've read and pieced together over my professional life,*" Russo said. "*An education, a fine job, a wonderful wife. I've had it all. But until now, I haven't had to accept the hard line of experience. That I must rely on what Gem-X has to bring to the equation, and that could mean never knowing how successful he was or wasn't. All the months of a route he absorbed day after day, session after session. In the end, he might not remember a thing, or if he does, it may be too late for him to do anything about it. And that*

is my final fear. That after all he's given, including this latest update,
he'll never be free to fly."

Russo looked tired. His explanation, a catharsis that Pritchard
understood, still puzzled him. What was it that had overtaken the
man's life? His experiment was still largely unexplained and his
personal life seemed mostly imaginary. The revelation of Colzer's
death threat was something Pritchard regarded as a man's final act
of revenge. But there was also avoidance to tell precisely his side of
the story, as if the very nature of what Russo planned shouldn't or
couldn't be fully disclosed. *For fear of what?* Pritchard thought. If
a man believes he's going to die, why not take down the almighty
curse with him? The fifth CD, though an indictment against Colzer, didn't absolve Russo of his own bizarre agenda. From what
Pritchard saw, he'd strapped a bird to a table and given him a
perpetual look at a world through one man's lens. This Gem-
X couldn't have gotten away even if he'd wanted to. Pritchard
rubbed his forehead, then looked at the thin line of grease outlin-
ing his fingers. "I can't get it out of my head what I saw there in
that compound at Wilson's Bridge," he said. "The hole under the
fence. You know, pigeon feathers all over the place. Whose plan
was that anyway?"

Mellon shook his head, then raised his shoulders in a body
question. "The broad's?"

It was possible, Pritchard thought. Women were more cun-
ning than men, some extraordinarily so, as he was witnessing.
If the widow Russo knew about her husband's experiment, she
might've been compelled to save the one small focus of his passion. She, of any person still alive, might know how to seduce a
passenger from under a fence, by now for her own agenda. But
there was still the nagging doubt of her husband's calculations, his
preoccupation with time somehow measured in the purest, clean-
est signal. Some ancient instinct, maybe. Escape, if that's what it
was, was far more likely the result of the birdman's computations
than the whimsy of his loving wife and her new boyfriend. Besides, the chain-link bottom had been pulled inward and pliered
straight up, something an insider would've done. Not some jack-
ass trying to impress Russo's wife. Once more he thought of the

numbers initializing the entire training exercise. June 21, 2005, at 5:30 in the morning. Almost to the day, four years ago. "Na, more like a wizard," he said. "A very patient one."

By now Russo was sitting down. He'd pushed everything on his desk aside. Only the eyebolt remained, a mesmerizing reminder of hours spent training a bird, offering him some kind of poetic justice for a life measured in blood draws. *"I have to say I'm not sure I'd have made this happen without Josephine. She came with me the whole way to Darby, Nebraska. Well, almost. We had a good vacation that June. Really good. Lots of sights, documenting at the medicine wheel in Wyoming—when the solstice gave me some idea of what birds must measure, must sacrifice. Hennings and I used to talk about it. Everything to fly. They'd give up any sense or security to fly sixty miles an hour, hours at a time. To extinction."*

The mention of Hennings caused Pritchard to tighten his hold on the laptop, a response intensified by thermals bombarding the jet, pitching it up and down through wind shifts Mellon could only drive through. Billings grew closer, then as if lifted into a space photo, the ground gave way to cross-hatchings and the wide view of a horizon displaced by a wall of smoke and an ominous orange glow. He watched the dip in instruments as Mellon adjusted for landing. "You might want to shut'er down," the pilot said, nodding toward the laptop.

Pritchard raised his hand in an attempt to stop time. There was only the smallest chance that Russo would answer the question of why he'd trained one passenger to migrate against all odds of survival and ultimately if he'd used his wife to set it all in motion. But even wizards occasionally spilled their guts.

"I should've taken her all the way in with me. I should've taken her to the man who understood the passenger pigeon more than anyone ever has. Yes, it would've given away this secret I've held, closed off in my life for over twenty years. It would've made her as privy to the adventure and the fear as I have been. But we'd have been together in it. All the way." Russo looked up as if searching his room for one last accounting of what he'd done. Or a place he could store it.

"Instead," he said, once again picking up the vials, *"I leave her with these. Ninety-eight percent. I don't know,"* he said, hesitating

mid-phrase. "*Up until now people have died in spite of Pass-Flu, but now, with this, they might die because of it. I'm sorry, my Josephine,*" he continued, dropping them into what appeared to be his coat pocket. "*There may come a day when you'll have to be the one to find out.*"

CHAPTER 24

By the time Mellon got them on the ground, the airport had been officially closed for over four hours. The twenty minutes he'd anticipated had turned into over an hour of circling, wide swaths that cut through the sky in increments, turning the jet into a decisive minute hand over the city below. Permission to land consisted of one man who interrupted the standard airport warning. "This is a medical contingency?" he repeated to Mellon. "No aircraft is allowed to land unless they have medical or military status. Please verify you can make safe approach."

In the last half circle before the jet settled onto final approach, Mellon looked across the cockpit toward the avalanche of air blackening the sky. The right wing pointed directly toward it, a white aluminum arrow scraping the side of a bloating monster. He looked at Pritchard. "We are a medical aircraft, right?"

Pritchard nodded while putting his laptop behind the seat.

"I mean they still have the power to fine," he added.

"Let'em," Pritchard said. "This cow town's probably going to be a ghost town in a couple days."

They taxied to the terminal by way of a series of parallel ropes. Mobile chain link fence cordoned most of the field into unauthorized area. A tanker sat behind the fence, conspicuous in its apparent grounding.

"This place is a tomb," he said to Mellon as he departed the jet. "I might be back before I get out of the airport."

"Don't even ask," Mellon said out his side window, reaching overhead. "I'm gone, man. Any problems from here on out are yours, paisano."

Pritchard watched the jet turn into a small white sliver, its take-off precise, away from the incoming cloud. He could feel his tongue thicken in the accumulating wind. Air turned dense as wool pulled tight over his head. He coughed and spat straight down between his suede sandals. "Chickenshit," he said out loud, then forced the terminal door open. One man stood at the only car rental desk in the building. After opening his laptop on the counter, Pritchard studied the blip on the screen for a full minute before he talked.

"You know what I've got here?" he said, studying the man's name tag. "I've got a medical crisis, George. Not only is this about the flu, it's about eliminating it." He put out a Colzer business card and watched George's face. "I need the fastest, toughest ride you've got. I need it right now. And I need it for unlimited miles."

George pulled up his choices on the screen, two newer model Luminas and a year-old Hummer.

"What color is the Hum?" he asked.

"Cantina Yellow," George said.

"I'll take it," Pritchard said.

"One more thing." George continued, unaware that he was passing on his bill to a man steeped in the day's perversities. "In these hard times, sir, I have to ask for a five hundred dollar security deposit. You know, my boss says it's the fire and all. A Mastercard or Visa would normally do, but our phone lines are down. I can't let a car out of here without a deposit."

"Even to Colzer-Bremen?" Pritchard said. "Even to the company that's keeping you alive, you meadow muffin."

There was a gap, and a serious one, in the mental capacity of small town America. Pritchard had seen it when he visited Hennings or in Fraser on the peninsula. Little, snippy dogs is what they reminded him of. Ankle biters. People who meant to please the boss in the middle of apocalypse. He imagined Elsa, her atrocities hidden from the world by a barricade of brown-nosers just like George. "I'll tell you what, George. You see that blip on the screen?"

The car rental man studied Pritchard's finger as it tapped the laptop's satellite reading.

"That's a bird you're looking at there. He's what they call a passenger pigeon. He's been tagged as a potential source of bird flu. There's only one of him right now. Just like there was one

Typhoid Mary. Remember her, George? Sorry to say, he's headed your way, spreading it as he goes. Kind of like one of them crop dusters." Pulling his hand out of his pants pocket, he buzzed the agency man, swiping his hand through the air, dropping a thousand dollar bill from high above the counter.

"You know if I was you, I'd go have a good time tonight, buddy. Because one way or another, from east or west, you're going to be expired within days, maybe hours. And that's something none of us can do anything about. Even your frickin', car junkie boss."

*   *   *

The attempts at confinement ended as the road into Billings widened infinitely, asphalt just another attempt to ease the crossing, leading men into believing they'd conquered the soul of a native prairie. Bunch grass held the whole thing together in a deep, conniving resistance to change. Pritchard accelerated, leaving the road at fifty miles an hour, bracing himself against the tufts hard packed beneath him. The Hummer slewed, then gripped the table, stabilized and gained speed. No wadi would stop him here. A land of nothing, he thought. Mile markers, fence lines, ambling cattle trails separating nothing from nothing. The Empty Quarter of North America. At seventy, the dust behind him finally obliterated the darkling twilight in his rear-view mirror. He braked and in one last easy motion plowed the Hummer head-first into a stop sign. The edge of town was tolerant, he decided, or morbidly apathetic. As he rolled down the window, not even a dog barked.

Curious for the first time in hours, Pritchard checked his messages. Elsa must've given up after about the tenth or twelfth try. Russo's final CD came to mind. That's what interrupted her tailspin, and he knew it. Combined with his refusal to respond, it made her shut up. But it also made her lethal. He brought up the number to Wilson's Bridge realizing this was no longer just Russo's death that filled Elsa's portfolio. Paul Garner had disappeared over the brink of an aqueduct. Thus, it didn't take much deducing to visualize himself pinioned under an overturned Hummer, pulled from under its still hissing wrack in rips and shreds.

Pritchard turned into a gas station and once again called Wilson's Bridge.

"That CD you just sent me," he said to Morris. "We both know who else is looking at it, don't we? You think where you're sitting is overgrown now? Well, well, my friend, Ms. Elsa's just now figured out how many ways Russo stiffed her. She knows that I know Wilson's Bridge is about to collapse, and her corporate remedies could bring her prison time. All because the bitch got greedy." He said the last part hoping to send Morris into a fit of worry, maybe even remorse, for his witless loyalty to Elsa. For everybody's unconscionable loyalty to duty in the midst of overriding, even deliberate death.

"Sir, I mean Mr. Pritchard, I don't know anything about that, but I've got something here you might want to see," Morris said, his voice an unshakable drone. "Camera nine. At first, I didn't think to look at it. But something told me to go back through from the night before. You know when the birds all died. I started backtracking from this other camera, and this thing happened early the morning after. A shadow, it looked like. But I think it's him, #522. He got out. Under the fence, then took off. Real quick. You was right, Chief," he added. "The bird wasn't stolen, not right then anyway."

This unexpected turn softened Pritchard. What had been a modest liking for the security guard morphed once more to appreciation, then back to doubt. His feelings erupted into action when he saw the last standard price of gas had been scratched out and above it seven dollars and eight-five cents a gallon was highlighted. Fill-ups were restricted to one pump. "Christ almighty," he said, his voice a low rumble that he hoped carried to the masked figure behind the station's streaked windows. "Every bastard here deserves to come down with the Stretch."

"What do you mean, sir?" Morris answered, clueless except for Pritchard's curse. "We can't get sick. We're forbidden to get sick, even if we didn't do right by the birds."

Stretch-18. That's what everybody in the lab had called the flu from the time it struck the sledders in New Hampshire. Pritchard might have coined it himself, likening the virus to a toboggan, a snow flyer in a wilderness of unprecedented disease. It could've been SARS or Ebola or simian foamy virus that struck down humanity. As it turned out, the passengers had been a reservoir species for flu as extinct as the bird. They were untainted by the virus hidden in their DNA or their organs or the cramped lodgings of their brains. They had been a common denominator of success, bypassing extinction and providing a blurry vision into a world of medical tinkering. The passengers were a chimera, a two-headed monster, and to Pritchard's way of thinking they should've gone extinct. Then medicine would've had to look elsewhere when the likeness of the 1918 flu blew up all over again. He wondered now if Russo had thought the same thing the last few days of his life.

It was true Wilson's Bridge was a different kind of place than the outside world. Not only did the workers live there round the clock, they bought into the vacuum it created. When Morris said he couldn't get sick he really believed it. When he was told the passengers weren't diseased, he believed it. Theirs was a solidarity built on dedication, but not necessarily to the science of drug mining. It reminded Pritchard of the nuclear refugees of Chernobyl whose lives had been rearranged by an exclusion zone, who couldn't leave it despite the carnage. They drifted back to their small villages, even to the plant itself, to clean and restore what they could. As yet, some of them avoided pockets of radiation as if it was simply puddles in the road. They didn't get sick, and they still believed the RBMK-1000 reactor could've, should've worked. For the greater good. Altruism captivated and distorted reality, he knew, even in the most gruesome die-outs.

"Look, Morris, everything around you just went kaput. You can probably skip the sick phase." He wanted to say, *"Don't you ever wonder what the inoculations, even the authorized ones, really did to the birds?"* Did anyone understand a virus in hiding? A random, fiendish gremlin that decides for itself when conditions are prime to explode, then rips through a reservoir groomed for months on the teetering edge of an outbreak. Or did they just pretend, Elsa to her employees and the world, and Russo self-absorbed in his experiment with a virus-tainted passenger. "I'm not sure what's going to help me most right now. You either for that matter. But send me the shadow from Cam nine. And, go home, Morris. You and your family, you might outlive the whole infected mess."

"Sir, it's on the way." Then Morris added in the expected Colzer brainwash, "I'll be here if you need anything else."

Half of a Montana sky distilled sunlight into a narrowing, brilliant prism, fractious in violet-blue and orange-rose that sometimes trails behind thunderstorms. Driving into it, the caution-sign yellow hood of the Hummer reminded him of the paradox he'd become. Pritchard realized he could well be at the leading edge of a giant Kuwaiti plume, a hell-tinged firestorm heralding the insatiable appetite of a natural disaster. Yet, from here on out he was also a warning, an easy-to-spot target that intended to tell the world, if necessary one-by-one, what a fraud they'd bought into. Even if it kept some of them alive.

Swerving onto a side road, he brought up the picture from Cam nine. He watched a bird preen, fold and re-fold its feathers as though squeezing out any excess air. The passenger disappeared in a kind of pulsating blur, no doubt in a thrust under the fence, then took off at an attitude that had been described by Morris as a shadow. But after several reviews of the video, he realized there was a subtle, gleaming strand attached to a retracted leg, an identifier that still pulsed across his screen in exact alignment with the freeway. If it was #522, the famed Gem-X, he now had the proof of his escape. And the proof was more mystifying than his imagining.

If Russo had been preparing the bird to escape and "migrate" to Darby, Nebraska, what triggered the incident? He might've started scraping the hole under the fence a week or two before he died, camouflaging it in moss, returning to it day after day as secretive as a prisoner of war. But what would guarantee his subject would ever use the slit no bigger than an open zipper dug under eight-gauge wire? Why would the bird wait over four months to make his move? And why was Josephine Russo there when it all went down?

Pritchard looked up, scratching the corners of his eyes, then working over his whole head as if he was shampooing this disaster out of his life. He turned to look over his shoulder at the impervious wall of atmospheric soot behind him and wondered at his own capacity for stupidity. First, he'd taken this job dumped on him out of Elsa's desperation. With Garner and Russo dead, it was obvious she used more favored alternatives. But he was like the manic phase of a bipolar disorder. She'd always swing back to him, telling him it was his simple understanding of how things needed to work across medicine's top priority that kept Colzer-Bremen the forerunner in the war against the flu. That Mexico City, Nairobi, Damascus, Belgrade and Prague would have to stand down for a shipment of updated anti-virus he'd be delivering to Vatican City by nightfall. "We'll get our best to them all," she'd say. "And, as it's always been, Martin, the rate of success from moment to moment is entirely up to you."

Maybe he was less expendable than the two conjoined scientists, he told himself, but it was a deadly spin of numbers she'd laid at his feet. It wasn't meaningful trust or even a substantial belief in his abilities. Elsa coordinated the production of Pass-Flu because she could manage men like Russo. But she couldn't outguess the idiosyncratic plague that infected places like Dharavi, where it descended deep inside human organs and pulverized tissue to a warm, molten skim. Flu couldn't be managed in a calculated epidemic. It swung back and forth, the spitting tongue of a bronchial fire stoked by mutation and cellular holocaust. There were places in the world where, in the first months, 12 percent Pass-Flu had fit the lock, driving the international hope that man could stem the epidemic. But as weeks passed and the flu flipped its mutations end-for-end, updates, especially outdated ones, became only a trickle of interference. It was Pritchard, more than anyone else, who knew the numbers and the game, and, except for once, had kept it in Elsa's favor.

He drew a line across the increasing sooty smudge beginning to cling to the inside of the Hummer's side window, then drew another line bisecting the first. There were four parts to this equation, most of it just supplied by Russo's final CD. Pritchard's writing, mostly symbolic, was exaggerated in the way of genius. *Never 100 %* was in the first block. In the second he wrote, *To Darby?* The third said, *Bird captured, maybe.* And in the fourth he wrote, *Two 98 % vials.* He studied the patterns, realizing he'd just created the reason to go on, the manifesto of his ability to re-route the entire plan if he had to. He grinned and shook his head hard as if he couldn't believe his eyes. Barely beyond the symbols he'd just written was a small herd of pronghorn grazing as repetitiously as if they were a screen saver. Behind them was a short expanse of duff, then a tract of housing. They were so close he could see their tongues flick an occasional woody reject.

Driving past the only entrance to the community, he could see where Billings was attempting to isolate itself. The eastern U.S. had shut down their freeways. The west simply cordoned off suburbia with cement barricades, making it impossible to enter or leave except on foot or by some ingenious means other than a vehicle. A horse stood in a sleepy daze attached to the bumper of a lime green VW. The street and lawns were studded with broken trails of manure, and someone had backed a horse trailer lengthwise against the cement barrier. Circling the wagons, Pritchard thought, was about as useless as tracking thieves. But everybody, including him, wanted to feel some semblance of normal.

He pulled up to a flashing stoplight on the frontage road to I-90. Above the last length of city road someone had stretched a swath of white material between two light poles. By now, it had the abandoned droop of a flag torn almost in half, but the black and red hand prints scattered across it had apparently survived by fading and running into a familiar collage of tribute. A visual message board, especially in smaller cities, families smeared their hands in paint, joining together vast sheets of hand prints in a final embrace over their sidewalks, their roads, even their graveyards. The effect had long since eluded the man who now accelerated under the graffiti above him. He just wanted to get to the junction of the freeway with Highway 25. That was the place where the future would all come together.

He kept thinking about the vials Russo had abandoned to his wife. Everything was linked to the woman Pritchard had only seen in pictures. She could pass right before his eyes, and in all this emptiness he still might not recognize her. But the junction was the only logical interspace where the funnel would become narrow enough that he could make an instant decision. Where an ambush, figuratively, could take place. If she and Sterns went on to Miles City, they were, in all good reasoning, headed toward Minneapolis and Haviland Labs. But if they made the turn south onto I-25 they could be headed to Nebraska, just as Russo had planned. They could also be headed to Denver, and that, Pritchard knew, would be the real conundrum of this goose-chase. Because, despite all of Elsa's venomous suspicions about Haviland, there was another smaller lab in Denver. A lab named Intermountain Species that Pritchard heard about through the grapevine of corporate stealth. A place that believed zoonotic disease, that is disease between animal and human, could only be eradicated through cultivated extinction. They were, in fact, the agency enforcing the government's nationwide crackdown on migratory birds, doing it, he'd heard, not too differently than when the passenger pigeon was decimated one hundred years before.

The junction consisted of the usual tangle of signs and a small wooden building called The Outpost where two gas pumps were fenced in caution tape, and a sign on the island said, *Don't even lift a nozzle. We've been dry for two weeks.* A grassy, cottonwood-studded lot bordered the freeway-side of the building. Part statuary and part junk pile, the space contained two sculptured billy goats with a garbage basket between them. The bin was full, and cans and paper spread across the small conserve, refuse that reconfigured itself every time the wind shifted. Pritchard parked between the goats and a near-by dumpster and soon after heard the sound of cans grazing each other in a microburst of wind. Some of them rocketed against the Hummer, then settled underneath. The place was alive, literally prancing with shit.

But this, Pritchard knew, was the place to be. This strip of prairie he'd studied the night before, a miniscule bend in a continuous green splat on Mellon's sectional of southeast Montana, was a channel through which all travelers must pass. Last night he dragged a bottle of Mezcal in a straight, wet line across the map until he outlined the city of Billings in a ring of condensation. He watched Mellon flick darts across one corner of the cantina's bar and knew, now that he had what was left of Ortez' cortisone, he would be heading toward the pale northern break between sky and more sky. Once there, all he had to do was wait for a bird and a woman. They weren't, he was sure, very far apart.

Nothing, even at this checkpoint, changed about the bird's transmission, except it kept coming closer. Its insistent ping reminded him of how slam dunk this all was. He took another look at some of Russo's training, slipping the first and second CDs into the laptop, irritated by the clatter of tin cans around him. "She's always been a mule," he said out loud, watching Josie playfully tie her shoelace to her husband's, then point her hands overhead where Russo filmed the steady thrum of a great blue heron, then climbing higher, digitalizing, until pure elevation filled the eye of the great bird. Until he was only a part of lift and scent, a ghost in a world swirling below. Far above forests, long straight gouges between peaks, the hard scrabble savanna of the Great Plains. The video was no more than a pathway, a devised system from overhead. It was a sectional, and according to Russo, it was memorized, down to the very fence lines by Gem-X.

Amazing as it was, perhaps even plausible, there was something off kilter about this man's scheme. Schematically it seemed perfect, but the timing bothered Pritchard and had from the beginning. He sat now at the junction just outside Billings thinking there was every reason to believe Josephine Russo would emerge from the very place he'd just been. She and her friend would drive past the nauseously yellow Hummer, probably never seeing it. Or maybe looking right at him as he made his decision about their decision. Either way, they were being monitored by their own stolen goods. Why hadn't they taken the transmitter off? And what did stealing have to do with Russo's program, especially the bird's long-awaited escape?

In repetitive, coordinated annoyance, Pritchard re-played the escape from camera nine's angle over and over. Finally, he noticed the recorded time of the bird's breakout was exactly the same as the blinding sunrise initiated in the third CD and a digital display varying little from four years before. *06-21-09 at 05:24:12.* Some place, some source had come together for Russo. A knowledge of birds and their glands, their strange, pecking, beady-eyed intelligence. Something he was able to rely on and the bird would recognize, no matter what happened to his trainer.

In a faint disturbance hardly discernible from the cans thrashing about beneath him, Pritchard sensed encroachment. A stem of blue lights flashed from behind, just even with the band of his rear-view mirror. He could see the officer grab his shotgun from the rack behind him, then walk to the side of the Hummer, the barrel pointed to the ground. *Precautions had flooded the world in spite of its mortal weakness*, Pritchard thought. *And so had assholes.*

"Need to see your license and registration," the man said, tapping the window.

"Yeah, yeah," Pritchard said, shoving his license up the window while the cop squinted, then said, "Roll it down, mister."

"Don't you think that could get a little prickly, officer? I mean you've got this place sewed up like Bagdad. We could . . ." Pritchard said, throwing his hand back and forth, "You know, exchange something. Like germs."

The cop then tapped the Hummer's window with the butt of his gun. "You should've thought about that before you parked here. No parking on freeway sidings. Now, roll down your window."

Pritchard barely cracked an opening, then slid the paperwork out, hanging on until the officer jerked it away. He studied it for a moment and pushed his hat back on his head.

"Well, Mr. Pritchard, I can see you're a long ways from home. Sorry for the delay, but I'm going to have to follow through with this. Interstate protocol, you know. Experienced man like yourself should know there's no parking on freeways or sidings to freeways 'til this thing is over. Place would turn into a regular Trail of Tears, you know."

An unfamiliar beat-and-a-half filled the containment of Pritchard's car. He checked the transmitter, watching its simple echo near the junction, the extra half beat a positive startle. Josephine Russo, the bird or both were about to pass in front of his eyes. Pritchard rolled down his window and studied the cop examining his license. "There wouldn't be a chance I could come back for this?" he said.

The officer looked up, scrutinizing Pritchard. "I've got this theory. People like you tend to show up at predictable times. Full moon, woman's bleedin' time, solstices. You fit right in," he said, starting back to his car.

"Son of a bitch," Pritchard said without lowering his voice.

The officer turned around, pulling his shotgun to his waist.

"No moon. I got no vagina. So what's the last one?" Pritchard asked.

"Solstice," the officer said. "People like you, they never pay attention to the turns of nature 'til it gets them in trouble. You're one day past the summer solstice, Mr. Pritchard. And I'd like you to stay right where you are."

CHAPTER 25

Sometime in the late afternoon Josie awoke to a whirring sound, a fan maybe, and slowly realized Sterns had started the pick-up. The idle emanated through the trailer, a vibration that soothed, then sent her into a frenzy. Only after she started to open the door did she realize nothing had changed since earlier that day. Coffee was still on a burner, his shirt was hanging on the edge of a picnic table. She turned around and studied the bed. One side was barely rumpled, the side she'd been in. Then she took a downward glance and saw she was in a T-shirt and sweats—his.

It crossed her mind what might've happened. She was sick, and she'd imagined things for two days now. Sterns might've finally had enough, lured her in, and took advantage. But there was nothing to show for it. In fact, when she pulled down the sweats, she was in her underwear, and the underwear was clean. She rubbed her fingers between her legs, then traced upward, touching herself for the first time in weeks. All she remembered was the smell of aloe, and she smelled it again now.

She pulled up the sweats, cinching them as tight as she could, then sat on the edge of the bed. The vibration continued, reassuring and slightly domestic. *A man fixes his home while his woman sleeps*, she thought, staring at the coffeepot. *But I'm not his woman, not anybody's woman.*

"Why am I thinking this?" she said out loud, pulling at the bedspread. "Right now I'm alive. I'm just grateful," she said, holding her breath, "to be alive."

It was never far away—being grateful. For everything she'd had. For a life without worries in a home filled with windows and drapes the color of sweet corn. For winged back chairs and a small cherry wood table that eventually separated her bed from Rob's. For doves who sang to her of life behind bars with the one you love most. There was never any doubt she'd been grateful, and silent, and suspicious.

It was as though another life had been agreed upon, just between the two of them, after the trip to Darby. There was intimacy with him in Nebraska, closer than anything she'd ever known with Robert. But at Lanscom she agreed, without so much as a pause, to let him go. And, after that, he went day by day into his long-enduring world. Coming home to do laundry, fix a meal, move the birds, pat her underwear into an even stack on her dresser. They'd agreed that the thing between them was too big to talk about. And after awhile, it was.

As she opened the trailer door, she saw where Sterns had tied her husband's head rag around the porch light. Probably an absent-minded act or maybe he hung it there one step before throwing it away. She untied it, then gave it a quick shake, watching it fall away from her in the light evening breeze. It was, she knew, what was left of her husband's skin, his sweat, maybe even his thoughts. And she was setting it all free in a stand of Montana timber. Because the best of Robert, the last of Robert was in Darby, Nebraska. Exactly where she was going.

The main path into the campground was lined with strands of Christmas lights, some of them twinkling off and on in the bruise of dusk. A strand nearby had gone out, and Ned was bent over trying to jiggle it into working again. She could hear swear words sizzle under his breath. "Fuck," he kept saying. "What's Mr. Washington man going to think if I can't light up the woods?"

Josie looked over her shoulder and couldn't see Sterns. She considered walking past Ned into the grip of people who were avoiding her, but who might see her differently in the soft glow of luminarias or, in the dark, might not see her at all. Already, she could hear the rattle of dishes, and somebody kept re-playing James Taylor's I've Seen Fire and I've Seen Rain. But it was Ned's preoccupation with Sterns and his rig that cinched her comment. "I don't think it really matters, Ned. I'm leaving for Nebraska by dawn."

Ned twirled, his roundness captured in the trail of flashing lights wrapped around his belly. First a red one, then green, then blue and white, they flashed upward under his chin and under the bags of his eyes. She wanted to laugh, to spin him outward and see how far he'd roll. But there was something else happening behind her. She could tell because Ned straightened, then took a step backward. "Hello, again, Mr. Sterns," he said, extending a bulb-covered hand. "Understand you're leaving in the a.m. Going east?" he asked, then began what he really wanted to say.

"You know what you're driving into, don't you? Or have you heard? They're calling it the Great Plains Massacre. You know how they have to name every goddamned fire. Even the ones they can't fight." Ned's hands were busy unraveling the tangle about him. He kept pulling out duds, keeping one in the corner of his mouth until he found another. It was obvious he didn't want an answer from Sterns—just unprecedented awe.

"We here at the Rattlesnake take such things seriously. People here know you can't expect services like there once was. Gas is hard to find. Damned expensive. People are losin' faith, pickin' fights, burnin' their dead. My guess is that's how it got started. Anyway, it's got away from them and burnin' right on down through South Dakota, Wyoming. Fanning out they say to Nebraska. Maybe even parts of Colorado. Nobody out there to stop it, folks. You know that. They's just lettin' that incinerator burn."

She could feel Sterns' hand in the middle of her back, nudging her forward, down the path away from Ned. An ache at first, it felt more like a claw inside her pushing one fiendish nail into her abdomen, then another and another while the man beside her seemed determined to make it worse. "I can't believe this is happening," she said, doubling over. "You're never leaving here are you?" she said, looking up at Sterns. "Or maybe you're turning around and going back."

"No I'm not," he said, "Staying here. That Ned back there, he doesn't know what he's talking about. He's not even from here."

"What do you mean? He's the mayor of this place," she said, holding herself around the middle.

"I mean he calls pigs javelinas. Around here, they're just plain pigs. That's all they'll ever be." Sterns looked up, studying the melting contour of the sky, the way it worked its way down into the space between them. She knew he was saying what had to be said to get her through.

"You came into the bathhouse after me, didn't you?" She watched him turn his face back toward Ned. "You brought me back to the trailer, didn't you? Then you walked out and milked the cow, fed the chickens, and squeezed the orange juice. You expect me to believe you? Somewhere in there I was naked, Sterns. What did you do with that?"

"I looked," he said, putting his hands in his pockets, the lines of his face fading into darkness. "I looked a long time."

A light steadied itself beyond them, a lantern maybe. She could see faces gathering around it, drawn to its energy instead of Ned's stringers of electricity. It didn't seem to faze Sterns, who seemed better suited to turn-and-face-it truth than she ever had. Who stood there at an opening into her life and was considering what would happen if he walked in.

"I could tell you we're leaving for Hennings' tomorrow for sure. I could tell you I can drive this rig through anything. Flu, a goddamn fire, a state of national emergency, any other kind of killer. I could say it and right now make myself believe it. But I've been low on fuel since the start. You've been sick across three states, I mean really sick. There's been times I didn't think you were going to wake up. And I want a pancake so goddamn bad, I don't think I can leave civilization without one."

She watched his face, the quirky truth bouncing back and forth between fear and funniness, his eyes slightly crazy in the episodic pulse of camp light. He wasn't hiding anything from her, his problems, his appetite or his infatuation. It was as though he'd made up his mind, here at this place of no return, to give her everything and see what she'd do with it.

There was a quickness of her thoughts, as if the last few hours of sleep had restored her senses, sharpened them into ideas that waited, untapped, until Sterns turned another key. Until now, he'd looked at her through illness. He said so himself, over and over. But he'd also shared something secretive, something magical with her. Not now, after all these miles. Right at the beginning when he hardly knew her. Telling her about the passengers and her husband. Telling her the truth far away from where it started with him. The truth of the last twenty years. She looked at Sterns, the way he held there, slightly embarrassed, more human than masculine. Hardly enough for the world coming at him. "Got any Bisquick?" she said, watching him work a small bolt between his fingers. Not waiting for an answer, she walked into the deep shadow between Christmas lights to the open door of the trailer.

* * *

She busied herself with preparation, mostly a couple cups of flour formula that with a little milk would automatically create the impression of competence. It settled her mind and localized all the problems down to one—hunger. She realized for the first time since leaving home she was truly hungry. The heat from the gas burners felt good. There was a change going on thermostatically inside her, a feeling of coming back to normal.

He sat there reading, the Coleman's steady hiss reliable in the deepening night. They'd decided to eat outside on the picnic table, she thought because there was some reconsideration going on. In muted darkness he might cap off some of his vulnerability, and she might better avoid his glances. She could see he was making notes in the corner of the paper in front of him. Beside him on the picnic table was a binder she'd never seen before. "This is the first time I've seen you perfectly still since we began this trek," she said. "You're always fixing something, including me." She pushed the majority of pancakes on one of two plates between them. A glaze of butter gave them a chubby, toasted quality, and far better results than she usually had with cooking. It struck her they might be disappointing when he broke into them. "Must be interesting, whatever you're reading."

"Yes. Thanks very much for this," he said, holding his thought while pulling the plate closer. She handed him the syrup and watched him flip open the top, then pour exactly in the middle of the stack without once checking. He seemed more intent than ever on the paper. "It's some data on passengers I printed out a few days ago. Sometimes I'd take notes up on the platform with me. It seemed fitting to read about them, to reassure myself that's what they really were. You know," he said, taking his fork in his hand, "There was belief that large flights of pigeons would be followed by sickness."

She could sense his doubt, the delay that extended even into his eating. He put the fork down and looked at his hands. "I haven't even washed," he said.

"Does it really matter?" Josie asked. "If we're that surrounded by death, does it really matter?"

He seemed unable to make up his mind about the thing that mattered most. Hunger, yes, but he was agonizing, she knew, about this thing with the bird. She watched him roll one cake in his hand, almost caressing it into jelly-roll shape, then take a slow bite off the end.

"You know, I remember when they thought they found one Ivory Bill," she said. "I remember because of something Robert told me. Something I don't think I'll ever forget. Something you should know because you've brought it up all over again for me."

Josie pulled her bench closer to the table, closer to the lantern that illuminated Sterns' hand, the lean webbing between his knuckles. "Robert told me one of the last true sightings was of a female in the Singer Tract in Louisiana. She wouldn't leave her nest even though they were logging within a stone's throw from her. She would rather perish, and I've no doubt she did, than abandon all that she knew."

Sterns looked up. She could see him swallow, not out of pleasure, she thought, but just to stay alive. "I'm that logger, then. To you."

"Well, I'm more perceptive than that, I hope," she said poking at the syrup coagulating on her plate. "I guess I was getting sicker by the minute, and you were the face of the enemy. You have to remember living with an ornithologist is like living with an all-seeing feather-god. They know ramifications."

"Yeah, I know," he said. "I figured that out when I met him. A sense that he knew the worst."

She could feel herself staring at him through the Coleman nimbus around his face. Wanting to get inside that visit he'd had with her husband, but even more wondering what it was about Sterns that kept him secluded, even from his home. "What is it about this place that's so hard for you?" she asked. "You say it's where you were raised, but you've never once said you need to visit your family or even call them."

"It's been a long time. They're all gone now." He put his hands together above his plate, prayer-like, and she wondered if it was some gesture telling her to back off.

"Well, then at least you don't have to worry about them getting sick."

"No, all I have to worry about now is being judged. Even a woman who doesn't know a thing about me has got me pegged." He took a hurried final bite as if he'd lost all enjoyment.

"You mean being a logger? Oh hell, that's been going on a long time. Nobody's going to listen to what I have to say, even if there's a solvent paper company left when this is over."

"No, I don't mean being a logger," he said, his eyes moist and unblinking. "I mean being a smoke jumper."

There was a slight delay in the way he separated the words, as if he couldn't acknowledge the continuity. He was looking past her, through the Rattlesnake's boundaries, straight into the twisted charcoal of deformity. Sterns was as expressionless as a man burned in the worst place of all—his face. Only the weight he assigned each word gave her an inkling of his real emotion.

"You were one," she said, "Once. Maybe here."

It fit, she thought. This man who didn't seem to want a lot of accountability was really locked in a stranglehold with duty. Stripped of protection, he'd learned to let go of a man-made cage, to exchange breath with something that devoured from above, from below and across entire mountain ranges. He didn't need to report to anyone. His governor was deep inside. Watching him now, she could sense his struggle and remembered how he'd said to her earlier, "I looked a long time." Now, even more, she believed him.

"There's never the perfect landing," he said. "But I've come close. I've gone over and over somebody else's landing though, a hundred times, a thousand times more than those almost perfect ones of mine. Because his was a mistake after all the perfection. I guess that makes it a perfect mistake." Sterns looked up as though holding back tears by sheer will.

"I don't know why I need to tell you this," he said. "Maybe it's because I've watched you unfold a little over the last couple days. You probably didn't even know what you were doing, but I learned about you. Really you, not just a woman I found in my life and shared my first secret with. You did so well with that one, maybe I figured you can handle the next one."

She wondered if he wanted her to hold still and wait or turn off the lantern so he could say it all in the dark. This stuff that came so naturally to women. To encourage or hesitate, to ask for permission or pop off an order. None of it seemed worthwhile anymore. She realized with Robert, after the first few months of marriage, she'd rarely consulted him and never told him what to do. After the beginning, he never let her get close enough. So Josie said nothing. She waited, her hands alongside her plate, her mind a tangle of indecision.

"It was my second summer jumping," he said, pushing his plate off to the side. "We were here." He angled the lantern closer in, right between them. "Rampart Lake makes a big curve, almost a U-turn in the wilderness. Guys used to say if there ever was a fire there it would boil water in the middle of the lake. A funnel, kind of, the lake just following the contour of the land. My brother, Mark, got the call on a Saturday night. I remember because Kitty told me he'd just finished cutting the lawn. Always a Saturday job, you know." Sterns seemed to be anchoring himself in details, she thought.

"I was working another fire about three grids away. That summer Missoula divided The Swan into grids. A precursor to giving fire a name. If it's on the northeast corner of the third grid, then it's still a baby. Maybe we just watch a while. See if it means to make a name for itself. But there were at least four babies that Saturday in August. And it was forming up to include Rampart Lake."

Rampart, she thought, was probably a name well suited. It was not a word used much anymore and suggested an archaic obstacle. Which was it? Walled in or cut off? Its shape implied a warning, even without Sterns' prelude. For the first time she could hear the tendency for him to condense an event, to prepare it in his mind, then to recount it in episodic bursts, as if his voice could only describe an intangible outline.

"They told us what happened was unlikely. Unlikely. Not a freak accident or the work of an inferno. It wasn't the man or his training. It was just events." Sterns waited. "But I knew better," he said. "Because I used to watch Mark sometimes. When he didn't know." Sterns rubbed his forehead, then pushed away from the table.

"There were times in square training when he wasn't always deliberate. That's what they told me later, after it happened. The Rampart Fire wasn't one to leave many clues. And it wouldn't have spared a jumper who wasn't sure, even when he was still above it. It burned its way from God all the way down. There was no sense. I've sometimes wondered if he was on fire before he even hit the ground."

"Then I got to thinking back," Sterns said. "The old clothes chute at our house on Morgan Street. My folks moved it one year. It still came down out of their bedroom, but Dad moved the entrance to a corner of their closet. It was black in there and dusty. I remember Mom never even used it after that. She bought a hamper instead. I don't know what it was, but Mark started having me jump first. I remember I'd have to suck myself in on the way down, the hole was so skinny. I'd wait at the bottom on an old glider cushion. Wait for Mark. Listen to him push his way through."

Sterns began again, a formulaic rhythm to his speech. She could hear the increasing steadiness between his words, as though he'd finally, after all the doubt, resigned himself to trust his own instincts. Or that he'd long ago figured out what was wrong. "Mark must've been about nine. I kept noticing he'd take longer and longer to come through. He was my older brother. I thought he was making it last longer. Maybe found a way to come out of there by slickin' himself up with Mom's VO5 or something. But sometimes the spot where he landed, after he'd done it a time or two, was pretty wet. I knew it wasn't anything I was supposed to talk about. But, I think what happened at Rampart might've been something that went that far back. It was a reverse logic that lingered in his brain."

"What do you mean?" Josie said, finally aware of how close Sterns was coming to her own life. "It seems pretty straightforward to me your brother might've made a bad decision or might not have had time to make a decision." She remembered Robert's plane, the way they said it looked like it had hopped through trees. Leaving rivets and flanges and the trailing edges of his life strewn across branches that merely bent, then held him secluded from sight for almost a week until they found him.

"Yeah, that's what they said too. No time. But that's the part I wish I didn't know. Because I think he did have time. He just had no vision."

"There's a strange irony here." Sterns continued, she thought, with such a simple observation, something he'd valued enough to hold across the years, until his brother's death and all the way to now. "He had time, maybe too much time, in that old clothes chute. He was stuck, mid-air, while he festered up the gumption to give himself the final shove. It was dark above and below. Havin' me down below didn't make any difference. Rampart was like Dad moving that entrance. The chute this time was above him, a drogue invisible in the slate black of smoke. Could've been, for one surviving moment, smoke was below too. Darkness. Wanted to put it all on hold, stop in the chute. But he couldn't. They exploded hot and poker red below him, then around him. Trees. Piercing through the smoke like scalpels. Less than twenty yards from the lake."

Josie could feel the question arise from the same place it always did, a place foreign to intellect and reason, stricken from consciousness. "The reality that someone you love has died is its own tragedy. But it's separate, isn't it, from the way it happened?"

Sterns' voice gave little recognition to her only comment. She knew he didn't want to disturb the ache of a lifetime or to be talked out of his resolution, whatever it was. He was as close as anybody could be to defining someone's death, and it didn't belong anywhere close to the human ear. "I left Missoula that summer. Nothing could bring me back, not after what happened that year. Not even my mother's passing years after that. No, I couldn't. It never occurred to me I'd be here ever, ever again."

CHAPTER 26

Camp lights sputtered, dimming the Rattlesnake Wilderness. There was punctuality about it, an evensong as routine as the hush of candles on a Sabbath altar. After what Sterns had told her, she watched the pulse of halos, the way they transformed, then melted, some slowly, others in less than a breath, and wondered what was there to replace them. Weariness couldn't offset the night's inevitability. She realized, more than anything, she wanted to call home.

Sterns left the background of fading light, his sadness re-opened, but for Josie his momentary unraveling offset the doubts she'd had about him all the way along. The loss was palpable, as much a part of him as the woods she found him in. If he hadn't told her, she'd have rooted out the scar the best way she knew—supposition. But, he told her the truth or as much as he could stand. And then he simply lapsed into his thoughts, closed his notebook, and walked to the cab of his truck. He left the door open as though the dome light might change his mind. But she knew it didn't have to do with convenience or with her. Maybe, she thought, it was for Mark.

She gathered plates, intending to dump what was left of the pancakes. One last lantern flare came from the campground. The only remaining light was the Coleman and the cab of Sterns' truck. Shadows bounced across the picnic table like elongated ghosts. Josie shuddered, feeling the ground through her feet, its dimples suddenly undulating chasms. She hesitated, then swayed backward.

"If you fall, I'll have to put you back in bed," Sterns said, coming up behind her, the Coleman now dangling from his hand. "And neither of us wants to go through that again."

He gripped her fingers over the lantern's handle, pausing, as if considering saying something more. It occurred to her this would be the time to tell him she was still married. That even when a marriage wasn't good, even when it had been interrupted by death, it was still a commitment. *A commitment*, she thought. No longer the gentle hold of even a distant husband. "I'm sorry," she said, "But mostly I'm sorry for what happened."

"Yeah," he said. "So am I. Everybody lost on that one." Then he added, "What I have to concentrate on is the present. You've reminded me of that. With how sick you've been, where we've ended up. I'm not sure of what to do next, Josephine Russo. And that's not like me. Let's see how you are in the morning. In the meantime, just pile the dishes in the sink, cakes and all. Or we'll have visitors."

He handed her the dishes, him standing at the bottom of the trailer's steps, then flipped a penlight on the ground in front of him. "Is there anything else you need?" he asked.

"I'm really missing my mother. I guess I've avoided so much, including her and those two silly birds she loves."

"Call her," Sterns said, bringing his cell out from under his shirt. "Keep it for the night." He turned, following the light's thin etching across the ground. "Just remember signal's best outside."

"Sterns," she said. "Thanks for everything. I know I've told some wild stories the last couple days, but one thing you can know for sure. No matter what happens in the morning, I appreciate what you've done. And what you haven't."

She thought she saw him raise his hand in a careless salute, then close the door to the pick-up. He'd retreated into the smallest, the most inconvenient of places, and there was no doubt that's where he meant to stay. She sat on the last step of the trailer rubbing the cell phone between her hands, for a while wondering if he was watching her from his interment or if he was propped behind the wheel weighing the reasons to go on. But she knew he wouldn't sleep, maybe for hours. And she doubted she'd ever know exactly what would settle it for him.

By the time she reached the threshold to the bathhouse she was rehearsing what she would say to her mother. She might be in bed by now but probably sleepless. She would answer smart and snappy, "State your business," then be mystified why it had taken her daughter so long to call. After a moment, she would cry.

Timelessness surrounded Josie, a back-and-forth notion, neither safe nor vulnerable. She kept wanting the conversation to already be over. "Mom, I'm okay. I'm in Montana. I'm not alone. And, yes, I found out Robert wasn't making his way out of my life because of another woman. He was unable to tell me what was happening. Extinction, virus, serum, treachery. It was all of them, Mom. You understand, don't you?" She could think it all so quickly, but the mistake was she'd try to explain. And completely disregarding, her mother would listen only to her voice.

Raising the lantern to the bathhouse window, Josie hummed a tune she used to hear her mother sing and for a moment tried to recapture the words. An impatient swoop from behind startled her. It was no more than a single rush of air, almost as if her voice was being jerked away, followed by a single, guttural *keck*. The lantern light patterned across the face of the building, then dropped away, a soft angle swallowed by the night. If it was Gem-X, he was merely another shadow, unflinching, holding his bold red eyes right on her. It occurred to her he'd been watching her all along. "This could be heaven," she said, ad-libbing the words. "Or this could be hell."

"Gem-X? It is you, isn't it?" She kept the lantern in front, waist-high, afraid she might spook him and walked completely around the bathhouse. She knew if someone from camp happened to see her, they'd report she'd totally lost her bearings in the middle of the night, spinning round and round the house in flu's delirium. Ned would whisper to Diane what a shame that a man like Sterns should waste his last few days on her. Once again, she stopped at the entrance and waited.

She opened the cell phone, picking through the blue-lined numbers. There was a faint ring, a connection so fragile she suspected a night moth could easily interrupt it, then the sound of her mother's voice. "Is that you Josephine?" she asked.

"Yes, Mom. How'd you know?"

"Oh, a mother knows when her chick is in trouble."

"It's not that way at all," Josie said, adjusting to her mother's pre-meditated calm. "I'm just a long way from home."

"And, why so?" Laurinda asked. "I mean I expected you to poke around in the rain forest for a while. But there's only so much you can answer, dear. The rest is up to eternity."

"It's something I found, Mom. Something that has its roots in Nebraska. I'm on my way there. To find out what Robert was working on. He was involved in a project I can't even describe, something bigger than the flu."

"Is that what killed him? I mean, Josie, if that's what killed him, then you have no business going forward with it. Come home, dear. I'm still well."

Josie could hear the resolution in her mother. The stilted, one-way vision that would only permeate her life once again, sitting among the geraniums until someone down the street got sick. And then the god-awful dawning, the crazed accusation. "You brought it back with you."

"That's good. I mean, be careful. I'm not going to dwell on death anymore. Robert's or yours or mine. There's other things, more important, that will survive death. I don't know what I'm supposed to do about it, don't know why it involves me. But it does. I love you. You know I do."

"Love you too, darling," Laurinda said. "Can't doubt your reasons."

Briefly, it hung mid-air, her mother's assurance in the midst of one last anguished pull. Josie let it go, the call becoming a blip in the night sky, then closed the phone's shell. When she did, she heard ruffling. She realized during the call she'd left the Coleman on the ground several feet away. The intensity of its light was behind her, and in the deepening shadows of the building the sound of a thousand aligning feathers took on disproportion. She wondered if it was Gem-X after all. Owls, she knew, could stand by for hours waiting for a meal, their patience, like their heads, tied directly to their instincts. And pigeon, no matter what kind, was easy dining.

She opened Sterns' phone and one-by-one touched keys. It was senseless and probably a death-blow to a techno-gadget, but she continued pressing, watching the screen glow from within and wondering if it was an irresistible attraction to the creature somewhere about her. Colors deepened and blinked, as bright as the switches on autoclaves and incubators. Sounds accompanied, similar to a drawer full of baby spoons being thrown down a flight of stairs. Josie watched the cornice in front of her and realized she was looking at the butt end of an ax driven into the outside wall of the bathhouse. Maybe, it was meant to hold lanterns or even towels, she thought. But there was something else on top of it now. And she saw it move.

She moved closer, the phone having become a silent blue screen in front of her. The bird seemed perplexed, his slender head down-turned as if he was studying the familiar in the middle of a wilderness. Josie cooed, a soft guttural sound she sometimes did with the doves. "Well, blue meteor, you've got the world in a real fuss. There's people thinking you're flying death, and there's people, like me, know you're far worse than that."

She reached upward, watching him shift his attention to her hand and the soft blue light she held underneath him. He seemed to nestle, looping his long neck back and forth in arc-like motion while his chest ballooned and his legs disappeared. Everything about him suggested mesmerization. Everything but the trembling antenna beneath him.

Josephine captured this moment. She gorged, as a hunter does when he sees a buck come to the salt lick he replaced two weeks ago or when a woman discovers among her things a bottle of perfume that once was her mother's. She wanted to touch him, to rub the soft underbelly until he no longer trembled. But all she could do was hold the cell's faint light under him, afraid it was his only reassurance. The moment, so close she could hear the gurgle in his throat, pushed through the last few hours, as if they'd hardly existed. She was granted a look at something not only extinct, but a creature as enchanted as she was. "You know me, don't you?" she whispered. "You've seen me through Robert. I mean something to you or you wouldn't be here." The cell's light blinked out.

She withdrew her hand and waited for him to fly. But all that happened was stillness, forthright, something chosen. Slowly, she put her empty hand below him, feeling the soft fuzz of down and a motionless leg, then perceptible, steady breathing. "Gem-X," she said, "Can I hold you?"

He didn't move. It was as if the consent had been there in the darkness and would stay if she could just keep her balance. She braced against the wall, recalling the dreams of the last two days. The sharp outline of his flock huddled in death, packed and sealed in plastic until someone could study their remains. Rows, and then a warehouse-full of serum broken from cases, poured into hazardous waste that would someday seep into the Sound. All his work, all his living destroyed.

He relaxed, his body filling her hands as though nesting in a human cup, lighter than she expected and somehow condensed, as if he'd measured her capabilities and re-arranged himself to suit her. He didn't tremble now, and she could feel the antenna rub against her fingers. It was slight as a tie-wrap but inflexible, banded around his leg without a crease. "Legs shouldn't have to grow around such things," she said fiddling with the apparatus.

The bird shifted and began the head bob he started earlier, withdrawing, swerving to the side, then settling his beak in a keel-like furrow center-breast where it disappeared in mottled plumage. When she began to pull on the antenna, he went through the head maneuvers one more time. But instead of coming to rest at the end of the circle, he pecked her hard, right on the chin, then flew into the anonymity above the bathhouse. There was nothing, no sign he'd been near her. Just the dwindling warmth of her hands and the impatient sting. He'd slapped her, she thought. Maybe because of his pain. Or maybe because he realized she wasn't Robert.

She thought about waking up Sterns, telling him what had waited for her at the bathhouse. But even if she told him everything without exaggeration he would assume the peck had been an outright attack from a disease-ridden bird. He wouldn't listen to what she was really saying. That the antenna could be snapped off the band. And she was sure at some point Gem-X would let her do it.

Before she went into the trailer, she looked up at the window awning, The recess, no bigger than a tree knot, was empty.

Hardly adequate to hold a stowaway, let alone a meteor. But Josie felt comfort in knowing sometime during the night the slender body that had spent hundreds of hours alongside her husband, absorbing images and internalizing boundless flight would tuck into the awning cave as inconspicuous as she was only inches away from him. Would Robert have ever encouraged this aberration? Or would he have considered it straying from the purer truth, the one that included Josie as a simple, nonadjustable control.

The bed softened as she crawled into its center, and she rolled back and forth, tightening sheets around her in constriction as intentional as the passenger's awning. She thought about her husband's devotion and silence. Robert worked between worlds comfortably because he didn't confuse one with the other. It was assured on the Gem-X side. Explanations were hidden within pictures as rudimentary as a Wyoming landscape, fed over and over through some kind of program that allowed his special bird to get the idea. And most of all, to want to duplicate it. She'd heard her husband say dozens, if not hundreds of times that birds, in fact, most animals picked up cues we weren't aware of. Vibrations and earthly rhythms beyond the scope of seasons and weather. Was that information locked into Robert's silence? Did he understand what Gem-X needed to experience and fed it to him daily? And when he tried to bring it home, to his other world, that same silence was misinterpreted. Over time it became rejection.

There was hollowness to the space of her dreaming mind. A feeling very different from the earlier flu-dreams where memories stood naked as salt cliffs. This was a sense of fluidity, of gliding and intense freedom. She realized she was no longer asleep but energized. Skittering on the edge of a plateau, then flying high over it. There was nothing below her, and she seemed to drift away from it, as if air itself was a soft blue light at her underbelly. First, she heard them shouting. Four men, probably Native American, below her. Someone took a shot. She didn't have to feel it. She saw feathers fall like wayward dots toward the ground. And she followed them, watching the crack in the earth beside them get wider and wider. It wasn't going to happen the way the men envisioned. She wasn't going to end up in the stew pot. She fell past them, their hungry eyes fixed on her. She fell far down into a grove of trees. Their evergreen spines caught and held her long enough to see the wreckage beside her. Giving her time, maybe only a moment, to see the man she'd slept with for twenty years.

But this dream was not a replay of the past. There would be no picture of her husband's plane being detached from the forest piece by piece. Her imagination wouldn't stay with him day after day, hunting down the reason, tinkering with the engine, dislodging Kerrie's hind feet from the crumpled seats. Now, she was seeing it from some other place. Other than looking overhead, she was coming down upon it. She was feeling it from inside at a rate she could hardly comprehend. It was a place of birds and all they knew.

She could feel their mind. It was their mind, but it was one, inseparable strand. It made them passengers. Rolling clouds of bodies moving within seconds of one another. Cylinders that swarmed with birds hundreds of feet thick. On the ground it was their brains that ticked away the long distances between flocks, waiting for the mass to take them up as if in the suction of one giant wing. And when they finally flew, they pulled the sky apart in a thin seam of delirium.

It didn't last. For whatever reason the birds had amassed, she began to sense a sort of hesitancy never known before. They waited for flocks that grew smaller, for feed that blew away on the wind running below them. They were descending more and more to wait in the wrong places. And by the nightfall of her dream, the passengers had fallen, slaughtered beyond survival. But that was the dream, they told her. Because the reality was they would never have to face the world alone. And, in fact, they would never face it again.

"But you have," she said. "You never completely went away. You performed the disappearing act men have regretted ever since. But there was one man who found what was left of the passengers and gave them to my husband."

It was as though she'd removed a shield, as if a thin filter of disguise re-adjusted itself, and in the tight flock around her she saw Robert. He smiled more at them than at her, his hands held out, gesturing for them to keep coming. They obliged, focusing their energy on one single man, leaving her another helpless witness to their history. Josephine would no longer tamper with hallucinations, she heard him say. When the time was right she, like Gem-X, would know what to do.

The bed's warmth enveloped her, the dream and its dissipation hard to leave. She kept rolling back and forth, wanting to see him again. Hoping the passengers would let her through, the glimpse of Robert pulling her back into the vanishing fragment. She drifted just outside its peculiar, impatient spin. If only she could get close enough to tell him what she was doing. *I'm with your bird, Robert. There's nothing to worry about anymore.*

It was a relentless ache in her left upper arm that finally woke her. Curious, she reached across and felt a small hot lump in the meat of her arm about the size and attitude of an inoculation. Then she touched her bottom lip and realized the flesh still burned, that the flu she thought was over was still playing with her deep inside.

No mirrors were in sight, but all trailers had one somewhere. For Sterns, she imagined it remained wherever it had originally been installed. She began with the upper cupboards, one of which had a bracketed mirror on the inside door. Too high to see herself, she moved a chair in front of it, then stood, crouching close to see a red halo on the back of her arm. She couldn't remember it hurting before now and touched the place lightly.

"What's this?" she said to herself, feeling the immeasurable fear of amnesia. The distrust that had begun with Sterns' rescue in the bathhouse now included a feverish overcast on her skin, starting at a pink center outlined in radiating yellowish-purple. Josie stared at it for several minutes in disbelief. Nothing, not even Robert, had prepared her for this kind of raw blemish. "This was something from the outside," she said into the mirror. "An injection."

She could see Sterns' first aid kit behind some dishes. There would be insect repellent and maybe a tincture of some sort. He'd have band-aids, probably gauze. Or maybe something soothing, she guessed—even for his horses. Opening the box, she saw two Pass-Flu vials upright in the corner. Hesitantly, she pulled them into her hand, rolling them back and forth, not sure what to do. Each one was 98 percent. And one of them was empty.

She sat down trying to imagine what this all meant. Robert had always said no one should take any of the serum until they knew assuredly they had bird flu. This flu, like no other, was lethal, sometimes within a few short hours. But as long as you were able to exchange oxygen, there was a good chance the antidote would work. If you took it too soon or didn't have bird flu, it simply had no effect, or so he'd said. *But what if he was wrong?* she thought. *What if it could cause bird flu, if only once?*

Josie shivered, a kind of insidious vibration that crept along like an insect trailing up her spine. Whatever was going on, part of the answer was in her backpack. Her own kit was closed deep down inside the pack, and she took a minute to think about it, to give herself time to consider what might be wrong. *Once before he didn't lie. He told me flat out he looked a long time.* She pried the kit open, then stared at two empty depressions. "My, God," she said, running her fingers inside its pre-formed tissue paper. "What has he done?"

CHAPTER 27

The night, what was left of it, compressed into random, sometimes desperate thoughts. After finally putting the vials back in her own kit, Josie realized her life had been slipping between worlds, maybe since Robert's death. She'd kept looking for him. And when she finally found him, it was as though the barrier he'd so carefully erected was all that was left to hold onto. She sat in the chair at Sterns' table, first completely befuddled. Her husband had constructed a life, not with her but within judgment of her. He'd drawn a line down their marriage and waited for her to find out. Every vial should've led her closer. Instead, she stored them like some people store bullets, thinking she'd never have to use one.

Slowly, she reasoned if Sterns took the vial himself, then she probably wouldn't notice any difference in him. He would either have guessed right and outflanked the plague or he wasted a perfectly good vial. But if he gave it to her somewhere along the way when she was too sick to recognize it, then he saved her life, wasted the vial or secured her place in God's Death March. There was nothing in any first aid box in the world that could help her now.

She pulled Robert's laptop from under the table and began searching the notes she'd read that first night in the rain forest. Only once had Robert mentioned something about training, but she remembered it because he simply passed over the term as if that was the last thing he wanted to discuss. She re-read his reference to Mr. Hennings as the "perpetual Oz of this operation" and knew, with that understanding, he might not say anything further about methods. But as she researched, Josie began to link her husband's ingenuity with his avian student. In a circuitous way, Robert had filtered his techniques throughout his notes.

SAF was a system he'd devised through many hours of observation and probably some instruction from Hennings. Between them, they conjured up an apparatus so easily assembled and disassembled that Robert could train Gem-X in increments equivalent to a daily exam. A series of monitors had grown from the original two to a "sense-surround" system of eight. From what she could tell, the streaming video played repeatedly to the bird was the exact route she and Robert had driven four years ago, a compendium of all his photography between the Olympic Rain Forest and Darby, Nebraska, or something he called *a documentary incorporated into a satellite migration template for known flyways.*

It turned out *Sensation of Accomplished Flight* was no small thing. It engaged the bulk of her husband's fieldwork, some of which had been studying finches but most of which was in pursuit of fine-tuning. Apparently, he'd been researching thermals and various tones and temperatures picked up by birds as they were swept up canyons and alongside mountains. Hence, his own increased hours in the air over the last few months of his life. She could imagine the parameters of flight taken from one-dimensional film to Robert's final trifling with focus, adjusting for the uplift of one wing while the other might logically obliterate rocky outcroppings below. He might've added a stream of air from a fan or even faint natural odors, once mentioning pine musk, to the experience. Increasingly, he'd enhanced the daily ride for Gem-X. But there was no doubt in her mind her husband had one purpose in mind, and that was to free his prodigy.

The night air gently paced through the trailer's open windows and seemed to clear the small space of doubt, of chronic flu-infested dreams. Josie looked at her husband's work, his life's real calling. She scanned screen-by-screen his infatuation with the passenger pigeon named Gem-X and his total devotion to the one thing he could influence. Less and less he mentioned the flock at Wilson's Bridge. It was as though they existed only as a featureless detail. Yet, she sensed his promise was to them all. That they would live as they always had, through the spirit of one. She went to the door, opening the screen and took a long look at the dark pick-up in front of her, then picked up the cell phone Sterns had given her earlier. It was exactly four in the morning. And it would be that same hour in Darby, Nebraska.

* * *

His voice was close to what she would've imagined. He dropped the "s" sound at the end of his name, and the "n's" in the middle were derived through sinuses more like echo chambers. "Henning," was all he said.

She could still hear it now after all these miles. The way he accepted her call in the middle of the night, not questioning or ignoring. It never occurred to her he might have caller I.D. and that a phone call from Sterns' cell might not be all that far-fetched.

Sterns had been silent since they left the Rattlesnake. He kept looking in the rear view mirror as though he was convincing himself they were one curve away from being apprehended. But there were no curves in this part of Montana. There were no buildings, no fences, no side roads. Nothing but a long stretch of freeway where anyone could be seen for miles. Through the side mirror Josie watched the sky behind her awaken in a series of sloping clouds overlapping each other. The ones in front had become gray escarpments ready to collapse on the fragile, decaying layer below. There was an energy building above and beyond them. She knew she could be looking across a thousand acres. But there was a sense it was becoming shrink-wrapped in a fiercely trotting inferno, cut down to size mile after mile. It was an inevitable collision course, and right now there was nothing more to say.

She'd asked Curtis Hennings what he knew about her husband's project, whether he knew the cause of his death. She hadn't minced words because at four in the morning no one wants to procrastinate. And they might be too foggy to lie. But the old man seemed practiced or maybe so comfortable he just never said things differently. *Victor Borge falling off his piano bench*, she thought.

"You know, Ms. Russo," he said, "It's never been explained to anybody what happened. Seems to me he was doing what he did best though. If anybody understood flying, he did."

"You think so, Mr. Hennings?" she said. "You think men who love birds understand flying?"

"Not so much as they can manage an emergency," he said.

She told him briefly about her emergency, the flu and its outcome. That she was on her way to see him when she got sick and had reason to believe she was injected with Pass-Flu. "I'm traveling with an acquaintance, I guess you'd call him. He must've panicked, and now after two days of being out of my head I discover he gave me a vial without my even knowing. I don't know what to make of it. My husband told me very little about how it works. Do you know anything about it? I know what it's made of," she added, as if to simplify her worry.

"Well, there, that's the most important part," he said. "You know what it's made of. Robert must've told you something or left some clues behind, did he? Did you know if you got the last update it's all from one bird?"

"Gem-X?" she said.

"Why, yes. Have you met him yet? Pure extinct passenger. If you're comin' to see me, you might as well know that. For sure."

"Yes, I know," she said. "I figured it out, and yes, I've met him. Did you expect me to?"

"Uh huh," he said, "At least I was hopin' so."

She could feel the way sweat on her hands had turned cold, how the old man knew the story before she could live it. "Look, Mr. Hennings," she continued. "I'm up for some truth here. I don't know if I'm seriously ill, and I'm in the middle of a wilderness area in Montana with nowhere to go but back home or on to you. And the fright is now I don't know if I'll make it either direction."

"Well, your friend, what's-his-name, he probably saved your life. That Pass-Flu is the purest strain there is. And it come from none other than Gem-X. That's one racer, he is. He's got it in him to fly all the way to Nebraska. But you're in his sights. That's what's keepin' him in the envelope. You."

"Are you saying I've somehow lured him into confinement? Because I haven't. He just appears out of nowhere, then disappears again. He's even traveled some of the way with us in a trailer window awning."

"Clever," the old man said. "Even Robert couldn't have foreseen that one."

Josie knew the conversation was being deliberately interwoven within a long history of secrecy and that Hennings was not about to tell her anything he couldn't completely digest first. More and more she was convinced he was the man behind the man she loved, and again, she wondered what he knew about her. "You know, I have reason to believe somehow I was used in my husband's project. I don't know why, but there's some reason this bird has taken on this journey. Am I with him or is he with me? Frankly, I understand my husband was trying to make this animal's life bearable under the extremely questionable circumstances. But I can't believe a wild bird would keep me in sight, even let me hold him. That makes no sense."

"It makes no sense now, Ms. Russo. But it will, especially if you keep coming this way. Your husband trained his bird with love and expectation. To survive. It wasn't easy, and for a while I didn't think it could be done. But I'm wonderin' now. I'm really wonderin'."

"By the way, Ms. Russo, that bird has a whatchamacallit on its foot. One of them transmitters. And, if I've got my wrinkles lined up, that outfit Colzer will be tracking him. Which means, they'll be tracking you. A big guy. Blond. Probably a better guy than he lets on. But he ain't goin' to give up, Ma'am. And he don't have to. Because that bird's going to bring him right in. If I was you, I'd get that gear off him somehow. And damned quick."

The thoughts of what he said made her shiver, and she pulled her sweater from between the seats wrapping it tight around her middle. Sterns would be watching her for any telltale relapse, but his awareness couldn't possibly penetrate the way Hennings' had. "What makes you so sure Gem-X is not going to fly off over some mountain someplace and get shot or eaten by a coyote or something?" she'd asked Hennings. "Why would some bigwig from some pharmaceutical track me down? I've done nothing wrong."

"Oh?" said the old man. "Neither did your husband. And that bird, well believe me, he ain't leavin' your side for long. He's got you in his circuits. And you got him in your antibodies."

She remembered how she sat on the bed wanting to go back to sleep. To go to a place where she'd never heard what she'd found out in a three-minute phone call. She couldn't remember ending the conversation or what she did to get ready to leave. But after a few minutes she closed up the trailer, then pounded on the driver's door of the pick-up. Sterns opened it with a jerk.

"Do you need some help? What's the matter, Josie?"

"Unlock the other door," she said. "Please."

"What is it?" he said, as she moved into the seat, carefully placing her feet one beside the other on the floor and her backpack on her lap.

"We have to leave," she said.

"What? It's barely dawn. I haven't checked everything yet."

"Too bad. We have to go."

"Wait a minute," Sterns said, gripping the steering wheel. "What's bothering you? Are you having another . . . uh . . . situation?"

"Well, if I am I'm thinking it might be your fault." She had watched Sterns, not straight-on but corner-wise as one looks for a lost kitten. Waiting for a quick, unwitting movement, something done out of the instinct to run. Josie reached into her backpack pulling the first-aid kit close onto her lap and retrieved the two vials, then specifically the empty. She laid it on the truck console. "Explain this," she said.

He acknowledged the moment in a way that offset her accusation, funneling it right back down to the core suspicion she'd felt hours earlier. Sterns didn't stumble or pause to consider the answer, whatever one he could fathom, from the myriad of possibilities. He simply got out of the truck and walked around the entire length of it and the trailer, giving things an occasional thump as he went. He got back in the cab and started the engine. "It was a decision," he said. "An accident that led to a decision."

"There are no accidents in this, Sterns. You went through my stuff. You found something potent. And injected me—obviously."

She slipped the sweater from her left shoulder, pulling his sweatshirt down until the bruise spread corona-like across her arm. This time Sterns looked. Pallor enhanced dark circles surrounding his eyes, and he visibly cringed. "Jesus Christ," he muttered. "I mean I'm sorry. I'm no good at this, this medicine. I just knew you had something in your pack that might save your life. I couldn't tell how sick you were. You just . . . couldn't breathe."

She readjusted herself, taking her time. Thinking. There was so little to berate him for now after what Hennings said. Yet, his judgment had a subtle dominance over everything. This stranger had made her the focus of his life, even his confessions in only a few hours. Was it guilt over what he'd done at the very beginning? Was this the reality between them? That more and more he had become her caregiver, starting with an injection meant as a last resort, that even Robert would've questioned.

"Maybe I should be thanking you," she said. "But you've spread your own doubt. What is it with you? You don't trust anything. Me, the bird, even your own instincts. And then I start to question what's happening here. Why I'm here with you, when I should be doing this alone." She handed him the cell phone, cutting off the momentary drench of words. "I called Mr. Hennings a few minutes ago. I asked him about the Pass-Flu."

"And what did he say?"

"That you'd done me a favor. Probably saved my life."

"And do you believe him?" Sterns asked, hardly moving his lips.

"I believe him," she said.

Sterns turned toward her, bracing himself against the door. She could see how tired he'd become, rumpled and slightly estranged. But he seemed to be lining himself up to tell her his version of the truth. "You know when we were at the top of Lookout, how you went off in the bushes? I e-mailed Mr. Hennings then and got an answer back. The same question. The same answer. It's the only thing I can believe in. That an old man knows I didn't try to kill you . . . or take advantage of you."

He wasn't talking about caregiving anymore. With every word, every turn of his hand he was telling her something else. It was the flu, she realized, that had derailed him many hours ago. "I've spent most of the night thinking about what I should be doing right now. It's easy to think you're through the worst of it.

That bruise," he said gesturing toward her arm, "Might be the end of it. But I kept thinking what if Hennings is wrong? He's just a witness to what the experiment was all about. And the provider. What if he's got something, some motive to keep you coming his direction?"

"Yes, well," she said. "By now, there's lots more than him keeping me doing this." She thought about the bird, his elusiveness, then scanned the side mirror on the hunch he might be in the awning. No feathers protruded. No antenna. But there was another demon in the mix, someone far more capable of pursuing them than Gem-X. It wasn't just Ned and the Rattlesnake, a lethal illness that barricaded whole communities from getting help, or even a fire eating away at the meager few able to defend the Great Plains. Now, it was a personal inquiry from Colzer-Bremen itself. A blond man, a tracker, *maybe better than he lets on.*

Josie knew it was trackers, most of them Native American, throughout western history who'd been impossible to shake. Darkness or downpour didn't slow them down. North or south didn't matter. They thrived on experience. And habit. Tracks weren't pressure. They were thought and intention. Running or hesitant, hungry or dripping blood. This man read her moves through technology. But he also knew something about pursuit. Enough that an old man in Nebraska could promise he'd never stop.

Sterns began the descent without further comment. He feathered his way, hardly touching his brakes. She knew he was concentrating on decisions that were his alone. They'd entered Missoula through a bottleneck. A road restriction sign indicated they were on a designated byway, and it was no longer an option to enter certain neighborhoods. The maze led them through a town of purple-colored banners, of windows boarded up or propped wide open. A pack of dogs looted dumpsters in a Wal-Mart parking lot, shredding disposable diapers lettuce-like across at least two city blocks while at the same time and from the opposite direction an old woman picked up the bigger pieces with her grabber, never letting go of the cart she dropped them in. Finally, Sterns pulled up to a security station. In the background was a complex of buildings, a square of uneven skyline. A tower stood in the middle. Mounted at the top story was an illuminated cross.

"What's this?" she said. "I thought you were going to get gas."

"Not your worry," Sterns said. "I can't let this go on. This is a good place, Josie. St. Pats Hospital. They'll take care of you, of what I've done to you."

"So this is where it ends?" she said, unable to take her eyes off the chain-link perimeter. "It looks a lot like what we found there in the rain forest, doesn't it? All fence and authority."

Sterns pulled the emergency brake and put on his hazard lights. The trailer, by now, was blocking traffic from a side street leading into the complex. He seemed preoccupied with the obstruction he had created, but there was also a security guard coming. As if clearing his head, he opened his door and looked behind, then withdrew into the cab looking straight at Josie.

"I talked to your husband in Fraser one day, a time I haven't told you about. But maybe I better. Because he warned me to stop going up that tree. Apparently, he'd been watching me. He said I'd regret it someday. Well, that day is here, Josie. In fact, I think the exact moment is."

She felt herself fall, the kind of drop that happens completely in your head. It was not graceful or even slow-motion. It was a horrific scramble of feet and hands, of the sharp unforgiving angles of her elbows and a fleshy tear across her stomach. Everywhere she could feel was embedded. With gravel or glass or both. It was a hard fall. And she thought she could hear the hiss of a rock-warmed rattler.

"Don't do this, Sterns. If I go in there, I don't know if I'll ever come out. But if I do, if I somehow make it through, I won't go back home. Don't you see? Everything, the dawn light, the pictures he took, my husband's virtual plan all included me. For some reason, maybe it was the marriage we had or didn't have. Until Pass-Flu, I could only guess. But that injection, whatever it's done, has made me see one thing clearly. Clearly, Sterns. If I'm the control, then until now I haven't been the test. It means almost everything that happens was established long ago by my husband and his avian student. It became the norm, just like life was before this pandemic. Can we ever get back to normal?" she said, holding herself rigid, watching the guard approach them straight-on.

"But now this has become our test, yours and mine. We're living it. If I don't follow through with what made me a daily fixture in a plan I don't understand, I'm leaving my husband's lifework to a twist of fate. Everything he did, I'll minimize. By now, with a world that's about to explode, I'll ditch what little hope there is. This isn't me, anymore, Sterns. It isn't us. It's a final say in a world that may never know. But we will," she said, spreading words as if unbreakable seed between them.

The guard waited, pulling his hat down over his eyes, then made a quick perusal of Sterns' outfit. He wrote something on a note pad. "Yes, sir," he said, "I wonder if you know what this is. We're in semi-quarantine here. But if you need to come in or drop somebody off, we can take over from this point."

Sterns made no reply. It was, she thought, as if he was watching an internal dilemma of his own.

"Sir, we can't have you sit here much longer. We have accommodations inside. By the way, how many does your rig sleep?"

In the passing miles between Missoula and Billings, she wondered what it was about that question that caused Sterns to put the pick-up in reverse. To follow the turn-out exactly without a single mistake and to lock the doors, all of them. There was an exactness about every mile spent headed east as though the man was planning to drive as far as fuel would let him and save every square inch of doubt for another time. For her, though, the distance between outposts consisted of sky and plains and a feel of grit in her mouth. Once or twice she thought she saw a falcon jab herself into the earth. From any direction there was nowhere to hide. Except, perhaps, in the trailer awning behind her.

CHAPTER 28

Patience had never been Pritchard's long suit, and when the white F-250 passed in front of him he almost floored the Hummer. They looked so incongruous, the man and woman gliding by as if on a leisurely vacation in the middle of a holocaust. The trailer was like a beacon. There was no doubt he was looking at Josephine Russo, her boyfriend, and probably the bird itself all wrapped up in a recreational package, turning south onto Highway 25. "Great fuckin' balls of fire," he yelled. "There goes my retirement in Guadalajara."

As he watched the faint outline of the trailer disappear into a thread as slender as the center line he turned the receiver off. There was no use in listening to the taunting wail of transmissions. He was as close as any outsider was likely to get to Gem-X. And, it might not ever happen again.

He watched the rear-view mirror, jerking it back and forth, hitting his head on the headrest until he saw the trooper look up and study the frenzy in front of him. That's all he did, finally dipping his head back into paperwork. Several more minutes went by, and Pritchard settled down. He slid his gun from its holster and held it between his legs, then, absentmindedly pressed a key on his laptop. A replay began, a chiseled prism of light no more than a speck that expanded and rippled as if barely holding on until it was overcome by an impervious sun. The timed beginning, a solstice beginning. An exact replica of yesterday morning.

Pritchard pulled back the gun's slide in smooth familiarity, more like a caress. He thought about the simplicity of training with a single object like a handheld camera that could record every step of a journey. How simple it would be to depress a button. Everything would be right there, mile upon mile. Landmarks, bends in the road, things that would never change—a self-contained tool. And yet so unlike the suspended violence he held in his hand.

He could see the patrolman leave his car, propping his gun alongside him. A clipboard hung from his other hand. He was so careless with the last few minutes of his life. Pritchard waited for him to get to the side window. Then he said what had just occurred to him. "Solstice, huh? You're right, officer. Nobody pays any attention. Except one passenger pigeon."

The officer steadied the clipboard against the side of the Hummer, holding it there with his stomach. With his empty hand he signaled for Pritchard to lower the window. "Did you say something, mister?"

"Nope," Pritchard said. "Just fantasizing about patience. What it must be like to have it." *It could be too late,* he thought. *Too late to catch a bird and to give this one more death any meaning.*

Papers came through the window slot. It was an odd, unappreciated dilemma that Pritchard was in. So close to blowing a man's head off while he adjusted his sunglasses against an aplomado sky. "Keep to the right side of the road," the cop said. "Wouldn't waste your time going any further east."

Pritchard lowered the window studying buttons dead center on the officer's chest. Nothing ever moved in the desert, he thought. It just reflected. Tiny things. A man's wedding ring, the thin fringe of a moving tongue of oil. He wanted to scream, then felt the steadying weight of the gun in his hand. "It's too late," he said, looking straight up at a man who could be forgotten within hours.

As if in idle amusement, a Mexican melody went off. In short, screeching bursts Pritchard's cell phone fractured his growing impulse to eliminate the only thing between him and another half million dollars. He pushed the gun under one leg while accelerating with the other. "Business," he yelled, "Hope yours turns to blood-spurting plague, you nose of a she-goat."

He could feel Elsa's tension as soon as she pronounced his name. When she was most piqued it came out with emphasis on the backside where the "ard" became "chard." He could see it in her teeth, even now. The way she chewed his name into pieces.

"Pritchard, where have you been since last night?" Elsa demanded. "Tell me exactly where you've been with my plane and my pilot."

"I went to Mexico. Palomas. A pharmacy. And I got cortisone. Something you don't provide anymore."

"I have bigger concerns," she said. "Accountability goes two ways, and you've been ditching yours since you left here."

Hoping he'd somehow accelerate beyond cell range, Pritchard concentrated on the angle of rippling grass along the freeway, smoothed like the hair on a dog's back. He noticed it never stood straight, no matter which way you were going. It was simply born to bend. Finally, he said, "Well, you haven't done so well with yours either."

"What do you mean by that, Martin? I'm the one who can wipe you from the face of this earth without so much as a single inquiry."

"Yeah, unlike Russo and Garner, I'm goddamn disposable, right? It's just easier to keep me alive for rides like this. And the unsuspecting bastards at the ends of the earth."

In a smooth, deliberate monotone she began. "I've accessed everything. All five training CDs and the image from Cam-nine. You think you can bribe people to provide you with classified information. But you've underestimated them and my sense of propriety. I've known for a long time what Robert Russo was up to. I knew he was stealing vials and training a valuable bird. I let it go because of his dedication to the project. His success was questionable. And all the while he was making us millions. He failed and Garner failed when they thought they could influence the future by keeping vials that should've been destroyed. They didn't know what decisions I've had to endure. What a risk it's been."

"Uh huh," Pritchard said, smelling the distant heat of carbon and timber and grassland burning at the roots. "A risk you chose to take without me. You know, the guy who peckers his way through slums and carcasses, through bed sheets soaked in urine and pus. The asshole who brought your personal, guaranteed update to Tibet. You've been had, lady. While I was away doing your bidding, Russo packed it in. But not before he shut down your chance for

100 percent. Wonder what it felt like removing the last four vials of the highest percent? Not destroying them, like he told you he'd do. The only regret I've got right this second is that it wasn't me that had that distinct pleasure."

The pause, Elsa's most deliberate weapon, seemed to sweep down across the road in front of him, surrounding the Hummer and engulfing it and him in a silence so disapproving he slapped the cell hard on his knee. Less than a minute went by.

"You can throw in your usual distractions, Martin. But unless you want to forfeit another small fortune for a job only yards in front of you, you'll concentrate on your part of this picture. It's really very easy. Bring me the bird," she said, her voice a solid wall of vibration. "If it's Russo's widow who has him, kill her. If it's her stooge, kill him. If it's you . . . Well, that's not smart. I have your Rachel under protective custody. It's all relative, Martin, what I can do. And, if necessary, I'll clean up the mess in Darby myself."

He turned on the receiver and adjusted the volume into one undeniable tone, then felt the first tingling spasm in his hand. The sensation caused him to turn off the receiver again, instead listening to her, concentrating his thoughts on her threat. This was a departure from the usual way Elsa did business, at least with him. Pritchard knew instinctively it was only a matter of time before she got to his daughter which would lead Shanna to slaughter as well. But for her to warn him was something calculated far beyond her signature discipline. It caused him to decelerate and to think about his words before he said them. There were many he could embed in her flesh. But, there was a shred of reticence in him, a cool, guarded patience he realized might be a counterbalance for time and the declining chance of his ever seeing Rachel again.

"The anti-virus, Elsa." he said. "We both know what it means to you. I don't think Russo ever intended to destroy the last run. It looks to me like he planned to destroy your chances of getting it and whatever else followed. That's the no-brainer. What isn't is that he trained a passenger to fly to Nebraska, and now the widow Russo seems to be moving right along with him. Didn't steal him. Did you hear me, Elsa? Moving with the pigeon. Cam-nine didn't lie. Some cue, some ornithologist's hex, and our little buddy is out.

But if she holds the bait just right and does get a hold of him, now we have a problem. Because, as you recall, the road forks out there. The woman might decide to go to Denver instead of Darby. And remember there's a lab in Denver. A small, bird-eating factory. Interspecies will shred him into a pigeon pillow. If she does go on to Darby, then that makes him Hennings' star pupil, and he'll probably kill the flyer rather than let you get him again. Either way, Elsa, you lose."

Silence filled Pritchard's ear. He could sense her unmistakable repugnance. "You think I don't know what you're planning," she said. "You're running with the thought she's got the 98 percent updates Russo gave her. You said so yourself when we first talked about this. The vials would be worth more than the bird himself in the right lab. But what you don't know, what you haven't hacked into, is that the flock was indeed stressed. Russo wasn't the only tender. Others saw the birds losing their edge. It was up to me to make the fatal decision to extract 98 percent, and I did so knowing it could well prove the end of the flock. And it was, Pritchard."

"But that update you think she has is tainted. As he customarily did, Russo pulled those first vials of 98 percent anti-virus from Gem-X. He stopped the run with the other birds, as he had also sometimes done in the past. First, I accepted his decision. But it troubled me that he continued to train a bird that was destined to die. He would, you know, on the next update that was planned in June. Even Russo said so in his e-mails. And, mind you, I was reading his e-mails. But when it became apparent Gem-X survived this devastation, I finally knew why. Like so many disease carriers in the past, Gem-X is alive—maybe even safe to handle. But his antibodies somewhere along the line underwent a disquieting aberration. Right now his anti-virus can boil a brain. And you," she said with unmistakable accentuation, "Are the one I entrust to bring him back to me, alive. Head and all."

In the minutes that followed he realized the chasm, the almighty drop below him. There was only the illusion of flatness, of a chronically level plain in front of him. Two women had him distended, so much flesh parceled out in a stranglehold. He'd have to choose which one was worthiest, which was most vulnerable.

Which one would die without a struggle. Because he couldn't have it both ways. Josephine Russo meant to succeed, whatever her motive, simply rolling down a freeway littered with the increasing thunder of fire trucks. And Elsa Dupree wouldn't stop until she took out the very last of what Pritchard could only call his life.

In his mind he thought of Josephine Russo as a duplicate of himself. With or without permission, her husband had used her image to coax a bird into virtual reality. She was a focus without being a destination. The woman had reason to steal her husband's plan. She also had the impetus to take over his life's work and make a fortune doing it. Pritchard could've interrupted all that. So easily. But now there was a holy war, and casualties, maybe even the one who meant the most to him, would mount.

Purposely, he drove the Hummer off the freeway, shortcutting to a frontage road that paralleled it. He picked up speed, watching a caravan of fire trucks being led by a six-truck convoy of National Guard, all heading toward the Bighorn Mountains. It was desperation, he thought, to fight a plume fire from the ground. And it was madness to expect to see the man and woman in the F-250 ever again.

There was no sign, just a T-bone intersection in the middle of nowhere. Pritchard slammed on the brakes. He'd been driving with his knee for the last several minutes, his hand virtually shrunken into a peach-sized clench. With his other hand he pulled his gun from beneath his leg, then rolled down the window. He selected a quadrant of space that included a telephone pole. A small knob straddled the top, occasionally moving a head silhouetted like black felt against a darkening sky. The head tilted down. Pritchard aimed, and with a single explosive crack the hawk fell, a straight-down, graceless stoop that ended in abrupt death. He studied the feathers ruffled by increasing wind and felt for the first time since he was a boy being lifted weightlessly from the long, sure course of indecision.

*　*　*

He cut back into traffic just beyond the Little Bighorn Battle-field. To Pritchard the necessity of a vehicle was only superficial. He was bearing down on a problem. If he could've done it from the air he would have. He'd have told Mellon to execute a dive and driven a post-hole right through that miserable twenty-eight foot trailer he saw less than a half hour before. The road and the bitter char below the sky's luminous orange only accentuated his pace, and he realized he was locked onto a very restricted path. The receiver picked up the bird's ping, but it was faint and infrequent and somehow irritatingly resilient.

The fire truck in front of him slowed every few hundred feet. Sometimes he'd see a driver coming toward him lower his hand after having waved. There was always such adoration for fire crews. Maybe it was because they were on their way out, and most everybody knew it. Headed for hell, capping off what they could. Nobody acknowledged flu like a wildfire because there were no dramatic signals in the sky, no gusts of declaration. But they weren't really so different. When you finally got tapped on the shoulder, there was only sudden unbearable suffocation and for a few recognizable moments an exhaustive fear of being alone. That look, he could still remember, in Rachel's five-year-old eyes.

She'd been in bed a couple days. They'd all three had the flu before, but this was a relapse only Rachel seemed to get. She couldn't sleep and then suddenly she did. Her skin slowly rip-ened, first a honey-bronze. Then the creases around her wrists and throat turned dark brown. For a while it was jaundice, Shan-na kept saying. "Something wrong with her liver." It was in the middle of the night when they took her, her body compressed like flattened leaves. No one said the possibilities. He remembered rid-ing alongside her. The bumps in the road, the way her eyes would flutter open. He leaned over her brushing her lips with his hair. Just to tell her, to let her know he would never be far away.

"The flu," they said. "That's what set it off. Addisonian cri-sis. But we've got it under control. She'll be fine."

He'd asked them what would happen the next time she caught the flu. Would she be fine then? No one seemed to blink. They had it gauged. He remembered wondering whether any of them had seen Addison's before or were they just reading up and spewing? He should've asked them what would happen if it was the bird flu that she got. "What would you geekin' monsters do if it was your normal kid who got the bird flu?" Pritchard said out loud. "Well, you're finding out now aren't you?"

His impatience was bottle-necked, wedged between a caravan and a ridge of imposing mountains. The Wyoming line fell through all of it, no more than a crossing with a way station surrounded in young Douglas firs. A temporary sign indicated a fire staging area would be accessible at the junction with Crazy Woman Creek. *Fitting that no fire truck could proceed into hell without a visit first with a crazy woman*, he thought.

Pritchard threw back his head and laughed, a tight howl that showed a man not amused, but pleading with the universe. Women, the very creatures he'd avoided, now surrounded him. They all wanted something, one of them without even knowing he existed, and that he'd be the one stopping the whole show. It occurred to him that, of them all, Shanna was the crux. He'd never been able to shed her even though she walked away from him some two years after Rachel's diagnosis. Somehow, there was this feeling they were both responsible. Genetics maybe. But it was more than that—worse. They'd volunteered to take a chemical bath, something that unleashed itself in their child. Addison's disease might not have happened if it hadn't been for the Gulf. They should've quit at a little desperate sex. Now, one came attached to the other. A benzene ring dreamed in the night, and it was too late to break the reaction.

There were still answers, he thought, listening to the receiver's increasing thrum. He could take his daughter to the Sky Islands along the Rio Grande. Watch her skin bronze naturally in the shadows of the Chisos Mountains and sunlit stands of oak and Texas madrone. There would be crystalline pools where she could bathe and soak out the predators of immunity and butterflies that danced across never-ending grass. It would feel right to take her into the Chihuahuan Desert after what she'd been through, a place where magic still existed in plants. Where Ortez could send more cortisone, and Shanna would decide to stay. Never mind that it was slipping away, the future with his daughter dissipating in flu and in Elsa's threat. "El Pipila," he whispered. "You woman turkeycock."

He watched the brake lights of the truck in front of him flicker a warning. Transmission beats that had begun in accompaniment were, by now, a steady honk. Pritchard took his foot off the accelerator, senseless, except that he wanted to see if it would change anything. The solid ping indicated directly overhead, then, according to the read-out, drifted slowly to the left. He braked and opened his door, craning his neck to watch the sky above him. A truck behind him waited then began creeping forward. Pritchard retracted into his seat and pushed on his hazard lights. He had to think about what was happening. Not Shanna or Elsa, but the woman with the bird.

The beep tripped along to the left of the freeway, then veered right nearing the apex above Pritchard. He began to connect the dots in his usual back-and-forth strategy. Josephine Russo didn't have the bird contained. He was flying the programmed route pigeon style, his body no more than an arrow dragging a finely tuned wire. Thermals would lift, then plunge him across the tormented plains. Gem-X was a mere scrap ingested by a conflagration picking up steam from below and towering thousands of feet above him. He couldn't last, Pritchard thought. But his mistress might.

A fireman from behind jumped out and made a sideways motion with his hands as though to push Pritchard out of the way. A steady screaming horn now accompanied the bird's transmissions. The roar that was never far off, the rumble of oil escaping at sixteen hundred pounds per square inch distended the freeway like a grid of Kuwaiti desert. A long-ago heat seared his face, and he knew the plumes were out there, shafts of fire boiling from burning wells thousands of miles away. They would form a black cloud of smothering, then deafening convection. And no one would get through.

He began again. Some traffic exited at Powder River Pass, but Pritchard stayed in line with the fire trucks. He thought about what a woman with a man and a twenty-eight foot trailer would do. Then what she'd do if you threw in a couple vials of record-breaking Pass-Flu. It occurred to him Josephine Russo was telling him the answers mile by mile. Unfazed, she made steady progress across the terrain of suffering. She was doing it without quitting and without changing the trajectory of her husband's plan. But, like Pritchard, she didn't know the evolution of a serum, except to believe it was the world's best antidote. She might not realize the single passenger overhead could have the constitution of a cave full of bats while, at the same time, spread infinite destruction in one deadly vial. For that reason, she might still entertain the idea of selling it to the highest bidder. And if Elsa was right, just this one time, that could break all the death counts for plagues.

He thought of the painstaking two hundred miles it was to Denver. In one more decision, she could drive further south than anyone had expected, imbedded in a line as tight as a funeral procession. Whatever connection she had with the bird would be tested just getting to Interspecies Labs, and he realized there might come a time when the two would no longer be traveling buddies, the telemetry a mindless blip of a bird on a doomed journey into hot air. But if she managed to corral him or decided to approach the lab with only the two vials, they would likely concoct their own trade name and market. The world would be looking to Denver to stop the scourge. Would Interspecies know, would they care whether the bird's serum was tainted? Or would they grow fat, like Colzer, and pay Russo's widow handsomely to do so. No one, except Pritchard, had the beguiling thoughts of what kind of havoc that could unleash. And this time it didn't matter whether Elsa was right or wrong.

Pritchard kept moving his head while swerving lane to lane. He watched the sky, the road, even telephone poles for any sign of Gem-X. Beeps had crisscrossed the freeway several times as if he was in an aerial ballet, tormenting the man below for killing something avian, even a raptor. It was strangely intimidating knowing the pecking order was beginning with a bird and working its way down to a woman without predictability and possibly without scruples. He knew if he was going to have any kind of influence over the situation he would have to get to her before she passed Glendo Reservoir because, by then, Interspecies was less than an hour away. Hemmed in, front to back, she'd literally have a traffic escort.

For a brief moment he watched the horizontal pallor that hung in the sky, creeping upwards as a fine blush of increasing temperature. He knew, by now, fire was in some places as much as fifteen hundred degrees, melting asphalt and trackage, buttes and ravines into billowing funnels and flaming turrets of gas as bright as a star. The boiling clouds were only a corona overhead, a warning to run. *But where?* he thought. *Where could anybody run? Dumb asses. It burns without mercy on a map without a name.* He tossed the Billings sectional from his window, the fold-outs fluttering open, then pitching back and forth on the side of the road.

Once more he turned his head front to back. Pritchard wasn't sure what he'd just seen in his rear-view mirror was really happening. In smooth deceleration a white truck and trailer exited the freeway on the Powder River turn-off less than a quarter mile behind him. The road clover leafed, and as the familiar pick-up angled west into the center of the mountainous horseshoe that separated the Rockies from the Great Plains, he realized this deviation was the reason for the bird's recent overhead scramble, and far sooner than he expected.

Pritchard groaned. In the hapless wasteland that stretched before him was a free-flying passenger pigeon and the only viable reason to keep moving forward. A steady signal echoed from straight ahead. The bird pulled away as if on a tow-rope. At the same time a woman was deliberately separating herself not only from her charge but the only two places on earth that made sense for her to go. He wondered where she'd been and how she got behind him, then, with one steady look ahead, the question evaporated into incredulity.

The caravan pushed on at barely forty miles an hour. Pritchard could watch the pigeon systematically out-fly the traffic below him, hurling himself outward in the same direction, but on the grid at least twenty miles an hour faster. In his mind he could see the bird's determined stare, his wings in a low, aerodynamic arch, sliding upward above the stagnation below. *He might roast*, the man thought, *but he'll have a good time right up to the end*. "There's a lesson here," he said, swerving the Hummer onto the dry cake of road shoulder. "And it ain't goin' after some flu-crazed bird."

CHAPTER 29

The railroad crossing sat at the top of a low-grade hill, one of the few undulations in the road since Sterns had departed the freeway at Billings' final truck stop. She wondered why he'd waited three exits to finally search for gas. He'd been silent for hours. Sometimes the only movement he made was scratching the beard on the side of his face or extending his neck to look overhead through the windshield. It would've been wondrous, that sight he saw. Of reddening cumulus piled high against the slant of a high-riding dirty overcast. But she knew what it meant and that it was testing his recollection of youth and fire.

The crossing arms were locked down. She watched Sterns pull the truck as close to them as he could, then honk the horn in aggravation. It was as though he finally wanted to be heard in the middle of a landscape of indifference, unpopulated, except for a single driver sitting near the opposite entrance to the freeway in a garishly yellow Hummer and the state trooper behind him. "Can you drive this rig?" he asked, pushing the side door open. "I mean just get it across the tracks."

She thought about calling him unfortunate or a procrastinator or just plain stupid. For waiting until the last chance to fill the tanks at the most expensive outskirts of town, then asking her something that steamed with his frustration. But she knew why he'd come this far without saying anything since Missoula.

"I can drive it to Nebraska if you want," she said.

He lifted one crossing arm, barely raising it, as though knowing his effort was better spent behind a wheel. Its twin rose upward, and the accompanying bells and flashing lights stopped. Josie studied his outline, the thin upward crag of his body, the way his belt cut him perfectly in half. He was tired, she thought. But unwavering.

When they got back on the freeway the gauges showed they were less than a quarter tank full on each side. She hadn't bothered to look until the two gas stations he passed posted signs that they were out of fuel. It wasn't anything she wanted to think about. Just like what was happening inside her head. Things that simply came back over and over to re-visit you. That wore you down with their simple demands.

She remembered more things Robert had mentioned over the last months of his life. How he'd read an article, usually something less scientific, then recite its heartbreak in one sentence. One morning after breakfast he'd said, "Memories of my wren will stop the final beat of my heart." He paused in a kind of dreary sadness rubbing a cold coffee cup between his hands. "I wish I could've said that."

"It's too sad," she'd said. "I hope your work is more, well, enlightening. After all, you look hard for your finches. And they're still out there."

"Yes, Jo, they are. But Murray Long, one of the best, knew about extinction. Finding and knowing a bird are two different things. And then there's the extinction. The final phase. Something that can bring a man, an ornithologist, to his knees."

"What if there was a fourth stage?" she'd asked. "What if a man thought he saw the last of a kind and then months, maybe years later, someone found another? And it had a mate. Like we could be looking at with the Ivory Bill. What if sometimes there's a throw-switch, Robert? When the bird and the divine plan hook up. And in some stretch of lonely forest the bird survives."

He'd looked at her with the only description she could think of right now. It was a momentary spell, so unlike himself that she could visibly see him shiver and push it back where it belonged. "It doesn't happen," he'd said, turning his back as he poured the coffee down the kitchen sink. "No reprieves. Man is too thorough." This mystery he'd known for twenty years, now so new to her, was something insurmountable. There was no reliable witness. Not even his notes could tell her what she was experiencing.

"There are feelings that go with extinction," he'd said. "Feelings of extreme fear." Was he simply unable to separate himself from the passengers he so loved? Because what she was feeling now, about extinction, was more like an extraordinary sense of continuance. It had come through in the hallucinations. Even among the dead flock at Wilson's Bridge, the regret was strictly human, her husband's for the passengers and Colzer's for their by-product. The soft blue haze of the pigeon's laboratory world was a constant, something they'd retreated into long before and after every blood draw. It was the most natural place to die.

* * *

"We need to talk about Gem-X," she finally said. "I know the bird is trouble to you, Sterns, but one thing is right. You made the only decision you could. You gave me his serum. It probably saved my life."

Sterns hardly moved but turned on the right-hand blinker signaling miles ahead that he planned to get off at the next exit, the Little Bighorn Battlefield. The tink-tink-tink implanted itself in Josie's brain causing a slight deviation in her optimism. "But the fact is that bird is wired. Maybe you've figured that out with all your months of spying. I tried taking it off back at the Rattlesnake, but he wouldn't let me. He's a flying tattletale."

"Yeah, well, what's got my interest isn't his fascination with you. He's only doing what he was trained to do. What I can't figure out is your obsession with him. Ever since I gave you the injection you've gone on and on about seeing him or knowing he was around. So what, Josie? He's just a goddamned trained bird. An extinct one, to be sure, but really, what can he possibly mean to you? People the world over have been given Pass-Flu for months, and they don't come unhinged every time they see a pigeon. In fact, they don't even know what they've taken to get them through. So tell me, since you want to talk . . . tell me why he's so important to you. I mean aside from the fact he's telling somebody right now exactly where we are."

She could hear now where his thoughts had been all those hours on the road. What he'd been thinking about besides pressing forward into doubt and a long, thin line of traffic. She didn't know if she could keep up with him. But really, she thought, the job would be for him to keep up with what she was about to say.

"I keep being reminded of the only thing I was supposed to be. And, you know, I failed even at that. I was supposed to be the control. That's a simple thing. Just the average, non-stimulating control. But control of what? Not my marriage. I lost that. Not the bird. He's an opportunist and totally out of bounds. Not this trip. You're the one in charge, and you could leave me or turn around anywhere along the line. I'm not even in control of myself. I think . . . No, I'm convinced I had bird flu. I think I'm better because of what you did. But I've had the craziest dreams of my life. I've been somewhere else far too long, Sterns. Somewhere inside another's dream. I've watched my companions die and curiously followed Gem-X's escape."

"What do you mean, watched?" Sterns asked, getting a look on his face like he was about to enter yet another hallucination-by-proxy.

"To Gem-X escape was never the goal. Training was the goal. In order to fly the route, he had to withstand Colzer's technology. He waited through inoculations, blood draws, the excessive handling for a clamp that sleeved his leg. The pattern would begin with let's call it beads. Beads of light. In dreams I've seen them pulsating against the horizon. Pearly dots of quick light. Something that incited his curious nature. Maybe triggered some dim collective memory. Over and over before the beads evaporated he knew the height of mid-summer sun. So that when the trainer, my husband, no longer brought him to the beads he followed a track-line he'd memorized. Something mapped inside."

"He began eating biliously. Bugs in the aviary became addictive. He dehorned slugs and bored through acorns while he waited. And then, the morning after you showed him to me, he found the trigger. It wasn't me, Sterns. It was the solstice. June twenty-first at the Powder Medicine Wheel in Wyoming. That's what Robert used to start the training every day for months. Aldebaran, bull's eye of the constellation Taurus. The quick light of a perfectly photographed dawn." Josie considered her perspective, now so clear, and what an aberration it was becoming as she related it to Sterns.

She wanted him to look for her explanation, to search hard to believe it, yet he seemed to concentrate even more on what was in front of them. He squinted into the subduing light and pulled down his visor.

"It took me a while to figure it out. Because it didn't all come pieced together so tidily. Gem-X had to train me. And he did it his way, just like Robert did with him. In my flu-dreams when I went to this other place at first I was a stranger unable to feel the only thing I can describe as familiarity. It came to me in clips, segments I can only describe as intense determination. There was light and then an absence of it. There would be a descent slow and steady into a cave where the slightest impatience would mean forgetting the way back out. Sometimes light moved away, sometimes toward, a fusion of color and motion but always darkness at the center. He was alone, Sterns. Steering toward the cold, dark eye of a plague. He was doing it for months. For so long, I guess, that his serum became something of a truth serum. The control I've become is not what my husband intended. He had no idea it would be his training coming full circle. Through something mankind mined from a bird."

She stopped, feeling herself as tightly wound as the day she'd first met him. She was dumping a lot of data, forming words where only sensation had been. It sounded like she was on some fatal cocktail of hallucinogens, just getting out the words before they melted into reality or fractured into death. But it was time for Sterns to listen to what he'd started, even if it furthered his regret. Because he still wasn't allowing her absurd reaction to take shape, to give it a name. He didn't have a clue what she was thanking him for.

"I don't know why it's me. If Pass-Flu has these side effects then, you're right, why haven't we heard about them? I can only suggest that this is the grid my husband created between himself and Gem-X. This feeling of extinction, as he called it. Perhaps the serum, at least from this one bird, is a conduit to the past. Something we've never been able to do before, to look at the 1918 flu up close. But it's here now, among us, as close now as it was the first time. Maybe it caused the final die-out of these birds. Maybe, from one point of view, it's worth mentioning what that world was like."

The battlefield was a little over two miles away. She looked ahead across the stark, weather-scoured ridges, mere grooves that, even yet, concealed matters between Indians and a cavalry on a June day in 1876 and momentarily wondered about what she couldn't see there. A place as mysterious as Wilson's Bridge had been studied and rehashed at least once a decade since the battle itself, and still men couldn't come to terms on exactly what happened there. It was interesting, she thought, that the whole thing had started with one chieftain's vision.

As if he'd distilled her description down to something he could verbalize, Sterns said, "You're still in love with your husband, aren't you? It's right in the middle of everything you just said." He slowed down even more, pulling away from the ambulance in front of him and pushing headlong across one of the ridges to Garryowen.

"First you called him the trainer, then your husband. I know who he was, Josie," he said, steering into a line of pumps at the Hunkpapa Trading Post. Leaving the truck running, Sterns turned his back to begin the walk inside. Even so, she could hear him say, "And he's still all that and then some to you."

She sat there looking at the mixture of quick stop, rest area, and historical marker. A small group of men had cordoned off what seemed to be a perfect circle to one side of the trading post, huddled inside a ring of separate, evenly placed flags, each staked in the ground to about the level of their shoulders. The flags' four colors kept repeating themselves. White, green, black, and gold. The men were Sioux, she was sure. The colors were unmistakably what the meeting was about. This country was sacred, all of it, from the Black Hills to the Powder Medicine Wheel. And this battlefield, in particular, was alive with spirits. Theirs was a declaration of a place of beginning. In the middle of disease and on the outskirts of deadly fire, these men went back to the Medicine Wheel, even if it was in the shadow of a convenience store. They would probably be there for days, if they hadn't been already.

Sterns pumped fuel. He took a long time filling the mains and reserves, even an auxiliary tank in the truck bed, periodically craning his head inside the cab to check gauges and tapping the last drops from the nozzle with a hideous clank. He didn't say anything. No offers of refreshment or advice on how long it could be before the next break. Just the overhead radio broadcast kept time with his anxious fueling.

"Black Hills Fire . . . Estimating already a million acres . . . Mostly south and eastward moving . . . Fastest, hottest inferno since 1910 and similar in place and character. Few resources, but individuals are digging trenches around communities. There's some National Guard outside Rapid City. Have saved only half the metro area. Now spreading already thin troops to Scottsbluff, Nebraska, with even further extension to Cheyenne, Wyoming, and Denver. Evacuations imminent, particularly flu-stricken. Any fire fighting vehicles, equipment and healthy qualified personnel are asked to contact local command centers."

"How many more miles to Darby?" Sterns busied himself pulling switches in front of him, his hands moving about the dashboard in hurried skill. The air bristled, electrified as though when he re-entered the cab he was ready to let go, to scream if he had to. "Or didn't the bird tell you that?"

She could see the gates to the battlefield had been closed and padlocked. Little was open in Montana any more. Graveyards were as desolate as shopping malls. Right now, they were only a reminder of a privileged past where even the defeated were named on headstones. It would take an inferno to cleanse the earth for the next generation. The "Autoclave" some people were calling the Black Hills Fire. A purification from a viral monster that some said they welcomed.

"I don't think Darby is where we need to go right now. I might as well tell you, seeing as how we've come to this anyway."

"You mean you've been changing your mind in the middle of hallucinating? The bird's decided to go to Halifax maybe? I'm pointing this rig to Darby, just like I did hundreds of miles back. So, let me tell you something now," he said pointing toward the deepening glow on the horizon.

"I don't like fire. More than most. Have spent most of my life working from the other direction, making cuts, thinning, pulling out the slash. But right now, right this very minute, I've come this far. Not for me. For you. The very reason I got involved. That first minute I laid eyes on you, all wet and befuddled, and then I showed you something I should've walked away from months before. Robert warned me to stay away. But no, I had to keep hoisting my ass up that tree. And then, I'm sure, we got caught. Not because anything was any different, except for that bird that's overtaken your brain. I gave you his serum, I packed you across country, I listened to your stories, real or unreal. And now I'm hearing all this mystical shit."

"I hope it's not too late for you." Sterns' voice softened as he found an open stretch of road, a place where the wind swerved around behind them and barely helped them past fifty miles an hour. "I've prayed for miles I haven't destroyed your brain. What you know would take me the rest of my life to learn, and that's without this entire incident. But now, I don't know. Visions. Hell, the only vision out there is the god-forsaken passenger blipping away on somebody's screen. If you're following him, you're losing us, Josie. To my way of thinking there's only one choice. If the old man knows the real story, you deserve to know it. If he doesn't, then you've seen through your husband's dream or at least part of it. And that's what this is all about. You and your husband."

It seemed to her that Sterns had mulled over what he'd seen at the bathhouse. That all the miles of suffering she'd put him through paled in comparison to two brief moments for him. One of them he'd just mentioned—taking her up the tree. But the other, she knew was at the soul of his claim. This wasn't about Robert anymore. It was about a man who'd offered her something she'd never experienced. The spareness of his love, the empty edges that might never be recognized. In fact, he was concealing it under a new layer. Drawing her away from his heart. Something other men through history were famous for.

"Speak for yourself," she said.

"You're not ready for it," he said so quickly she knew she'd glimpsed something abiding, perhaps relentless.

"Yes, I am. I've known since the Rattlesnake, maybe longer. Maybe I knew from the moment you sat next to me on the platform. I knew, Sterns. I just haven't seen it like this before."

Sterns looked at her across the wide expanse of the cab. The furrow between his eyes didn't lighten nor did his resolve. "I can't promise you anything worth having except what's happening right now. This is what I can give you. This trip, however you want it. Whatever it takes. It's worth it to me. Just to be here."

CHAPTER 30

He'd said so much in so little time that Sterns felt himself flailing. A sensation as if his foothold had been reduced to pumping air, then clamping his bare shins against a swaying six hundred foot Doug fir. He was out of control over this woman. And she knew it without him uttering a word.

She was on the verge of asking him something, and now he was apt to oblige her, even if it was based on nothing but her insight. He was going to put more at risk. But it was happening anyway. The gas tanks he'd taken so much time with were only about a quarter full. He re-distributed most of the fuel to keep it balanced and had concentrated on filling the tank in the truck bed with another twenty-five gallons. But, truth was, he'd drained the pumps at Garryowen, and they'd charged him just over nine dollars a gallon because he had. It might be they'd make it only a few more miles anyway. A wall of darkness was heading them off, dissecting the Great Plains into a deepening bloom of tangerine. Lightening strikes tracked through opposing colors uniting earth and sky in sizzling strands of ignition. The fire was feeding.

During the silent, introspect miles Sterns had vacillated between the thought of a flame-engulfed future and the 1910 fire he'd learned about in his youth. It was an odd comparison, not only for its combustibility but for the year it happened. Parallels kept linking this time with a comparable ten-year stretch a century before extinction of the passengers in 1914, the Spanish influenza in 1918, an oft-forgotten world war during that same period, and a fire that redefined the terror of wildfire fighting. He wondered if he should tell her what he knew. If she would tell him to turn around now and face the rest of her life on the other side of annihilation.

"We're coming up on the Wyoming border," he said. "I don't know what you have in mind, but I can't just pretend this is going to be easy. They could have a turn-around there. An option to turn back. But my guess is traffic is just going to get worse at Sheridan. More fire fighting stuff. Any equipment they can truck in. This is no California fire. Maybe a few helicopters, if we're lucky. It's too big, Josie. It'll slam the Midwest. It's too goddamned dry out there."

He didn't want to look at her, not even once more. He kept remembering the fire he'd been trained on, the one every hotshot remembered just by the ax he carried. He kept thinking about graves the color of lampblack. The way they'd faded into an overgrowth of red cedars, untended amid lady fern and Solomon's seal. Forty granite markers on the outside, seventeen on the inside. A wheel within a wheel.

"You've heard of the fire of 1910?" he said, asking, but sure that she had. "Obviously, I wasn't there. But if this is like that one, it's hard tellin' where it will end. That one merged over a thousand fires in Idaho, Montana, and Washington. The men fighting it wet down everything they could. They covered their horses' heads with wet blankets, and the fire fighters, sometimes at gunpoint, were forced to lie down in creeks with other blankets over their heads. Some of them went mad enough to dance around and sing. Others saw floating bodies of fish suffocated by ash in the water. Wind so strong it threw burning bark, shards of trees. Cedars, trees that hold tons of water, burned hot enough to explode. Sane, healthy men died. At least fifty-seven of them. It didn't happen in the middle of a plague, Josie. It happened on two hot summer days."

Sterns heard her rustle in her seat, pulling the seat belt two or three times as far as she could, then letting it snap back against her. He wondered what he was doing to her, holding her mind as close to flame as he was.

"I know. I know," she said, her voice strained, higher pitched than he'd ever heard. "Believe it or not that scares me less than what's following us. When I talked to Hennings he said a blond man is tracking us. The fire is moving away east and south. This tracker, whoever he is won't stop. I've got to get the transmitter off Gem-X. That's what Hennings said."

"Shee-it," Sterns replied. "He'll risk every life left on the planet to save his birds. I'll go as far as you want, but not because he says so. And not because some hitman is crazy enough to chase through this hellfire because Hennings says he will. Don't you see, Josie? Everything points to Darby. The experiment, maybe even some dumb-ass tracker. All I know is I said I'd take you there. In the middle of flu and in spite of my own doubt. It doesn't matter whether you take the transmitter off. The bird is making his way through this, and so is the serum. And thanks to me a vial of it's in you."

"Don't let it get in the way," she said. "You've been letting that run the show since you gave it to me. I could be dead if it weren't for you. No one else was here to do it. Maybe no one else would've. Maybe not even Robert."

"But that's who was meant to do it," he said. "That's why there were two of them. For him and you."

"And now, you could be the one," she said. "I've thought about it, Sterns. You could take the other vial. Maybe if you did, you'd see what I see. You'd understand that whatever strategy is happening out there doesn't decide the end. It's too late to reason out why this happened. Pouring over Robert's notes is the closest we're going to come to knowing what made him do what he did. The only thing Hennings can tell me now is what will happen to the ones who are left. The real passengers. If we get tracked down, I want it to be because Colzer just got lucky. And they've got to work hard to get lucky twice. Robert was easy to kill. In fact, I think he was expecting it. That's not for me, Sterns. Or for you."

He could smell it now, the rank beginnings of fire, its spill-over fuming through the atmosphere. Still just a far-off, mind-numbing warning, but enough to set him firmly in the middle of a forest scratch line. "If it's not Darby, where is it?" he said.

"The medicine wheel, the one at Two-Dot, where Robert took me four years ago. It's where Gem-X will go. Where it all began for him. He's been keeping up with us. I know, because I've seen him in the awning above the trailer's window. Sometimes he's so close the signal is right above our heads. We could lose the tracker by just turning off early and trashing the antenna. And then go on."

"What about the bird?" Sterns said, wondering what she was really thinking behind the solid, reasonable plan. "Even if you can get his wire off you're setting yourself up. He might not make it, but he might come close, and you'll never know. Neither will Hennings."

"He'll make it. If there's any possible air current that will carry him, he'll make it. He's not anchored to the training route anymore. In my dreams, I've seen some of where he's going. Somehow felt his strange aerial passion. He's no longer an object of submission. He's free-flying. And it's happening more and more."

Traffic had bunched together, platelets on a road winding its way toward a bleed-out of men and equipment. She didn't know what a grass fire could do. How it could spiral a thousand feet in the air, gusting into devils that spawned more funnels, and move faster than a running man for hundreds of miles. She hadn't seen animals scorched, their hooves melted into shapeless ooze. Or birds fall from the sky, dismembered as if from a giant burning hand. Survival would be minimal and only for those who embedded themselves in the few, unnamed islands between torchings. Not likely for a laboratory bird on his maiden voyage. "You believe in miracles, don't you?" he said.

"I told you that hundreds of miles back when I discovered Gem-X was with us. My mother used to tell me we don't trust each other, and because we don't, a line for every painful experience will show in our face. Look at me, Sterns," she said, "I wonder, is there even one sign left of where the flu used to be?"

*   *   *

He watched her now standing outside a barn admiring three quilts, all of them flecked in some arrangement of red, white or blue. Two-Dot wasn't sparing its finest handwork, even if it was draped over a paddock door. Oddly, there were no price tags, but if somebody wanted something badly enough, a quilt, a jar of honey, a bag of homemade pretzels, all they had to do was ask the town's minister, Prestonia. She'd likely give it to them and tell them to keep the recipe or the pattern and someday make more just like it. There'd be some who'd do just that, she told people. "It's not very often a whole town dies."

They'd gotten there about mid-afternoon. Tucked on an inside ridge of the Bighorns, Two-Dot wasn't much. A couple blocks of worn-out buildings, a gas station that doubled as a funeral home, and a dispensary on the backside of the post office. Even if the sky had continued to pronounce the world going up in flames, there was a feeling here of deliberate reserve. Maybe through the years they'd experienced shelter through most any storm and simply traded one day for another, not anticipating intervention of any kind. For whatever reason, a big blue hole sat directly over the town and through that hole came a sizable amount of sunshine. It was a gamble, Sterns thought, to stay here very long.

They'd driven in through a winding valley that reflected the course of the Powder River. It broadened as it diverted to the side of the sleepy town, establishing remnants of trickling water and the croak of pond frogs. Three huge grain elevators clustered on the outskirts leading to the rodeo grounds, grounds that also paralleled the river. It was here where once a day everyone gathered. And it was here where Sterns made camp.

Josie, indeed, didn't have a mark on her face. The flu that had frayed her mind and deadened the spark of her eyes had retreated. What was left was a woman he'd never seen until now. He did look at her, a couple times for a very long time. Once she caught him and smiled back, not impulsively but with the corners of her mouth slightly pouted. She put a finger to where the sore had been, then shrugged her shoulders. It was over, she seemed to say. That part was over.

He went back to the truck and pulled a section of the handbook on fuel consumption. The trailer was a liability they could no longer afford. It was an expense, and it was a target. So he began the business of unhooking. He went inside and tried to account for what they couldn't live without. All the while Sterns watched the river road that was the only noticeable way to the campground, and just once he checked the awning over the front window. Both were empty. Mostly he gathered blankets and shovels, rope and a couple buckets, then moved his climbing gear from the truck back to the trailer. It was the feeling of being a settler in the new millennium. Trading off his life for the unknown.

It, however, wasn't all unknown. Earlier on the road, she'd seen it first. The yellow Hummer in front of them, weaving back and forth, crossing into oncoming traffic coming out of the south, then back again. Just two cars ahead, a blond man kept leaning out his window and sometimes pounded the side of his car with a clenched fist. Once he threw what looked like a folded-up map out his side window. If he hung out there too long traffic started to slow, and Josie would lose sight of him swinging back in and onto the shoulder. But Sterns could see him unbuckling his seat harness, protruding from the window like a yellow-headed wingwalker. "He looks like that idiot, Custer," he said.

"Wasn't he back there?" Josie said, throwing a hand over the back seat. "Wasn't he at the Billings stop? You know, the one with the cop behind him?"

"Yeah, I remember. Pretty obvious the cop should've slapped him with a DWI."

"I don't think drinking's the problem. I think we're the problem," she said, holding onto the place she'd just grabbed.

"He's the one?" Sterns asked, rubbing the back of his neck, then studying the quarter-mile marker to Two-Dot.

"Yes," she said so low he wasn't sure she'd answered.

"You're sure," he said one last time as he climbed the F-250 toward the lazy S-overpass to the Powder River. "To the medicine wheel?" he asked.

"Yes," she repeated, barely nodding her head.

It was that turn off the road where the whole thing had changed. One horse, nose-high to a barbed wire fence studied their progress, his heart beating just fast enough for him to turn his head when they passed. Slumped mounds burdened heavy with grass were becoming the saturated green of a river bottom. The town of a Wyoming highland would become a momentary shelter. And Sterns was sure this might be the only place left to spend time with the woman who'd overtaken his life.

CHAPTER 31

The cell phone showed a nervous orb dancing across the screen, a call that moved between Pritchard and his daughter. She probably wouldn't pick it up, in which case her voice would connect with him in soft, timeless humor. "Please leave your number, darling. I don't want to be alone." He wanted her to change the greeting, had for months. It always stirred up an admission in him. That he'd left her too soon and for the wrong reasons and that, even yet, he was still wasting time.

"Not for long," he said into her voice mail. "I'm not sure what's happening there, but don't let Colzer-Bremen shake you up. Taking care of business, that's what I'm doing, Rach. It's never enough though. You know how it is. You and Mom, just keep doin' what your doin'. I'm going to be back in less than a day, My Lady. No flu, no fire, no feeble-minded boss is keeping me away. The pills . . ." he added, "Just don't stop taking the pills."

He could feel twinges, nerves that pulsed then relaxed. He didn't know if he could trust his right leg on the accelerator, then moved one buttock onto the console in an attempt to reach the pedal with his left foot. "God damn circus act," he said, settling back into the seat, then pulled the emergency brake while he stomped the two floor pedals intermittently. The Hummer glanced off the side of a guard rail, then gripped the shoulder in paralysis. Unable to see the cut-off behind him, Pritchard got out of his car and stepped into the middle of the highway. The exit, lined in white metal girders, reminded him of a delegation of starch-coated hospital personnel no longer dutiful members of a medical promise. *First do no harm*, drifted through his mind. Then, *First to take the serum.*

Pritchard pulled hard on his right leg, dragging it along the pavement as though he was offsetting a charley horse. Keeping it on the center line, he paced the distance between him and the motionless fire truck in front of him, then decided to make another phone call, this time to 911.

"Emergency status only. We're on stand-by," a voice said. "Please state your emergency."

"Yeah, out here on Highway 25, about a quarter mile past Powder River exit. Collision." Without compunction, Pritchard added, "At least one injured. We need ambulance from closest town. Like stat."

"That'll be coming in from Two-Dot," the voice said. "Make way for a red Jeep Cherokee that should be there in about twenty minutes. Medical equipment and personnel on board. Can you keep situation under control?"

Pritchard pinched the furrow between his eyes, then, as if aligning his whole body, propped his legs together in a stiff salute. Still facing the cut-off, he smiled. "By all means," he said. "Two-Dot? How far's that?"

"About fourteen miles. Steep terrain. Sometimes rock slides."

"Well, just get here," he said, re-entering the Hummer and starting to pull into traffic.

He wondered how soon the Cherokee would meet the F-250. How they would simply pass, a trade, one for the other, never knowing they were each fulfilling one man's scheme, giving him a location and log jamming the heartfelt practice of rural medicine at the same time. The system, Pritchard knew, was strained. That 911 was even answering out here was phenomenal. But it told him one more time medicine was always begged for, never the beggar. And it goaded him that any American citizen, even a lying one, could demand a medical priority. "God help 'em with their Jeep ambulance," he said, reaching across the seat to turn up the receiver. "Ain't going to protect 'em from dying like sissies."

Suddenly, Pritchard heard an ear-cracking screech. With the downturn of a button, the steady ping faded into the overstuffed pads of the Hummer's seats, but there was no doubting what it meant. The bird was probably easily noticeable, perhaps no more than a car-length away. Cat-and-mouse, he thought. Chiding or maybe flu-ravaged. The thought came to him of once seeing a cormorant polished in oil walk purposefully away from his life toward a desert hot with death. This bird was really no better off, just for the moment less pitiful, still flying his tangled destiny.

Confusion broke loose in front of him. Someone screamed, "Jesus Christ, what's the matter with that thing?" It wasn't easy to see, so he climbed out, keeping his hand on the side window, following the heads of onlookers. Nothing, he thought. Just people on the edge of fire, watching its promise trail across the sky in billowing smudge. He realized the heads in front of him had turned and were holding a course directly in line with his. It was then he sensed something approaching from the right as streamlined as a collapsed umbrella that shot wide open as it approached his temple. His face tingled, as if every nerve ending had been spliced. Everybody waited, and Pritchard waved a hand in front of his eyes, clearing up any misconception, then realized he'd been declared the target.

The passenger came at him from the opposite direction, gaining speed from a sweeping arc. As the bird pushed forward, Pritchard realized he was full throttle and turned his back hoping to get in the car before impact. He looked over his shoulder, clipping his nose with the Hummer door, then saw the leg antenna sheer across the upper left side of the windshield. He crunched into the seat, leaned forward, and for one brief moment accelerated. Too late, he realized the bird's maneuver had diverted his attention. Pritchard ran his hand alongside his face, feeling for blood, then saw the truck's headlights blink off-and-on just before the Hummer slid down the side of the Great Harvest tractor-trailer in a sideswipe choreographed to end at the truck's rear axle. An involuntary shudder passed through the car's frame as it settled, hood open, eye level to the mountains in front of him. And on that hood perched Gem-X, an acrobat coming to rest directly in front of his intended audience, his blue powdered head craned forward as if inspecting for damage.

No one had prepared Pritchard for this kind of attack. It wasn't something so fleeting he could tell himself he'd imagined it. The passenger continued to preen, rolling his head to one side as if it was skewered to his upper wing, and in that position he blinked and opened his mouth. The thin membrane around his eye intensified like a small red garnet. He was close enough to stab with a back scratcher, but Pritchard knew the bird was lined up with the most prevailing wind gust, merely tantalizing.

"You all right?" a man asked. "I kept thinkin' you was just pushing your nose out to get a look at that fucked up bird." Pritchard could sense hesitation, then the trucker added, "Shit, is that the son-of-a-gun?"

Gem-X continued to concentrate on cleaning, slicing through down, separating flight feathers with cautious preoccupation. Yet, somehow Pritchard knew this wasn't a ritual, at least not on the hood of his car. "That there's a flu sentinel," he said to the trucker. "My guess is he's not sick enough to keel over but goofy enough to be contagious. Nothing normal would do that."

The Great Harvest man backed away, steadying himself on the side of his truck, then vaulted into his cab. It was tempting, Pritchard thought, to just sit there and see how long the bird would continue to entertain. But traffic was nervous, and hesitation would only bring on more onlookers. The pigeon was not able to calculate, he was sure. An idea passed through Pritchard's overly saturated mind, however, and he decided to give the bird a taste of his own past.

Finding Russo's fourth CD, he plugged it into the laptop, bringing up the aerial landscape identified as Sheridan, Wyoming. At times the view would be from a thousand, two thousand feet and other times it was road level. He identified the mountain range beside him and even thought he saw an interrupted ribbon of the Powder River. Slowly, he lifted the laptop, screen outward through his window. Gem-X took little heed.

"Here birdy, here's a refresher course." Pritchard balanced the laptop using both hands to hold it alongside him. A man-made satellite dish came to mind, and for a moment he considered how inane he looked. But there was a visible reaction in the bird, an excitement or perhaps agitation. He scratched the leading edge of the hood, then propelled himself upward, almost like being lifted by a string. Pritchard wondered if he suddenly realized he was off course and was winding himself up, spindle-like, to an exact heading. Whatever was happening, the event served another purpose entirely. As he brought the laptop back into view he could see the exit that now coiled away into the Bighorns, where it led into a town named Two-Dot and a medicine wheel on the outskirts of the community. In fact, Russo had inserted a long view of the wheel's uneven stones, the way they pocked the land. Then the lens left the ground, and the stones had the symmetry of mushrooms. And, finally, from fifteen hundred feet the wheel became a cylinder that shimmered in daylight, an illusion of a slow spin, like a space station. Pritchard took it in and realized Josephine Russo was not only holding to her husband's dream, it appeared she was revisiting it frame by frame.

When he left the freeway, he was doing forty miles an hour. He'd driven down the wrong side for as long as he could, the yellow hood bouncing, cutting his view into short clips that provided windows into his future. Another truck got closer, then disappeared into a cloud of gravel as Pritchard veered into the golden long-stem that clumped as thick as a dog's winter pelt. He had the sensation of skidding from mound to mound, a space man free of the shuttle, holding on by a thin umbilical cord. He saw the sign to Two-Dot.

Elsa would never get here, he thought. She'd expect everything to come together at Darby where she'd puncture a couple of dreams. It wasn't in her to let someone else, something else lead the way. As he drove a line to the Powder River exit, Pritchard watched a million birds lift from a catch basin right below the rim of the overpass. They rose in a membranous circle, a tide of bodies that spread from the close weave of kinship. There was a vast uncertainty in the air, he thought. An impatience he would have to guard against or he might never see his daughter again.

CHAPTER 32

"Come with me," she said to Sterns, who kept pulling chain from the back of the truck. Finally, he withdrew a tool, an ax at one end and pick at the other. "The Pulaski," he said. "It goes with us."

"You don't mean to stop him with that?" Josie said reflexively.

"Not planning to. But the trailer has to stay. And it's one more way to even the odds."

She forced herself to consider his priorities. Moving his life from one rig to another. Gathering blunt instruments to defend against deranged impulse.

"Yes, you do plan on stopping him . . . it . . . the mess we're in. You know how I know?"

"Nope," he answered, throwing the whole works behind the driver's seat.

"Because you didn't push me out at Lookout or the Rattlesnake or St. Pats. You knew it would come to this. Somebody would want something connected to me. And now you. You're connected to me."

His stride back to her quickened. But he didn't change his pattern except to pull Robert's head rag from under his belt. "Here's the real connection," he said. "To both of us."

"A few minutes, Sterns," she said, smoothing the material between her hands, then pulling her backpack from the floorboard. "We have some time. Really, I believe that." She thought of the way it was lining up, a bizarre chase dependent on the turnings of a bird. His predictability could be traced moment-by-moment, minimized into fractions of light that spread, then re-aligned into a single beacon accurate enough to guide the path of a maniacal tracker.

They stood at a place where the Powder River came toward them, not straight on, but completely at ease in a gentle, hidden percolation between banks, lapping over warm rocks and the drone of insects. An arena emerged from the river's edge, a natural landing that might've begun as a set of picnic tables or a willow kids tied a rope to, then launched into a hole dark with pencil-thin trout. It was impossible to avoid, even now that it was being swallowed once again by its ancestral foliage. Sagebrush tinged the squared off edges of the grounds, thinning out to wild geranium and dandelion. Fence rails formed two corrals at one end, and a chute, gate open, was left suspended from the backside of a couple rows of bleachers. Even so, there was a long-ago feeling this had been the crown jewel of the town. For now, two signs stretched across the arena's midsection. *Jubilee with Everything You've Got*, one said, and the other, written in the scrawl of thin rope, *Horseshoes Will Take You to Heaven*.

"We've come to a nice little town," she said. "I don't remember it from before. But I know we were here. At least passed through. The medicine wheel . . . it's over there." She pointed off the far side of the arena, away from town, toward a point of rising ground. "I'd ask you to come with me, but I know you're not in favor of getting too close to the passenger."

"This isn't my decision." Sterns put a hand in his pocket, then extended the crook of his arm to her. "Your bird, if he's there, is showing up because of training. Or maybe because of you. We both know the best way to send him the other way is to bring me along. Is that what you really want?"

She could feel him lengthen his stride. She wondered if he was as aware as she was of the brief reality right in front of them. That this was the closest moment, maybe the only one, in which she'd been able to pull him out of his orbit, out from under the imposing shadow of her husband's influence. It wasn't intentional, she told herself. But it was strangely liberating, as if she'd found someone who knew her long before Robert did.

"You know I'm really kind of jealous. That bird over there," Sterns said, nodding toward the trees, "He's always going to mean more than I ever bargained for."

"I know," she said. "But I'm jealous too. You had something with my husband in just a few short moments that I never had. He warned you. But he also confided in you. With me he discussed the poetic injustices of wrens and the indiscriminate sightings of Ivory-Bills. But with you he talked of passengers, no matter what the context. You were the haven of a stranger. I wonder what he'd have done if I'd stood one night with a toothbrush in my hand and said, 'Sweetheart, how many times do you expect to run that video before he gets it all figured out? When will you trust that bird to his own devices?'"

"He might've told you everything," Sterns said, slowly making his way to a small building at the furthest edge of the arena. "And everything might've been too much."

"You know," she said, "It turned out to be too much anyway. I doubted him, Sterns. I picked up on the cues and twisted them. I thought he was having an affair. When I walked into those woods on the peninsula I was convinced he might've died trying to get to another woman. For God sakes, not another bird." She could feel her voice tremble remembering her mother's tirade, masked low, behind the kitchen counter where Robert would never hear.

Sterns brought her up to the small woman she'd seen earlier, the woman named Prestonia, who was waking up the chihuahua in her lap and tapping a microphone as big as he was. There was obvious affection between the woman and her pet as if they'd worked this rodeo many times, stuffed in the dusty shack on the outskirts of arrogant bulls and horses tied to men in configurations nobody understood. Today, she was manning the rodeo by herself, calling the rides she'd remembered over her lifetime. It was peculiar witnessing her lonely showmanship, and Josie kept looking for at least one horse and rider, even another spectator. But no one arrived, and Prestonia continued as if it really didn't matter. "Between mountains and the Great Plains," she began, her voice belting across the expanse in front of her. "Betwixt man and animal. There's a place that will touch your heart or chill you to the bone. And that place is the Two-Dot rodeo, folks. That place is right here."

Prestonia took a long breath and smiled with the kind of mouth that showed even, gleaming teeth pressed into a stable chin. Her neck and eyes matched a chronically sunburned woman. Skin folds overtook in those places, but didn't distract from her face which remained balanced by the prominent blue of her eyes. It was these that she focused on Sterns. "You're a horseman, aren't you?"

"Yes, ma'am. Belgians."

"Oh good horses," she said, "Deliberate."

"Pull logs in a rain forest," he said.

"Well, then, they're real deliberate." She laughed and asked what had brought them to her rodeo.

"I'm going to the medicine wheel," Josie said. "Saw it one summer about four years ago and wondered if it's changed."

"Oh, it just stays the holiest place there's ever been. You going to the wheel too?" she asked Sterns, concentrating on him once again.

"No," he said. "I got a job to finish back there." He pointed over his shoulder in the opposite direction.

"What little story can I tell you in these times that'll help young folks like you? She's going to the Wheel. You're goin' to your truck. You's either about to be married or never goin' to be."

Josie could feel how he pressed her hand to his rib cage. How still he was, holding that one part of her to the sparest part of his body.

"Oh I don't know about that," he said. "She's been my teacher more than anything. I don't know if she'd ever consider marriage, at least to me."

It seemed to Josie it just happened that way with men. They could tell someone else in one sentence everything they couldn't tell her. She grasped his arm, brushing it quickly against the side of her breast. "Some things take a while," she said. "Like waiting for someone to level with you."

The rodeo queen smiled again, this time picking up her dog and squeezing him into the front of her red and black shirt. She turned up the microphone and looked across the empty arena that comprised Two-Dot's rodeo. "Ebony Black," she said. "Remember him? Famous stock horse of the 1940s. Man by the name of Valdez trained him. I'm old enough to remember that," she said, pushing her hat back in a manner that conveyed confidence, almost belligerence. She looked beyond Sterns, yet Josie knew this story was for him. A way to make him an indelible part of her world—of horses and men.

"Val taught by repetition. Persistent but gentle. The horse converted all that training to reflex because he could use all his senses. Whispering? Maybe. But I think Val sometimes just let the horse think for hisself. He didn't over exert. Everything was positioned between the two of them in pure efficiency."

"Then," she said, pausing and thrumming her hand on the mike, "There came the National Horse Show in Santa Barbara about '45 or '46. Working cow horse class. Valdez and Ebony Night stood center ring without a move. At the far end of the ring a big steer come through. Big horns. Big everything. Went right to the ring's center. Every time the steer aimed to get by, Valdez and the horse would stop him. A fence or Ebony Night. Both of them pissed off that animal, and he made a drop-head move. Val swung that horse completely around and threw him against the side of the steer, then spun Ebony around so he could knock him from the other side. It was enough for that bovine. Bawled and ran clean the other way. One for the scorekeepers, I tell you." Prestonia thrummed the mike again, then brought the shivering dog from somewhere inside her cleavage. She placed his paws together in a quick clap.

"My audience day after day," she said. "Might be the only one left to listen before long." Prestonia paused, wrapping her friend in a soft lap blanket. "Two-Dot's not goin' down easy. We keep to the daily life. But, God O'Mercy, we've lost a lot of good folks. I see a man and woman like you, and I hope there's a world to start over again when this is through."

Sterns seemed to follow her sadness, reaching across the short ticket counter to clasp her wrist. "It can't last much longer," was all he said. There was detachment, Josie thought, a deliberate touch without offering hope. The comfort, she thought, lay behind him in a place where he'd avoided the flu's destruction for months, not at this junction with pandemic and its solitary victims. In a single motion, as he withdrew from Prestonia, he wrapped the same hand around Josie's arm and began to turn toward the trailer.

"I can't," she said. "Not before I see this through."

Slowly, Sterns began to retrace his steps, moving away from her but drawing her into a conversation she'd started only moments before. She sensed this was where he was out-maneuvering her, perhaps what he'd been planning for mile upon mile of silence.

"You said you thought Robert was having an affair. He was, Josie. He was involved with a bird, a species without hope. He couldn't leave their side. I know that, but it's taken a long time to understand why he spared you. I couldn't understand that for the longest time," he said, as if taking one last look at his own delusion, the way things were fifteen hundred miles ago. "That's because I hadn't thought about love, old love, for a long time."

He began again, holding his body still, his hands straight down now, open and unaccusing. "Something happens during love, doesn't it? Something unexpected. Sometimes it's hard times. Or a baby. Or too many opportunities. Or not enough. But wear and tear, it takes over. It can scour you out. Even so, it leaves you with a memory. Call it approval. That no matter what you did wrong, you always did enough to make up for it. It can take a long time to hear that approval when everything's ending. God, how you don't want it to end."

"I never wanted to go through it again," he said, his voice low and strangely preoccupied. "Losing someone, a woman who's been sick. Giving it all up. Where you wanted to go with her, sleeping with her the rest of your life. First you want it to go away. Then you want it to be you, not her. Then you watch what you can't stop. When I left Missoula twenty-some years ago it wasn't just because of Mark's death. She was alive then yet. There was always room for a miracle, I told myself. I might come in and find her sitting up in bed one day, asking me to help her on with her slippers. You know, crazy as it sounds, that's just about what happened. One morning she was just sitting there, and I told her what

I thought happened to Mark. She looked at me with a kind of gentle wisdom, I'd call it. 'Don't wait to find out,' she said. 'Don't let this moment take over your life.'"

"I'm going back to the truck," Sterns said, his reflection stark and predominating as if he'd mastered the words without uttering them until now. "Your husband knew, Josie. He knew if he once started telling you of this unbelievable plan he was part of he'd never be able to stop. You'd have known every idea, every hope. You'd have been sworn to secrecy until the world was ready to know. And we know that's not going to happen, is it? The world's not ready to know."

She nodded her head but held the rest of herself still, entranced by his admittance.

"He gave you the vials. He knew what it could do to you. But he didn't know what it would do for you. The gift in all this isn't the serum or the bird or even my having had a chance to be with you. It's the power of a man's dream. How it spins and reforms long after he's gone. How it moves through time taking his wife with it. She learns and she teaches. All of it . . . began with him."

He was so calm, she thought. She just wanted to hold the reverence of what he'd said. And for another moment she did. But when he turned back toward the campsite saying, "Don't be gone long. Please," it was no longer easy to walk the other way. In the dirt below she could see a simple, penetrating line of tears. Her awakening, she thought. Or the long shadow of her husband's plan.

* * *

She was convinced the medicine wheel had been part of Two-Dot's hope. That being in direct line with the westernmost cairn was a way of securing prosperity or at least longevity. As mysterious as this site was, it also seemed invisible. No litter, no bullet-riddled aluminum cans, yet no signs limited traffic. It had the charisma of an old graveyard. Josie stood there taking it in, aware of her own disturbance. She put her backpack against the limbs of a bottom-heavy fir tree, then walked to the stones, now realizing at least two of them were horizon markers. She looked at the symmetry tendered in overgrowth and outlined like a skeleton against the earth. What was its meaning? Medicine wheels, in everything she'd ever read, were unexplained, their value lost in the oral traditions of the plains Indians. But there was conjecture, and had been for a long time, that the ancient spokes had signified specific time, as if they were the first and most lasting endplates of the seasons.

He'd been so open, talking the plain truth about both of them, then let her go. Maybe all those miles Sterns said nothing was so much armor plating, because you can't get very far from your partner inside a truck. But Two-Dot was measured distance. And it was asylum. Safety was nonexistent, yet there was undiluted blue sky all around them. It was an illusion, she thought, and he took a breath of it and for a moment slipped free of perhaps the only reason he'd pushed on in the first place. Intimidated by death, it had worn a groove deep inside Sterns, a constricting harness around his soul until two nights before. When he made the decision to give her the vial of Pass-Flu, it wasn't just to remedy death. In fact, it wasn't even to solve a crisis. She realized now he'd waited half his life to decapitate sickness, to snap it without resistance from her body. To watch it, and worry it, and punish himself for having the audacity to raise his hand against it.

Josie looked through the low tangle of trees and brush that joined the wheel with the town and watched for him, parting the grass in front of her, then hesitating, studying the path of her own feet. Somehow, she wanted to believe Sterns would follow her. Her mind went back to Robert, his frenzy over her in the beginning, and it occurred to her guilt had led him on too. He'd held her in the dim-lit corner of Stuart Anderson's more than once telling her his son's softball game wasn't going to be over in time to see her the next day. She wondered now, after all the years she missed with him, if he went back to that memory when he was training his bird. If all the pent-up guilt fell away in the name of progress.

It wouldn't take much to imagine most anything here. Leaves twittered, and there was an unexplainable, almost electric sense of another presence. She began to walk the spokes, thinking of the dawn image she still remembered and Robert's restless night before. It couldn't have been this overgrown, she thought. The morning stars had been low on the horizon. Yet, right now, any direction she took was obstructed by young evergreens and the slow creep of river willows. If a bird as routinely trained as Gem-X was trying to orient to cast-off light from Aldebaran, he simply wouldn't be able to. But the signposts for his flight emanated from here. He would come to the wheel if for no other reason than familiarity. And, perhaps, he'd come to see her.

Again, she circled the misshapen stones perforating the ground, rising in mounds with nothing to prevent them from scatter. Yet rumbling earthquakes and the scour of wind and sun hadn't disturbed them. There were architect's fingerprints, she thought, still pressed into the construction, saying the same thing over and over. *You come here for the same reason we did.* She said it out loud, uttering the only definable sound she'd heard for several minutes. Then she kissed the back of her hand several times sucking in her lips to make the sound Robert used to. She waited and did it again.

Movement startled her, so close she had to bend over to see it fully. The soft glow of an overhead sun melted between fir needles and spilled across her backpack at the tree base. Squinting, she looked upward. Gem-X, wings outspread, settled on an interior branch a foot above her in a barren vacancy between layers. For whatever reason, maybe vanity, maybe the necessity to feel the sun between his primaries, he kept his wings spread in a dazzling transparent gray-white, the color of a snow sky. She kissed her hand again and watched him fold them one at a time until they were merely part of his barrel-shaped body.

"You're being predictable all of a sudden," she said, letting lower branches envelope her. "Have you found what you're looking for?" He cautiously stepped down while the wire filament protruded but didn't seem to waylay him. "You know you guys always look so ridiculous all trussed up," she said, softening her voice, pulling him in second by second. His chest expanded as he neared her, revealing the underpinnings of pale yellow down, then he made a thin, peevish scream. The first thing that touched her hand was the wire. "That's my boy," she said withdrawing her arm from the tree with Gem-X balanced on it like a small, heroic falcon. "Kisses? That's probably what Robert used to give you, huh?"

She thought she could sense the bird's readiness. His feet gripped the small of her arm, and for the first time she could see the transmitter's streamlined efficiency. Indomitable, crack-proof, weather-resistant, it would probably outlast the bird. She began to finger it. Attached with only a small metal clasp that resembled a tie-wrap, she knew she could release it with one determined flick of her finger. But it would snap away, and the startle might terrify him to the point of self-injury. "Or you might not come around me again very soon," she said, pulling on the wire a little harder.

"Oh I'd come around you anytime," she heard a voice say. A man entered the perimeter of the medicine wheel from the opposite direction. Lavishly smiling, he looked as though he'd walked through a thicket just for the fun of it. His blond hair stood in a peak above his forehead, and two rivulets of hard packed earth were pressed against his temple. "Name's Pritchard. Martin Pritchard. I think I might be the dude who was intended to pop off your husband. Instead, here I am catching you with his bird. I mean our bird."

Josie looked at him, then beyond, studying the impenetrable wall of bramble he'd just stepped out from. "I can't believe anybody could get back in here except the way I did," she said. She could feel perspiration break out below her arms, an instant flood that would penetrate her shirt within minutes.

"What's it matter how I got here, Ms. Russo? I've got you and the bird, the one they call the blue meteor, yeah?" He kept grinning and pulled out his I.D. police-style. "Colzer-Bremen. You know, the corporation your husband was fuckin' with. Well, now, you can make up for all that. Just hand him over to me. No, better yet, just bring him along for the ride."

She'd heard people say never let an assailant get you in their vehicle. Do anything. Scream, scratch, bite your tongue and spit blood, say you have leprosy, AIDS, and irritable bowel syndrome all at the same time. But this was not a man who'd put up with gimmicks. As he walked toward her, she could see he was easily over six feet tall with a hand pushed up under his turquoise studded shirt.

"You just make sure you carry that little birdy this direction," he said, putting a pistol midway between his waist and her head.

"I don't know if he'll stay with me," she said, hardly breathing.

"It's a bet he won't leave your side."

Josie forced herself to look away from the gun and the man pointing it at her. She studied the bird, the only sign left of her husband's existence. She knew he was extraordinary. That he merited every frustration, every worry her husband ever had about him. She also knew by now he'd experienced freedom, the kind born on high winds and in the awnings of trailers. He was no plebe.

"Follow your heart," she said, unsnapping the transmitter between her fingers. As she pitched the bird forward, Josie screamed, "God willing, I'll meet you at the finish line." The downstroke of wings vaulted him instantly into a flurry of racket, and somewhere in the middle she heard a single shot. Neither she nor the man moved. The bird had vanished.

"Ever heard of a blaze of glory?" Pritchard said, tucking his gun into his waistband. "That's where your bird's headed, Ms. Russo. Right to his kin. All of 'em," he said. "Burned to death right there at the finish line."

CHAPTER 33

On his way to the truck Sterns gave a quick wave to Prestonia who was putting up a sign on the counter of her shack. *Baptism? Meet me at the river*, was all it said. An older couple waddled duck-like around the building's corner, obviously the first and maybe only in the day's line-up. It didn't seem right to leave Josie, and he knew it. But he wanted her to succeed. Not only would it free the bird, he knew it would free her. He thought about the final thing she'd said at St. Pats. How she'd told him there wouldn't be any going back. Only forward to Nebraska. But she'd also said something else.

If you've given me the vial, I'm serum. If they're tracking, they'll find me because the bird and I are together. We're both hot, Sterns. You can leave, and it won't change what's going to happen. Only getting rid of the transmitter. That could change things. To mislead is all I can think of to do.

Wind chimes resonant, almost anxious with vibration went off. Strung from tree to tree he hadn't noticed them until now. They continued, and he realized the wind had shifted setting them astir. Contrariness in the atmosphere, he thought. A high to a low or maybe a cold front to a fire.

Jiggling a connection, he realized the fuel line should've been changed early in the spring. Comfortable with his own logging ways, he and Gil would siphon fuel from the spare tank if they had to. But now, if the line was plugged or split from pressure, with as little gas as was left in the mains, he and Josie would go begging. Any fuel could blow at any time. But Sterns feared a monster far greater. To strangle in his own indecision or worse yet, to wait. He realized he better follow any route he could count on.

Mislead. She'd said it way back where he could've helped her. And before that, he should've done it himself. He knew about the antenna and that the bird wouldn't leave her alone. In the awning. In the tree overlooking the bathhouse. As close as he was, it wouldn't have been hard to grab the center of his head and wring.

"Fire continues to move east . . . Now, just two hours before sundown we get the worst winds of the day. Tornado-force, they make it inadvisable to leave Grand Island, Nebraska, going east. Citizens there say it's like nothing they've ever seen. A column of fire. Some say it resembles Hiroshima. Wind shifts expected to shift it south. Right now spot fires within fifty miles of North Platte River. Concerns mount for Nebraskans in Hay Springs, Alliance, and vicinity of Scottsbluff."

Sterns could see it. Turning the radio off, he realized if they didn't get moving the spots would turn to pools, a fire that liquified, instantly becoming a landlocked tsunami. The ocean would move in waves with only an eery silence between. Then a forest of trees would explode creating another slam. He reached into the glove box and pulled a map. There were only two ways into Darby, two ways by road. The rest, he knew, would have to be ad libbed.

He thought of it again. The extra vial. Josie encouraged him to take it, enticed him, even when he wasn't sick. *Maybe he'd see things the way she did.* Was she joking? Was there a part of her looking to get even? Or maybe the opposite, feeling sorry for him, watching him grow desperate, suddenly asphyxiated by his own memories. He glanced at the floorboard and remembered she'd taken her backpack. For some reason he thought of Russo and the updates with notations in a first aid box that implicated him over and over. He wondered if the ornithologist had taken a hit of serum himself and knew, just like his wife, how to navigate the realm of extinction, yet didn't have the foresight to save his own life. Sterns turned the key to the ignition, then heard a gun shot, distinct and sharp above the sound of the diesel. Nothing else, just the crack settled in his brain, and he realized by staying behind he'd done the worst possible thing.

By the time he drove through the medicine wheel's furthest slope, he could see an opening that meandered into a small, reed-infested meadow, too soggy for most vehicles. He stopped and studied the tracks fast filling with water. Tires from a heavy-duty

SUV. He thought of the yellow Hummer they'd seen earlier and for a moment let an image overwhelm him of a woman flatbacked against the side door while a fiend spread her legs. It can't happen to her, he thought. She's got to be out here somewhere. "Josie," he screamed. "Josephine Russo, answer me."

It seemed irrational what he saw next. A glint, a golden thread on the bottom tier of a fir tree. He picked it up. The antenna felt substantial. *A pinion*, he thought, and Josie's devastating achievement. On it was inscribed the number 522.

Sterns pulled the steering tight, then held back, barely accelerating through the mire. He'd seen her best that night at the Rattlesnake when she'd sat across from him in the camp light and listened to the way it had been before the logging and the peninsula. He wished he'd told her then what was happening. That his dreams, like hers, were hallucinations. That when she looked at him in the darkness of his truck, it was indelible. It was the last time he would ever be alone.

CHAPTER 34

The North Platte kept rolling into sight, a steady consciousness as enduring as the freeway. In the middle of growing invisibility, Pritchard found himself navigating by occasional glimpses
of the river. A kind of rebellion slipped between its banks, every
eddy and tumble of water a refusal to burn. There was refusal all
around him, especially in the woman he'd chased over half the
United States. She withdrew into the Hummer's seat and watched
the landscape turn to smoke.

He laid his gun under the seat, letting it fall into a pocket
in the carpeting. A gun, he thought, was like a credit card. Just
a reflex for a man like him. And a total enigma to the innocent.
He welcomed the contemplation she gave him, the hundred ways
he could bait her. Oddly, it wasn't the possibility of this moment
that had intrigued him those last few miles into Two-Dot. It was
Morris.

"Hey, Chief. You might want to hear this," he'd shouted
through the cell phone. "Had coffee with Mellon this morning.
Told me Shanna called him when he got back to Vegas. Said she
and Rachel are looking for a ride to Cuatro Cienegas. That you'd
be happy. No need for sprinklers there."

"No shit, man." Pritchard suddenly felt light-headed, as if
the unexpected contact was pitching him forward to someplace,
until now, off limits. "Marshes, four of them," he translated. "In
Mexico. Tell her I'll be there, gringo. Tonight. With fifty million
Pass-Flu dollars."

Morris also said Elsa looked like a storm cloud the last two
days, giving orders and isolating technicians one from the other.
She kept repeating the same thing. That their jobs weren't threat-
ened, and there would be a fresh supply of birds before the week

was out. She also said to prepare for the largest supply of serum yet. At 100 percent.

"She's a fraud," Pritchard said. "She's so damn sure of herself she's let up on my family. But it doesn't mean any of this is over. I know that. Because Elsa never caves."

"I think you're right," Morris said. "Corporate jet's filed for Darby, Nebraska, for later this afternoon. I know 'cuz some guy from the tower called here trying to find her. Told me to get a message through. That she's on her own on this one. Not even sure she'll get radar coverage because of fire."

"Well, then," Pritchard said. "I guess we got ourselves a real hot hootenanny." He wondered if Morris was finally for real. Maybe this one last promise had thrown the switch for him and a dozen others. For once, they wanted to go home, to face a flu-infested world with their families, not bargain for another round with the serum's weakness. But holding out for a promotion, Morris might have just inherited the other half of Pritchard's million wedged under a paperweight on Elsa's desk. Still mulling over the call, he studied the Nebraska smoldering before him. Elsa might really get him this time, he thought. Not with persecution or fucking with his family, but by the simple act of waiting patiently in her corporate coliseum while he drove mile by mile into another financial mother lode centered in the middle of hell itself.

Even without the graying blur of smoke, Pritchard didn't know what Nebraska should look like. Flat. A place not far from tarbush and catclaw. But what was happening brought back a picture of stricken wells and plumes that could be seen from the moon. A man far out in a low burning field was leading his horse across its unbroken grass while a team of firemen dragged truck hoses around the charred perimeter. It looked crazy attacking it this way. "You know what I said back there. About eliminating your husband. Maybe that was too much information. Can't imagine what I'd feel if somebody said that about my wife."

He wondered where he was going with it, letting himself feel immense, momentary pleasure. She was sending a message. Even if it was a hoax, Shanna's name had re-entered his mind. And, for a change, it wasn't to get her attention. Possibly, she was trying to get his. He'd set a sprinkler right in the middle of their broken relationship, and now she was putting it out there like a peace offering. Probably, it was a phone call or more likely a visitor at the car lot, but somehow Elsa peered in a little too close and Mexico, never a consideration before, became the destination for his wife and daughter. To the borderlands, she said. Directly to the heart of Pritchard's fantasy.

"I almost forgot," he said, driving a little faster. "There's someone else now. A man named Sterns, I believe." He watched Josie, the way she flinched when she heard his name. "S'pose he's in hot pursuit, huh? After all, looks like you two planned this thing. Boy meets bird. Girl meets boy. Then, bingo, bird meets girl. A regular little triangle."

Again, she flinched but said nothing, simply turning her head toward the orange line basting the horizon.

"Good work. I really admire what everybody's done. Your husband trained his pigeon, then put him on autopilot. Great move. Only a nerd and a bird could figure out just the right dawn. Solstice," he said, raking the "Ss" between his teeth. "That way he didn't need to be around to blame for the escape. And you, my little pobrecita, you'd be overlooked in the whole nasty affair. That's what it's become, hasn't it? First, you spied, then you took, now you've got a critter who can't leave you alone. Smitten or just plain looney?" Pritchard continued while steering toward the patchy glow of fires, one after another, like hesitations across the prairie. "Which is it, Ms. Russo?"

"You don't understand," she finally said. "I didn't take him."

"Yeah, I know. I've got the evidence it was a lot more premeditated."

"I don't know what evidence you mean," she said. "If it's my husband's notes, they describe a theory. One that may or may not work."

"Oh it worked all right," he said, patting the lump in the pocket of his shirt.

Once again she grew silent, mute to everything but the firecracker sounds that permeated the car's metal and heavy glass.

Momentary pings of explosion that seemed to grind through her reserve. He wondered how she'd manage war.

She'd been easy to find. Two-Dot's sign posts consisted of "Exit, North Road, South Road, and One-Stop Gas & Eats." Curious, he might've driven through town just to see how it all fit together. He had plenty of time. The receiver hovered at the same rate for several minutes, and he wondered if its constancy was connected to the woman, the medicine wheel or both. It was obvious, just from Russo's training CD, the wheel was a focus to be reckoned with.

So Pritchard took the South Road, a turn delineated by a crude sign braced between two rock cairns. Winding down across a cattle guard, the road picked up elevation while it disappeared into a twilight of cottonwoods, then punched on up through new growth firs. A deliberate cut-away had long since grown over but seemed to be intended for parking, and this is where Pritchard got out. He found a trail almost gouged away, now soft in summer mud, and pivoted his heel deep inside the slippery belly. It didn't hold. He kept falling, a ricochet of mud and rubble, him catching sight of his hand isoscelesed between two shafts of rock. When it ended, he was upside down with his head in a chunk of bark.

He thought about it now, how he must look, and rubbed the side of his face, then angled the rear-view mirror closer to his head. The road was empty behind them except for a pinpoint, a continuous dot that waved mirage-like in and out of ground smoke. Pritchard kept his eye on the particle, still thinking about the glory hole he'd found at the wheel. "You know I never expected you'd have a 98 percenter on you. I mean right there in your backpack. Didn't your hubby tell you?" he said, pulling the vial from his pocket, "This shit's like gold. Naturally, makes me wonder what happened to the empty." He paused and clicked the vial against the front of the mirror, then placed it in the ashtray. "Wouldn't be that Sterns has anything to do with it?" Pritchard rotated his head, tilting it back and toward Josie at the same time.

"What are you talking about? I'd even forgotten I had them. It was the last thing I'd think of," she said in disgust.

"Uh huh. Well, we'll see about that when your little friend back there wonders where the hell you're goin'."

"The only place makes sense to go is Darby," she said. "My husband built the whole program on it. You'd know that if you've seen his work. It's where the bird will end up. And that's what you really want, isn't it?"

"Not necessarily. You think your husband figured on a fire almost as big as the state we're in? Like I said, I don't give the passenger a chance at anything except roasting. And if he doesn't roast, he's going to follow you. And until a few minutes ago we knew exactly where that was, Ms. Russo. Every step of the way."

"Not every step," she said, looking directly at him. "He's been free flying since the beginning. Wouldn't you after one hundred years of never leaving a compound of one sort or another? Of being officially extinct?"

"I'm not quite that anthropomorphic," Pritchard said. "But now that you've brought it up, how's it you didn't take off that transmitter 'til now? You know that bastard attacked me on the way into Two-Dot. Just up and dive bombed me. You think maybe he's sick? Is that why you led me right in, Ms. Russo? Because you was afraid of the bugger?"

He kept his concentration on the road, realizing the approach to Glendo Reservoir meant a choice, and one he didn't want to make alone. Even though the freeway paralleled the lake, it was becoming impossible to see beyond his hood at times. Smoke drifted past in waves like early morning fog and a wind, almost like sprites, tantalized him with glimpses of range land, then a malignant downpour of ash. At twenty miles an hour he was suddenly speeding, and a roadblock, unless it was concrete, was as good as useless. He turned on every head and fog light the Hummer had.

"If you don't turn off this freeway, we're not going to make it," Josie said. "There's nothing but a wall of darkness ahead."

"Yeah, well, you ain't got over fifty million at stake either. I figure that's what I'll get for delivering the bird or any update of Pass-Flu to Interspecies. Probably can up the ante to a hundred mil in this shit. Oh, you'd love that place, Ms. Russo. They adore birds. Got'em all over their walls, in the freezer. Heard they make jewelry out of bones from dead specimens. Endangered earrings. Shit like that."

"They might as well be selling fuzz off my butt," was all she said.

"Fetching idea." Pritchard paused, amused, but also vaguely incited. "So how'd you like to see your buddy Gem-X under the lights at Interspecies Laboratories? They're going to want to see how far the virus has gone. An outbreak bird. Volatile. Separated from 1918 about as far as he is from being a reptile. They're going to take one look at him and start testing. Ninety-eight percent? Shit. They're looking for a killer. A flying rat turned bubonic."

"All we gotta do is get you there and keep you there. If he makes it through this blast furnace like you say, then it's just a matter of time. He'll show up and bingo." Pritchard rubbed two fingers together while he squinted through the incessant char.

"Well, you might get your whatever million with that vial in your ashtray," she said. "But you won't get your bird. He's on his way to Darby. And right now I'd say he's brighter than you are."

Pritchard veered to the side of the road, then scratched at the windshield as if to claw away the ceaseless smoke. He switched wipers on, then off, and finally got outside and climbed up on the hood. Spreading his legs apart, he bent over swiping the windshield with the fat side of his hand while glaring at Josie, looking down at her, oddly vulture-like.

"You bitch," he screamed. "You've drug me across this godforsaken hellhole where even a gopher can't breathe. You've ambled right in front of me as you meandered across this Solitario, this dead butt of the world, me listening to a cackling bird on the other end of a wire accurate for about a city block. Now you sit there studying the geography of this goddamned fire. What the fuck, woman? You think you're some kind of psychic or something?"

"'They tried to confine me,'" she said.

"What?" he said leaning even closer, rubbing his eyes and parting his lips in a freakish grin.

"Crazy Horse," she began again. "You know, a quote."

Pritchard stopped grinning and enunciated his demand. "Speak normal English."

Quick Fall of Light

"I am," she said. "You can't confine me, Mr. Pritchard."

Sitting on the hood he slowly pulled his shirt over his nose and let himself breathe in the situation, then systematically, rhythmically felt relief. This was no easier just because Russo's widow was sitting on the other side of the windshield. Her serenity was infuriating. There was also a memory-tricking eeriness that went right along with the fire, but this, he recognized, was the time for confession. He could tell her what he'd done all these years for the biggest pharmaceutical in the world. The "Processor," they'd called him. A man who makes things happen. That he worked on the opposite end of her husband's efforts, transporting updates all over the world to every human population deemed worth saving. Gave it to them and still watched the corpses pile up, toe tag to toe tag. All of it would never make it out of his mouth. Only one thing still permeated his instincts and seeped around Pritchard's façade in a stink so intolerable even a throat-clogging fire couldn't suppress it. One putrid memory he wanted to inflict on her, for all the miserable indifference. Hers and the flu-buggered world's.

Pritchard re-entered the Hummer and in one jerk pushed the steering column upward. "A few months back I was given orders to take updates to Tibet. I want you to hear this, Ms. Russo. Because this is what's goddamned real out there." He pointed with one steady finger straight ahead as if defying her order to get off the freeway.

"I'd just been brought back from India for the infraction, I guess you'd call it. Done the best I could, but I pissed off corporate. And she decided it was time for repentance. So, along with a box full of vials, she sent me to, what do they call it? A Tibetan monastery. Frickin' amazing. Fourteen men, monks living at 10,000 feet probably wouldn't need 82 percent Pass-Flu. I kept thinkin' it couldn't get much more sterile than the Himalayas. But she told me these men had been exposed to flu, and they were indispensable. And I knew it too, after I'd been there a while. They live in thin air you know. If you're not prepared for it, it's magical."

He let the words hang there intentionally, keeping them sparse and uncomfortably loyal to what he remembered. Pritchard knew she was listening because her chin had measurably lowered, and she stared straight ahead, the last of her resolve dissolving into curiosity. He knew it because words well executed affected women, and he was being unusually strategic with this one. "After one of them helped in a nearby village, he brought the bug back to the rest. They were showing the usual signs. Cough, spitting up blood. So I administered the vials personally. Each man, one vial of 82 percent. All in a line they sat. Red robes. I remember that best, Ms. Russo. How trusting they were."

"In only about twenty minutes, they began to bleed. Serious, from their noses and ears. Then from the naval and the genitals. They hardly moved while they sat in their own death. Prayer, maybe. No help. Not a soul could help me. I'd injected all of them. For hours, maybe days I cleaned up. I kept all the vials. Nothing was left but the monastery. I burned everything else. Everything," he said.

"When I finally got to civilization, nobody at Colzer would answer my calls. I thought maybe it really was the end. For everybody. Then I looked at my e-mails. Corporate didn't say much. Just that she hoped my journey had been a safe and successful one. 'Success, Pritchard,' she wrote. 'Is sometimes passing on the responsibility I've endured. When you doubt me, you doubt your future. Take a look at your empty vials. Heparin, Pritchard. It's always available. And from me it's never a mistake.'"

It surprised him that he could remember exactly what she'd written. Here with little more than a lane change difference between moving forward or, with one twist of the wind, burning to death, there wasn't one glitch in his memory. Empty as old inkwells, the deadly vials were still lined up in the top drawer of his beside table. Sometimes he heard them vibrate when he fell into bed, fourteen hollowed-out tubes rattling the names of holy men. Yet, it was the image of their hands, their still, deliberately cupped hands that woke him from sleep. Seeing it over and over. Forgiveness and blood let loose in a torrential act of human betrayal.

He sat across from Josie stupefied at his own reliable accounting. Almost half a year had gone by since he'd left the monastery, so high and until him, so untouched, it was like leaving an astral plane. Snow had deepened on the night of the deaths, enough that it absorbed, then covered blood like gauze, and he remembered thinking they didn't die in vain. This was the shortfall they'd all prepared for. Maybe, they'd even known what he was about to do. But merciful as they were, they couldn't revive his soul. To Pritchard, Tibet had marked the end of his life's work, and culminated in the final, ugly disposal of trust.

So when he asked Josie why she hadn't made a move for the accelerator or at least for the gun during those few minutes he sat on the hood in front of her, he was really asking her why she hadn't fought for what little chance she had left. "What is it with you fuckin' pure in heart?" he asked, bending over to take the gun out from under the seat, then putting it in her lap. "You figure things are better on the other side. You know they are, right? You're goin' there in about half an hour anyway, so you might as well give me another demerit. Nah, not this time, babe," he said, looking straight ahead too. "This is your chance to call it even for fourteen others who didn't get one."

Out of the periphery, the only clear vision he had left, Pritchard saw her pick up the gun. Small movements, he thought. Consequential, as if she was handling Austrian crystal. He closed his eyes and breathed inescapable clinging soot. It surrounded him now, just like it had in the Gulf. Nauseous death, no longer insidious but declaring itself, waiting alongside him.

"I don't even know if it's loaded anymore," she said. "I've seen way too many movies, Mr. Pritchard, to fall for that one," she said, placing it quietly on the console. "Besides, your suffering has obviously prevailed more than anything I could do." Her voice trailed behind her, and he realized she'd rolled down the window in perhaps the desperate effort to breathe. "I don't think we're going to die, either of us," she said. "But we're at a place where we've got reminders, frightening reminders of how it could end. That's where you are. Where my husband was. And now where I am. I can see the end, Mr. Pritchard. Every tree line, every meadow. Even the moss on Mr. Hennings' roof."

He listened carefully, but it wasn't until she said the name that he knew. It was so clear what she was describing because he'd seen the brown-green fuzz edging the barn's roof every time he picked up passengers. As though the whole dwelling was intentionally layered in comfort. "How would you know about Hennings' roof?" he asked. "Have you ever been there?"

"No. It just came with the experiment."

"You mean for a change I'm looking at a survivor," he said, eyeing her carefully, then putting the gun under his armpit. It fascinated him, and he wanted her to know it fascinated him, that the discovery of an empty vial now intrigued him as much as a full one.

"That would be me," she said. "At least up until now."

CHAPTER 35

She watched the road, expecting at least embers or the glowing outline of a tongue of fire to cut through smoke. It was as though they were guided by a rope anchored between the concrete edges of freeway, vacillating back and forth, often feeling the vibration of shoulder strips or gravel or an overshoot into prairie itself. Pritchard wasn't listening, continuing through the darkness on a line as thin as if balancing on rim rock.

Glendo Reservoir was only the first of three lakes, all sparkling charms in the long southeast-running chain of the North Platte River. Josie knew where they were, not by memory, but by an internal reference which repeated itself, a stencil against the murk still in front of them. She and Pritchard were in the interior. It was the edges she could see, the fractious light of three small lakes and the sloping banks of a river, simple water-strewn cutouts on the way to Darby. She knew if they failed to take the exit to Scottsbluff, they might not survive, and she couldn't tell if that would, in the least, bother the man alongside her.

Remembering part of her husband's notes, she thought of the program he'd used to train his passenger. "*Sensation of Accomplished Flight,*" he explained, was more than video repetition. It called into play a second level of physical reality. Gem-X, he wrote, was influenced by life forms around him within the physical sensation of flying but even more, and harder to understand, within the urgency of his trainer. *There is an intention by the man to influence the bird. It's hard to believe that could carry across, but I believe it has. Intention boosted by my crude technology somehow has connected with passenger #522.* Could he have ever known it would transmit through derelict strands of virus, permeating deep into his bird's antibodies, then pass into her body assuming a form as surreal, as unexplainable as the conjurings of her mind?

She realized now that Robert had built on simplicity, step-by-step in a process neither perfected nor entirely accepted. Perhaps out of all his credentials, it was his years as lonely observer that had determined a species, even a single member of that species, had to be promised some measure of normalcy. A mindset, daily and ritualistic, had begun between an ornithologist and one passenger. Perversely, the demands grew as the relationship exceeded all expectations, but the result was the best anti-virus in the world. It must've been heady those first few successes. Then Robert must've found out about the selective distribution. He came to realize his methods were only fueling Colzer's ambitions. And then he heard about the work of men like Pritchard.

"You know your husband started a hole under the fence there at the Bridge," Pritchard said. "That part bugged me the worst. Seeing those little bits of fluff under the wire where he'd set the whole thing up. When that bird probably belonged in an incinerator."

She wondered what he was talking about, why he was thinking about escape the same as she was, but oblivious to the cluster of windmills off to their right standing straight as soldiers, legs motionless, burned to fiery shreds in a field of charcoal blur. He kept gripping the steering wheel with his left hand, pulling it from one extreme to the other, relaxed enough to believe nobody was coming toward him.

There was nothing she could do except watch. And think of Sterns, who was left to the hazards of a world without any guidance, even that of a madman. She stared at the vial rolling back and forth in the ashtray, then ran her finger over the side mirror as if she finally might see him. But it was like he'd said. The power of this dream was re-forming, moving through time, taking her with it and not necessarily the man who brought her face-to-face with herself. She sensed she might never see him again, him trapped inside the freeway's shadow, looking straight up into a boiling sky.

"I never intended for this to happen," she said, holding onto a thin sliver of side window. "And whatever my husband was trying to do, I don't think he foresaw my being here right now, and certainly not with you. But 98 percent Pass-Flu changes your life.

First you live, and then you find the life you possess is no longer the same. Yes, I have a vial's worth inside me, Mr. Pritchard. It would seem it's given me what little good sense we have going for us at this moment."

Pritchard grunted, laying the flat of his gun on the steering wheel. She watched him balance it there, his aggravation focused on the barrel which he tapped rhythmically on the leather casing. "What does it matter to you whether we get to Hennings?" he said. "You never met him, seen his barn, carted his birds all over hell's half acre. Probably just heard about him three days ago. He doesn't want company. Never does. You're just an experiment to him, even if he knows about you. So what the hell, woman? You tell me something I don't know. Something I can believe, and I'll turn this piece of shit right into his driveway. In this pitiful soup, just give me some of that goddamned good sense you claim to have," he said.

"How about a place to start over?" she said, barely aware of what was coming out of her mouth. It resounded in the back of her thoughts, a dim pulse in haze as dense as the one they were driving through. Inside a dark night of brackish fever someone had seen her waiting on the edge of her life. He'd forgotten to ask where she was going, really going. Instead, he gave her a taste of the worst kind of plague since 1918. All of it would've never happened without Sterns. Her life, she realized, might've never changed without him.

A sign emerged out of the gloom in nothing short of a momentary clearing. "Leaving Wyoming," it said. Pritchard steadied the Hummer, then with finality shoved the gun back under the seat. "You say a place to start over, Ms. Russo. That's a reason. But, more important, it's the end of my reason." He seemed to measure the moment, his hand unfolding enough to grip the wheel alongside the other. As he turned towards Nebraska, Pritchard began a song, a strange parody that seemed to Josie to come from another time wrapped in a tune that seemed manic, probably self-invented.

"*I had a little bird,*" he sang. "*And its name was Enza. I opened the window and in-flew-Enza.*" He repeated it a second time, then began a slow, silent parallel alongside the river leading to Darby, giving her time to consider a bird, weightless, tumbling in the atmosphere high above and the intractable decision the man beside her had just made.

*   *   *

Sterns left the freeway taking a paved road that skirted above the reservoirs, not so much because he wanted to, but to keep line of sight with the whimsical notion that he could see and that he would finally see Josie. He knew it was chasing an illusion. The snags on fire between him and where the fire had swept through were slow-burning ingots. Heat radiated into the truck in pulses. Yet the torches, some of them still a hundred feet high, were like windsocks, their glowing heads pointed away from him. He knew the wind was pushing the smoke straight forward and for the moment clearing a path, so he accelerated, and accounting for periodic curves, kept it at seventy.

He didn't know how many times he'd said the only words he could say out loud. "Why Josie? God damn him. God. Damn me." The last couple days she'd overtaken him as if the serum inside her was set to poison the closer he got. Her body, her voice, her love for another man, her impulse to drive them into hell all drew so suffocatingly close he suspected the burn itself was part of the seduction, pulling him faster and faster into a jumper's fire.

Ivanhoe Creek passed beneath him reminding him of soup, a brew of ash and dead fish about to dump its broth into the only hope Nebraska might have. He knew the Platte paralleled the highway into Scottsbluff, but on the wrong side. If a gobbler fire continued downward from the Black Hills anything north of the river was destined to experience the sound of a half-dozen freight trains colliding overhead. Only the river itself could protect the place they were heading. And it might not be adequate. But there were signs of a relationship occurring, one that firefighters used routinely. Out of the soot-dappled overcast Sterns saw a helicopter, its silhouette reminding him of a pterodactyl, airborne, yet lumbering above a mist of burn-out. Maybe its persistent drops had been enough to clear the space in front of him. It didn't matter, he thought, because he'd keep pushing through the edges, from island to denuded island, until he got further into a fire than he ever wanted to again.

The yellow Hummer drifted in and out of his consciousness. The driver, to Sterns, was an aerialist, a concoction who annoyed a trooper in the middle of a flu-infested community, then zeroed in on Josie at exactly her most vulnerable moment. This man with hair the color of palominos had circumvented the law and the highway. But there was also a nagging doubt about her. She'd told him there was time. Time for what? Time to unhitch the trailer, to make love? She knew what he wanted. Her nakedness, the fragrance of pine mixed with damp earth crossed in front of his thoughts, lightening quick. Wanting to kiss her under the running shower. Then walking away if he had to. Waiting, wordless, until she was ready. He searched the unconscionable, the place inside himself he'd resisted since he met her. That she might not ever have a chance to tell him how close he'd really been.

Pockets of burn collected in the scant woods he passed, luminarias that might glow for days. They lit the underbelly of smoke as it thinned moving east, then created their own self-fulfilling haze in a cycle no longer controlled by anything but wind and the lack of it. He was free to drive hard, and Sterns did, but he kept glancing at the fuel tanks watching the drop-off, then pressing harder. The speed, the flickering, moody obscurity catapulted him into a far-off memory. He thought of a picture his brother used to keep in his locker of a smoke jumper dangling one hundred fifty feet high in a ponderosa, the chute itself draped over the tree's crown like a petticoat, the man hung stratified between branches. It seemed to be the one thing Sterns could leave at Mark's grave. A fragment of the eternal question. What had really happened?

It occurred to him now as he watched the ferocious spark in front of him that no theory could replace a man's paralysis. Pictures, diagrams, practice, all proven, all tested couldn't overcome human instinct. It was vision that freed the soul, that breathed life into the impossible. And it was cumulative vision of an ornithologist, one he'd hardly known, who set hypothesis on fire.

The vial he'd given Josie was just the beginning, yet it probably was the end result of what Russo already knew. Something happened over the months of training to change the relationship between the man and his bird. It spilled over into the serum which, in turn, became, as Hennings said, "The best there is." Even if Russo had wanted to reassure his wife, to explain to her the reasons for the strange resurgence of the passenger pigeon, he couldn't have done it near as well as the serum itself. He counted on her vision when the right time came. And at a place far from science.

As he made the final turn south toward Highway 26, Sterns could see her again, in his mind too young for the man she'd spent the last twenty years with. She'd lived her life waiting, maybe for this very day. Without her husband, the one she had, she might've had children, lived on a houseboat or kept an ocelot. Instead, she fell into a rain forest that held obsession, generations of it, that flitted between trees and altered the destiny of a plague. The only thing clear in front of Sterns was her disappearance. It was as if it could end no other way.

He ran his hands across his eyes, trying hard to focus on the depression ahead. The road ran straight and slightly upward to the horizon, a thin, obsessive ribbon barricaded on both sides by spot fires. Dust rose behind him and converged into a funnel. He remembered how calculating she'd been. How she'd taken her backpack and walked away from him toward the wheel. She had it all, he thought. The vial, the bird, they were just extras. She had the vision, the unmistakable ability to see what had become the flight path of a passenger. And, now, there was the agonizing possibility she'd known who would be there at the wheel with him.

It was a sight coming down off that ridge. In front of him spread the highway and beyond that the river, both of them untouched except for a still smoking cut-away that signaled the end of Wyoming. He squinted, then realized the only thing moving in front of him was a yellow square, an insect in amber, and the woman he wanted to spend the rest of his life with. Sterns punched the accelerator keeping his eye on the target, then remembered something he'd read about the 1918 outbreak. In Montana, they said, there'd been a lack of flu among loggers, and now, with as little logic, it seemed he was repeating that statistic. He looked at the flat-out terrain in front of him and felt a sudden fleeting twinge for the lost forests of the peninsula.

CHAPTER 36

"I thought you said it would clear off," Pritchard said, leaning forward. "This shit's rolling in faster than black satin."

She could feel the Hummer groan as he left the highway and began plowing through switchgrass waist high. Clear immediately ahead, a continuous halo of fire burned on the horizon in a rising tide of embers. Somewhere in the past she'd read the Plains Indians called this kind of combustion the red buffalo. A snorting, body-slamming animal that devoured everything, even its own kind.

"Keep toward the river," she said, knowing it was there beyond the acrid pall hanging perpendicular to the ground. But she was only guessing the route. Magic had gone out of her head the moment they turned east, and the only reason they'd gotten this far was damned luck. The passenger had fallen away from her. His obliteration, like smoke, was capricious, and there were a few minutes when she simply waited, starved for visibility. Pritchard drove into Nebraska, the textures of grass and isolated draws in front of them, the river eerily placid alongside. But the atmosphere was thickening, baking into layer upon layer of traps.

She'd heard Robert talk about it. What weather could do to a pilot. How he'd keep venturing further in, drawn by a familiar contour and, perhaps, the overwhelming urgency to land. The horizon would dim, then disappear, the body of the plane fast becoming an erratic projectile. Nothing more than haze and a man not ready for it. But this was a one-pound bird embedded in a stratospheric storm. Here at the edge was no consolation. There simply was no more homing.

Pritchard kept accelerating the Hummer until it bounced, fully airborne a couple times. Worked up, he drove back onto the highway. "You're shittin' me," he said. "You've been puttin' me on." He took his foot off the gas, then stared at her, wet streaks running down his face. "You don't have a clue where we are, do ya'? Do you?" he screamed.

"I knew back there," she said, holding her hands across the bulge of her stomach. "I still know we stand a better chance out here."

"Fuckin' A, we stand a better chance." He floorboarded the car, a straightforward jet until he lost the asphalt. Again, the Hummer bounced, veering back and forth as it spun on gravel. It wasn't until he'd backed off and steadied the wheel that Pritchard turned his head to look out his side window. She could see it, a methodical move in the middle of his frustration. "What?" he said, hitting the window lever, "Is that?"

She couldn't tell what he meant until Sterns pulled ahead. The white truck sallied back and forth so close she tasted soot and dust, his brake lights flashing dull red as he cut toward Pritchard. They kept to a vicious pattern, sometimes coming so close she could smell fuel along with a waft of Pritchard's underarms. Ludicrous, she kept thinking. Vengeance in the middle of catastrophe. Yet, as she gripped the dash she wanted more than anything to send Sterns a signal.

"That the other half?" Pritchard said, slamming on the brakes, pulling sideways off the road. The Hummer skidded, then careened from dip to dip, the F-250 right alongside. Josie kept reaching into her backpack while keeping her head eye level with hellbent energy, then found the red head rag. She couldn't believe what Sterns was doing, pushing the truck beyond limits, forcing Pritchard to turn even tighter toward the river. Finally, he pulled in front, running with the hill. Something flew off. A chunk of metal hit the windshield as she wound the rag around the outside mirror, forcing Pritchard to deviate left and when he did, she saw Sterns for the first time. A glimpse, she thought, of straight-backed steel.

As they crashed across the earth, one leading, then the other, a narrow border visualized in front of them, and she realized it must be the edge of the North Platte. The way it looked as they approached reminded her of the Sound, its stillness, even composure in the middle of humanity's incessant churn. Nothing moved except two vehicles pulled by gravity. Like magnets, she thought, about to collide with the only life force out there. "What are you going to do?" she asked Pritchard.

"Follow the bastard," he said. "There's a bridge ahead."

She thought about this man, and what little she knew told her it wasn't in Sterns' favor to be in the lead. The gun was probably only a passing advantage. Pritchard was maniacal, strangely in tune with the fracas around him, maybe welcoming one more adversary. She kept wondering if he'd reached the end of the line. If the monks he'd inoculated were only part of his head count. "Is there a kill order?" she asked. "Are they, are we, going to die?"

Pritchard waved his hand at her as if to motion her away. He said nothing but made a small, sideways flinch as she watched his hand fold in on itself. A wounded leopard, she thought, tears without remorse at flesh of the living. He kept the Hummer right behind Sterns, the two of them in consort, leaving the bridge behind in a spray of ash. In less than a mile a sign appeared. "Darby, Nebraska. Population 251."

She wondered if Hennings was part of that. Maybe the highly valued "one." It was possible he was slated for death as well, and by the end of the summer the sign would be adjusted to two hundred fifty souls. A lingering sadness overcame her as she watched an adjacent field of horses, their noses deep in unburned grass. After Hennings, no one here would know what had been in their midst. The birds would've vanished in one last massacre, and she and Sterns would be listed in the obituaries as carriers of incoming flu.

A sizable barn appeared on the right side of the road set deep within a grove. Elms, she thought. Trees meant to brace against the elements. Some part of her hoped it wasn't his place. That nothing like Pritchard could come up his lane and wipe out the old man and his obsession.

"Your friend up there," Pritchard said, slowing through the back-churn of road dust, "Cracks me up. Acts like he knows where the hell he's goin'. Thought that was supposed to be your job." He paced the Hummer putting his left hand under the seat. She knew what he was feeling around for, all the while staring at the vibrating tremor in his right hand. She tried the locked door beside her, then pushed herself deep into the seat corner facing him.

"Tibet. Maybe now, after all that, you think there's nothing worse. It's horrible what you did. But there is something worse. It's happening right now. Everything, from this moment, you can still change."

"Shut up," Pritchard said, his hand thumping under the seat.

She waited, watching the stir all around them, air heavy with the smell of sweet grass burning. "We can't go back. I'm not even sure how far forward we can go. That man up there, he's as lost as I am. You're the only one who can make something happen. Something decent. Because from the looks of things I might be your last witness here on earth. If what's happening matters to you, Martin Pritchard . . . one other person," she said, pointing hard to herself, "Me, I'll know."

The clearing, by now, was a road width, then hundreds of feet in front of them. Pritchard took it as if he was chasing something wild. Something inside, she kept thinking. The Hummer slid back and forth, bar ditch to bar ditch, then picked up an edge. Like flying, she thought. A bird turned loose after a hundred years.

A familiar outline emerged. Sterns stood facing them, the side of his truck crosswise in the road. Waiting, she thought. Waiting for whatever the fool "Custer" was about to do. Pritchard let up, one hand, then the other on the wheel. He craned his neck toward the windshield. "He's got the address right. But standin' there with a goddamned ax?" he said. "What do you call them things? A pick ax?"

"A Pulaski," she said without hesitation. "You know. Smoke jumper."

"Yeah? That son-of-a-bitch?"

He turned the Hummer directly in front of Sterns, toward the Hennings' mailbox, then rolled down his window. "Whatcha' take for that weapon, Mr. Sterns? I got a feelin' I'm going to need one of them before the afternoon is over."

She bent down looking at Sterns. He didn't take his eyes off her, then said to Pritchard, "You let her go, I'll give you anything, including this piece of shit behind me."

"I tell you what, Smoky. You just let me make up my mind about a couple things. Ms. Russo's one of them. Another woman's going to show up here, could be any time now. That's the one you gotta' watch out for. Bring the Pulaski."

They drove through a long field, the lane splitting it as far as she could see. A small white house was at the end of the division surrounded by all sizes of blue and green spruce, their shadows foreign, reminiscent of unending forests. It was a shame if they had to burn, she thought. A shame if this day ended in terror of another sort. She watched Sterns as he pulled alongside her. He got out of the truck stowing the Pulaski at his side, then stood quietly next to her window. Just once he made eye contact and only momentarily. She saw nothing of the man at Two-Dot. This was the Sterns she'd seen that day on the logging road, a man weighing options, moving tons in his mind.

Pritchard got out and shouted over the top of the car, "Throw me the keys, man."

She watched him unfold them, an old fashioned, metal bottle opener included in the chain, then throw them underhand, easy, like cut limbs from a giant hemlock. She thought about his hands. How steady they'd been on the long ride from home and considered the advantage he had now against a man with an old wound.

"Come on out," Pritchard said. "This way." He motioned over the top of the console. She wondered if he'd stick the gun in her back. Back and forth, she thought. He was unpredictable with things. The vial was gone. He kept his hand, his fist, in her back pushing her forward until he met up with Sterns. "You first," he said. "You and the Pulaski. The old man'll be in the barn. Always is."

They walked first down, then up a road that finally curved into a dimming horizon. It seemed such a long way for an old man to walk every day. More back and forth to something hidden in plain sight. She concentrated on Sterns, measuring her steps to his, watching his stride lengthen as he climbed the knoll. He stopped at the top, waiting or maybe perplexed. "A runway?" he said, looking back over his shoulder at a long sod strip paralleling the road.

"To the barn," Pritchard said. He withdrew, then nudged her harder than before. He had the gun, she thought. If it wasn't before, it was there now. Ready to blow through her abdomen.

Hennings came out, a gentler looking man than she expected, small and steady-paced. He wore a yellow shirt under bib overalls giving him the appearance of a wind-worn sunflower. In his hand were two squabs about the size of baby chicks. "Well, lookee here," he said, first looking at Sterns, then Pritchard, then her. "The whole fam-damly."

"Fam-damly, shit," Pritchard said. "You knew we was comin'. You just didn't know when and if somebody'd come in on a bubble stretcher."

"Well, so far, most of you's made it." Hennings pointed to the top of the barn, squinting hard, then grinning.

Josie followed his gaze. On one of the upper shingles stood a bird. From where she was, it appeared to be of average size, in every way resembling a passenger. He let loose with a stream of cacks, what could only be described as a buzz, like moths hitting a bug light. "Is that who I think?" she said.

"Yup, Ms. Russo. Just like your husband planned. I see you got the hardware off him. Didn't work though, did it?" He stared at Pritchard, the smile evening out to an empty grin. "And you son, why don't you let her go? Ain't nothing can hurt you here."

Pritchard pulled back, letting her stand alone. She looked at Sterns who, she assumed, saw the gun. He extended one hand, as if to keep her there, then laid the Pulaski on the ground. "Hey, Mister, whatever you're thinkin', don't do it," Sterns said. "It's the only one left."

Josie turned to face the man behind her. To feel the bullet straight-on. That's what Sterns was trying to tell her. One bullet. She wanted to close her eyes. Instead, she watched Pritchard bend down and empty the vial of Pass-Flu, squirting it into the Nebraska dirt. "That's for all the shit," he said. "All the goddamned death."

She wondered what else would follow. Whether this was only the beginning. They were all standing there. People, not passengers—yet just as open for death. She thought of birds, millions upon millions, trapped and netted. Burning in roosts a hundred high. Troughs of birds fed to hogs. Burned, still alive in fires from Manitoba to Leavenworth, Kansas. People and birds. Alive, starving, sick, imprisoned. They could die without words, without mention. Remembrance was only a headstone, a female passenger in a zoo in Cincinnati.

"Well," said Hennings, "Just like now, it didn't always work so well in the beginning, did it Pritchard? He can tell you more than I can, but it took quite a while to get the kinks out of the serum. Then Gem-X come along, and . . . it was like unlocking the secrets of the universe. *An intention field*, Robert called it. They got so good at it Rob told me he could feel the bird's scheme. I guess he meant that it kept going back to the training day after day, starting with that star Aldebaran. Then seein' you over and over, Ms. Russo. You know that was all planned, didn't you? Robert using you as a trainer. Strictly visual at first. Now this. I bet you're real proud."

"We've got a visitor," he then said abruptly, bringing her back to the unsettled sky above. A jet touched down on the far end of the runway, it's incessant white interrupted by a stylish red script, "Colzer-Bremen International." A woman appeared from the cabin and began a brisk walk to the barn. As she got closer, it was apparent she carried a cage.

Hennings moved quickly, pulling something from a pocket in his overalls. "You deserve the honor," he said, patting Pritchard on the back then handing him what looked like a remote. "You two," he said, bringing her alongside Sterns, "You need to go closer to the barn. Where you can watch."

Josie took another look at the woman coming toward them, at the cage, and the bird in the middle of a vocal meltdown on the roof. She realized the old man was simply putting on the finishing touch as if, he too, had been waiting for a hundred years. Pritchard walked toward the approaching woman. There was something in each of his hands now. Back and forth, she thought. A man who'd waited long enough.

She didn't look at Sterns but could feel his steadiness behind her. His presence wasn't comfort, but an awkward freedom. They were back to the beginning in a forest without hope. She wanted to thank him for climbing a tree, for taking her beyond Missoula, for uncovering what it meant to love a man who'd fallen into a silent, deadly passion. She wanted to tell him how little she knew about smoke jumpers, but if he wanted, she would learn.

Without skipping stride the woman named Elsa yelled across the men in front of her. "Ms. Russo, I want to talk to you." She stood stiff legged, holding her skirt in place with the cage while fiddling in her pocket.

Josie walked a step closer and stopped. It was the right place, the in-between place she'd been all her life.

"I'm going to ask these two gentlemen what they know about the state of things. In other words, what they can provide. Can you provide anything, Ms. Russo? Do you have anything of mine?"

"No," she answered, suddenly aware of a cacophony above, of coos and low hums. A cut-away appeared in the barn's roof, very much like looking into the open side of a doll house. In it were cages, rows upon rows of birds. The roof slid into another section of roof, all of it edged in brown-green moss. She wondered how this could happen, then looked at Pritchard's right hand where just the tip of the remote was showing.

Undaunted, the woman merely sat her cage on the ground. She pulled a very small silver gun from her pocket keeping it pointed at her shoes, then began again. "Would you like to give me that remote, Martin? We can't have any birds getting loose can we?"

"My pleasure," he said, scarcely grinning, handing it to her as delicately as if it was set to go off.

"Martin," she said. "If you don't come up with something for me, namely Gem-X, the two vials or any of the above, I'm going to have to make some administrative changes. You promised me results. I have a check for another half million if you can produce. I'm here. You're here. Now, how can we make this work best? You know, serum is serum. It doesn't matter whether it's in a bird, in a vial or in a human. It's all marketable." She patted his arm, then moved forward to just about a half inch away from Josie's nose.

"You know, Martin, science is inexact and so is business. I knew if that 98 percent run was allowed, it was close enough to a full 100 that we could no longer determine control of foreign populations or of individuals in the United States. I could give two vials to the President and the First Lady, and idealistically there'd be plenty available for their children and grandchildren. But what if something happened, like so many times before? Where people would give away their vial to a child or sell the anti-virus on the street to some junkie. This would happen and I knew, with that percentage inside them, the wrong people would end up living. They would end up running the world."

"You, for instance, Ms. Russo," she said. "You're one of those who shouldn't be alive." Elsa's stare was uncompromising, and Josie knew Pritchard hadn't been exaggerating.

Maybe it was an accident, or perhaps there was another button on the remote, but as suddenly as the roof had partitioned, this time the front panels of each cage rose up in unison. The racket, like automated cell doors in a prison, overcame every other happening, erasing what she'd just said in a whir of wings. Every pigeon descended from the barn. Maybe a hundred, maybe three hundred. Josie couldn't tell. The cascade was as if she was under a waterfall, the wing beats a pulse inside her skull. They pulled together immediately and circled the building twice, a small band of powder blue cumulus that siphoned up Gem-X on the last arc. So quick it had all been, a fall of light no one could rescind. And most of humanity would never know.

It passed like a shockwave through the woman named Elsa. She threw the remote at Pritchard, then walked up to Hennings, holding the gun at his head. "I've had enough," she said. "You and Russo spent your time and my money building escape hatches and furthering some kind of delusion that you could build a phoenix out of a pigeon. You took some of my best men with it. One way or another they compromised the real purpose of the passenger. They made it a mockery. A stooge. I want a vial, Pritchard. And I want it now."

"You know, Elsa," he said, holding the empty out in his other hand, "I think you're lucky if that's all I call you in front of these folks. And I also think you make a lot of mistakes. A big one was Russo. I bet Colzer doesn't know the kind of mistake that was. I didn't . . . well, finish him off. And nobody does things better than Martin Pritchard." With that he tossed the vial in the air.

When it landed at her feet, Elsa turned from Hennings. She picked it up and, empty as it was, gave it a shake. Unfazed, she went up to the man who claimed to be the best. "My regards," she said. "I came here ready to kill you. I didn't expect you'd have anything. Especially anything to fill that cage I brought with me."

"Well, that's what you got, Elsa. Nothing."

"Only to the naked eye, Pritchard. You see that's what's the matter with men like you. You haven't met the scientist who can make Pass-Flu out of a trace, a teasing in the bottom of a vial. There's a million doses of anti-virus in there, Mr. Pritchard. And all of it, thanks to you."

Josie watched her walk away from Pritchard, leaving the cage right where she'd dropped it. She could see by the way he stood, by the way he held his hands, open to the wind, that he'd never brought the gun. By now, a breeze was beginning to cartwheel around them, raking through the long soapweed lining the runway. She noticed the acrid smell of fire mixing with rain and for a long moment thought she heard the faraway pummel of wings. Then the jet began its skittish whine.

She could feel Sterns come up behind her saying something about birds. He steadied her, bracing her shoulders as if he was waiting for some sign to release her. She wondered what he sensed, intent as he was on watching the jet in its low airborne dynamic, turning upward and curving away from the field. It was hard to see them at first, their wind-blown bodies spirited across the sky like a cloudburst in front of the plane, but when she concentrated, in that second when she recognized they were finally unified, she wondered if that was what Sterns was trying to tell her. She smiled and leaned back into him, remembering the audacity of a blue meteor.

Then she heard only a spit of silence, a warning. An impatient bell without a ring. She watched the passengers gather and connect in strands of gray-blue, once more perilously close to death, appearing to absorb the jet veering out of control between them. It corkscrewed first low to the ground, then turned on its back riding the field like an exploding sled. Birds rose steadily away. *They move through black cumulus as if they'd never ceased,* she thought. Josie shivered in a reaction as uncontrollable as all the hours of illness had been and sensed Sterns, unyielding, behind her.

"On the graveyard of those who don't survive. Just like 1918. That's the way it will be with us," he said. "We'll rebuild on top of the world's grave. Only this time, we'll know the way it happened, Josie. Some of us will know because of you."

Author's Message

Ideas for this book began almost like a snowstorm—snow-flakes, like ideas, some solitary, others conjoined. First, I wanted to do a story set in the Olympic Rain Forest of Washington State. There needed to be a strong sense of impending doom, but not full-blown apocalypse. An epidemic, maybe. Through all the warnings, all the waiting, it would approach. Not as one would think of an outbreak of monumental proportions, but as a trickle, building steam.

At the same time, I was fascinated with the long-ago effects of the 1918 flu. As a medical transcriptionist, I've documented the course of disease through hundreds of lives. But it wasn't until I realized my grandmother's lifelong problems with diabetes, digestive problems, and unexplainable lethargy that I found out she suffered and survived the flu of 1918. In fact, her illness brought my grandfather home from World War I. This was the second major element that brought me to the story.

A third element was the love of flight. In my early 20s I learned to fly single engine planes, finally accumulating a few hundred hours of flight time. Though flying never became anything more than recreational, rare encounters with birds did happen. Fortunately, these were always incidental, but lasting. I realized I was in their space and sharing their world. When it finally occurred to me that the passenger pigeon became extinct at almost the same time my grandmother might've died from the greatest influenza of all time, I began to work a plot around the idea of retrieving a bird from extinction and pushing it for an anti-virus to stem a new and lethal virus—a modern-day influenza. And with that, the story of *Quick Fall of Light* was born.

About the Author

Sherrida Woodley lives with her husband and four dogs on a few quiet acres not far from Turnbull Wildlife Refuge in Eastern Washington. She pursues writing from the perspective that nature provides unlimited inspiration, and that, combined with human mystique, creates story. The mother of three daughters, she dedicates this book in part and website to her youngest, Deanna, who recently passed away of breast cancer.